PRAISE FOR

"A beautiful, bloody, harrowing mashup of all the best elements in gothic horror set against the backdrop of a (more) demented version of *Grey Gardens*. An absolute stunner."

—Emily Carpenter, author of *The Weight of Lies*

"Only the crazy-brilliant mind of the super-talented Shannon Kirk could channel Stephen King and Edgar Allen Poe—and create this unique and contemporary horror-mystery-love story. Only a skilled writer like Kirk could dive into the dark madness of the mind and soul—and come up with this chilling tale of broken hearts and desperately twisted love."

—Hank Phillippi Ryan, Agatha, Anthony, and Mary Higgins Clark Award–winning author

"*Flowers in the Attic* meets "The Tell-Tale Heart" with a dash of *Psycho*, Shannon Kirk's *In the Vines* is as dark, tangled, and twisty as the title would suggest. A fascinating portrayal of madness, wealth, and decaying family legacy, Kirk's superbly crafted gothic thriller will have you gasping the entire way through. This is an insanely good ride into the mind of a madwoman . . . just remember to hang on, lest you not make it back out."

—Jennifer Hillier, author of *Jar of Hearts*

"A dark and twisted thriller, both poetic and page-turning. A treat for the discerning suspense lover."

—Mark Edwards, author of *Follow You Home*

IN
THE
VINES

IN THE VINES

SHANNON KIRK

Published by Thomas & Mercer, Seattle

www.apub.com

Amazon, the Amazon logo, and Thomas & Mercer are trademarks of Amazon.com, Inc., or its affiliates.

ISBN-13: 9781503901940 (hardcover)
ISBN-10: 1503901947 (hardcover)
ISBN-13: 9781503900752 (paperback)
ISBN-10: 1503900754 (paperback)

Cover design by Damon Freeman

Printed in the United States of America

First edition

Dedicated to Halibut Point State Park, Ocean Lawn at Coolidge Reservation, Fort Constitution State Historic Site, and Odiorne Point State Park, for the science, the solace, the history, and the inspiration.

The Haddock Point State Park of this novel is a fictional location in a nonexistent sliver of space between Rockport and Gloucester, combining various elements of these parks.

And for Max: always visit gardens, reservations, forests, beaches, and points, whenever in life you want or need to. This is where the peace lives unfiltered.

In the Sink

I have been in the sink
The cycle down, down, around
Can't stop
Darkness, walls, fading light
Thoughts on cycle, looping, racing
I have been in the sink, the stink,
The ever-choking loss of breath, can't think
Can't grasp a hook or a hole or a knot or a root
Too slick, thoughts swish, on cycles, all grim
The madness
The flickers of tricks of reason, lucid not
Of laughter echoes above from deniers
Who too will feel the walls as they slide
I have been in the sink
I know the signs
The sink, she widens, greedy, relentless
Slipping at the lip, ground loosened and jagged
Deniers trip, hands knees in mud
And will know, their silence, delay
Made wider ways, for all to fall
In the patterns made by wicked men
Time and again, history's said
We're all in the sink, as we've always been

—SCK, November 13, 2016

CHAPTER ONE
MARY OLIVIA PENTECOST, AKA MOP

Present time

It was the note that led us here, in the dark, trembling. Bloodstained. Hiding. It was the note. It crinkles in my hand, wet with sweat, in the fortune-teller's creases of my palm.

Although I didn't write it, I can recite it, here in this hole in which we hide, in my head.

> *I am the mistress. Say it. Say it. I am the one sleeping in your bed. The nights you're there, I'm there, a whisper. My body snakes in your sheets, swimming in his head. He doesn't say "I love you" anymore, not without the stick of me in his throat. The sob you hear in the shower through the walls, that's your delusion, draining down the pipes. I am the mistress, know it, know it. I am the one sleeping in your bed.*

I found the note in Aunty Liv's guest room. I wasn't supposed to be at her near-seaside house in the first place. For two years now, ever since my mother, her sister, launched herself into the ocean just beyond

Aunty's house, she has kept a lid on, blocked us out of her life. Yet here I came, her twenty-five-year-old, still-grieving niece, breaching all her literal barriers and boundaries as if they never existed. I needed her help. And I found that damned note one week after first arriving two weeks ago, when we lived aboveground, like most humans, not hiding in a hole. As shocks go, the note is tame by comparison to the other shocks that crashed like asteroids in the last two weeks.

Now I'm in the basement remains of a burned guest cottage on Aunty's property, hiding. I hear a woman who wishes to kill me—or rather, wishes to kill me and my companion. She's scraping and scratching, clawing and hacking her way through the otherwise impenetrable tangles of five-foot-high hedges and tornadoes of oceanside brambles. Her skin must be ravaged like a savage's, the thorns, the heavy dead sticks off twisted trees, the relentless vines that wish to hold you firm for their forest friends, the nettles, to slice skin. All around us topside is a New England jungle, as if nature wishes to coil vegetation into a barrier between inland and the glorious roaring ocean it protects. And the goddess ocean, she's angry tonight, yelling at us mortals in the middle of a personal war. Her thundering waves warn of the coming hurricane.

In the last two weeks, I've come to view my world in dramatic terms, and as this night is either a magnificent resolution or our climactic end, I find comfort in anthropomorphizing nature as Earth's army, the Atlantic as Earth's one goddess, and the sky her faithful servant. I must consider something greater than the woman who hunts us, focus on something more forceful than her murderous evil. Because this is the literal last ditch: we have nowhere else to run. Like lab mice in a glass box. No clear, safe escape. If we try to exit from where we entered, out through the hidden hinged board among other boards that cap this burned basement, she'll hear us and hack us. Again. I lost too much blood before I tied the kerchief tourniquet around my wounded shin. I'm weakened and pale, slouching in a lean against a dirt wall. My companion is even worse. Nature now is our only hope.

The woman above who hunts us, she treats the boundary of nature's twisted knights like trash. A thwack, thwack returns, her slicing through vines and overgrowth, cutting a path with a hatchet she took from the barn. "You bitch," she screams. "You biiiiitch," she screams again—the word *bitch* is a bat's sonar, sending out waves of sound to detect us, her insects in this hole.

CHAPTER TWO

AUNTY LIV

Two years ago—Boston

This is the story I'll have to commit to memory and live with, forever. This is my story now. I will never, I cannot, forget the details. Even as I watch the facts unfold and I burn this story, the one I'll tell if asked, I am confused at my current reality. It's like the emotional delusion I felt upon Daddy's death and my two miscarriages, but this is not delusion. *This is not delusion. Watch, listen, burn these details to your mind. Everything is wrong, everything is off. This is not delusion. This is real.*

I watch her, because, I admit, I want to watch her disintegration. I am not an evil person—at least, I thought I wasn't. I am, I was, happy. I have a great family. I live in a pink house, a shade of light rose, by the sea, on a large parcel of land that neighbors Haddock Point State Park. The brightest blue morning glories crawl up my outer walls, netting the creamy rose like blue crocheted lace. It's possible I am insane now. I should maybe get professional help; I sometimes don't recognize myself. But I don't think any medical intervention would clear my mental plague. What I suffer is the insanity of being in love. The type of insanity for which there is no cure.

I trailed *her* all day, and she led me here, to Proserpina's, the oldest Italian restaurant in the universe, but somehow regular vintage in Boston. The walk down the alley to Proserpina's, the buildings we pass, all made of bricks.

It's early June, so it's friggin' cold one minute and hot the next. I say spring is like a menopausal woman. Mop, my lovely nerd niece at Princeton, is more *giving* in how she describes spring. Last night in a phone call, she said, "Boston weather is bipolar: hot one day, cold the next, high, bright sun one minute, biting chill the next. Spring is a selfish bully, clawing to hold more time away from our beloved New England summers." So that's one way to put it. I responded by telling Mop I love her, and to go on and finish up for the semester with her nerd poetry and philosophy courses so we can enjoy the damn beloved summer—which, as of now today, I'm almost certain is lost forever.

For me, however you describe New England spring, this weather sucks. Brings every strain of cold and pneumonia to Saint Jerome's, where I work, one block away. I've taken off and put back on my green cashmere sweater fifty times while trailing *her* through Boston Common. The pink flowering trees are in bloom now, so the scent of sharp sugar and a dusting of pollen lingers in my nose.

We enter the restaurant. She sits in a circular booth with padded walls with another woman. I'm in the likewise circular booth adjacent them, the barrier between us high, so they don't see me. The woman I follow, she doesn't know me. Doesn't know the impact I'm about to make on her life. I have no clue who this other woman is, and I wouldn't care, except for what I heard and what I did see and what I didn't see, as I expected to see, in the park.

Nothing made sense about *her* path here. My simple intention was to follow *her* until *she* met up with *him* and watch from afar as he told *her* about *us*. Simple. By now, she should have returned to Danvers, a forty-minute drive north of Boston, to *their* big Victorian across from the baseball fields. She should be sitting in her car in her perfect-paved, suburban driveway, her head on the wheel of her ridiculous minivan, the color of drab and dated yet evil, like her, maroon. She should be burrowing her etched face, etched of her madness, into her steering wheel, grappling with accepting what *he* should have told *her*. But this did not happen.

Instead, I followed her following another woman. *If she knew the truth, she'd be following me.*

Do I know everything? Am I the sucker? Is he making love to this other woman too? No. We're in love. He's meant to tell his wife today.

He was supposed to tell *her*, his wife, in Boston Common, where I waited and watched. But he never showed, despite her being there, and she waited under a flowing willow, and I across the pond, watching. Then *she* saw this other woman traipsing through with a Lord & Taylor shopping bag, and *she* followed her, so I followed her following this other woman. A total twist to my intended spy session. *Who is this other woman?* I wondered. I continued following.

The wife I follow cornered this other woman at the edge of the Civil War cemetery on Tremont, across the street from Suffolk Law School, a half block out of the park. With one hand wrapped around the black iron of the cemetery's fence, and one foot away from a cracked, gray grave, I caught only fragments of their heated argument, but pieced together enough: this other woman is a neighbor friend of the wife I follow, and the wife thinks this neighbor woman, whose name is Vicky, is having an affair with *him*. But she's wrong. *No. This Vicky is not sleeping with him, my love. MY love.*

Out there, aside crumbling graves, a cool wind swooped in and swirled Vicky's hay-bale hair, washing out her words to me. When the wind slowed, I heard *Vicky* deny the wife's "false accusations." Oh, little Vicky with the twitchy nose, she was pissed, but she must empathize with the wife, or hold some diabolic ulterior motive: she convinced *her* to calm down and join her for a late lunch at Proserpina's. I followed, and now we're separated by the curved booth wall.

All staff of Saint Jerome's, where I work with *him*, come to Proserpina's to unwind. My place of employment takes up the entire block behind. The other regular inhabitants of Proserpina's are law professors and law students from Suffolk Law, and, of course, Freedom Trail tourists, who are obvious as the only ones wearing the "Paul Revere Rode Here" and "Wicked Pissah" T-shirts they purchased down at Faneuil Hall.

With the law school on the same block and the hospital behind, this is our regular spot, us nurses and doctors, us hospital workers, us budding lawyers and professors. Hell, *he* could walk in any minute, still in his white doctor's coat, stethoscope around his thick, muscled neck, the one I've sucked after getting too liquored during Proserpina's happy hours. I scan the crowd with furtive eyes but find no one I recognize. The bloodred paintings of Tuscan poppy fields litter the dark paneled walls. I hide my face behind the extra-large menu. The tension in Proserpina's, for me, is like a plaza held captive by a backpack bomber.

I had pulled the waiter aside upon entering and said with a pleading smile, "Please don't interrupt, please. I need to finish this book. Please bring me still water and the penne Bolognese, thanks." This way, the waiter won't interrupt my eavesdropping or call too much attention to my presence next to *her* and *this Vicky*.

At first, her and Vicky's conversation in the adjacent booth was inaudible. All I captured were excited whispers. But now I hear the wife, because I calibrated my hearing to the cadence of their conversation, and *she's* just opposite me. I note how the restaurant's music forms a barrier between her voice and the sparse inhabitants far away at the bar. The bar folk are further insulated from her talking, given how they conduct their own loud conversations by leaning in to one another for better hearing, what with the television squawking mindless drivel about the Red Sox game tonight and the outfits a state senator dressed her two daughters in to tour Boston on vacation. The wife I follow shoos the bow-tied waiter away. He snaps a basket of bread on their round table in retreat.

"I'm done with this. He's been saying he wants to talk to me tonight, and I know what he's going to say. I thought you were my friend, Vicky. He wants to leave me for you," the wife says to this Vicky.

No, that is not what he is going to say to you tonight. Not the plan at all. He was supposed to tell you in the park today, where I was to watch, he's leaving you for me. Me. Me. Me. Not this Vicky. And you have no clue who I am, Cate. Cate, your name tastes of metal in my mouth. Like a metal pin in my mouth . . . like the metal shirt pin that cretin shoved in my mouth when Daddy tried to save . . . no, stop. Stop. Don't go there. Don't think in the past. You're here, now, in the present, in a restaurant. You are forty-some fucking age, not fourteen. Listen.

I need to spit just to think your name, Cate. Everyone thinks Cate is an innocent, best-friend name, so yellowy and pristine, untroubled by problems and poverty, the epitome of sanity. But that's not you, Cate—foul, I spit your name. You are the opposite. You don't deserve your own name, much less him.

He never showed in the park, and instead you saw her, and you followed her, and now here we are. Where is he? And who the fuck is Vicky?

I know a panic attack is closing in on me. I force a cavernous inhale and push the air around me with flat palms. I drop my head, close my eyes, and breathe. *No. Heart, stop. Stop going crazy. Listen. You must listen. Relax. Five . . . four . . . three . . . two . . . one . . . breathe.*

The waiter is back, timid in his approach to Cate and Vicky's table. "Madams, I am sorry to interrupt, but my shift ends in five minutes and I could expedite your order now, before shift change, please."

Cate grunts and orders "spaghetti and meatballs," because she's an obstinate child. "And ensure the chef places exactly, ex-act-ly, three meatballs, not two, and not four," she adds, because she's a fucking psycho. I flip a page in the book I swiped from a park bench, sticking my nose to the cracked inner spine, appearing enthralled in this thriller—although it could be a romance novel, I don't know. Mop would know. She'd be able to read *and listen*. But I couldn't possibly hear the real world around me if I were reading. I suffer consumptions. I need consumptions, for safety. For sanity.

Right now, I'm in Proserpina's, pretending to read a book of questionable genre, while listening to *Kent's wife*, who just accused a woman named *Vicky* of sleeping with *him, my love*.

Fortunately, I minored in drama in college, to lift the burden of premed, so I believe I'm pulling off this reading act. Proserpina's night shift filters in, so too, the night ambience, and so the late lunch classical is replaced by an upbeat jazz through a plug-in CD player behind the bar.

"In ten minutes, turn the volume up," Proserpina's manager shouts from within the music moat between our booths and the bar. I know restaurants. He wants the music change for the lingering late lunchers to be an ease into a warm swim, rather than an abrupt cold jolt reminding them they're still eating and drinking here, late in the afternoon. Before they know it, they'll be ordering the happy hour specials the bartender is chalking on his blackboard, and they'll be begging for one more hour out with friends in cell-phone calls to wives and husbands. The whole world is socially engineered. As *he* was socially predestined to marry *her* and expected to stay married to *her* until *death did them part*, even though he no longer loves her and she has become morose and hypercontrolling in every sense of the term. And evil, serious evil, a truth I can't dwell on now. I'd shudder and lose focus to think on what she holds over him, and thus, us, and specifically, me.

Instead, I concentrate on the superficial awfulness of *her*. How she doesn't clean clothes or their home, only barks at him to press his pants with deeper creases and fold her underwear in three folds, not two, like she's demonstrated for him "numerous times." He's Saint Jerome's chief surgeon, yet he does this laundry charade on Sundays to keep the peace. It's sickening. It repulses me. He tells me of the routine every

Monday morning over coffee in the break room, or after a good solid fuck at the Kisstop in Back Bay. Cate could fold her own underwear, and underwear can be fist-shoved into a top drawer in a lump, because underwear doesn't wrinkle and it doesn't matter. He owes her, she says, because he shoots blanks and can't plant her with kids. Which is absolute, 100 percent horseshit.

Why do I hate her so much when I'm the mistress? I should hate myself, true. And I do. But I hate her more. I have a profound and frightening reason, a validated example, but I won't, I can't, return my thoughts to real reasons now. I stick to these facile underwear reasons. I need to listen.

This is insane. I should leave. I should move on. I should return to the person I was before him. I am a different person now, a person I never wanted to be. Who am I? What have I become? I can't return to who I was before. Things are different now. My life will be very different now.

I'm stuck here, transfixed. Listening. This is dangerous. *I'll listen and then leave. I'll talk it over with Johanna tonight.* Thank God my sister's staying with me this week and not coiled up in her stifling estate in Rye, New Hampshire, our family home, the one she agreed to take over when Mom died. I don't understand how Johanna can live in Rye with those awful memories in the walls. I guess I'm the only one with the awful memories; she skated them, because she's blessed. I'm not.

Everything will get better after I talk to Johanna and confess to her what I've been hiding. *I can't believe I hid this affair from Johanna.* We'll cuddle up in the guest cottage behind my rose house, the cottage I had built for her, decorated just the way she likes, "beach elegant." I'll feed her a bottle of bordeaux. I'll confess that I'm sleeping with a married man, that I'm unfortunately struck by a disease of love, I'm sick with it. I'll give her all the details about the state I'm in, too, and my sister will still love me regardless. She'll soothe my heart with her hand on my hair, and we'll figure it out, like we always do. Best friends. Sisters.

Soul mates. We've always been. She'll fix me. She'll listen. She'll smack me with tough love. And we have time to ourselves before her daughter, Mop, my beloved niece, returns from Princeton for the summer. *I'll tell Johanna tonight. This is insane. I need a fucking cigarette. I don't smoke. Who am I? Shit.*

This Vicky woman orders. "I would like a plain breast of grilled chicken with nothing else on the plate, please. I have allergies."

The waiter is in a hurry to end his shift and doesn't inquire as to what allergies, which I think the new law requires, or at least common sense and basic decency. "No problem, madam," he says and shuttles off to the kitchen.

Vicky must turn to *Cate*. Her voice is more audible, facing Cate, and thus, facing my ear. "I need to go to the bathroom. I'll be right back," Vicky says. "Cate, you need to calm down. We've been friends ten years. We live across the street from each other, for crying out loud. So I'm going to forgive you and talk—we'll talk this out. But you need to stop this. I hope you didn't say anything about any of this to my husband. I didn't sleep with Kent." The last sentence doesn't sound very convincing to me, but then again, my antennae might be up and misfiring.

If someone accused me of sleeping with a married man, out in the open, I wouldn't stick around. So I'm presuming Vicky sticks around for this volatile conversation only so she can control the messaging, the neighborhood gossip, and, likely, save her marriage.

Vicky reappears after a good long five minutes in the bathroom; I thought maybe she fled. She doesn't sit, says she needs to make a phone call if they are going to continue talking, and she leaves again, back out to the black-and-white-tiled foyer. Cate gruffs and grunts and says, "Whateva," in a heavy Boston accent, which grates and grinds my nerves, so I cringe. My shoulders are up around my neck.

It's WHATEVERRRRRR! Enunciate, you lazy bitch!

As Vicky slips away, their waiter slinks up like a shadow creature in a Dracula film with their food. I continue to pretend I'm reading my absolutely amazing, enthralling thriller or romance or *whatevER.*

The waiter disappears to the kitchen, and *Cate,* the wife, is alone. I hear her unzipping what must be her purse. I hear crinkling of plastic. I hear a crushing, a rolling crinkle, and a slight rip of something. I do not stand to look over this leather wall. I cannot allow her to see me, or me seeing her, can't give away my listening post. But these noises compel me; I am riveted. *What is she doing?* It takes all I can to not kneel on the cushion and periscope over the booth. Vicky returns. The jazz music is still soft, but I know I only have a few minutes before the volume is cranked to happy hour. I need it to remain a steady sound wall. My ears are adjusted on this side of the rhythm. I need to listen.

Cate and Vicky say nothing to each other. I hear forks on porcelain plates, some knife slices.

"So do you eat here with him, then? Is this why you're downtown today, Vicky? The hospital's just behind us. Is this why you know this place?"

"Cate, good grief." Vicky pauses to cough. "I've never"—cough—"ugh, been here before"—cough.

"What then, after you eat here with him? Do you go to the Kisstop and fuck after your shitty chicken? I bet he orders the veal. He loves veal. Is that your routine?" Cate says and puffs loud and swallows into a drink. I hear the swish of the liquid. "Of course he would go fuck some loser with allergies. He likes his women weak."

I'm not weak. He likes his women weak? Am I weak? No, I am not weak. I accept I'm crazy at this moment in my life, but I am not weak. I need to get up and leave. Tell my sister. Johanna, help me climb out of this hole! I am not weak. And yes, Cate, yes, indeed. He does order the veal, and then we fuck at the Kisstop, we, he and I, not this Vicky.

Vicky clears her throat, doesn't speak. She keeps clearing her throat, a low, constant gurgle. I set my ear over a pocket in the puckered leather.

Vicky has not spoken. I don't believe she has scraped her fork across her plate since she took her first bite. She clears her throat again.

Vicky is now clearing her throat in a desperate blizzard of rising coughs. The bartender doesn't notice; he's moving over to the volume knob on his CD player. And when he's one step away from blocking the voices behind me, I hear Cate's virulent whisper.

"Whoopsy, are you having another one of your anaphylactic reactions, Vicky? Gee, I'm a nurse and all; I should have an EpiPen on me, but I don't. What? There's one in your purse? Oh darn, your purse is over here, under my jacket. How'd that happen?" Cate says, without an iota of alarm and with uncut sarcasm.

Cate stands and shouts for help. "Help, help, my friend is choking."

The bartender shatter-drops a glass mug. The people at the bar jump from their stools; one stool tips back and crashes in a deafening bang on the floor tiles. The chef, opposite our tables and in the open kitchen, throws a steel bowl of salad in the kitchen, sending lettuce shrapnel to spin midair. The waiter flings a tray of saucy ziti and ravioli to the side, landing the pasta missile in a miracle on a table, before velocity takes over, splattering the table's seats with murder sauce. The waiter and the chef and the bartender and two Saint Jerome's doctors, who just walked in, surround Vicky. Her face is a bulging bubble of welts and hives, her throat swollen to the width of her jawline. Cate stands off to the side, acting the part of a shocked woman. I stand behind Cate, strategically so.

"She has a peanut allergy," Cate is saying in such a high, forced, phony fluster, I wonder if any of the fools in this restaurant appreciate good theater. *Can't they tell she's acting?*

"There are no peanuts on her chicken!" the chef is shouting.

"I think just peanut dust can kill her," Cate says.

So this is how this will go down. There will be an autopsy. The cops will investigate the contents of Vicky's food, her medical history, the makeup of Proserpina's kitchen. They'll question Cate by visiting her at her home; no doubt by then she will have burned her purse with all the evidence. Nobody will suspect murder until much later. Nobody will be thinking about preserving any evidence in the critical first minutes, hours. Just another allergic reaction in a restaurant. There are no hidden video cameras in this joint; it's an old-school hangout for lawyers and doctors and also some of the politicians from Capitol Hill, which is behind the Civil War cemetery. It is quite possible this restaurant fed some of those dead Civil War soldiers. No wiring for cameras, and no enterprising owner would dare drill into the original wood paneling to retrofit modern technology.

No one will be able to connect any dots beyond a reasonable doubt. No one but me, that is. I'm the only one who heard. The sound of plastic opening, Cate crushing something, only one thing that could have been: Cate, Kent's wife, *her*, crushing a bag of peanuts, so as to dust Vicky's chicken. And with no surveillance and the cops not here yet, Cate has plenty of time to play the part and hide the minuscule evidence.

Stop. Don't do it. Leave. Stop! No.

I don't know why I do this—it is so counter to self-preservation. Cate's murderous act must take over my reasoning skills, which are blotted anyway given my heart's misfortune, my mind's weakness in love. My rage is unstoppable. Passion controlling my moves. I walk up behind her; she doesn't see my face.

I hiss in her ear, "You killed the wrong woman."

I slip my green sweater's hood over my head and turn, slipping between the swarming crowd, before she can see who spoke.

Why don't I out her? Why can't I scream to the cops to look in her purse for the remainder of her crushed peanuts? I can't. She would soon uncover the dirt she holds over Kent is dirt she holds on me, and I must return to being invisible. And this dirt is not our affair, nope. Rather, it is the type of dirt that'd get me fired and my reputation ruined, my Mighty Mary charity obliterated, and I'm not quite sure but maybe some jail time, I don't know. I don't need to nurse for the money—far from it. I have more family money than all the Kennedys ever had, combined. The Vandonbeer riches go back centuries. We're the wealthiest New England family by several digits on the balance sheets, and to make money matters even more insane, that fortune doubles when you consider the fact that Johanna married into the second-wealthiest family, the Pentecosts. And maybe we'll go and triple all this lunacy, since it looks like Mop is about to marry into the fifth-wealthiest family. I suspect my neighbor boy, Manny Acista, is going to propose to her when she gets home from Princeton.

La-de-freakin'-da.

Because none of it matters.

You can't buy sanity, and I need to nurse to stay sane. I need my occupational consumption. I can't lose my license, can't lose my job, can't lose my hold on reason. The dirt Cate has keeps me up at night, but it was all an innocent series of mistakes and misjudgments before Cate got involved. She caught Kent, my love, with the evidence, the very dirt in his hands.

In pushing through the clotted crowd, I consider my options: send an anonymous note to the police commissioner or handle the justice for her crime myself. Cate's a nurse at my competing hospital, Mass General; I'm a longtime nurse at her competing hospital, Saint Jerome's. There are ways to wage this war that don't involve the authorities.

I slip out among the clatter of chaos, and I know Cate hasn't followed. She can't. She has to stay and play her part in all this, her fictional, malicious, awful part.

Away from the hell of Proserpina's, I'm back on a green bench in Boston Common. My shift at Saint Jerome's doesn't start for another hour. All I want to do is go home and talk to Johanna. But I have to put in a half shift tonight—I promised to cover for another nurse. I have to, and maybe that's good, so I can get distracted in my consumption. They'll bring Vicky to Saint Jerome's now, and I don't want to go there while they confirm her body dead, so I need to sit here, sit tight in the park, and wait out this excruciating hour. And this is the worst time, time when I'm stuck and can't move and am forced to do nothing but think. To fucking think. I'm anxious to go on and get my shift over and get home and hash this all out with Johanna.

Why—and I don't understand why—have I allowed myself to be alone in all this? Why haven't I said anything yet about my affair to Johanna, who would love me regardless? Or Mop, my niece, who is more like an adult daughter?

How can I connect so well with her, and with Johanna, my love, my sister, and yet neither of them knows about *him*? Mop came home from Princeton a few months ago for Easter, and there was a moment on a silver platter, a perfect moment in which I could have admitted to my affair, admitted out loud to my imperfections. We were at our family estate in Rye, New Hampshire. The Rye chef had made a traditional Catholic meal of ham and peas and predictable mashed potatoes, all of which we ate after saying grace, so as to be respectful to Johanna's sister-in-law, the *former nun* Mary Pentecost, the only one who actually celebrates the resurrection of Christ. Full and finished with our family obligation, Johanna's husband, Philipp, said he had business to finish in his study, so we three—Johanna, Mop, and I—returned to my rose-hued house by Haddock Point for a girls' night. Each of us got hugs and kisses from Philipp when we left, and we gladly gave them back to him. Former Sister Mary nodded to Johanna and Mop, and nodded to me, and I returned the gesture, but neither of us could meet the other's eyes.

The Easter night was unseasonably warm, and a sea breeze carried salt to us as we got out of the car. Crawling her wistful eyes up the clapboard siding, Mop asked, "Some 'Die Rose,' Aunty, in the rose house library?" referring to the Schubert classic "Die Rose," and the color of my home in one.

Seeing as Mop's boyfriend, Manny, was committed to his own family Easter dinner, that meant we had the night to just us three. And so, comforted in knowing we had a night in our own curated bubble, we entered my rose house in a practiced choreography. Mop and I went to the Mermaid Library. Johanna hummed her way down my bird-wallpapered hallway to the kitchen, to cut us some coffee cake and make us chai tea. I refuse to have servants in my home.

As I started Schubert's "Die Rose," set low for ambience and not to disturb, Mop lit all my battery candles, twenty in total, so that our reading haven became an "ancient tomb of glowing amber"—that's what Mop calls it, at first in eternal drama, only to reject drama with, "I mean, a nice, soft light."

Mop propped three books open on her crisscrossed legs, sitting on the middle cushion of one of two leather couches in the center of the library. She skipped from one book to the other; I'm not sure of her reading methodology. I took the middle cushion on the couch facing Mop, choosing a nonfiction travelogue on Chinese restaurants, because I had no appetite for any additional drama in my life.

Johanna entered the library with a tray of cut cake and three cups of tea, humming her favorite Paul Simon song and click-clacking into our subdued, amber solace like a bumbling, sparkling fashion rainbow. "You girls, already reading, my nerdy loves," she sang. She plunked down the tray on the coffee table between Mop's and my reading couches, kicked off her shiny Christian Diors—silver, of course, on Easter—grabbed her tea and cake, found an old *Vogue*, and plopped in her tulle-lined, polka-dot Easter frock into a puffy turquoise armchair in the corner, behind the couches. I set that chair there for her, because she said she'd join us in our reading if only the library's wood and leather had a little "happy pop." Such was born this routine we embarked on for the umpteenth time this last Easter.

Mop smiled from her leather couch to Johanna in her upholstered chair. Mop's smile was wide and her eyes sentimental, revealing she was not bothered by her mother's intrusion on her concentration, nor troubled by the white reading light Johanna flicked on to read her *Vogue*, thus shaming a corner of the room's amber glow—a bright reminder of grounded reality. The unstated message being *It is not practical to read by candlelight, my lofty loves*. Johanna blew Mop, and then me, several air kisses.

The operatic lyrics of Schubert's "Die Rose" gave way to calm instrumentals, and this was the perfect lull, the moment at which I could have confessed to my closest confidantes. But, in that same moment, Johanna looked down at her *Vogue* and gushed, "Oh my goodness, this is the one where they featured classic Valentino! Valentino!" She dived into the magazine's pages, while Mop looked to me with a mocking but loving eye roll about her mother, my sister, all of which confirmed, for the thousandth time, that my niece might see perfection in me, might identify with me, even more than the mother she loves to distraction.

So I couldn't break Mop's trust in me by admitting to the room of my affair. And breaking Mop's trust—where would that lead? Would that lead to other ugly truths about me to her, and indeed, to myself?

I won't think on it further.

CHAPTER THREE
MARY OLIVIA PENTECOST, AKA MOP

Present time

> Superstition is to religion what astrology is to astronomy,
> the mad daughter of a wise mother.
> These daughters have too long dominated the earth.
>
> —*Voltaire*

Everyone calls me Mop. And I'm glad, because my name is ridiculous: Mary Olivia Pentecost, like I'm some dowdy, black-dressed colonial awaiting a witch trial in Salem. But since our family money tracks to *Mayflower* days, I was burdened with a *Mayflower* name.

I don't wear any of the gold crosses given to me on birthdays or my confirmation, not the one with embedded emeralds bestowed like an heir-apparent coronation sacrament at my Trinity High graduation. There's a drawer in my room in our Rye estate filled with crosses, literally filled with crucifixes of all kinds, shapes, metals, and woods. I never open that drawer except to plop another in, and when I do, a drop in air pressure causes my stomach to lurch, and an ice chill slaps my cheeks, as if a demon is being released from the bowels of my dresser. I slam the drawer shut to feel benevolent warmth again. Lessons on religious wars scarred me. Babies impaled on spikes? Who could ever get behind a *religion* (different from faith) like that? Who could ever get blindly behind any man-made religion? I'm not an atheist. I'm just troubled by the way money and power motivate the undercurrents of churches.

What is a church? What is mine? Is it okay to ask these questions? I believe, I think, it's okay to ask these questions.

Here I am in a hole in the ground, waiting to die. My companion is passed out. I have nothing to do while the woman above tries to find us with her shrill voice. Shouting on repeat, "Bitch!" All day I've been in here thinking and fading. Thinking and fading and cowering and hot.

In my mind, I keep getting stuck on the sharp and sudden contrast between our cheery, rosy life before and the dark life after the fire, my mother's death, and Aunty Liv's devastating abandonment.

Her abandonment.

Her sudden, awful abandonment.

No warnings.

But were there warnings?

I worry, too, about my love, my Manny. I wonder if he's alive. These questions I'm asking myself right now while I wait an eternity to find a way to escape—*What is a church? What is mine? Were there warnings before the fire, before the abandonment?*—perhaps these are just the untethered questions one asks when they've lost grasp of reason, when in a total existential and physical crisis.

I don't visit priest chambers to atone for my or my family's sins. I don't necessarily respect my father's sister, the nun, just because she's a nun—*was* a nun—and the biggest source of all those crosses. Maybe I respect her for other things. Sister Mary Patience Pentecost: I was named, in part, after her. That's my aunt the nun, from my father's side, but I gravitate to my mother's sister, Aunty Liv: Lynette Viola Vandonbeer. My mother, Johanna Vandonbeer Pentecost, called her Liv or Sis—when they were alive at the same time.

I need to rest. I lie on the dirt ground and cradle into the crescent space between my passed-out companion and the dirt wall. Timing the distance between my companion's faint breaths, I hope our bodies form a camouflaged shadow under the wooden cover above. *Are we willing to recognize each other yet? I can't even say my companion's name, so as to acknowledge how we're both prisoners, in such danger, together. So maybe not.*

All it will take is for the woman above to hatchet through the right bramble bush and see the paint-chipped and weathered wooden cover, which looks like one for an old well, but much larger and square, and she'll know where we are. She's as crazed as the devil in a desert fire, but she's not dumb. Our only saving grace is this lush high August, hot, with leaves full. Recent reports of coyotes give me hope that my wild brothers will come upon the hacking witch and nip her ankles, trip her long enough for me to spring from this hole and run.

But I won't make a flaming mistake and launch myself in the ocean off the cliff wall a quarter mile off, through the twisted paths, like they said my mother did. I won't leave my body on the ocean floor, unfound, rolling with waves, left as prey for sand sharks and lobsters. Cringing from such a thought, a panic more profound than the panic of hiding from a crazed woman drills into my chest. I shiver, although the humid air is so hot, sweat is not dripping down my neck; no, I *am* sweat. My entire body is encased in a blanket of sweat. I cry inside, although I'm paralyzed by fear and anger. My companion is the same. We're the same. One of us is going to have to get a grip, turn robot, and calculate a way out. One of us is going to have to wake up, not slip, be alert. One of us . . . but which one? Which one of us is the bitch, the subject of the crazed woman who beckons from above our ditch? She must mean both of us, for I think the lunatic up top is confused. I think I must be confused too. Here now, she shouts again, "You bitch!" . . . and she's closer. I can't tell if she's south of us, west, east, or north. But seems one right slice in the vines and we're toast.

The hole we're in, of black soot and clay, jagged, blasted granite, too, is the remains of a basement for a guest cottage on Aunty's Cape Ann, Massachusetts, grounds, forty-five minutes from the estate where my father and his sister, ex-nun Aunt Sister Mary, still live and where I grew up in Rye, New Hampshire. I'm home, in between finally graduating from Princeton—I took a few years off before starting college—and heading off to grad school in Manhattan. I'm doubting I'll ever make it to grad school now.

This guest cottage burned to the ground two years ago, alighting my mother and forcing her to jump into the sea. The next day, when Aunty abandoned us, she also abandoned her spot as a respected nurse at Saint Jerome's Hospital, in Boston, Massachusetts. That fire ruined everything for our family. Over the last two years, I did consider scouring the ocean floor, risking hypothermia, the bends, everything, to dredge my mother back to us. The loss of her hollowed all the happiness. All lights extinguished without her. I don't hold a candle to her brightness.

And while I've had trouble accepting the truth of my mother's death, today, in this hole, I remain stuck on the starkness of Aunty's abandonment of her job, which meant so much to her, and her abandonment of her family, me, who I thought meant so much to her.

Back when everything was cheery, rosy perfect, Aunty was the one nurse with the work ethic of a tireless, commanding general in a violent war, but who wore ten-carat heirloom diamond earrings, out of respect for her "grand ma-ma," who bequeathed them to her. She was the one nurse who wore a blue or purple or red or green 100 percent cashmere sweater over her nurse's uniform when the hospital wing was cold, because her charity-ball mother once instructed, "If wearing a sweater, my petite cher-ahhh, only ever wear cashmere." In her most private charity, she manipulated the records of postpartum mothers suffering postpartum depression so they could remain inpatients longer than insurance would otherwise provide—insurance companies more readily recognizing tangible symptoms, such as "can't urinate" or "continues to hemorrhage," than intangible observations, such as "Mother listless," "Mother appears vacant and apathetic when child presented," or "Mother cries all day." She thereafter provided living assistance to these mothers until their minds cleared through her Mighty Mary charity, the trust to fund such things.

Growing up, I just wanted to love Aunty Liv, the one I found so similar to me in many ways. If I split myself in three, Aunty Liv formed part of my identity. My mother, another part. Myself, the third. And maybe if I'm being truthful, there's another foundational woman I should have identified with in part as well, Aunt Sister Mary, maybe, but such identification cuts too cold. These foundational people with whom we identify, they are never exclusive, and the personal definition we hold of each is often shifting. But if you select the memories about them you call to count, then that definition can appear whole and stable, and thus you might feel stable, because ultimately you're defining the whole of yourself. But stability of foundational identities is a mirage, a fleeting fog, a lie. I think I know this now, as I tremble in the truth in this hole in the ground. What have I blocked, what have I caused, what have I enabled, because of my fog?

After the fire, Aunty Liv was not to be inquired of. She wasn't to be dropped in on "without prior express and written approval." These social restrictions were made crystal-chandelier clear in an impersonal, embossed letter from her lawyer to my father. One time we sent a grief counselor to her house, the same counselor who'd counseled me and my father, coaxing us to overcome my mother's disappearance and fall from the cliff wall, as the papers reported. We were afraid Aunty was suicidal, likely from the guilt of surviving the death of her sister on her grounds. But when our gifted counselor showed up, Aunty threatened to shoot her in the face with her glass-cased, collector's hunting rifle (something rumored to have been used by Teddy Roosevelt), if the counselor didn't get off her property "stat." Soon after, the locked chains at her driveway mouth appeared.

I'm thinking of Teddy Roosevelt right now. The glass case holding his gun is bolted between shelves in Aunty's Mermaid Library. The barrel of the gun points out a library window, aiming for Aunty's lawn. I'm thinking on how Roosevelt hunted big game in the African savannah. I personally find such an act disgusting, murder in violation of nature's highest sacred law, but I'm also thinking that right now, the woman above is justifiable big game to me.

I'm thinking of slinking out the south side of this hole, out through the hidden board, braving the brambles, weaving out behind whatever lunatic path she's cut, and smashing open the Roosevelt case with one of Aunty's metal mermaid bookends, one from several sets in her mahogany library. But is her Roosevelt rifle loaded? How do I load a gun? The bullets are in the glass case, too, so no need to worry about finding bullets. It's loading them I'm concerned with. Crazy still hasn't found us. She's still shouting from the out beyond, within the brambles, I imagine.

"You BITCH!"

I shimmy my shoulders backward so they nudge my companion's arms; we're still a combined body on the dirt floor. When this produces at least a light strain of audible breath in response, I close my eyes. Just one more rest, just one, before I wake us both and force an escape. Or at least sit us up to wait for some idea or natural force to save us.

But I rest. I shouldn't. I rest. I slip.

My mind wanders back to two weeks ago. After two long years of grieving my mother and my aunty who abandoned us, I ignored the flashing warning on my red Volvo, stretching the warning long enough to weave around the snaky bends along the ocean from Rockport to Gloucester. Perhaps fate, perhaps the whims of an evil wind, perhaps I'd listened to something, perhaps some haunting, calling me for help, perhaps intent—intent to see my own lost love, Manny, who lives nearby—blew the gasket in the engine at just the right time to roll the Volvo dead in front of Haddock Point State Park.

You can get to Aunty's house via a long driveway through vine-twisted, gnarly trees, hardy enough to withstand nor'easters and the relentless salt air. Or you can trespass through protected forest after breaching a restricted side trail, which might as well be marked by literal skull-and-crossbones warnings, but is barred by looping chains and rows of boulders. These obstacles are intended to prohibit parking lot tourists from accessing the sprawling properties of adjoining residents. Since Aunty barred the street end of her forested driveway with several ropes of interlocking metal chains two years ago, I left my dead red Volvo in the park's lot. Of course I trespassed over to Aunty's by breaching the restricted trail and traipsing through the protected forest.

I planned on ringing her doorbell for help. I wished she wouldn't turn me away, ignore me, her once-loved niece.

The idea of even having to ring her doorbell bristled my nerves as I crossed over her dirt driveway. Up until two years ago, I used to practically live part time at Aunty's.

I think about that moment now, in this hole, the bristling feeling of being a stranger in a place that was once a home. I reverted to being a child, and as I did, one memory stood out, as one chock-full of evidence of the nascent—or chronic or manic, I do not know—turmoil in Aunty. In real time and to a child's mind, the day was bright and happy. It is in retrospect only, as an adult, and now lying in a hole, I rethink this memory.

I was thirteen. I was spending the weekend at Aunty's same pink Haddock Point house. Manny was over playing with me. We'd just dug two potatoes from Aunty's kitchen garden, the one below her kitchen's bay window with the yellow-and-green curtains and the flower box stuffed with hot-pink wave petunias. Blue morning glories crawled up lattice on each side like twenty-foot exterior drapes, framing all her colonial's first- and second-floor warbled-glass windows, and scraping high to meet the newer windows on the dormers in her refurbished attic.

Manny stayed outside crafting a round target out of vines so we could play a game of rubber-tipped-arrow archery. I held the dirty potatoes, one in each dirty hand. My feet were bare and dirty, too, and since the grass I'd sloshed through was wet with dew, my muddy footsteps marked a path through Aunty's marble foyer, onto her turquoise bubble-print runner, and slip-sliding to the honey wood floors of the front hallway and living room.

My Pippi braids were coming loose, and several twigs pinned my hair—before the potatoes, Manny and I had chased one of the ubiquitous wild bunnies into a butterfly bush, because I suspected him in a line of possible culprits of stealing Aunty's bloomed roses. Manny's theory was more romantic than mine: he guessed that a seagull named Frank was one by one picking off the rose petals with his beak so he could build a giant rose on the cliff wall each night, trying to attract the love of a mermaid named Vanessa. Manny was like that, dreamy. *Is he still like that? Is he still alive?*

Back on the day when we were thirteen and I entered Aunty's house with my muddy feet and the muddy potatoes, Aunty stared out a living room window with sheer white curtains, tied in the middle with a dried starfish affixed to bendable wire. All around her, squadrons of sea turtles, rainbows of fish, and varieties of mermaids swam among raspberry coral in the colorful-patterned wallpaper. She plucked double pendants in the divot of her neck as she twisted from the window to see me and my cyclone of soil in the hall. She always wore those double pendants—gold baby shoes for the babies she lost before they grew full term.

I offered the dirty potatoes with outstretched palms. She fisted one in each hand and stared at them. Then she puckered her lips and braced one arm across her belly. Raising the dirt of one potato to graze her face and soil her shiny hair, she lifted a hand and pointed out the window.

Silt rained around her and onto her starched apple-green dress. And as I look back on the memory, here in this hole of lunacy, her actions and words were untethered, I believe. Disconnected from the reality of what she was doing.

Disconnected.

Right now, I pop my resting eyes open in reliving this childhood memory and I stare, like Aunty stared out her window that day. I stare at a dirt wall one inch from my nose. Smells musty and thick in this hell. Perhaps I'm disconnected too. I shimmy my shoulders again into my companion and procure a weaker breath in response, but a breath nonetheless, so I close my eyes. And I'm back, I'm back to my memory of twelve years ago, when I was thirteen.

"This bird," Aunty said, breaking out of her silence and thumbing backward toward her favorite willow. "This red cardinal in my tree where Manny's hanging the vine target. He's very funny," she said in all seriousness. "He's—" She shook her head. "All morning he's been chirping jokes while you two played, but the twigs in the tree are too ignorant to get the punch lines, and the leaves are too snobby to laugh. I think the cardinal needs to work on his timing." She shook her head again, then appraised me and my outdoor self, indoors.

"I'm sorry, Aunty. I made a mess."

"What mess?" She squirreled her eyes at me like I was hallucinating. "Go talk to that funny bird. Give him some tips, funny girl."

I don't know why she called me funny girl; she was the funny one. I was just her audience, the one who would laugh, because she was funny, and I loved her. Now, as I think back on it, survey our shared history while I await death, this lightness of her making twigs and leaves sentient is confusing. Aunty was always otherwise so clinical and realistic, funny usually, yes, but a hard-boiled humor. And yet, there were these light times when she entertained a more mystical outlook on life, which I wonder now, for isn't it clear after what we've gone through: Was this twig-leaf moment one of high mania? Back then, I was just happy she was happy.

As I walked out, leaving her with the potatoes, she kept talking to the window, not to me. "They should laugh, the twigs and the leaves. They should laugh at the bird's jokes. He's trying so hard for them, working really hard, chit, chit, chitting on and on in his routine. But nothing. Once he figures on them, he'll use the dumb twigs for a nest and he'll leave droppings on the uppity leaves." She turned to see me in the hall where I'd stalled and listened. Again she stared in a total blankness. Then she laughed her big bowl, echoey, aunty laugh that always made me laugh, too—like one sneeze leads to another's sneeze. I was a little muddy girl with messy braids, giggling with her shiny aunty in a sunny living room.

After, she sliced those potatoes into shoestrings and fried them up for an impromptu midmorning snack for me and Manny.

The same day as the funny bird incident, after Manny was called home by his father, Aunty and I spent the day nailing together a birdhouse. I painted it the same pink that adorned her home and then decorated around drawn-on windows with painted blue morning glories, all to make a perfect matching home for that funny, funny bird.

"I love that we have Manny here for you to play with," Aunty said while we worked. "Keeps you close to me, funny girl. At my house, not that stuffy Rye estate, right? We have so much fun here," she said with a twitching nose and kitty-cat smile.

I recall feeling an odd conflict when she said this, perhaps the way she said it. As an adult now, I think I can better interpret what I then felt as a child. Perhaps a guarded possession is one thing I felt, for *I* had chosen Manny. Manny was *my* friend, someone separate from everyone else in our tight family. In retrospect, as I shiver in this hot hole twelve years after she said it, as I probably die of fever and shock and blood loss and terrifying fear that my companion will die a worse death than me, I don't think I liked Aunty's use of the word *we* in the context of *having*

28

Manny. But I think I also felt ashamed for thinking Aunty was claiming, stealing something of mine, a piece of my separate love, because that would allow an imperfection in her perfect shine, how I'd grown to define her, a definition that gave me great comfort and freedom. I recall my physical wince. I recall shaking my head to shake out, in a tangible way, the brewing conflict. I recall beating the flash of darkness away by nailing into the birdhouse a little harder a few pounds, and all was well again. Blocking out darkness is a family trait, a family strength I've come to hone.

Aunty designed a trapdoor on the bottom of the birdhouse within which to hide a second set of her ring of house keys. Everything she has ever built, as far as I know, includes fake doors or rooms or hidden compartments. She always used to say they were part of her security system, what with not having a man living on premises in any permanent way. Even when pregnant with her longtime boyfriend's babies, she still didn't allow him to move in, and she certainly didn't allow him to move in after both miscarriages. He's long gone now. Been gone forever. But her multiple secret doors and hidden keys remain.

So we built that funny bird a birdhouse with a trapdoor for her duplicate ring of house keys.

Aunty showed me how to use her circular saw and drill.

Aunty handed me her hammer and nails.

Aunty never hired a live-on-premises caretaker, like we have in "stuffy Rye." I loved that at her house we had no servants or others hovering over us. We buttered our own toast; she, not a governess, not a maid, would bring cups of water to my room at night. She was "free" to do as she "please," she said. "Free as the wind."

What does it mean to be free as the wind?

I wish a wind would swoop into this hell and cool and wake us, make us both alive and alert.

I pop open my eyes again. The dirt wall is still there. The musty stench. The wetness of humidity. My sweat. My companion's sweat. I sit up, cross my legs. Still sitting in my companion's crescent space, I place my hands on the dirt wall and drop my head. Breathe in through my nostrils slow, controlled, so as to stem a rising nausea and to gather what strength I can. Our time is coming to act, to do something.

As I contemplate and calm my body, I fast-forward from age thirteen to two weeks ago, when all our current traumas coalesced into leading us here to this hole.

Two weeks ago, I clutched my crazy, loving, childhood impression of Aunty, as I trudged through Haddock Point's side trail, the protected forest, and trespassed onto her summer lawn, which had been so familiar to me growing up. I assumed the place would be in disrepair or some other visible sign of neglect would match the neglect she'd thrown us, her family, for two solid years. So it angered me when I stumbled upon her green, cut lawn with no weeds and her perennial beds bursting in rainbows, accenting her still-pink house. And when I saw those window boxes stuffed with hot-pink petunias and the crawling blue morning glories on the backside, so too the pink birdhouse I made with her and for her and for her funny bird and house keys, I felt a ringing betrayal. If life went on for her unharmed and still fresh, why did she refuse us a place in her life? For me? Her once-loved niece.

And when I caught her humming a happy tune in leaving her natural wood barn, one big enough for horses and tractors and a high loft, the place in which she taught me to use her hammer and nails, her drill and circular saw, the tune angered me further, for how could she be happy, alone, out here, without us? My mind could not understand her humming to herself, so naturally high, when my mother, her sister, remained swallowed by the ocean. Right there. Right through the brambles, across the rocky boundary, an eighth of a mile hike is all to the sea, her grave. My mother's hair strands snagged in the nasty vines, which were proven singed by her burning dress along the path; her burned dress and one of her shoes washed up on the cliff wall where they say she jumped; her footprints. Everything. All the forensics.

What had we, had I, done to Aunty to deserve her abandonment for two years after that awful night?

When I stood in her driveway, stunned at the apparent perfection of Aunty's property, having expected to find only disrepair, she turned around and saw me. Her humming stopped, and so did the mirage of perfection. In a snap, Aunty's world was no longer a cartoonish summer of Disney birds and heavenly flowers, no. It all changed to horror. Like a torch lit the Technicolor film of reality and the whole reel melted. Twenty yards away, her face was as clear as one foot from mine in the waning summer light. Her punctured eye, punctured two years ago on *that* night, remained dead and glazed in a milky film and, indeed, unpatched, brazen and naked to the day. The scar she acquired that night rivered from above and through her dead eye, straight down like a bloated and malformed earthworm. She clearly hadn't had it subdued by a plastic surgeon, as I'd expected. Standing staring at me like a zombie, her mouth slack, she revealed her broken maw: several smashed, missing, jagged teeth, so she also had not seen a dentist. And her hair was no longer a shiny chestnut, but wiry gray, flying in the sea wind, like she for real transformed into one of those fictional, cranky, hunchback witches we used to dream up for stories when I was a child.

Aunty's only in her forties, but she appeared to be a neglected, perhaps depraved, woman in her late eighties. Why no eye patch? No doctor? No dentist? No personal maintenance, but attentive care to her grounds? And her humming as she exited her barn, was it a song of happiness or lunacy? Now, two weeks later, looking back to that moment, these mysteries are mere superficialities, what with the profound shocks to come.

I could not contain my jaw from flapping open, in awe of the transformed woman I loved and missed an eternity. Oh, how I needed *love* and still do. The space in my chest where my heart should be felt like a sucking, swirling black hole.

Before saying hello, she held up a timid index finger to shush me, turned, and took quick care to loop a chain several times through the barn's sliding pocket door and lock the links with three separate bike locks.

Then she said, "Hi."

What's in the barn? She's never locked the barn before. Locking from the outside, to keep what within? To keep what—who—out? Her property is secluded, no homes around. Why the shushing finger? We're alone. What's in the barn? What the fuck is in the barn?

Perhaps when I first got here two weeks ago, I should have followed my instincts and fled when Aunty locked her barn and looked at me with her crazed, broken face. In that moment, I should have walked. But shock—the worst of mental thieves—forced me to slip back into the well of my mind fog. Aunty turned, shh'd me—face naked with bloated earthworm scar across her dead eye—locked her barn twenty yards from me, and stared me down with her one remaining eye. She tried to smile, which made her appear deranged or wicked or both, what with her villain's face, full of busted teeth. A passing sea wind picked the dry strands of her hair, grayed 65 percent, and lifted them like electrical frying.

"What! You turn us away for two years and now you . . . ? What do you have in the barn? My car broke down. I need your help," I shouted, still standing by her pink home's blue front door.

Why did she lock the barn? Why is she shh'ing me? No one is around. No neighboring homes. What the hell is in the barn?

And what did she say? Did she answer my questions? No. She flipped me an evil smile, like someone who she is not, like someone insane, and said, "Get in the house, funny girl," in the flat affect of the criminally depraved—or perhaps like someone trying to keep a lid on something about to boil over and that would burn us whole. I couldn't tell which persona she was: villain or protector.

In that moment, with her confusing directive to "get in the house, funny girl," I think I too turned insane, desperate to find traction and climb out of my well of fog and denial and grief, but slipping. I focused on the barn.

The barn is huge. Natural wood siding and two giant doors that, when opened, allow you to drive a tractor on in and out. I remembered the back door to her barn, the hidden one behind which Manny and I would wait to make grand entrances for our theatrical performances, on a stage made of shipping crates, with stage curtains made of old sailboat sails. I ran around the back, past the herb garden, catching a ground cloud whiff of rosemary, beyond the side of the barn, burst to the hidden back entrance—which you have to know exists to find—and found it barred from the outside with a crosshatch of boards, which had never been there before. *Why the barring from the outside? Why bar the possibility of leaving the barn?* But I was outside, so I removed the boards and threw them on the ground.

After clearing the door and entering, I slithered to the center of the barn, which looked the same as always: a mottled-lit middle where one might park two tractors, and on each side, two horse stalls, all four of which Aunty had converted to hold the stuff of four different hobbies. In the house-works construction stall, there remained her circular saw, the hammer, the nails, all her tools laid in perfect placement on a workbench. And a hatchet on a hook. The smell was of dry dirt.

Everything in the inner part of the barn was the same too. Manny's and my shipping-crates stage with the sailing-sails curtains waited in a corner, prop box taking center stage, the lid on.

I looked around in a frantic way until I saw lights on in a temperature-controlled side addition to the barn, a place Aunty used to say she'd built to use as an all-season potting shed, but actually used to store all her nursing stuff. In I entered, discovering the side room upgraded with functioning medical gear, flashing monitors, a stand with a saline drip, a metal medical bed, and in that bed, connected to the monitors and the drip, a woman, out cold, eyes shut, oblivious to me in the doorway.

All this two weeks ago, the start of our descent into total, unhinged madness. Or maybe we've been in this dark sink of madness for two years anyway, ever since that damn fire. Right now in present time, a woman with a hatchet has found our hiding spot.

She just crashed in on our hole, and I hear her roaming around up top now, circling the wooden cover with her heavy stomping.

"You BITCH! I'll end this now!"

She must jump with both feet on top of the wooden cover above our heads.

Dirt and paint chips cascade and snow our hair.

The storm is picking up mad winds, howling, slicing winds above. I hear the wild sea out beyond. And I'm sure the sky is about to release a biblical flood. I want the strength to haul on out of here, push on past her, break into Aunty's house, crack open her glass gun case, and grab her Roosevelt gun. I want to see if Manny's alive. But I'm frozen. The woman up top stamps her feet on the wooden cover above.

More paint chips and soot rain down in our hair.

I can't tell if the whispers for "Mop, Mop, Mop," are from the wind, the ocean waves crashing beyond, my imagination coiled in my fear, or real from my companion.

CHAPTER FOUR
AUNTY LIV

Two years ago
Aunty's property
The guest cottage

"You know what you should do," my sister, Johanna, says. She's sprawled on the queen-size iron bed I put in her guest cottage, behind my barn. The open window catches the sound of the crashing Atlantic, past the acres of corkscrew trees, brambles, and vines. The salty sea air washes in with each seismic wave.

Johanna's atop a pink-and-green quilt I purchased at the local artisan fair in Rockport. I just told her about my affair with Chief Surgeon Kent Dranal, and I'm leading up to another truth I must reveal, and also today's allergic murder I witnessed, by hearing. *Allergic murder I witnessed? What has happened? Get a grip. Focus. Say the words. Tell her.* I keep trying to interrupt my little sis, rushing through facts and telling her I'm upset and traumatized. But the problem is, I can't get her to focus. And I can't focus either. I feel untethered, unable to grasp a lasting thought. Like my brain is drugged and my mind disembodied. Like the night when I was fourteen and Johanna was out with Mother shopping, safe, and I was left home, dragged to the brick coach house by the estate manager, and he shoved a metal pin he used to affix to his shirt, the color, blue it was, with the shape of California as the image, in my mouth, and my father came in and . . . Like the two nights I miscarried. Like when I lost hold of all reason when I found out why Johanna's sister-in-law, Sister Mary, really left the church.

I should have been stronger all those times. I should be stronger now. But has each event left me weak? *Am I weak? Is that why Kent keeps me? Like Cate said? No. Stop. Don't think of the past. Don't think of weakness. Think of today. Tell Johanna. You need help. Get help. Don't turn in on yourself this time. Don't.*

When I got home in a fluster tonight, I found Johanna drunk on bordeaux. Of course she cracked the entire case during the day while I was working (spying and then working in Boston). The turquoise polka-dot bedside lamp is tipped to the side from her flailing arm, which she's still thrusting in fruitless attempts to flick ash ends off her Marlboro into the oyster-shell ashtray. The oyster shell is mouth down to the wood floor, ashes everywhere. I pick it up and move it along with her moving hand, like a net holder under a man about to jump from a building. As soon as she smashes the butt in the shell, I reset the shell to its decorative place on the white wicker nightstand. It's not supposed to be an ashtray. The nightstand should be holding a clean shell, the turquoise polka-dot lamp upright, and a sweet summer romance for bedtime reading. Instead, this cottage is a soiled dorm room for a drunk girl.

Johanna, unstoppable, lights another cigarette. I correct the lamp. *Son of a bitch!*

My sister, Johanna. Jo-Jo Beans. Sis. Jo. She's not an alcoholic, but she's a damn goldfish whenever I get a shipment of this bordeaux in from France. It's a specific vintage she and Mop and I found a few years ago when we rented a cottage in Saint Rémy de Provence. Mop was only sixteen, but *quand en France*, so we lent her two sips: one from Jo-Jo's goblet, one from mine. Mop drank her minor first sips in a solemn silence and declared the event a "sacramental taste of family blood." Then she twisted her lips like she does, in a shrug, and added (and Johanna and I froze our goblets midair, awaiting Mop's expected dismissive tagline), "Well, not really. It's just wine." Jo and I clinked a cheer once Mop delivered her predictable line and then rolled eyes at the girl who turns everything into some profound religious occurrence only to flip to ambivalence, like she's juggling an internal debate between dramatic faith and sterile reality.

What I would do for a stitch of Mop's depth, her introspection, her willingness to seek traction into things unknown, only to deny them. The girl is a complicated ball of contradictions, but she is colorful in her personal cyclone and thus alive. I'm jaded. Losing my colors. I don't pose questions about anything anymore. Doing so would require me to consider events of my past, and whenever I do, I fail in a scary psychological way. So I must remain clinical. Even today. Even after what I witnessed. I went to Saint Jerome's an hour after leaving Proserpina's. By then, they'd already cleared Vicky for removal to the morgue. I played dumb and jaded and callous: just another dead woman. Who cares?

What happened today? How? Is hearing witnessing if you do not see with your eyes? My God, Cate murdered her neighbor, someone named Vicky. I want my peaceful life back. I have grown insane, lost my grip, the world around me, also insane.

"The lamp, Johanna! Dammit! Johanna Vandonbeer-Pentecost, stop, listen. My God, you with the cigarettes. You don't even smoke," I say, righting the polka-dot lamp, *again*, on the wicker nightstand. Her white cotton nightgown reminds me of when we were girls, but her braless boobs, tanned to a summer pumpkin, sweat through and remind me she's very much a grown woman. And here she's going to give me grown-woman, drunk advice on what to do about my extra-marital affair, and she doesn't know the whole truth or the real horror yet. My heart's about to bust through my rib cage.

"Oh, Livvy, don't call me's by my first name. You're not Mumsy-Mom." She giggles, then grows drunk serious, so with a fighting devil smile. "I smoke whens I drinks, Liv! And no!" She stutters, blubbering her lips, her eyelids dragging to stay open, the right one drooping more than the left. "You listen to me-ze-me, Sister Pister. You knows what yous should doooze? You should write a big, mean letter to this wife. Be super-duper mean, as mean as you can. Get it all out. And then you rip it up! You . . . but you-wooo . . . da dum dum, you never send. Rip it up! To the up-up-up!" She makes like she's ripping her pale-pink cotton top sheet like paper, which is impossible, because of course I got her precious, waxed ass the one billion thread count from Frette. "Bad paper." She smacks at the sheet for not ripping like paper. She doesn't notice facts; all she sees is the last drop of bordeaux I'll allow her tonight. She's done. I know the signs.

"Go to sleep, Jo-Jo. We'll talk in the morning."

I tuck her in, like I always do, or she always does for me. As I kiss her hairline, I take and extinguish her lit cigarette and gather the remaining pack. I skid across the high shine of the pine floor and place the half pack in the jewelry drawer, which sits like a cherry on a cake, top center on the coral dresser. I gather the spent bottles of bordeaux—somehow she drained two on her own today. I'll hide the rest of the case so I can at least have a half glass, perhaps save a sip or two for myself—she'll drink, I'll sip, tomorrow night. I work the evening shift tomorrow, so I'll bury the bottles in my house good and deep—behind the false bookcase to the secret wine room.

Johanna doesn't have a formal job to worry about, but she is supposed to be orchestrating the Mighty Mary charitable trust gala our family hosts every year at the Saleo Country Club. *Shit.* That's in three days. It feels so far off, and it seems, how odd, I won't make it to my own event. Feels like insurmountable mountains of stress and horror and reality lie between me and the event. I hope Johanna has the arrangements settled, the caterer squared off, like she always does. If all Johanna has scheduled tomorrow is a liquid lunch with the valet captain to ensure the Rolls-Royces are parked just so, she still needs to make decisions and be somewhat functional. So I'm shutting her down for the night.

Mop isn't back from Princeton for another few days, so I have this time to unravel for Johanna. Time for Johanna to patch me back up.

I trip on her absurd animal-print Tory Burch flats on the way out of her shingle-shake cottage, so I scoot them under the sand-dollar couch—sand dollars embroidered in blue against the couch's ivory. Johanna and I have the same size feet, but we definitely do not share shoes. I'm a nurse and often in white Naturalizers; she's a glamour girl in prints and colors and couture. At charity galas, I wear classic black spikes; she's in items designers make once and only for her, so it will say so under her picture's caption on the society page of *Northshore* magazine. The animal-print Tory Burch I scoot under the couch must snag Popover. From under the nether regions of the third cushion comes an angry meow from the gray shorthair with lime eyes who travels everywhere with Johanna. Everyone's pissing me off today, so I pull-slam the door in response to Popover. *Damn cat. Damn everyone.*

How do I make any sense of this day? I'm a nurse. I've seen death many times. I'm numb to it, immune. But I am not numb to murder. I am not numb to madness. I don't know how to clear this fog I'm in. *He* hasn't called me. I'm too afraid to ring him. Won't email him. Actually, neither of us use email anyway. Our lives are medical, and the height of our technology is inputting patient stats into electronic records. I carry a beeper and flip phone—Mop is always busting my ass about this—and I don't text, no such capability. I use the internet to check the tide schedule and weather, maybe copy some recipes; no Facebook, no Twitter, no Instagram. I garden and paint and sometimes land a supporting role in the Gloucester Theater in my free time. So there is no electronic trail of our affair for *her* to find, at least as far as I know. The Kisstop room we use, he expenses to the hospital, which is another story. And still, I have a growing fear *she's* figured us out. *I should never have whispered in her ear at Proserpina's.* I'm forty-three; I know better.

His name is Dr. Kent Dranal. Her name is Cate Dranal. The Dranals. A terrible last name. If I were to ever marry him, which as I clear an inch of my mind fog I realize I never will, I'd keep Vandonbeer as my last name. *Dranal, banal, anal*—I can hear the schoolhouse taunts. *What was I thinking falling for a man with a name like that?* Huge mistake saying his name to Johanna, because speaking it led to her laughing fit and a three-second swallow straight from the mouth of the bordeaux.

She sang, "Dranal is an anal, banal anal, anal ass, ass, ass."

If she only knew.

And now she's passed out in the guest cottage, and I'm alone with my thoughts, walking along the flower path in the backyard to my rose house. The solar lights in the perennial beds, the twinkle lights in the trees, illuminate my way. I pass my barn to the side, snaking a finger on the clapboards of the small room addition. I peek in the window and notice the overhead on in the side room, which was supposed to be an all-year potting shed but isn't any longer. No light should be on. I hear a footstep within. I shake.

Maybe just the wind or one of those coyotes. Maybe Johanna worked in there today and left the light on.

I've lived on this property my adult life by myself, no full-time man protecting me. I can handle security. *I must handle security. I can't be the cause, again, of someone's death. Oh, Daddy, I'm sorry. I miss you. Stop. What's that? That's definitely a footstep in the barn.*

A sliver of a shiver crackles up my spine, and I freeze on the spot. An ocean wind of wet salt air, humid and sticky, swipes my cheeks in passing. I paste my body against the barn's siding and walk on tender feet to the back of the barn. My WeedWacker leans beside the secret back entrance, which appears like the rest of the backside and not like a doorway at all. I grab the WeedWacker and hold it like a fighting lance as I enter the barn. Stalling once inside, I plant my feet and bend my knees, like I'm some warrior. As if a forty-something woman holding the right posture is surefire self-defense. The tea-length, poly-blend skirt and inner slip of my nursing uniform restrict the width of my crouch.

I see no moving shadows. I hear no shifting feet. I freeze within, wait for some breath from some corner, but nothing. The light in the barn's sidesaddle of a room crackles and dims and brightens in a soft amber with every blow of New England wind. I decide it's safe to move on to the light that should not be on. Still holding my WeedWacker like a lance, I'm halfway through the middle of the barn, which used to house horses. Under the high roof, you could park two tractors in the center and four horses in side stalls if you wanted. I converted the stalls to different crafting and construction purposes: one stall with my construction tools, saw, hammer, hatchet, etc.; one for making sea-glass sculptures, for Johanna; one for potting and gardening; and one for the stuff of painting ocean landscapes—easel, brushes, oils, acrylics. There's a pin light on in the sea-glass stall, a tiny desk lamp Johanna keeps there. From the outside, I hadn't appreciated this light was on too. In moving to the sea-glass stall, I swear another footfall creeps behind me, but when I turn, I note the noise is the bang of the false board that serves as the incognito back door, which I left open, so it creaks now in the wind.

Using my WeedWacker as a cane, I brace and bend to inspect the top of the sea-glass stall's workbench. Under the pin light, I see Johanna laid two sea-weathered, cobalt-blue bottle bottoms, both of which are so pitted and smooth they likely spent a century rubbing against the seafloor, against the coastline, gritted by sea salt. Truly rare pieces. She has out her copper wire, sterling silver, a foundry crucible for melting the silver, crucible tongs, a blowtorch, and wire cutters. Set to the side is another bottle of bordeaux, which pins in place hand-drawn sketches of the design she intends to paint on each bottle-bottom necklace. One sketch is of a heart with the cursive word *Sisters*.

The other sketch is an infinity sign with the cursive words *love forever*.

Beside the infinity "love forever" drawing, Johanna left a note card that says, *For my beautiful Mop, I love you forever*. I know Mop. She will never take this necklace off once it's finished. How deep she loves her mother, a fathomless well of love. Would my own child look at me like Mop does Johanna? Doesn't Mop look at me, too, like that? Don't I deserve it, don't I? She's more like me, more like me. *Stop. Stop it. Love is not exclusive. Stop. Stop thinking and look around in the barn for the noise you heard. Security. Make sure everyone is safe.*

This third bottle of bordeaux is half-full: Johanna must have stumbled away from it and forgotten. *Oh, Jo-Jo. So that's what you were doing all day.* I picture her in the day's summer sun, her white sundress, her big floppy hat, barefoot with flamingo-pink toes like the wild sea girl she still is inside. I imagine her snaking her way along Haddock Point's curvy, rocky edge, scavenging for perfect sea-glass pieces to add to her collections and projects. She's been hunting blue sea glass our whole lives.

I shut off the workbench lamp and take a short swig of the bordeaux. At this point, it's better I calm my nerves, despite my state.

There are more shadows now in the center of the barn. My side room's amber overhead still pulses, and on each undulation, shadows move. Another creak of the false door in the back bangs, but this time, I'm sure, I hear a scamper of feet outside.

I run into the lit side room to look out the window there, and when I do, I catch a glimpse of a shadow, nothing more, moving in the driveway, low to the ground. Once past my black Audi, beside which the black wisp of shadow further ambiguates, whatever is running disappears. I can't make out what it is, but it appears blockish, bent, possibly on all fours, maybe, so I presume a deer, a neighborhood dog, something large. *I'll call animal control in the morning to check the prints.*

I stand in the side room, the amber light pressing in on me like a warping trap. I crash the WeedWacker to the floor when I realize the ominous change in here. I slap myself, strain for my senses to come alive and make sense of things. *Am I really seeing what I'm seeing? I witnessed a murder today. I witnessed a murder today. I witnessed a murder today. Am I in shock?* I know the signs of shock. I am a nurse. And I believe I can diagnose: I am in shock. All the signs are here. I haven't talked about it yet. Mold clouds cover my tongue, scratchy, fibrous, and tasting of gray. I've gone about my evening in a haze. Haven't changed from my nursing uniform. Haven't called authorities. I'm walking in a barn chasing sounds and shadows. I need help. *I need help. What do I do? Am I really seeing what I'm seeing in this room?*

I try to swallow the strangeness in my life. From this room, *he*, Kent Dranal, took something *she*, Cate Dranal, bungled upon when she rooted through his Jeep, and thereafter extorted her own husband with the knowledge, and thus, by doing so, extorted me by proxy. She has no clue I'm the source of the vials of pentobarbital Kent took from this room, vowing to rid them for me through some obscure back channels, alleviating me of their possession. He wouldn't confess to her where he got them; he let her hold the vials over his head and extort him into staying with her. But he promised last week that he was done, that he'd take the consequences and protect me, protect *us*. We'd be together no matter what, he said.

Thing is, Kent didn't get all the vials.

Instead of clay pots and heat lamps and seeds and bags of fertilizer that I intended take the space of this side room, there's a medical bed, a heart monitor, an EEG machine, a couple of drip lines and holders, a generator, a heating and cooling unit, a sterilizer, syringes, blood pressure cuff, and under a floorboard under the bed, there should be more vials of the pentobarbital that Kent Dranal, my lover, the surgeon, thinks he rid me of. But he only got the vials I kept up top.

All this equipment and medical devices and paraphernalia, lots of gauze, too, all innocently gained. A little while ago, I worked a private nursing job in Manchester-by-the-Sea, on an estate called Willow, and when my private patient survived and revived, the estate gave me the contents of their homemade hospital room, suggesting I offer private services to others of their kind: wealthy New Englanders who scoff the brutal lighting and freezing cold of hospital wings. I don't know why I didn't decline. To make matters worse, in flagrant apathy of drug laws—the people of Willow acted above the law—they gifted a case of pentobarbital too. I should have turned it in. I didn't. I just didn't think it would ever lead to anything malicious. Pentobarbital is a Schedule II controlled substance, used to induce comas. At the right dose, some states use it on death row. We're not talking about an unfinished pack of Cipro you lend a friend for her sniffles.

So now I'm looking around this strange medical room in my barn, the light on, by—I had presumed—Johanna, and I wonder, as my eyes focus, my brain haze clears or muddles more, I wonder why . . . Yes, why the floorboard under the medical bed, under which the remaining pentobarbital should be stashed, is now leaning against the white metal cabinet. I hand-and-knee to the floor to inspect under the bed. The underguts of the barn's crawl space: empty. No vials. No nothing.

That was no shadow. No animal.

I race back to Johanna in the guest cottage.

CHAPTER FIVE

AUNTY LIV

Two years ago

I just found the floorboard disturbed in the side room of my barn. All my stashed pentobarbital is gone. I'm racing back to Johanna's guest cottage. Someone took the vials, and they must mean harm. That someone has to be Cate Dranal, Kent's wife, who killed Vicky today and knew about at least part of the vials. I'm spiraling in these thoughts. Had to be Cate who snuck in here, which means she knows about me. *I should never have whispered in her ear.*

I reach the cottage and at first can't open the door. It's barred. *No, it's not barred, you're pulling, but you should be pushing. Slow down. Calm down.* I'm so outright flustered and freaked, I'm not breathing. *Stop. Breathe. Breathe. Turn the knob, push.* I turn the knob and push. I am a nurse. I am better at panic. *I'm better at panic when I am a nurse.* I open the door and am afforded a quick relief.

My sister is snoring like a fat man after a turkey and a ball game and a trough of Bud.

But now that I know she's safe, relief leaves. I must protect her from whoever came here. I don't know what to do. *I can't let her be harmed, like I let Daddy be harmed. Johanna's my love, my light. Oh, Johanna. I'm scared, darling. I can't care for Mop on my own, I need you here, too, I do.*

Popover scowl-meows at me from the sand-dollar couch, and I won't sleep at all tonight.

I'm going to sit next to Popover on the couch. We'll both stand guard over Johanna, all night, forever.

Cate Dranal took my pentobarbital. She knows about me. What do I do? I haven't heard from Kent. Had to be her. She was in my barn. Where else has she been? In the house? What is she going to do? I need to call the cops.

I check my flip phone. No calls from Kent. I press nine, hover my finger over one, intending to hit twice, but can't. They'll frame me for Vicky's murder; Cate will say I leaned over the booth and dusted peanuts when they both went to the bathroom. The cops won't care that I have no clue about Vicky or her allergies. I'll be framed. *That's irrational.* Doesn't matter how irrational. *There's no video at Proserpina's—I heard the bartender telling the cops, and I've heard before, on other nights.* Doesn't matter. *There's nothing to prove my innocence or framed guilt. Cate's word against mine.* Don't call. *Don't call just yet. Think. Calm down. You're irrational. Wait for Johanna, she'll settle some reason. Keep this with Johanna, keep your cool, keep your job, keep Mop's trust, keep it together. Stay straight. Stick to the facts.*

And also, if I call the cops, I'll have to admit to my good-gotten but ill-kept drugs. At best, I'll lose my nursing license and reputation for having the pentobarbital in the first place. *Call the cops. You should call the cops.* I can't call the cops. I'll go to work tomorrow. *What if they jail me for the drugs? What has Cate done with the vials? Will I be framed for something else too? What?* Talk to Kent. *You need to talk to Kent. Where the hell is Kent? Call him. No, don't you call him.* I'll be a nurse tomorrow and settle on a better plan.

I'm talking to myself in first and third person, which I've never done before. *Yes, you have. Four other times you can recall, in fact, and likely more. When you let your father die. When you couldn't carry your first child. When you couldn't carry your second. When you discovered Sister Mary's secret and couldn't contain your outburst, your jealousy. Stop. Stop. This is different.* This is different. Am I mad? *I'm not mad. Scared and aimless is all. Don't know what to do.* I just need to get through this night. Tomorrow will be clear, and I will figure this out.

I sit and I stare and I pace and I inspect every window in this night cottage upon every creak of every tree. The light is a warping loneliness, shadowed in sinister evil in spots irrelevant in daytime. I sound like Mop. It's just night, no evil. *Stop freaking out, it's just night, no evil.* The blotch of black light on the floor by the heater vent is a hand reaching for me from hell. *Stop it.* The shape in the corner behind the puffy chair is Cate Dranal, standing still and silent, a shape-shifting shadow. I push an umbrella into the shadow's stomach and prove what I know: the night is the devil. As in, there is no being that is the devil. No. The devil is indeed the night.

Now I really sound like Mop. Equating intangible things with intangible things, dramatizing shadows into sinister beings, and anthropomorphizing objects and moving air. All of which would be fine if I could conjure and then deny such thoughts, like her.

Get a grip!
Be rational.
Think like a nurse.
Get through the night.

I need some sleep. My eyes droop, but then another sinister footstep outside, which I must inspect. I find nothing but the big maple in the corner of the cottage's postage-stamp yard. Big Boy, as we call the maple when we tap him for syrup, aches in the wind, which pushes the wood-plank swing into the brambles behind and forward toward the cottage door. I watch the swing swing for a ghost, spotlit by moonlight. *I wish I was dealing with just a ghost. A ghost would be easier than this, whatever this is.*

Maybe I'll sleep from morning until noon, after Johanna wakes. I return to the sand-dollar couch.

I curl my legs into my chest and cram my back into the side arm, giving me perfect view of all four windows, the bathroom to my right, in which I dialed the overhead to the highest blazing-sun setting, and the door in my sight line down the wall on my left, against which I rest my head. Only the coral dresser with the cherry-on-cake drawer, which holds Johanna's Marlboros, obstructs my view of the door handle, but not the door. Not the door. *I can see the door. The door is locked.*

The drip from the sink faucet is a clock pounding out the slow seconds of my mad vigil. I should shut the knob tight, but *tink, tink, tink,* drops of water pace my night—the faucet is a deranged conductor for a deranged situation. *Stop allowing this foolish drama! Stop the dark metaphors. Stop thinking! Count up to one million if you have to. Just stop.*

Popover pops to standing on my thighs, digging his paws into the fabric of my nursing skirt, and plops to the floor in a sudden slap of movement. He scampers across the floor and leaps upon the bed to curl into the sweat-wrinkled back of my sister's nightgown. She kicked her covers to the floor at some point in this warm June night, and her gown is hiked to midspine. Her moony cotton underwear, the type she sleeps in only when not with her husband, and thus, what I call her real underwear, is on full ass display. She snores. The lush. I love her.

Her husband loves her mad too. And she loves him mad back. Philipp. She sleeps here at this cottage I built her about once a week, because she always has. He travels for his family's business anyway, but not in the big, fancy-pants, aloof, has-a-hundred-global-girlfriends kind of way. He flies commercial—first-class, but commercial. No gold jet. No Pitbull hired to entertain a cadre of escorts on a rented yacht in the South of France—although Philipp could afford such excursions.

Philipp is a hard worker for the family trust and charities and always goes to and comes back as soon as his meetings are over. Johanna has traveled with him several times and says he's all business and boring on these trips, so she typically stays with me. He brings her the sweetest things every time. Nothing expensive, just thoughtful items. Sometimes he takes a picture of a beautiful flower and goes to the trouble of printing it, which no one does anymore, so she has something tangible to pretend to smell from abroad. Sometimes he walks whatever beach his hotel is on and finds Johanna a piece of her precious beach glass. He once found a rare orange, and Johanna went berserk. Now she wears the orange piece embedded in melted silver on a chain around her neck. She says it's the "most priceless jewel in the world, and, bonus, from my beloved, King Philipp." Philipp is not as rich as a king, but he's richer than a king in two key ways: he holds Johanna's love and deserves it. When Johanna was eighteen and he got her pregnant with Mop, not a person had a concern, not even I. Johanna has always been living her destiny.

Mop loves her father, yes. But surely not as much as Johanna, and I suspect, or rather hope, not as much as me. *Love is not exclusive. Love cannot be weighed. It's not a competition. No one is entitled. Stop this. Stop this slide. You know you won't crawl out this time. Stop.*

I never found anyone like Johanna found, just right. David, my boyfriend of fifteen years, and the source of two miscarriages, he was never right, even though he was my childhood sweetheart, just like Mop and Manny. But was David really a childhood sweetheart or did my mother force his pedigree on me a year after Daddy died as an acceptable "cure"? *Fucking stop your bullshit! Just keep everyone safe, now, and stop thinking! Stop your fucking thinking!*

Don't think about miscarriages now, don't let the delusions, the blackouts, back in. And now Kent Dranal, my married surgeon, *my love*, is all wrong. If not for Johanna and my niece, Mop, I'd have nothing, no one. Daddy, *oh, Daddy, I'm so sorry*, is long gone. Mother died of cancer years ago.

A blend of cotton and linen makes up the ceiling-to-floor drapes in this cottage. A rippling white set on each of the four windows. They hang from thick silver rods and frame the custom-fit gold blinds, which kiss the edges of the inner window frame. The gold blinds can be finger-pushed up from the bottom or down from the top, the dual action on expensive strings, because I never skimp on gifts for Johanna. When I presented the cottage to her, literally cutting a fat pink ribbon around the door, the white drapes were hung on the silver rods with the gold blinds behind. The drapes were curated to perfection with five wave folds per panel, and the decorator had pushed each of the four blinds twelve inches from the top, and eight from the bottom, all four windows identical. As soon as Johanna entered, she jumped behind one of the white panels and prodded me to jump behind my own, so we could compete on who made the best ghost curtain. She won, but I put up some stiff competition. I can never tell who's the judge in these games we've played our whole lives.

I think we ate a whole half of a chocolate cake after that first ghost curtain game in the cottage. A stain remains of one of Johanna's chocolate fingerprints on one of these panels, because she wouldn't stop touching everything and gushing over every single detail of her surprise. I can't find the panel with her chocolate fingerprint right now. The light in here is full of tricks, blinding me to all benevolence and showing only shadows and evil. My ears, too, they betray me—they detect only footsteps and banging, although I never find any verified source after racing to each window.

Tonight as I pace once again, I finger a white curtain and note how the panels no longer match in wave folds. One has no folds, stretched tight to the middle; his mate panel scrunches into one hundred folds on the end of its side of the rod, like a cowering teen, wincing from a grown man unbelting his pants. *I'm so sorry, Daddy, I should have gone shopping with Mother and Johanna. I'm sorry I let him drag me by my hair to the coach house, to tear away my clothes, to shove his metal pin in my mouth. I was fourteen, I'm so sorry I couldn't stop him myself. Stop! Stop thinking. Stop remembering. Focus on the curtains, survey what's in this room. Think about simple things. Get through this night. The windows are rattling in the wind, look at the glass.*

Another window's panels scrunch to opposite ends of their rod, like a long-married couple in a king-size bed. Another window holds newlywed panels, both scrunched together, huddling in the middle of their silver rod. *Like Kent and I hold each other at the Kisstop Hotel.*

At my window, I use both panels to pretend I'm a curtain ghost, sending soundless boos to my sleeping sister, hoping I'm making her laugh in her dreams.

It's three thirty a.m. I'm losing my mind. *Call the cops.* I can't call the cops. I'm going to the hospital in the afternoon, looking for Kent, and figuring this out like a trained clinician. I note I'm still in my nurse's outfit from my shift. I won't change before my next shift: the thought of being an inch from Johanna is unthinkable. I jostle my hospital ID, clipped to my breast pocket.

Thankfully Mop does not return from college for another couple of days.

Maybe I should write a mean note to Cate Dranal like Johanna suggested. I'll have to admit to the affair in my mind in a naked, honest way. Yes, I guess I should purge the virulence on paper. Writing would make me think straighter. I'll rip it up right after. I open the cherry-top drawer on the coral dresser and extract a note card and a pen, which lie adjacent to Johanna's pack of smokes.

I begin my note to Cate Dranal . . .

> I am the mistress. Know it. Know it. I am the one sleeping in your bed . . .

CHAPTER SIX
MOP

Present time

Still sitting here in the hole, my legs crossed, the dirt wall an inch from my face. I'm huffing wet clay, the most primal aroma. The woman who hunts us is stomping up and down on the cover above. Paint chips, paint chips, paint chips, and splinters rain into our hair. I'm nearly there, nearly to a point where my breath is calibrated to some semblance of a determined plan. Almost to a point where I won't throw up if I move. Thinking and calculating on a way to wake my companion and haul on out. *Why didn't I run away when I found the woman in Aunty's barn?*

Maybe my car didn't break down so suddenly two weeks ago. Maybe I was also being intentional when my car broke down where it broke down. Maybe I missed Manny in a sudden rush. A sudden light after two years of hiding, of denying. He still lives at the end of a twisted path from Aunty's house, across Haddock Point's sea-lapped, granite front face, and after a sometimes treacherous beach. *But does he still live there? Is he still alive after what's happened? I can't tell from down here in this hole in the earth.*

As I look back over the last two weeks, when I first approached Aunty's, I was excited to be *emerging* from the fog I waded in. To even have anger at her for her abandonment, to have longing for love once again, felt invigorating, new. Like awakening from a long sleep in which you remember no dreams.

Over the last two weeks, truths blew up in my face, forcing me to acknowledge them, all the life I blocked, and truths I ignored, for two years. One being the boy I love . . .

Manuel Acista. An old-school Spanish name. We kissed all the time, at first innocently. He's lean and dark and holds a foreign mysteriousness to those who don't know him, even though he's pure American. He carries a remarkable brown birthmark under his right eye. I'd spent incalculable summer weeks, fall weekends, winter weekends, spring weekends, with Manny, in his domain, Aunty's domain, or between those two domains.

Over the past two years, I thought I got only a few texts from him, my love. How strange, given the height our relationship did reach, all the way up to the night of the fire.

Long ago, Manny helped break the case on which creature kept stealing Aunty's roses. Spoiler: not the bunny I'd chased into a butterfly bush and not the mermaid-obsessed seagull named Frank that Manny dreamed up. The thefts kept up another summer after our thirteenth, so it was in our fourteenth year when Manny cracked the case.

One day, late in our fourteenth summer, we saw a fox slinking along the edges of Aunty's lawn, three rose petals stuck to his fur. Pushing through brambles and past bushes and berries, Manny found the fox's literal bed of roses, a matted pad on the floor of the forest, pink and red and yellow petals mixed with strands of his shedding fur.

I spent the next week writing a script for a play as a way to expose the fox—whom we named Mr. Gillray—to Aunty and her invited barn-party neighbors. Manny illustrated the set with Aunty's acrylics, and she didn't care. I played Mr. Gillray, the fox. Manny played himself, finding the bed of roses.

Aunty clapped and hoo-hooted and whistled, leading the longest standing ovation, when we drew the final curtain and dumped two buckets of tissue-paper rose petals: red, pink, and yellow rain, the particles of which still stick to props in the prop box. She'd promised to take pictures so I could show my mother, but I recall her only clapping and clapping and clapping with two free hands, no camera. So when Aunty drove me home, only forty-five minutes to Rye, at the end of that summer week, we sat by the Rye pool and regaled my mother with every single detail but no pictures. My mother giggled and laughed and petted my head and asked a million questions for even more details and reenactments, saying she would have come if she'd known. And as I look back on this memory, did it seem like Aunty sat with a condescending smirk as I retold my mother about the play, as if Aunty presented me and this story as a passive-aggressive consolation prize to my mother, her sister? Like I was a toy between them. No. No, that is just me overlaying our present circumstances on the past, recoloring things in a negative light. No.

At seventeen, Manny pitched a tent in his backyard, facing the sea, and suggested I sneak from Aunty's after she snored herself into the whispers of waves. I ran to him with a flashlight in my teeth. Hiking over the dangerous middle beach, I thanked *goodness* for delivering a cycle of low tide. Once settled in his yellow tent, he lifted my summer dress and showed me what it means to be one with another. Our sweet rocking movements matched the rhythm of the sea below the cliffs. We continued all summer like this, with a pregnancy scare in July—just a scare, no pregnancy, which fear I discussed in a bed cuddle with my mother one night in Rye. That night, she kept rubbing my head and calling me Lovebug or Smarty Tarty or Sugar Cheeks, Mopsy, Mop-Bop, and a couple of her other one million names for me. Now I'm just Mop, the recent college grad.

After that seventeenth summer and the pregnancy scare, Manny and I jetted off to our respective objectives, me traveling, him in his freshman year in London, quite tanned and satisfied. Minus the pregnancy scare, we repeated our summers like this for several years, me adding Princeton in the mix.

When our twenty-third summer came, I thought Manny and I would continue on, but in a more significant, permanent way, for we'd grown up some and went the opposite way of typical childhood romances: we got *closer*. In the school year prior, we maintained a constant—as in daily—stream of letters, racked up long-distance bills with nearly everyday phone calls, and in between, sent emails and texts and IMs. But our twenty-third summer came, two years ago, the fire happened, and Aunty barred my return. My life thereafter, a blur.

Is Manny still alive?

❦

I listen to the thunderclaps above us now; lightning cracks the sky, illuminating electrical air to beam through the cracks of the wooden cover. The woman with the hatchet is pacing like a panther, unable to find where we entered. She stops roaming, stalling, just above our heads. I can see up through the slivers of space between planks of wood to her ball gown, the ripped lining and the dragging remnants of the skirt's tulle lifted in updrafts of high wind that accompany the lightning. I cringe upon an explosion in the sky, another thunderhead howling like a million wolves.

She crouches and starts hacking away at the wood with her bloody hatchet. Splinters and paint chips fall more on our cowering heads. I pull myself up and next my companion, whom I shook awake a minute ago, and push us to the secret entrance point, on the opposite end of this dirt basement. We're going to have to haul out upon the song of the next thunder wolves and hope nature's furious voice masks our footfall.

This is an impossible situation. I'm relying on lightning and thunder to save us.

The woman with the hatchet didn't hear us move under her feet. She's still hacking away in the middle of the wooden cover.

"Bitch," she yells again and again. It's the only word she speaks.

Nature is the sorceress of physics, so she forms an early hurricane in the dead of summer, for fun or judgment or both. As we emerge topside, loud crashing waves collide with loud smashing heavens, and literal green veins of lighting rip the sky, as if to etch Earth's ceiling forever, like a witch's furious face cracking a mirror. All this commotion is a cover for me and my companion as we climb up and out, setting our bloodied feet in holes I'd carved in the dirt wall two weeks ago so as to create a natural ladder. Because this is where I ran when I found the woman in Aunty's barn.

❧

Two weeks ago, I arrived and stood in Aunty's side room potting shed, which, as far as I knew two years ago, was storage for her medical equipment, some nonsense some family of a home patient gave her. I burst in the side room and found a woman, asleep or unconscious, but not dead. A monitor noted her heart rhythm, and I heard the wheeze of her breath.

At the time, my mind couldn't keep and hold any of the fragments of multiple questions popping in my brain like poured carbonation. *A hospital room in a barn? With a patient? A patient?* The woman in the bed looked inhuman to me, with almost undetectable facial features, her face was so bloated. She didn't budge when I screamed. Her heart monitor, some other monitoring device, and her saline either hummed or dripped away, calm against the chaos I saw.

I curled my eyes at Aunty. As in, my pupils twisted near out of their sockets in a total derangement. I couldn't accept the gravity of such a secret. *Aunty has a woman in a hospital bed in her barn. She hasn't let us visit for two years. Why? What?*

Aunty stood in the doorway blocking me, watching with her one good eye and still-exposed dead socket. She clocked my moves with her head askance, appearing frightened at me seeing this woman in a bed in her barn, and perhaps frightened, too, upon thinking on what she must do, in her mind, to keep me quiet. I had never before allowed a feeling of fear of Aunty. I'd always permitted perceptions of safeness around her, so I didn't understand my own feet when I took two steps back and deeper into the medical room, away from her. I braced my hands behind me on a white metal cabinet stocked with gauze and sheets.

Aunty appeared a stone-cold psycho, not rising to my alarm and meeting it. She placed a straight finger on her lips, slow, controlled, and said, "Shh," revealing the triangles of her broken teeth. Despite the wicked visual of her "shh," the sound was not the annoying slap kind of "shh"; rather, it was the coaxing "shh" one uses to lead a witless cow to a jaded butcher.

Black boards blocked the side room's one window, the one that previously looked upon Aunty's herb garden, backyard, and the path to the guest cottage. Rusty nails secured the boards, all cockeyed and rough, into the barn's Sheetrocked wall, and I guess, the joists behind. Only the barn's side room was Sheetrocked, painted, and temperature controlled, while the rest of the barn remained like any drafty, pine, New England horse barn.

Aunty stepped into the side room and stood at the foot of the medical bed. I didn't hesitate. I pushed past her and out into the center barn, back out through the fake rear door, and down along the path to the burned guest cottage. All the barriers and garrisons and moats I'd erected and dredged to block grief crumbled to nothingness. I wanted my mother so bad in that insane moment, remembered her huge, long hugs so fierce that my body would shake. My mind sought to take my body to the place of her last sleep, to scour the soot and the basement for any trace of her. I don't recall the blinding run through the brambles. I recall being surprised to find myself in the middle of the mouth that opens upon the cottage's minor yard, as if a blink changed my location.

The snaky vines ate the twisted trees and unfurled their pointed tendrils to scratch my triceps on both sides. The day waned into a haze-blue evening, so my path was lit, but giving way to dusk shadows. As this was two weeks ago, the sky was clear and navy, unlike tonight, which is stormy and gray and full of green lightning, or, between lightning, blackened by lightless chaos.

Two weeks ago at dusk, my eyes burned to keep focus in the tricks of light and the tricks of rage. I came to the burned cottage remains, the first time since racing here with my father on the morning after my mother was reported missing off the cliff wall, after the fire. Aunty hadn't tended the path well since then, nor did she groom the grounds around the cottage, so those greedy vines and the brambled vegetation had taken dominion like a mutinous jungle, swallowing evidence that humans once slept here. In the interim, what Aunty did, however, was construct and set atop the now exposed basement a square, wooden cap, made of sheets of reclaimed plywood, spackled and speckled with layers of old paint, the various sheets braced by crisscrossed two-by-fours. I know Aunty never constructs anything without false doors, like the back of her barn, like the pink birdhouse we built for that funny bird long ago, or like the pivot bookshelf that is really a door to a closet where she stores wine. So I noticed in an instant the near-invisible hinges on one section of plywood at the far end.

Although she'd never admit it, Aunty has a tendency to view the world in dramatic ways, like me; this is part of our shared identity, something I accept, but, I believe, she tries to deny. So under a coming full moon and cloudless sky, so unlike tonight, and needing my mother so bad I wanted to die, I knew down to my bones that under that hidden hatch Aunty had built a shrine to my mother. I flipped up the section of plywood at the hinge, and as it banged on solid wood, Aunty crashed onto the scene.

"No!" she yelled. "Don't go down there. Don't disturb things."

"Who is the woman in the barn?" I yelled back as I ignored her walking closer, gaining on me. I looked into the hole, so dark down there, stained of soaked soot, charred wood, coal streaks everywhere, and scattered debris from the fire that was never cleaned out. Whatever fell from the cottage to the basement and didn't incinerate was left to rot under Aunty's patchwork cover. This was no shrine. This was a trash pit of my mother's last-touched items.

One of my mother's favorite animal-print Tory Burch flats sat beneath the opening I peered through and within a beam of the moon's rising ray.

If this shoe is here, what about the shoes the investigators say she wore, running to the ocean on fire? Which pair? She usually wore her flats when she stayed at Aunty's. That's what I questioned two weeks ago, what pair of shoes my mother wore to launch herself off a cliff to stop her body from burning. *Why is this shoe down here?* I told myself I was inventing irrelevant nonsense by questioning the shoe's presence and entered the pit to get her shoe—the only thing I had of hers to hug.

I considered the shoe a talisman I could rub to pry my mother away from the selfish grips of her afterlife. I didn't consider the implausibility of such a wish. I just wanted the shoe, wanted it more than I wanted Aunty to explain the unexplainable horror in her barn.

Two weeks later now, as I and my companion tremble outside the same basement hole, for we just used the clamor of nature as a cover to escape, I don't understand the total insanity that has overtaken my family. My companion and I shiver in silence, hoping the woman with the hatchet, still hacking at the wooden cover, won't see us. We're in the realm of the unthinkable, the unfixable, the unregulated by any laws, man-made or divine. I wish I and my companion could run, and we try, but more green lightning rips the sky, illuminating the night to a glowing green, veining the heavens, etching time, wrinkling space. I can't hear my own thoughts given the thunder dump trucks crashing into tractors in the sky. And with that noise collide all the hydrants in the world, which rise in tsunamis, only to kill themselves in screams against the cliff wall, a minute run away, but beside us tonight. My brain bashes against my skull, trying to escape.

We freeze, hoping the hurricane won't distract the hacking woman from her job to see us. Thunder rocks me, pushes me, and I trip. I'm facedown in the dirt above the hole, so my feet twist in vines. My face hovers above the open hatch to the basement. The woman with the hatchet still has her back to us as she swings down and cracks through the wood cover.

"Biiiiitchhhhh!" she yells into a new jagged hole.

I'm going to get Aunty's Roosevelt gun, I think, and as I do, like the woman hears me thinking, she turns and sees me and my companion, who has also fallen to the ground, a belly across my leg with the fabric tie around the calf, so as to stem the flow of blood from my earlier hatchet wound.

I should stand and pull my weak companion along, try to edge us out beyond the hatchet woman. But we're trapped. The vegetation is thicker than two weeks ago, and we can't bust through the hedges and brambles and pricker bushes surrounding us on all sides. The only way out is the skinny trail the woman cut, back out to the walking path, all of which is behind her and at the opposite side of this burned and covered basement.

Thunder cracks a few gray eggs in the sky, and the first trickles of rain sizzle down. The torrent of all the cracked eggs will begin soon. Wind whips in racing cycles around the three of us, the hatchet woman, me, and my companion, tying us in crazy invisible ribbons and holding us to our spots. The ribbons of wind also bring eggshells of rain to fly into my eyes and sting them with their sharpened velocity.

I peer down the hole from which we escaped, in which we were hidden, and given the storm clouds thickening more above, I can't see much. *Where are my glasses? My contacts?* I'm blinded by my natural eyes as well. Fuzzy in daylight even without the blurriness of a hurricane. Upon the next crack of lightning, the space below is lit like two weeks ago, only then illumination was steady, provided by a faithful full moon. I'm immediately transported again to the moment when I saw my mother's Tory Burch shoe in the dirt and *needed* only her shoe, coveting it with my withered soul.

As if two weeks ago were now, I hear Aunty say, as she said in that moment, "Let her go," meaning my mother.

"I will never let her go!"

So here I am, thinking again. I realize I must be fading into unconsciousness, for I should be focusing on getting me and my companion out of this storm and away from the hatchet. But it's easier to rest, just a second, and go where my mind wants to go.

Two weeks ago . . . I dug into the soil of the cottage basement, making foot holes in the soft earth to reclaim my mother's Tory Burch. At the bottom, I captured and clutched it to my chest and ignored Aunty above, until, hearing her scrabble on down into the hole to join me, I looked up at her and her mangled face like a rabid beast, like I was the one with the mangled face. How dare she keep this shoe from me for two years. I could have held it. I could have cried into it. I could have conjured my mother in a round of Ouija while wearing it. I could have commanded the shoe to return my mother back to land and out of the sea. I thought all these things and no, I did not consider the impossibility, or the implications, of the witch's spell I brewed in my mind. *Witch's spell? That's not real.*

"Who is the woman in the barn, Aunty?" I said in a growling, unnatural voice, me now the deranged psychopath, not her.

She puffed out an exhale, closed her working eye.

"Who is the woman in the *barn*?" I clutched my mother's soiled shoe tighter, merging the sole to my sternum.

Aunty breathed deep and creased her brow, but still said nothing.

"Who. Is. The. *Womaninthebarn?*"

"Don't yell, Mop, please. That's so unlike you."

"Oh, seriously. Seriously. For real? Who is the woman in the barn, Aunt-y?" I stressed *Aunt-y* as two distinct syllables in an intentional aggression to her face, challenging her identity before me. How dare she tell me what's like and unlike me, suggesting I don't know my own self. *Do I know my own self?*

She sighed, opened her one working eye, strained the lid on her dead one, but low, and inhaled in a long and contemplative intake, perhaps a calculating intake, like even she questioned every word she was about to speak.

"She's my friend," she said. "Um." She turned a circle, sticking her thumbnail in her teeth, slipping there when catching nothing but a hole. Her thumb fell farther in her mouth. "Mop, you can't tell anyone about her. I could go to jail. Mop. Mop. Are you listening?"

"Who is the woman in the barn?" I said, slow and gritted, the shoe in my hand like a weapon for a bludgeon.

Aunty shook her head and dropped her shoulders, as if in that moment, she gave up whatever battle she'd been waging. Whatever facade she thought she was keeping. Her voice cracked; she breathed in quick breaths through her open throat, a minor hyperventilation. "Fine, fine, fine, fine," she said to the ground, catching herself from falling by placing a hand on the dirt wall. Not looking up to meet my eyes with her one good eye, she said in a hushed mumble, "Here's the story with the woman in the barn." She looked up at me, her eye wide and glowing green like an alive crystal ball. I didn't recognize her still. "Mop, I hope to God you understand how serious this is and you'll not say a word. I didn't want to involve any of you in any of this."

"God? You hope to God?" I asked. How dare she invoke God in the basement where my mother last slept. We were on the most sacrilegious soil anywhere ever in the history of forever. We were in the epicenter of hell, and here she had the audacity to say the word *God. God who? God where? Where is my mother, God? I want my mother back, God!*

"Oh, Mop, there you are," Aunty said in a desperation, like she parted curtains between foggy dimensions, having scoured every multiverse in search of me. As if for the past two years I didn't live an easy forty-five minutes away in Rye, or a click or dial away at Princeton. Some spell broke around her, her face once again the face I knew, albeit scarred and toothless and missing an eye and sad, but warm and full of light. I could read the transformation and all the emotions she conveyed in a simple second, for I'd spent countless hours with her my whole life. I knew her best, as much as I knew my mother, more than anyone else on this planet, save Manny. We read the ones we love like the sightless master blindness, eons with the braille. And she was my braille.

And if I'm being truthful, I'd read her scary braille before.

One night when I was fifteen, I slept at Aunty's in my own designated room. She woke me when I heard her roaming the halls, talking to herself in a sleepwalk. Moaning like a ghost, she stood in my doorway; her white nightgown swished around her stick-straight legs from a sea wind blowing through my open window. I got up slow and tried redirecting her back to bed. It had been three years since her second miscarriage, also when she famously threw David, her longtime boyfriend, to the brambles and out of her life forever.

Swaying in my bedroom doorway, my bedroom in her house, Aunty alighted her green orb eyes to me and didn't blink. But I knew she wasn't seeing me. I knew, although I don't think I'd registered one before from her, she was in one of the catatonic states I'd heard the Rye servants whisper about. She said in a strange stumbling staccato, long pauses, and a warbling dropped monotone of slurring, like she'd just had a root canal, "Mop's the daughter . . . I should have . . . David. Daughter . . . should . . . mine . . . David. Why . . . *whyyyy* . . . can't you give me my own daughter, David, David, David, you fail." She picked up the pace of her warbling dropped monotone, as if she'd been shot with adrenaline, although she kept her bright eyes, which seemed filmed over, unblinking. "Why was I the one to lose the babies? Why was I the one with the metal in her mouth? Why was I the one with Daddy to die, Johanna? Why, Princess!" When she said *Why, Princess,* the phrase was full of hate. Spit seethed in a spray from her mouth.

I knew in reading the braille of Aunty, what she needed was a soft voice and a sterile reminder of reality, and certainly not fear, and definitely not pity. As I look back from my current age of twenty-five, here above this horror hole, I have to now recognize how strange it was for fifteen-year-old me to not shy in fright nor be surprised by Aunty sleepwalking and saying *Why, Princess* like a psychopath. I must now force myself to accept the definition I must have always known I should have always had for Aunty Liv. One far removed from perfection. *Did I allow her mental sickness to grow?*

I fear I enabled her. It was easy to enable this bout of psychosis from her, easy to hide, to bury, and focus on her shininess, because she was not all good and not all bad, she was not one thing, not one dimension. I could choose the safe parts of her, if I wanted. And I could do the same for myself, if I ever had to. These are the subconscious lessons I must now admit to myself.

Back then, during Aunty's haunting night terror when I was fifteen, I knew that all that would break her night psychosis was a clinical diagnosis and a firm action plan. This is how I liked her treating me when I slipped on ice and yelped in pain after spraining my ankle, or raged in anger at a nest of red ants that caused my shin to swell in a rash, or cried misery tears from missing Manny when he left one August for a month-long soccer camp. So that's what I knew she needed too: clinical reality and a plan—either that or my mother's smothering sugarplum-scented hugs, which I didn't have the perfume or breasts or authenticity to pull off.

"Aunty, it's Friday night at Haddock Point. You are sleepwalking and having a night terror. I will walk you back to bed now."

She dropped her hypnotic gaze, closed her eyes, and shook her head. "Oh my . . . what? Where am I? Mop?" She stumbled in the hall, her white nightgown billowing on the hardwood floor as her knees failed. I held her up.

"Come on, Aunty. It's okay. I'll walk you back to bed."

We never discussed the event in the morning, or ever. I didn't even mention the event to my mother, for Aunty's overflowing subconscious thoughts revealed a buried hatred for my mother, one covered and covered in layers of Aunty's fight to sustain a real love. I focused on the layers of love.

Perhaps I was wrong to bury such an event. I know now I was wrong to bury such an event.

Now at age twenty-five, two weeks ago in the burned basement hole, and again witnessing before me yet another breaking of one of Aunty's psychotic spells—this one with severe implications—all of Aunty's own walls and barriers protecting her from the reality of grief crumbled away, like mine. I saw it happen.

It ended up being a short window, though.

"Mop, oh, baby, I'm so sorry, baby. You have no idea how much I miss you." Aunty started to cry. Her shoulders lowered. She sank to the ground, her knees in soft dirt. I wanted to hold her, her to hold me. I missed her so much my arms stretched out for her, listening only to my heart and not my fogged frontal lobe, which separated me from my own self with a million questions and red flashing warnings. I had no idea how to understand the woman she kept in the barn, and there I was, holding my mother's soiled shoe in an abandoned basement with a makeshift roof, the scent of wet soil on a full-moon summer night. I stood confused within a pit of charred objects.

"Aunty, you're scaring me. I don't know what you're doing. Who is that woman in the barn? A friend? Why would you . . . ? What are you doing? Why do you lock the front doors and bar the back?" My heart choked my lungs. I wanted to vomit. Tears came out my eyes, out my nose. My arms wavered in the air. I didn't know what to do with my own hands, except grip the life out of my mother's shoe.

"Oh, baby. Don't worry. Baby. Listen." She clawed the dirt walls as a brace to stand again, widened her nostrils to intake air, and steadied herself to continue her story. Still, she did not meet my eyes; instead, she looked out beyond my shoulder to another dirt wall, staring straight, as if she still had two eyes. "She's a nurse at Saint Jerome's. A friend of mine. She came here two years ago, afraid for her life."

I stood straighter. "Two years ago? When Mom died? When Mom died!" My voice rose with each sentence. "Is the woman in the barn connected to what happened to my mother?"

Aunty's head vibrated, rather than shook, like I'd slapped her from her story into present-day reality and the two didn't match. Her head shaking seemed an effort to calibrate facts. "No," she said, controlled, in a bellow, like when she'd said "shh" in the side room in her barn. Then came another head oscillation of calibration and she was back to having an etched forehead of sadness and open grief, staring out beyond my shoulder, reciting her story.

"No, baby. This was after your mother. After the fire. My friend was having an affair with a married man. Um. And the wife of this married man wanted to kill my friend. Yes. Um. So my friend was staying here with me and hiding out. And. And. So one night the wife came here looking for my friend." Aunty turned two more circles, raising her voice and also the rhythm of her narrative, while bouncing faster the double pendants she still wore around her neck.

Aunty continued, "This wife, she slammed my friend's head into the foyer floor, in the house. My friend went into a coma. The wife fled. I, I, I, couldn't bring myself to bring my friend to the hospital, because . . .

because . . ." Aunty cast her eye to my mother's shoe. "Because, um, I didn't know who this wife was and I couldn't name her, so she got away scot-free. I didn't trust the wife wouldn't attack my friend in the hospital, so I kept my friend here. I had all the equipment, and I am a nurse, so I kept her here. And. That's all. I kept her here. Before I knew it, a year went by. Then two. And I'm in too deep. I don't know how it got so far." She seemed to think of something else and rushed out some final explanations. "She has no one in the world to care for her. She's an only child, parents dead, no friends. I was her only friend. The hospital and the cops think she ran off and committed suicide. That's a big statistic, you know. People disappearing to a secret place to kill themselves."

This last part, the piece about suicide statistics and medical facts, this was a glimpse of the old Aunty, but as she relayed it in the course of her crazy story and the false version of herself before me, the statement didn't fit.

I squished my eyes, confused. Held up a hand to stop her from continuing with her nonsensical words, which I could not accept. I'm not a flaming moron. I flagged the gaping holes in her tale. I logged her shifting eye, her stumbling stutters, her word fillers and repetitions. But two weeks ago, I curled into my mother's shoe and sobbed. And also, no matter what Aunty had to say, I still loved her and, it's true, I wanted to protect her, enable her to get well again. *Oh God, please, stop talking and just hold me*, I thought. *Please say you love me, because I love you.* Holding back tears and wishing for love took all the strength I had left for the day.

"Can we go inside, please?" I said with a trembling voice.

She jostled at the question, a look of terror on her face.

"Inside?" she said, as if her own home haunted her.

What the fuck is inside?

"Please?"

She did her head shake of calibration once more and returned to a cool, practiced calmness. "Of course. Yes, of course," she said. "Let's do that. Go inside."

CHAPTER SEVEN

MOP

Two weeks ago

Aunty led me out of the burned basement—the night not raining nor storming—a regular summer night with a full moon. When we neared the side room of the barn in which the woman "slept," I stared at the boarded window blocking my view of her. Aunty walked on ahead of me, brushing up the scent of rosemary and basil as she passed her herb garden. A couple of crickets sawed their legs in a solemn violin duet.

Aunty's various perennial beds spread out across and around her lawns like a multicolor patchwork quilt: yellows, purples, pinks, and blues lit by the big, bright moon on high, by strategic solar lights down low, and midair by twinkle lights, strung, like always, throughout the limbs of her willows and birch, maple, and oak.

Aunty's roses were in full bloom and pink, yellow, and red. The pillows of her white hydrangeas were baby clouds, and the blue ones electric sea anemone. Her annual round forest of fifty sunflowers was growing to its usual monumental height and about ready to burst into yellow-and-brown dinner plates atop swaying ten-foot stalks. She always planted the sunflowers in a spiral, and it seemed to me they were a council of elders convening a summit on how to govern Aunty's lawns and farther, the sea beyond. Guarding the entrance to the sunflower summit, a resident rabbit of gray and white froze like a stone next to his best friend, a granite cherub. Assessing me as a nonviolent threat, the rabbit unfroze and resumed his nonchalance. A blade of grass hung from his slow chewing mouth like a mechanic with a toothpick. The fattest, laziest sentry on the planet.

Given this intoxicating environment, I allowed a wave of nostalgia to comfort me for three seconds, amid the turmoil I felt inside. Nature must have sensed me needing sedation, for she sent a bullfrog to add thrums of bass to the crickets' violins, and a seagull to cut the sky with a cry of soprano, long-winded and mesmerizing. How I used to love this place, my happiness reflected in the concert of the creatures and the rainbows of the plants and the white-noise hum of the strung twinkle lights.

I was awakened out of my slip into familiar comfort and back into our new strange reality, when in arriving at Aunty's blue front door, flopping pink hibiscus stabbed a vapor of high-octane sugar up my nostrils, like a magician's finger snap to the hypnotized. But I wanted the happy hypnosis back. I wanted my mother. My aunty. Us. Our family. I wanted to conjure illogical, fantastical conversations with that lazy rabbit, and gossip with him in my mind about the snobbish severity of the sunflower congress, all tall and high and mighty and pretentious as always—like before. Carefree in my curiosity. I wanted to be better, less frantic in my mind, less grieved. Less fogged. I wanted, really wanted to *emerge*. I wanted to break down and hug Aunty, and I wanted her to hug me, so we could heal each other and at least be us together again. I'd take a fraction of our old lives. *Please, just a splash of happiness back again. Anything. Please.*

Her marble foyer, the Mermaid Library on the right with the multiple sets of metal mermaid bookends, the living room with the multicolored sea-life wallpaper on the left, the one with the blue-and-white rug I once muddied with potatoes: all the same. The hallway that ran center of the house to the kitchen in the back still held its own pattern of multicolored wallpaper, the hallway's pattern being of birds and vines, not sea life like the living room.

"It's funny you should show up today with a blown gasket, Mop. Manny called here today, too, looking for you. He's home from London. Graduated," Aunty said.

And another slap to awaken.

"What did you tell him? Did you tell him where I was?" I had just finished crying over my mother and her Tory Burch shoe, which I still held and didn't plan on letting go. What she said about Manny was a wallop of a slap. I stalled in the foyer, the white marble shining like an ice rink after a Zamboni pass. Expecting her to lead me up the stairs to my regular bedroom, I remained waiting for an answer and for her to head up the stairs, but she continued on through the Mermaid Library.

"What did you tell him?" I said louder, causing her to stop by the section of her library she called the Good Books section. All the good books' spines were cracked so badly you could barely read the titles, for she read or loaned them so often. But unlike before two years ago, dust now covered this frequently used section. It seemed the mermaid bookends were crying, but upon closer inspection, the tears were wispy strings of spent spiderwebs. Still, Aunty didn't answer me.

"Aunty, seriously, Aunty, what did you say to Manny?"

Her change of subject to something lighter, Manny of all *things*, my lost love, my one lifelong friend, was yet another disconnection to the insanity around us. I sounded frantic over him, and I didn't care.

"I told him I hadn't talked to you and didn't know where you were. I gave, as I've given him before, your Rye number."

"Before?" And *your* Rye number? She used to always say *the* Rye number. As if she could be reached in Rye too. The difference between *your* and *the* is meaningful in this context. I felt a stab of pain in my heart, like she abandoned me all over again and meant to stick with it.

"He's called several times over the last two years, Mop. Hasn't he reached you at the house? At Princeton?"

"No. Only sometimes, a text message is all, I think." I trailed my words in doubt for some reason I didn't then know, or yet acknowledge.

With all the strangeness and Aunty flitting in and out of being my old aunty and this other being of strange psychology, I couldn't even summon anger. How do I explain what fog feels like? Tastes like? Tastes like dehydration; feels like sitting at the bottom of the pool, brain pulsing, sight wavy, wanting only one thing. air.

I followed her to the first-floor guest room, the one off the library with gray-and-green wallpaper and a twin bed, which threw me as yet another sting of abandonment.

"Won't I stay in my old room?" This, this act of putting me in the gray-and-green guest room, which is what we always called it, a room she reserved for people who visited her maybe once a year, was so impersonal, like downgrading me to a mere acquaintance. I swallowed air so as not to choke. I fought back tears to be led to this room, a sign I was still and would always be a castoff. She no longer loved me, no longer wanted me around; she couldn't stand to look at me with her one eye, or worse yet, grew indifferent to my existence, that's how it felt. I wanted to lie down and die.

Parading through the Mermaid Library, I once again questioned the Roosevelt gun in the glass case and why such violence existed in such an otherwise love-filled room, pointing its barrel out the window at her fantastical lawn.

I had my own room in Aunty's house, upstairs. I stayed at Aunty's so much, both my mother and I did, the family joked how we should claim Aunty's as our permanent address. Obviously, it was Aunty's house and I would respect if in the two years since she shut us out she'd made renovations, but given the history, wouldn't she explain, acknowledge the change, and at least say why I couldn't use the room she previously, for my entire life, kept solely for me? She'd painted a sign for the door:

MOP CLOSET—it's not a closet, it's a girl's room with a canopy bed and lace curtains, a green dresser, a retro record player, a dictionary, a writing desk with all my papers, journals, too, and three of my favorite paintings of the sea, painted by none other than Aunty.

"Oh, baby—" And here she was being Aunty again. "I'm so sorry. I'm so rattled." She hugged me, which felt half-true, half-false, and too long and too short, all at the same time. Pulling away, she said, "Right. So your room. I didn't mention. Right. Um . . . So there's a raccoon up in the attic. Hmm." She held her long finger to her closed lips, then popped it off to continue. "He's stuck up there. Weird. I had to board the attic doorway and all. I've been trying to get him out of there on my own, but I need to get animal control out here. I'll try tomorrow. He'd keep you up all night with his scratching about."

She's been living with a raccoon in the attic? The attic is a finished bedroom with four dormers. It's not really an attic. It's a finished floor of the house with carpeting, a king bed, and a second master's bath. So . . . um . . . and . . . a trapped raccoon? Boarded the attic door? Which attic door? There's two. One from her bedroom, and one at the end of the hall in which my bedroom sits. I don't think, yes, I definitely think I don't believe this story.

I chose not to ask further. I needed space. Needed to sit in the guest room and hug my mother's shoe. Alone.

"Okay. I need some rest. And a shower. I'll deal with my car in the morning," I said. The guest room had its own attached bath, a single stall shower, no tub, and a white pedestal sink.

At some point while showering, a time that was a mental black hole from all the crying and confusion, I forced myself away from obsessing over my mother's shoe, which I kept in eyesight by keeping it on the lip of the sink and the shower curtain open. It took concentrated effort, but I had to stop spiraling into grief, or wind up like I did two years ago, sleeping in the fetal position for three weeks and not eating, not talking to anyone, and convicting the sun of a conspiracy with the devil to cause me debilitating migraines—my sentence to the sun being to blot it out by drawing blackout shades so tight and stapling them in place, I never knew the difference between night and day. A psychiatrist tried to breach the barrier of my locked door in Rye to feed me grief pills, and I told the bitch to fuck off or I'd staple her eyelids. Then I launched the stapler at the door and made a dent in the wood. Aunt Sister Mary Patience Pentecost sat outside my door the whole night saying her novenas, fifty rosaries clinking on her lap as she spent each one, either guarding others living in Rye (herself, my father, and the servants) from me, or guarding me from others, I couldn't tell.

I don't know why I shouted such violence through the door at the psychiatrist or why I denied treatment. I think I said the thing about stapling her eyes shut because that's what I was poised to do to my own self when the psychiatrist's knocks interrupted me. Simply put, it was a confusing time. Insanity is a well we might fall into, and with luck and hard work, we might climb out. Standing in Aunty's guest shower two weeks ago, I asked myself if it was still a confusing time. I asked myself if I had forgotten some things. But even thinking these questions caused me to swallow the shower water and choke, so I had to think on lighter things, like Manny. I didn't want to crawl out of the shower and submerge into Sylvia Plath poems again, allowing myself to consider how she stuck her own head in an oven—a logical conclusion. *Think of Manny, it's okay.* I switched to thoughts of Manny, as a gift to myself, something I realized in Aunty's shower had always been an option, but an option neglected. And so the images and the questions rushed in.

Did Manny ever call me at Rye looking for me? No one ever gave me a message, I think. I pictured his black hair, his blue eyes, his long legs, the birthmark on his chest, the birthmark under his right eye, the others on his arms, his thighs, his inner thighs, the creamy tanness of his skin, like new leather, and swayed in the warmth of the guest shower, training my thoughts on him so as not to fall in the stall and sit under the showerhead for hours—as my active mind wished to do. I looked away from my mother's shoe, shut my eyes, and pretended the white tiled wall and the wetness that steamed there was Manny's skin after a swim. I pressed my fingertips into the tiles and raked down, down again.

But in thinking on Manny and the fact I couldn't remember a call from him in two years, except occasional texts when we were at school, I wandered further into thoughts of my family home in Rye and who lives there still and who might have answered the phone and never given me his messages, maybe. I had to blame someone.

I thought of Aunt Sister Mary Patience Pentecost. I caught her once in my room, rooting through my drawer of crosses, the ones she's gifted me. I think this was about a year after my mother disappeared into the sea.

When I walked in, Aunt Sister Mary heard my steps behind her and froze, bent over my drawer. She stood slow, removing her hands, allowing the crucifixes on chains and rosaries to lace like hair through her fingers.

Facing me with guilty hands, which were glistening clean, as if she scrubbed them with Brillos every morning, she dropped her head to the side and sagged her mouth. Contemplative, like a sad ghost. Although retired from the church, she still wore shapeless house frocks, hiding the curves of her forty-something female body, condemning her breasts as original sin.

"Mary Olivia," she said, as a confession.

"Aunt Mary, please. My name is Mop."

"I know, child. Yes. I'm sorry. It's just, well . . ."

"It's fine. Whatever," I said in apathy. "I don't mind you going through my drawers. I've got nothing to hide."

"But why do you not wear any of the crosses?"

"We've been through this, Aunt Mary. You know why."

"I know your thoughts on the matter."

"I'm sorry. But I need to get ready. I'm going out. Do you mind?"

"With a boy? You know, you should, oh, child. I'm sorry. But without Johanna, I mean, without your mother here, I feel compelled. I hope you are respecting your body and the church."

I wasn't going out with a boy that night, but I wasn't about to correct her. I wasn't about to tell her, or anyone, where I was really going. They'd have locked me up if they knew.

I raised my eyebrows. I didn't want to fight with her. But this was sensitive stuff here, her in my room, riffling through my drawer of crosses, her mentioning my mother and in the same breath the church. It was all I could do to not push her out of my room and slam the door. I also brought to mind some snarky jabs Aunty Liv had woven into conversations about Aunt Sister Mary, quick comments that she didn't give me time to react to. For example, when cooking a fresh whole cod once, Aunty Liv said, "The eyes of the dead fish, like the judgmental eyes of a rich, hypocritical nun." And another time, when I told Aunty Liv about how Aunt Sister Mary didn't approve of my swimming laps every morning like I do, she said, "If you were performing for her, the grand master of approval, she'd be fine, I guess. Hmm. You do your laps here, in the ocean at Haddock in your wet suit like you do. Don't monkey around her byzantine rules, which she herself doesn't follow." She ground her teeth, crossing her own belly with both arms, hugging something missing there. And before I could question her severe reaction and the accusation that Sister Mary didn't follow every single rule and law in the universe, Aunty Liv said, "Enough of what's her name. Hand me the cake bowl," smiling away in her regular shininess.

These comments from Aunty Liv came after Aunt Sister Mary left the church under circumstances that were never explained to me. And these comments and Sister Mary's strange ex-nunship were what I considered when I caught her riffling through my crosses in my Rye bedroom, a year after my mother disappeared into the ocean.

"I'm sorry, Mary. Mop. I'm sorry. I'll leave now," Aunt Sister Mary had said, and fast walked out of my bedroom. And yet, she stopped in the doorway and looked over her shoulder, stiffened her back, and wide-eyed me with her big green eyes like she does, like possessed, and said in a low hum, "If you're to see a boy tonight, I will have to inform Philipp, rather, your father. And you know, and I just have to say, I simply do not approve. I don't know how to. The Lord has not provided me the ability. I must protect you from yourself."

Who is the best to protect you from yourself? Is it you? Is it family? Is it a spirit? Who?

Sometimes I think Aunt Sister Mary Patience Pentecost is the inverse of me. She seems to first think on practical facts, then dismisses those in favor of divine blind faith and grandiose meanings. Like she's an upside-down mirror, able to hold the inverted image of me.

"Anyway," she continued, pressing her clean palms down the no-pleat fabric of her stiff cotton housedress. "I'll have to report this to your father, and I'll pray to our Almighty for you tonight. You are so restless, child. I know your grief remains."

"Don't. Just don't. My father does not care what I do, and neither does anyone else, celestial or real. So you don't have to, either, Aunt Mary. I'm sorry, but please, I need to get ready." I kick-closed my bedroom door and slammed the drawer of crosses in one quick series of motions, not angry that she invaded my space, again, like she always did, which was annoying, but wanting to shut out in a definite slam any mention of beings, living in my drawer, in the air, in the heavens, who might access my mother when I couldn't.

I allowed Aunt Sister Mary and my father to think I went out with a boy, because it was easier if they chose to believe I was back to being a young adult—only about twenty years younger than both my aunts and eighteen younger than my missing mother. Actually, you could say I was a grown woman of twenty-four, so all of Aunt Sister Mary's fumbling about me going out with a boy was a lie of concern, and she knew I knew it. She just wasn't willing—no one was, certainly not I—to address the rabid tiger in the room: my mental state.

I didn't go out with a boy. What I really did, as I often did when home in Rye away from my safe, obsessive study at Princeton, was drive my red Volvo to a state park with an old fort, also in Rye. It was always dark and closed when I'd get there, so I'd stuff my Swedish car on a side street. No one ever suspects colorful Volvos of anything nefarious or, well, out of place, pretty much anywhere. Then I'd scrabble through the brambles that make up the barriers to almost all seacoast New England beaches. Out of the brambles and beyond the dunes, I'd enter the old stone fort, pretending it was a necropolis for those who died at sea, for the fort was twenty feet off the seawall. I'd imagine the current swept my mother's body from the Gloucester/Rockport line at Haddock Park and north to the Rye fort—such ocean physics seemed plausible in my grief. Grief was deep when I sat in that fake crypt in my made-up necropolis with a lit candle to wait for my mother to appear. She never did. But shadows did, and I talked to them, asking them to go fetch my mother.

So did Aunt Mary, the retired nun, who still labored under her own crosses, did she answer the phone when Manny called and never tell me? This is what I wondered in Aunty Liv's guest shower two weeks ago. And then Aunty knocked at the bathroom door, waking me from my consternations.

"Yes," I yelled from under the water, still not opening my eyes. The mango liquid body soap scented in bubbles off my froth-washed shoulders.

She cracked open the door, and with the vacuum of cooler air on her side, steam from within the shower whooshed out as though escaping me, preferring the metal mermaids in the adjacent library. Aunty whispered, "Manny's here. He saw your car in the Haddock Point parking lot. He's in the foyer. Please hurry. He can't be here long. Please, Mop. Please, please, hurry."

At least she didn't lie to him and say I wasn't there. This I tipped to the side of Aunty being the real Aunty.

In reaching the foyer with a quick-thrown, pink chenille robe and matching coiled towel on my wet hair, I didn't care that I hadn't seen the boy I longed for in two years, and this is how I would look. He'd seen me growing up, with briars in my bangs, the time I got chicken pox on my face, the time I got a rash on my back and butt from poison sumac, and he did, too, for we'd played prince and princess in the brambles. He'd seen me with braces, with casts, with the summer flu, and once with Lyme disease. I'm pretty sure we gave each other strep three times. And there was also the scare that I might be pregnant at seventeen and thus my sleepless three nights, each of which he shared with me. I wasn't pregnant at all. I was just late due to overtraining for my annual win of the Haddock Point Lobster Fin Challenge—a three-mile swimming race in the choppy Atlantic. I trained every morning at dawn, along the exact race route. Several minor maelstroms swirl along this stretch; a person might get sucked up and spun if unaware. Perhaps you spin, drown, crash against the cliff edge. I preferred to skate my swimming body close to the sucking holes. I called my oceanic pool the Sink.

I entered Aunty's foyer in the pink robe and towel coil, leaving wet footprints on the wood floor in the library and the ice-rink marble. Manny's eyes glowed when they met mine, and I wanted to cry. He rushed over and hugged me, but I didn't know what to do with my arms, so weighted by the thickest chenille sleeves they felt five inches thick. The toe of my mother's shoe poked out of one of the kangaroo-pouch pockets. Eventually, I did hug Manny back, but two beats after Manny's, and so our hug was, in retrospect, sweetly prolonged.

"Why haven't you called me?" he said, not wasting one second on pleasantries.

"I have the same question," I replied as my answer, looking at him sideways.

Aunty, I could tell by my glance down the center hall, wallpapered in those colorful birds and vines, and to the kitchen in the back of the house, worked in a fury, jamming boxed spaghetti into a boiling black pot, a meal that didn't require such an aggressive level of attention. The scent of roasted tomatoes told me she was baking the sauce like she did.

"Mop," she yelled out, "we'll need to eat soon, so maybe you two could talk over at Manny's house tomorrow?"

This I slotted in the column of Aunty not being Aunty. The real Aunty used to beg Manny to stay longer, to join her in the kitchen, so she could prod us with questions on every minute action we took during the day, always keeping a natural smile and longing glint in her eyes, as if we were memory doors to her own charmed youth.

I eyed Manny, using Aunty's suggestion that we meet tomorrow at his place as my own request, and he kissed my cheek.

"I really miss you," he said, staring into my soul.

I lifted my chin and saddened my eyes, confused at the depth of his words and the way he said them. *Why, then, didn't he try harder?* I thought.

"I have tried to understand your silence as grief over your mother. I do respect your grief, Mop. So if you need more time, I will leave." He held both of my hands, rubbing the tops with his big thumbs, and he continued staring into my eyes with his own blue, swirling oceans.

"But?" I stumbled. "But I?" I didn't understand.

Aunty's clock in the living room behind him chimed out nine times. Waves of hot garlic braided with waves of roasted tomatoes, turning Aunty's house into a North End restaurant. My stomach punched my emotions and grumbled. I looked to Aunty in the kitchen; she looked out down the hall to the foyer, pressing me to move it along and rid the house of Manny.

Why is he sounding like I disappeared? He's the one who hasn't called or kept in touch. Right?

"Manny, I, um, I don't know what to say. Can we please meet tomorrow? At your house? Late breakfast, like old times?"

"On my back lawn with a thermos of coffee and cider doughnuts. You got it. Ten o'clock."

"Ten o'clock."

I set a tenuous kiss on Manny's cheek; he caved his chest as though swallowing the minor affection to his core, and he left.

Am I wanted? How could . . . That can't be.

Dinner with Aunty was quiet. We ate at her kitchen table in the middle of her country kitchen, a place most newer homes reserve for marble center islands. Her black gas stove sat on the side wall, like always. The bay windows on the two exterior walls still hosted green pillows for sitting, framed by yellow-and-green curtains. The view of the cottage from one of them did not show the cottage, of course. Now it showed the impenetrable tangle of vines and brambles and saplings and twisty trees. The floor-to-ceiling open antique shelving unit, which showcased Aunty's prized collection of yellowware pottery, was different. Before, it was laden with yellowware bowls and cups and platters and figurines, but now it was sparse. A few bowls left, one mug, and a yellow Santa figure. I didn't ask why. Neither of us talked; we glared at our pasta in a mutual shell shock. Angry at the other, frightened by the other, bruised by the other. I asked one question.

"Where's Popover, anyway?"

"Oh," she said, twirling her spaghetti and looking around as if my mother's beloved cat were somewhere in the kitchen. "He's around, somewhere."

When I stood to clear the plates, she said to my back as I rinsed the dishes and put them in the dishwasher, "Please. Mop, please. I'm begging you. Please do not mention my friend in the barn to anyone. I have to trust you. I have no other choice."

I kept my back to her and ratcheted my neck in a roundabout way, like a fighter cracking knuckles to start a bar fight.

We'd scoff, the three of us, Aunty, my mother, and I, over the implausibility that any of us would ever abandon one of us. How if one were tried and convicted of murder, the other two would hatch an *Ocean's Eleven*–style George Clooney plan to spring the jailed one from jail, and we'd all three flee with fake passports to a villa in some southern climate. Didn't matter if we abandoned all the money and were left to make do with whatever cash we stole away with. So trust me? She should have trusted me two years ago.

"Aunty," I said, turning and facing and meeting her one eye and eye patch, which she'd mercifully put on before dinner. "I happen to know you. I happen to know you're not telling me everything. But I'm too exhausted over my mother to pry tonight." I patted the shoe still in the robe's pocket (I ate in the robe, too drained and starving to change into clothes). "But please don't say all you can do is trust me. You shouldn't have to say obvious things. You shouldn't have to ask for my trust. This is what is the saddest part of all of this. Beyond the fact that whatever is going on in the barn is insane, and you know it."

I think this is what my mother would have said to her. My mother would have slapped her with tough love in a way to say she still loved her, no matter what. My mother was no scholar, didn't read the non-fictions like Aunty and me, but she sure was the one we both went to for the real answer and the never-denied hug. My mother remained steadfast in the whimsical and happy, and all she ever did was pour love, or shop too much like a girly girl or write in her fashion blog, doling consolations to her readers to not fret over the dearth of fashion in Boston, for she had solutions! That was her job, love and frilly fashion. In many ways, she was my opposite. She called me her "Cherry Berry Reader Geek, perfect as is," and then stuffed my face in her cashmere chest to smother me in love and fashion and kisses on my head. But she was the perfect one, as is. Those of us destined to dwell in dark thoughts and doubt, in the dust of old books, and the misery of addiction to the topic of philosophy, we *need* bright, unencumbered souls in our lives. Otherwise we slide with no balance, no foothold into good.

Two weeks ago in Aunty's kitchen, after I called her out on the insanity of nursing a woman in her barn, Aunty hung her head, admitting defeat and perhaps saddened by what I was saddened by too: her terrible suggestion of a lack of trust between us, the suggestion alone a rank betrayal.

"You're just like your mother. Telling me like it is," she said.

And before I rose in another anger at her for mentioning my mother, she shook her head and left the kitchen for her bedroom upstairs, beneath the alleged raccoon in the attic.

That night in the green guest room, I couldn't sleep. I missed the mattress in my Mop Closet. I missed love. Missed my mother. Missed calmness of mind. Missed everything.

About two a.m., I heard a *chih-chah, chih-chah* in the house, like a mechanical heartbeat. My body straightened in the bed, muscles sprung as if in rigor mortis, my eyes round moons to the ceiling. I'm sure I took no breaths for a good minute. *Chih-chah*—it wouldn't stop. I swung my board-straight legs from the bed and followed the possessing sound. Did I blink? I don't recall, but I don't think it possible.

I crept up the long, grand staircase and saw Aunty's room light on through the cracks of her shut door. The *chih-chah* rhythm continued elsewhere upstairs. *Chih-chah. Chih-chah.* I paused, listening for the source. Sure enough, it reverberated from around the corner and down at the end of the hall that held my Mop Closet room. We called this the minor hall. A second door to the attic capped the end of the minor hall. The other attic door was in Aunty's bedroom, which is off the main hall. *Is the sound coming from the door to the attic, and is that door barred, like Aunty said? Because of a raccoon?*

I paused again to listen for the scrape of raccoon nails in the attic. *But it's plush carpet up there, the only carpeted space in the whole house. No way I'll hear raccoon claws. What?* I heard only the *chih-chah* coming from around the corner of the second floor and down the end of the minor hall.

I slid past Aunty's sealed bedroom and moved only when the mechanical heartbeat resumed.

Chih-chah, I slid, *chih-chah, chih-chah*, I paused, I paused, *chih-chah*, I slid . . . and so on.

I reached the corner and had only to poke my head around to discover the source of the *chih-chah*, but I froze, stunned by another sound that braided with the *chih-chah*: the labor of heavy breathing, which wheezed between each interval of *chih-chah*. I held my breath, hoping whoever sucked the world so hard for air had not heard me.

And then . . .

Chih-chah.

In sneaking a peek around the corner and looking to the end of the minor hall, I saw Aunty, her back to me, in a sheer, white cotton night-gown covering neck to ankles. She fired a pressurized, automated nail gun, nailing boards to bar the doorway to the attic. Lasering my eyes along the wall of the hall, I noted my former bedroom door was also boarded shut—for how long, I do not know. The nail gun in Aunty's hands must have been a newer model, for the sink of the nail under pressure was like a bullet from a pistol with a silencer. A soft *chih-chah*, like a heavy-duty staple into a stack of paper. *Chih-chah.*

I magnetized myself back to the main hall and held my breath. *Chih-chah.* I again timed my slide to the mechanical rhythm, this time retreating to the stairwell down to the marble foyer. In the moments when the nail gun paused, and thus so did I, a slight scraping, like metal on metal, subtle, rained down in nets of sound from above, from the attic. Didn't sound like a raccoon scratching at all.

Now, two weeks later, I rely on the depleting energy of adrenaline, which isn't much given the blood loss. And I believe, really believe, an all-black shadow in angelic form rises from the ground at the mouth of the path behind the woman with the hatchet. My companion faints. I succumb to delusions. I must be dying now.

I don't know if I'm dead, buried, blacked out, or in a complete delu-sional spiral. A black shadow behind the hatchet woman grows more solid. I suppose it doesn't matter anymore, if this is indeed the end and the black shadow is the angel of death come to cocoon me in his yards of black gauze, which whip around him in this hurricane wind. *Why do I assume the angel of death is male? Could be female? Could be neither.* Maybe the death angel will seal me in an eternal encasement, arms bound, legs bound, wrapped in shrouds of blackness, alone, beyond the comfort of time. So be it. I don't believe in such things anyway. Or maybe I should, because I believe I am seeing *something, someone.*

I'm not sure if I'm lying in the dirt still, outside the hole of the basement, although I do feel the drilling of hard rain on my back. The falling water could be a washing anointment, some universal baptism upon death, and maybe the boom I hear is not thunder, but is Saint Peter crash-stepping in his asteroid sandals to join his comrade, the angel of death, so as to jointly perform my final judgment. I should be tipping the scale of myself and telling my thoughts they are impractical. I should acknowledge environmental and medical facts about my injuries and the weather, which might explain what I'm perceiving. But I slip, unable to gain enough traction to open my eyes, much less harness the hysterics I'm sure come upon this definite slide into death.

Is that a person come to save us, or is that the angel of death?

CHAPTER EIGHT
AUNTY

Two years ago

I must be mad. It's five a.m. the morning after I've been up all night, playing ghost in the white panel curtains of the guest cottage, guarding Johanna, because someone—and it has to be Cate Dranal—stole vials of pentobarbital from my barn last night.

Five a.m. I'll get this over quick. Get back to my house and to Johanna before Johanna wakes. I spin out of my property, pass by the Wilsons' off the main road—they're still in Costa Rica. I need to pick up their mail for them later. I drive twenty minutes to Danvers to Kent and Cate's house. I want Cate Dranal to know I'm watching her, want her to know I know all about what she's doing. I scrawl on the outside of the note I wrote her last night, the one in which I proclaim to be the brazen mistress who sleeps in her bed. I write: *I'm watching. I know what you did to Vicky. Stay away from me.* The inside of the note says everything else, my taunting confessional about fucking her husband. But I didn't sign my name, so how brave am I? *You're not brave. You're a coward. This is insane. Go home.* I'm not going home. I must leave this note.

The note I wrote to Cate Dranal is in my purse, beside me on the passenger seat while I drive to *their* house. I should have ripped it up, but I can't. It's haunting me, poking out from an inner zipper, white paper against black silk. I tell Cate I'm the mistress in the opening line. I needle her in this note how he doesn't tell her he loves her anymore, not without the stick of me in his throat.

I don't sign my name. I just want to warn her to stay away from me, because someone, nameless me, is watching and *knows*. It is delusional to think this will protect me and whomever else she means to harm, but I can do nothing else. *Stop.* No, I can't. I must.

Cate Dranal's ridiculous maroon minivan is in the driveway, right behind Kent's gray Jeep. Why they don't park in their damn attached garage is beyond me. He sang to me once in his Jeep, his thick hands on the stick shift, singing aloud so unembarrassed and free. It was some country song by Martina McBride about finding a mutual love that felt like home. I leaned across the seats and kissed the deep dimple of his right cheek for singing so unabashed, and he smiled with sad, in-love eyes. I think we were driving on our way to buy coffee, a sneak-away break, a stolen two hours from Saint Jerome's. I don't recall where we drove, what we said, nothing specific. I only remember him singing as free as if the world condoned us being together out in the open. I turned my face and wiped away a tear of happiness. I loved him so much in that single moment, my heart multiplied into a million hearts, each heart a different fold of a heart accordion, which expanded and contracted in my chest. *I love him so much. I don't know what to do. I have to let him go. I can't let him go. When he looks at me with those eyes, when his dimples deepen, when his hands frame my face, I want to liquefy and blend with his body, be his blood.*

What a fucking illogical bullshit thought. Get your fucking shit together. But his hands on my face, our bodies combined, muscles and skin. Park the car. Get this over with.

I park two blocks away from their Danvers Victorian. The June dawn offers enough light for me to sneak up to her unlocked minivan in nets of navy blue. I want to boil my hands in bleach to have to touch the handle on her despicable car. I know her shifts at Mass General as well as I know my own. Kent and I set our Saint Jerome's schedules to mirror, with strategic blackouts, hers—so she'd never be home wondering where he is: her idle mind lending credence to valid suspicions, over which she might act.

So I know her shift at Mass General is a grueling triple today, and Kent and I have the evening shift at Saint Jerome's. This is usually the day we spend all morning and afternoon at the Kisstop. It's the best day of all. After a whole day of lounging naked together, we scrub each other's bodies in the Kisstop double shower, and no one ever suspects the scent of sex off us when we slink in to fulfill our evening shifts. But we won't be meeting today, not after whatever went wrong yesterday with Vicky. This much goes unsaid between me and Kent, the words not having to be said over a phone call or email neither of us make.

As I step up to her car door, a light flicks on in their master bedroom (I've been in it), forcing me to freeze. I can't swivel my head to look up and see if a curtain moves aside, allowing inside eyes to peer down on my naked face. If I were to flip my head up, she'd see me, if indeed it is she who flicked the light on. I stay stalled. If someone shouts down, I'll know I need to turn tail and run before I'm caught red-handed.

I wait. I hold my breath. Everything in my chest and neck beats at separate rhythms, my heart, my lungs, each rib, my sternum, my esophagus, the muscles. A chorus of pulses in my body.

I hear no shouts. I note the curtains haven't moved and now the light is off again. I scurry to enter the minivan, pop the door open— they don't lock car doors in this neighborhood—and in leaning in to leave my note, get snagged on the seat belt. I realize I haven't changed since my shift last night, so the damn pockets on my nurse's uniform and cashmere sweater tangle me up. I yank back, staying low, drop the note, and scurry back to the bush on the sidewalk.

I catch my breath, watching the upper window, and no shouts come, no curtains move, no lights flick on. I hope this navy dusk of a morning shields my identity, if seen. I backstep in a trot to my car.

At six a.m. sharp, Cate Dranal will enter her ugly car, where she'll find my note on the driver's seat.

I plan to get home and wake Johanna to tell her everything, so we can map out how to handle this mess and stay safe. More rides on this than a stupid job and my and Johanna's lives. Much more. Even more than my own sanity. And it has nothing to do with those damn pentobarbital vials.

CHAPTER NINE
MOP

Present time

I question everything but love, which, ironically, is the most intangible, mysterious leap of all. But not really. Love is fairly scientific, and there are undeniable signs, instinct being the biggest tell of all, the one no one can deny. Otherwise, I don't understand how people hold such staunch certainties. Truly, I don't understand, so I feel displaced, like something's wrong with me to doubt almost everything, which leads me to want to curl tighter to my safe places: love of Manny, my mother, Aunty, and books.

I still cannot accept yesterday's shocking secret, something I've been grappling with the entire time in the burned basement hole and now, too, outside in the hurricane, my companion passed out on my fallen legs.

Still.

Love is one constant true source. The only thing I trust. I had a dream one night. That dream is the single clearest moment in my whole life. It was black-and-white. I was in a topless car as a passenger, Manny the driver. I don't know if we were driving toward our separation or running away, but a heavy emotion kept us silent. I leaned into him, and he turned from watching the road, one arm remaining on the wheel. The road was straight, no other cars in sight. I think the land was brown and flat, but we were black and white. He said, in a tender and painful tone, as if my answer would dictate whether he'd live or die, "What is the greatest moment of your life?" I smiled as my answer, a smile that said, *This. This is the greatest moment of my life.* In the dream, he blinked in a way that swallowed his tears. He wore a crisp white-collared shirt. This dream sticks with me as a pure truth. In my life, in my mind, in my truth, that dream is indeed the greatest moment of my life.

So I'm not sure why I ever questioned Manny's love, when I know I love him. And I know how he looks at me when he sees me—that look, that starry, out-of-body look, the look no one can conceal. I give him the same look. A mutual instinct colliding, like two cannons firing for a Fourth of July finale. Clear sky, no clouds, pins of stars, and explosion upon explosion of colorful fire, stitching the air with an embroidered heart of light. That's how sure I am of our love. I knew the second Manny delivered me his discovery of the true rose thief. How breathless I became upon sight of his sparkling eyes of excitement, when he pushed a pine bough out of my way to reveal Mr. Fox Gillray's bed of stolen roses. I'm as sure about my love of Manny as I am sure I hear Poe's telltale heart whenever I read the description of it beating.

Today is two weeks after I first arrived back at Aunty's, and so much has happened since. So much revealed, so many secrets, so many changes in our lives. One of those changes, which might seem the most severe, is actually the tamest, by comparison: the hatchet wedge in my calf. And the woman who dealt the blow stands before me now with the same bloody hatchet, while I lie on the ground, cantilevered over the burned basement hole. My companion is still passed out and sprawled across my legs. My feet remain tangled in the pervasive knots of brambles behind. The angel of death I saw at the mouth of the path that leads here moves closer, sneaking in on the woman with the hatchet, who doesn't notice the shadow draped in black gauze. The gauze flies around in the storm's turbulent wind, containing the shadow in a separate and slower rhythm of time.

By the way the angel of death moves, tiptoed and silent past the creaking swing on the maple we call Big Boy, I wonder if he (or her or it, I don't know) is here for the hatchet woman or for me or my companion or all of us.

I close my eyes, rest my head on a rock. I find a smooth spot of stone for my pulsing temple. The sky is a furious army now, helter-skelter with axes and spears of rain. Limbs flying, screaming words of wind howling, and the sea threatening to breach the barrier of her foxhole and storm the field too. Crack of lighting, scarring the green sky with green veins and unrelenting, and stab of the straight-on rain, like endless icicles of glass. My arms above my head are sopping wet, but I feel nothing beyond wet cloth. I don't feel my bones or my muscles or the fat within. I'm armless, legless, helpless, slipping to the land of the dead. I'm dying from inside out. I'll allow the black shadow in flying gauze to handle this. I shut my eyes and wait for the end.

And when I close my eyes, I return to the morning after I arrived and saw Aunty sealing her attic with a nail gun.

I used to flashlight talk from my upstairs room at Aunty's, my Mop Closet, to my mother in her one-room guest cottage out back, tucked catty-corner behind the barn. My mother loved all things frilly and cozy and pink and blue and patterned in sea things. So Aunty made her that cottage; plus, whenever my mother drank too much wine after any of their constant charitable events, she'd smoke a Marlboro or two. So it was good for everyone to give Mom her own little shack. Wasn't a shack, though. Was a beautiful beach cottage, shingle shake and outfitted within by Lilly Pulitzer and the best upholstered furniture, straight from Zimman's in Lynn, Massachusetts. My mother's regular designer at the helm.

Anyway, two clicks of the flashlight from my upper bedroom to my mother in her cottage meant *good night*. And three quick flashes meant *I love you*. I would click out one *good night*, pause, and then click out one *I love you*. In return, she'd click out a series of eight to ten *I love yous*, until I would shake my head within my lit room, so she could see me through the dark, and then clap off my bedroom lights and shut the shade, smiling as I crawled into bed. It never mattered how old I was—when my mother said she loved me, I was a child again, safe and full, and my heart felt strong and warm. Nothing in the world could harm me for the blessed seconds around the bubble of time when my mother said she loved me.

When they called that awful morning two years ago, I was doing what I did every day. I was hanging my naked torso over the rim of a hot bathtub, so as to read a book splayed on a white bath mat. *Boomerang* was the book, a financial markets exposé by Michael Lewis. A phone rang, followed by shouting. My left foot collided with my customary cup of red-berry tea, which thereupon spilled and ruined *Boomerang*, when I fish-flopped and sloshed out upon the screams of an emergency and to hurry. My lifelong reading routine shattered, just like that. I can't read in water anymore. And the sight of a Michael Lewis book makes me nauseous—to think of all his hard work, which goes to waste in my small world, for I can no longer so much as brush the spine of one.

I never understood until I lost her and lost Aunty how peaceful life was, how much I loved and was loved back. Didn't anticipate how looking at a flashlight over the past two years would cause me to fall into a heaving pile of tears, didn't anticipate a relentless cold in my bones. Literal chills in my hands that hurt. Still don't understand the chronic fog, how I'd find myself somewhere on campus, not having remembered one step of the trek. Finding myself standing by a fountain or leaning against a quad oak or staring at the fall canopy outside my dorm, confused, darting my eyes for any witnesses to the wizardry that transported me from my bed, without my conscious knowledge.

Had I been able to breach the boarded Mop Closet upstairs the first night I stayed at Aunty's two weeks ago, I would have clicked out an infinity of flashlight *I love you*s, hoping my mother would see my beacon in the beyond and find her way to the shore of the living.

Instead, I woke in the green-and-gray guest bedroom on the first floor, a view of nothing but the basement bulkhead, and alone.

The wallpaper everywhere else in Aunty's house is varied, patterned, of every color in the rainbow, and involving parties of every animal or fish or bird in the animal-fish-bird kingdoms, and yet, this drab, muted, green-and-gray room is the one I woke in. I suppose I should have fled right away, having seen what I did the night before: the boards on my Mop Closet bedroom, Aunty in a mad-witch act of nailing more boards on one of the attic doors. Not to mention the unconscious woman in her barn in a hospital bed. *The woman in her barn in a hospital bed.* In waking that morning at Aunty's, a phrase floated through the fog, something some doctor, I don't know, said about me, I think, some weeks after yanking me from my locked room in Rye two years ago: *selective, evergreen amnesia.*

But two weeks ago, I didn't linger on the phrase, and instead laser-focused on one single thing: love. *Baby steps. Baby steps. Baby steps. One rung at a time.*

I dressed at nine thirty, after hiding away in my guest bedroom since I woke at dawn. I ghosted through the Mermaid Library at nine forty-five, snagged a front door key from a hidden well within one of the mermaid bookends, slid across the marble foyer, and snuck out without interacting with Aunty, who clinked and clanked and hummed in her sunlit kitchen. I waved to her in running through her back lawn, to meet the side lawn, and then cut through a path only Manny and I know of that hits upon, at some snaky point, an abandoned access path to the ocean no one uses. From there, and I could have done this blindfolded, I took curvy lefts, curvy rights, sharp lefts, sharp rights, through the bramble bushes and vines, the twisted corkscrew hazel shrubs on both sides, and trees hardy enough to withstand the constant offshore wind. I didn't stop like I normally do to consider how these ancient trees look like arthritic hands stretching up through the earth.

I broke out of the labyrinth of thin paths through the brambles to meet upon the granite rocks along the ocean's edge. These rocks lie in layered slabs, some as big as house roofs, and tiny tide pools pockmark the surfaces with worn grooves and cracks. The layering makes the edge of earth along the sea look like inland is a cake, and the edge a gray buttercream frosting dripping off the towering sides. Running to Manny's, jumping over tide pools and footholding in granite grooves, I ignored the low rolling ocean to my left, purple flowers growing out of cracks underfoot, and the knee-high mounds of bayberry and blueberry and pricker mounds to my right.

The mounds thrive in a tangled mess before the taller brambles and vines and red-berried catbrier and white-flowered arrowwood shrubs, the boundary from which I broke through using skinny paths, which is the first line of defense for the inland ring of the corkscrew hazel and arthritic-hand trees, which surround the innermost ring of maples and willows and perennial beds around Aunty's house. Rings of vegetation, each ring hardier than the next, form the layers of nature's militia. Imagine how defiant you must be to be a purple flower that pokes out of a granite crack at the ocean's edge, where freezing water beats and yanks at you with hundreds of billions of gallons of water and corrosive salt, every day, twice a day, at high tide.

On my way to Manny's that day, I stopped myself from wishing one of the purple flowers was the new incarnation of my mother in her next life. *No, move on. That's not possible.*

I plunked down into the middle beach, for it was low tide, and kept my back to the cliff from which my mother launched herself. I climbed up more slabs of granite to Manny's estate lawn, and there he stood, A-frame and smiling, waiting for me at the tip-top, a green thermos of coffee in his hands. Out before us stretched his perfect green oceanfront lawn; the rocky edge to the sea to my left, his pool and pool house in the middle distance, and to the far-right corner his brick estate, and behind that, the property's long-standing lighthouse.

"I love you," he said.

No waiting. That's how he's always been. That's why I love him. Such certainty. Such trust of his instincts. *Where has this certainty been for two years?*

"Why didn't you call me?" I asked.

He pursed his lips, looked up to the blue sky in a humorous contemplation, then turned a serious eye to me. "Come over here. I brought the blanket. And the doughnuts."

Manny had laid on the grass the blue Duke blanket we had stolen from one of his brothers many years ago. This older brother graduated cum laude from Duke whatever irrelevant year that was. He wasn't so happy we stole his precious graduation blanket. I think he said something crude about us using his collegiate gift for "fucknics," his stupid big-brother mash-up of *fucking* and *picnics*. Then he said something about how we could keep his fucknic blanket, now that Manny's jizz stained the letter *D*. But the stain wasn't jizz; it was icing from a cinnamon roll, courtesy Aunty's kitchen, for she'd made them special for me and Manny. She'd placed six rolls, each with an inch of icing, because Aunty wasn't a barbarian back then, in a pink box she'd saved from some bakery, because she used to be particular. Packaging things with care, baking things and slathering things with ample love, and icing.

She didn't walk around with a punctured eye and no eye patch, and the thought of having broken gaps in her mouth would have made her own skin recoil, before. She would never have walked around like a deranged woman pirate, hiding an unconscious woman in her barn. And as for boarding her attic with a nail gun, that wasn't Aunty, was someone else. I can't even. *This is so incomprehensible*, which is what I thought in actively blocking the thoughts as Manny led me to our stolen Duke *picnic*—not *fucknic*—blanket.

I took a deep breath to cement my intent on love. *Just love. Nothing else. Baby steps. Breathe.* Another deep breath.

Manny handed me a cider doughnut. We didn't sit. We stood close, face-to-face. I took a bite and chewed while staring into his eyes. He mirrored my exact actions and brushed a hair from my cheek. The temperature became irrelevant, except for the emotional flash in my core, a welcome sign I was alive. Not like now, two weeks later, as my core cools.

We spoke no words, repeating bites of our doughnuts, staring, and in microscopic, involuntary moves, for we were commanded by instinct and our physical bodies, inched closer and closer. The low tide listened, calming the waves like hushing a brood of children. The water sounded more like popping bubbles than its regular bar brawl with the rocky cliff, ten feet off. Those cider doughnuts were freshly fried, so the scent wafted and hung in the grips of summer air, catching with the humidity and thus expanding, lending us a lovely displacement to the safety of fall in the dead of summer.

I caught myself smiling, and thus, felt myself emerging. And now as I slip away to some other world two weeks later, I don't care about the haze of shock I was in. I'd give anything to relive a million times over my and Manny's reunion.

"I love you," he whispered straight to my face, his eyes one inch from mine. "God, I love you. I miss you," he whispered closer, holding my face in two hands, brushing his lips to mine, but not kissing.

Our doughnuts were done.

My mouth watered, my tongue twitched, I wanted to make room in my body to swallow him whole and join his soul to mine. I fixed on the mole under his right eye, a brown dot I covet like a vampire covets throats, like I need it to live.

"Where have you been?" I asked with a crack in my voice.

"Right here, babe. You weren't ready."

"But you never called. You never wrote."

"I called hundreds of times. Couldn't leave a message, because the box has been full for two years. You don't empty it. I wrote a hundred cards. No returned calls. Two cards in return. Do you remember writing them?" He pulled away and shook his head to stop me from answering. When he lowered his hands from my face to my covered shoulders, the loss of his skin on my skin felt like he'd scalped me.

"I passed you once on campus at Princeton. Did you know? I went to see you, I was so worried," he said.

I widened my eyes, confused.

"You were sitting on a bench. Dressed all in black. You had your glasses on. You were staring into grass. You had no clue I watched you for an hour," he said.

"But . . ."

"Listen. Hold on. Listen."

I shook my head, lowered it, and flipped my hand to indicate he should continue.

"Maybe you don't remember this, Mop, but"—he inhaled and blew out hard, indicating he was holding something painful inside, but would have to let it out—"maybe you're not remembering how my mother died when I was ten. Do you remember the summer after? How you kept coming over and wanting to play? And I kept telling whoever answered the door to tell you I was sick?"

"I thought you were sick. I made you cards."

"I kept all the cards. I wasn't sick. Well, I wasn't physically sick."

"Oh."

"So when I saw you like that on the bench dressed in black, when you didn't call or write or accept anything from me, I had two instincts. One, I saw no point in pushing you through grief. I remember resenting everyone who tried to push me. I still resent them. I'm still angry at my father for making me go to soccer practices, saying it would make me feel better. He meant only good, but he didn't know. That feeling of anger I'll never forget, because that part is almost worse than losing my mother. I feared so much you'd resent me if I pressed you. So I left, and I waited, and London has been awful without you. I thought of transferring to Princeton. Yeah. To finish out grad school in proximity to you. Got the papers and all, but I figured that'd be big-time pushing. So I waited. I've been miserable. My second instinct was, and is, stronger than the first. And here it is. In my heart I know one thing." He shook his head, chastising himself. "God, I'm sorry, I'm rushing through all this and I can't stop. I've had this speech in my head for so long. Mary Olivia . . ."

Manny only ever says my real name when he's at his most gravely serious. Like when I told him I was afraid I was pregnant, and he bowed his head and said, "Mary Olivia, we'll wait together and see, and we'll be together no matter what, so it's not a terrible thing because we'll make it great. Don't cry. Stop crying. I love you." Then he smiled and hugged me, although we were both scared.

"Mary Olivia, I'm serious here," he repeated, holding my face so tight but so tender, tears welled in my eyes. "The only thing I know is this: you belong to me, and I belong to you. I have no other certainty."

You belong to me, and I belong to you. I have no other certainty, he said. These words. These words are the vows I hold with him. And yes, I then considered the beauty of David Gray's song "Gulls," about how the wind belongs to no one. I remembered, too, Aunty proclaiming herself free like the wind, and I sometimes used to want to be like her. But I am not wind. I respect the wind too much to want to be like the wind: free of ownership, of connection.

In that moment on Manny's lawn, a rush of awareness hit me like a twenty-ton wave: I was no rock, like I think I'd been trying to be, alone, an island, for two years. I then, in that single moment, accepted a wish to belong to one man, the one I've loved my whole life. There is power in individualism, a safeness from loss, I don't disagree. But some of us are like an octopus, whose IQ neurons belong also in its eight arms in addition to the central brain. Like an octopus, those of us who thrive best when operating in the multiple might survive the loss of a piece or two, but we swim sideways when not attached to what makes us whole. Manny, my mother, Aunty, perhaps a few others—they comprised my insular world making me whole, a straight-swimming, complete being. It took a mountain of emotions to accept this fact, this weakness, perhaps, which I did, standing on Manny's lawn two weeks ago. *No,* I told myself, looking in his eyes, which matched the horizon and at once, reflected myself to me. *Stop fighting to be like the wind. You are not the wind. I am not the wind. I am Mary Olivia Pentecost, lover of Manny, daughter of Johanna, niece of Liv. And what other identities comprise me? Any?*

Manny took his hands off my shoulders and shrugged, pivoting off the Duke blanket to the grass.

"I need to confess something, though," he said. "I tried dating a couple girls . . ."

I jolted my head up, swiveling my struck face to his. My posture that of a ridgeback on the hunt.

Manny laughed. "I'm not a priest, Mop! You should be happy I tried. You know why?"

"Oh, now this is some serious bullshit right here. I should be happy you slept with some other bimbos?" I said, only half joking.

"There's no bimbo better than you. You're the best bimbo."

I hit him, of course. I love how he flirts, insulting my gender as if we both didn't insist on equality.

"No, seriously. Everyone I dated, and there were only two—well, two and a half—reminded me that nothing compares to you."

"That's a Sinéad O'Connor song—'Nothing Compares 2 U.'"

Manny rolled his eyes and smiled, pointing a finger, indicating a coming lesson. "Well. Actually, Prince wrote it."

"Right."

He grabbed me then, and while standing with the dramatic Atlantic to his back, we kissed so long and deep, working ourselves up so much our hands fought under clothing, trying to claw beneath skin, we had to race for shelter. We left the stolen Duke blanket behind, pinned to the grass by the still-full thermos, so we could make heated love in the swinging daybed in the pool house. The pool house doors remained open to the sea and the blue sky's approving breeze. We were the only ones on the property, except the estate caregiver, and she was stealing a nap with the cats, up on a third floor somewhere in the main house, Manny said. And the location of his father and brothers—well, this became relevant in the minutes after we calmed our naked breaths after round two in the pool house.

I stood, no clothes blocking the summer's sight of all my pieces and my parts, and stretched before the open door. The fishermen in bright-red boats offshore maybe could have seen me with binoculars, but they didn't care about me: they pulled on lobster traps and checked the tension on their lines. Seagulls sang in swoops through the sky, and the air smelled of salty water and the gardenias potted around the pool house, freed for the season from the property's hidden greenhouse.

"Babe," Manny said from behind, swinging in the hanging daybed, a white sheet on his lower half, which is where my eyes went, wanting more. "My father and brothers are in Milan. My father inherited another hotel there. It's weird, I know, random . . ."

I turned in full and showed my surprise at such an unexpected statement, jostling the only thing I wore, a blue sea-glass necklace my mother had started to make me before she vanished. Detectives found the starts of it and my mother's handwritten plan to paint an infinity symbol and the words *Love Forever* on the glass. Aunty told police to give the plan and the pieces to me: I finished it up and never take it off. How I missed the orange sea-glass necklace Mom always wore, the piece something my father found for her on a beach in Havana.

Manny's family, the Acistas, owns hotels around the world. That's where their money comes from.

"So what I was thinking was, and this is so sudden, I know. But the truth is, I didn't go with my father and brothers to Milan to see this new hotel, whatever. I came straight here after graduation in London, because I was holding out hope of finding you at your aunt's. Too much time had passed, and if you weren't here, I was going to camp out on your lawn in Rye."

I smiled. God, I love Manny and his brazen certainty.

"Anyway, please come with me to Milan. I know you're between schools. I talked to your father last night."

"You talked to my father?"

"Yes."

He stared at me, shrunk back on his pillow.

"Go on," I said, throwing only curious confusion. I stepped closer to him. Perhaps I also blocked my father's attempts to heal me, to fix my world into love again. Everyone knew I loved Manny beyond practicalities. As I thought on this further, some items came to mind out of the fog.

Perhaps my showing up at Aunty's with the blown gasket was not mere contrived coincidence. Perhaps I had listened this time to my father's pleas that I consider finding my "friend" Manny again, for he'd heard he was back from London. Yes, that's what I believe he did in fact say, after passing me the fresh-pressed orange juice for breakfast by the pool in Rye the morning before, two weeks ago. This fact slapped me in the face, a slap of realization to the clouds I'd let hover and were now clearing. Do others in grief undergo this slow waking emergence from a walking coma? It can be extreme, the things we tell ourselves to survive. A walking coma, a walking insanity, but who's to tell what is real, what is sane? There are billions of variations on how someone might react to grief. Perhaps I'm on the extreme end of the spectrum.

I focused on Manny, intent that he not stop talking, so I could retain certainty in at least one thing: my love for him.

In a tenuous voice, half-afraid he might misstep, Manny proceeded. I was still naked, not caring about standing with my backside to the sea, plucking the sea-glass necklace in the hollow of my neck.

"Please come for the next week with me to Milan. I want you to be with me and my family. We'll get our own room in this Milan hotel my dad inherited—how crazy, right?"

"My mother liked to go to Milan for fashion week," I said, my eyes to the pool house's tiled floor.

"I know," he said.

He clicked his tongue, started to say something, squinted his eyes, and winked. The kind of wink to indicate a decision and a deliberate intent to change the course of the conversation.

"Hand me my wallet, beautiful. Please," he said.

I walked to his wallet on the lobster trap–turned–glass-topped coffee table, handed him his wallet. He swung to me in the bed. I remained standing to the side. He popped a clasp on a tiny pocket and pulled out a ring with red, yellow, and pink pricks of stones set in a rose gold.

"The rose thief asks you to marry him," he said, extending the ring, the colors the same as the petals the fox stole. "I was going to ask on the night of . . . I've carried this, well . . ." He shook his head, knowing he'd misstepped. He was going to ask on the night of the fire. "Never mind. I've held this for years." His eyes watered, although his voice was sure, a steady steel steam liner cutting through ice.

I looked up, defiant to the past two years, defiant to Aunty, and wanted for the first time ever to run away. Ignore whatever I was supposed to remember or notice, some vague sense of a nagging responsibility. Something happened on the night of the fire to Manny and me that cut the romance, but I specifically closed the option of going through that memory door, the one he almost opened, upon his pool house proposal.

"Yes," I said with trembling lip. "And yes to Milan too."

He slid on the ring.

I slithered onto the swinging bed, yanked the sheet from Manny's lower half, settled astride Manny's bare hips, felt his immediate stirring to strength down there, which I coaxed along with my hands and then mouth, before moving up like a cobra in control upon his golden-brown body to lick the freckle under his eye like I owned it, which I do. The third time we made love was solemn and long and neither of us smiled or closed our eyes. I consider this third time the consummation of our ocean-lawn, priestless wedding, for he was the witness and I was the officiant and we were the betrotheds, all at once.

And that was that. Our reunion, quick and simple. Painless for us as a couple. Painful, however, for me as an individual, for, if I was being honest with myself, it meant I blocked the last two years.

And this mental grappling only spiraled more when Manny turned to me on the flight home from Milan a week later and shattered my delusions that perhaps all could be settled now. He brought to mind a critical memory concerning the night of the fire. I had suppressed this memory, because, I accept now, I suppressed a scattered field of items that might hurt me, anger me, deliver guilt, or abandon me. Manny and I had had such a fine time in Milan for a whole week. Eating fried zucchini blossoms, drinking ridiculous reds, buying insane fresh flowers for our hotel room, which we did not leave often or for long.

On the plane home from Milan one week ago, I turned to Manny and kissed the corner of his sapphire eye, which I do when I want to convey how much I love him. He smiled in a serious way and wrinkled his brow.

"Mary Olivia," he said, and my shoulders sank as they always do when he means to be so grave.

"What?" I said, concerned.

In our two-seat row, he leaned in to whisper in my ear, "Listen, we had a great week, right?"

"Yes, Manny, so this is why you're freaking me out right now. Why are you so serious all of a sudden?"

He did not lift the graveness of his smile, the type of smile that says, *I'm going to hurt you with the next thing I say, but I'll smile to trick you to listen.*

"I'm a little concerned," he said, while rubbing my arms as if I were damaged from an accident. "We've been together for a whole week, and it's been amazing, and I love you more than I ever did ever before. And I'm going to ask your father for permission to really marry you, just so you know, although this seems a foregone conclusion, right?"

"Yes. Right. What? What's going on? Whoa, whoa, whoa, my father's permission?"

"Mary Olivia, that's not the point."

"Then what is the point, Manny?"

He bit his bottom lip and held a finger up to me to *hold on*. He squeezed his plastic cup of champagne and guzzled. A flight attendant knocked my elbow with her cart.

I held my breath, afraid.

"The thing is," he said.

"Holy shit, Manny, you're scaring me."

He didn't smile to lighten my fright, which meant he really meant to hurt me with the next line. "The thing is," he repeated in an almost inaudible whisper into my ear. He grabbed my hand, held it to his lap in both his hands. "We've been together a week and you haven't mentioned what we saw and what that woman said on the rocks, the night your mother . . . anyway . . ."

It was this moment, right about in the middle of his sentence, for in his preceding tone and the way he looked, I heard what he didn't finish saying: I remembered the night of the fire in a flash. I stood, walked down the aisle to the bathroom, shut the door, and stared in the mirror as if watching that night on a movie screen.

I remembered in a total rush what I blocked on the night of the fire and what Manny and I saw. No one else knew we were there that night.

CHAPTER TEN
MOP

Remembering two years ago
Manny's property/Haddock Point State Park

Two years ago, early June, to be exact, everyone thought I was finishing things up at Princeton and due home the next week. But, truth be truth, I got to town a week early, a day before I lost my mother. I didn't go to our Rye estate. I didn't go to Aunty's. I didn't tell anyone in my family I was home from Princeton. Instead, I went straight to Manny's to live in Manny's pool house and also his yellow tent, for he had likewise returned from his school in London. His father and brothers were off to who knows where in the world like any other globe-trotting international hoteliers. We preferred camping with each other to anything else, anyone else. Neither of us wanted to get tangled with our families yet. We wanted to be young lovers on his ocean lawn. I still wonder if everything would have been fine for my mother if I would have been there to save her, had I gone home or to Aunty's, *had I not started my path to definite identity distinction, a clarification from the pack, a betrayal to the trio.* Or if Manny and I acted upon and not ignored the woman we encountered on the rocks the night of the fire. *It's my fault* is an accusation I carry to this day.

I am certain now of one thing. Guilt played a large part in the equation that made up my extreme reaction to grief, the walking fog, the constant denial, my mind's ability to identify with only items of study at college.

That night two years ago. Manny and I sat on the ocean's edge, our feet above crashing waves. His yellow tent sprung and waiting for us, lit from inside with amber-glowing battery candles. The sky was clear. A perfect June night. A freight liner's lights of green formed a line above the navy horizon of ocean, and above, the domed sky allowed a light blue beyond the moon's white path. We were sharing a bucket of hot and salty buttered popcorn, sprinkled with a heavy pour of M&Ms, and laughing over misheard lyrics of famous songs.

"And the wee-wee cur," I said. "That's what Tom Petty says instead of whatever he's saying in that song."

Then we both sang, "And the wee-wee cur," laughing, because those are the heard words of whatever it is Tom Petty is singing.

"Mary Olivia," Manny said, reaching for his wallet.

I braced my arms on the lawn, kicked my dangling feet on the rocky edge of the sea face we sat upon, and tried to stifle my racing heart with a deep breath. The way Manny had set up this perfect June night, some hints he'd made, the way he said my full name. I believe this was the moment he meant to pop the question.

So this peaceful, humorous, romantic moment in life should not have been sliced in a thousand strips by the screams of a woman farther up the granite coast, back in the direction of Aunty's house. But it was.

Manny and I looked left along the sea and up the granite-lined edge, but the scream was outside the moon's illumination and into the black, the devil of night. We stood, dropping the bucket of chocolate-clumped popcorn, and ran.

The ocean shifted midway to high tide, halting our plan to plunk into the middle beach to avoid the longer way up through the brambled paths and back down onto the roof-layered granite along the water. So we stopped short and went the labored long way through the paths, weaving our way around the middle beach, scraping our legs on the thorns of the mounds of bay and blueberry bushes. We were a step from breaking through when we stopped short, my hand flying to Manny's mouth and Manny's to mine.

Sitting sideways before us, high up on layered granite slabs, but dangerously close to the roiling, rising tide, sat a woman in a pale-blue-and-navy-patterned ball gown. Midforties, about Aunty's age, and puff faced. The moon had moved its spotlight to this perspective, and given her close proximity, the tear lines on her cheeks glistened and sparkled, having mixed with her glittery powder and literal circles of blush, circles like on a clown. She turned to the sea and screamed at the water from the depths of her toes like a howling, grieving wolf, and we shuddered.

She twisted her head fast toward me and Manny and stared in a vengeful malevolence, as if possessed and pulling us into possession. She stared a good, long four seconds, I think to make a point, not so much to focus. And then, after that, she yanked out a sloppy smile and, up from her side, a bottle of wine.

"Whoops. Party up in the park grounds. Sorry," she said, calm and cool, as if we hadn't stumbled upon her howling scream at the ocean.

"Are you all right?" Manny asked, standing sideways, one side blocking me from going forward, the other with his arm outstretched, as both a brace against her and a peace offering—talking to a hostage keeper while protecting a crowd.

The woman pulled her face in, bugged her eyes, and shook her head like a paint can in the mixer at Home Depot. The fastest of oscillations, crazy, crazy oscillations. Still shaking her head, she popped her lips in an audible smack, jolted to standing, and ran. As she sped by us, her arm holding the bottle of wine swung back, her hand choked around the neck. I gasped, clutched Manny. *How can she have a bottle of Aunty's French bordeaux? She orders it special, right?* But then she was gone, out of sight, into the black. And I shook my head in fretful doubts, wincing into the bushes, away from this, from Manny, from her.

Frozen, stunned in the middle of a path between two blueberry mounds, Manny and I watched her run along the rocks, fast and slipping, looking back at us twice, while hiking up her blue-on-blue ball gown. She didn't step light nor flinch, didn't once circumnavigate pointed parts of rocks or roots to protect her bare feet. Crashing so hard and straight down as she did, I find it impossible to believe she didn't shred her soles or mangle her toes. She stopped abrupt atop the cliff, and, not looking back, not acknowledging Manny now yelling at her to stop, she tossed her bottle of wine toward the sea, only to miss, sending it to crash upon the rocks. In retrospect, I regard this act a prophecy for my mother.

Manny started toward her, to help, I suppose, but I pulled him back to me. I feared her.

What if I hadn't pulled him back and he stopped her?

At the time, we convinced ourselves—although, truthfully, I had a bad nagging sense about her, call it a sixth sense, call it the real sight of the wine, which I denied and didn't voice, and herein lies the guilt—she was an innocent drunk, who had indeed gotten away from a late-night party up in Haddock Park. Haddock is seventeen acres of seaside parkland, which hosts a small watchtower lighthouse, surrounded by sweet picnic tables. This area abuts a rather famous quarry that partygoers like to breach at night. It's incredibly dangerous, but on full-moon nights it's especially popular, since the bowl of the quarry is a bowl of light. And yet, the park rangers had grown hip to these insurrections in recent years, and security had been tightened. So we should have questioned this woman's story. Plus, the ball gown. Plus, her screaming howl. Plus, the bottle of rare wine. She disappeared into the dark devil of night again. We couldn't see which way she went, for the moon stuck with our perspective, not hers.

Oh yes, we should have questioned her story. We should have followed her.

But we shook, shaken on the spot, and traipsed back to Manny's house, and then his car. We decided in this return walk to skip the tent, and thus skip, I presumed, the marriage proposal for another unscarred night. We instead drove over to Rye to stay there the night. We thought it better to surprise my parents when they woke in the morning, for I didn't know my mother intended to stay at Aunty's that night, and also surprise, I suppose, Aunt Sister Mary Patience. Back then we were innocent and charmed students, and all we wanted to do the next day was use the new lap pool my father had installed. And the ground zero of guilt is this: I was pissed the woman ruined my night with Manny, so selfish, in fact, I ignored the obvious fear I felt, the instincts I sensed, and the vision of the wine. I knew better.

Everything changed the next morning when authorities called the Rye estate, jolted me from my tub reading of *Boomerang*, and reported the fire, my missing mother, and how Aunty had serious injuries to her face.

Manny and I did raise the incident the next day after all went to hell. But no one ever found a trace of a woman in a ball gown; she'd run on the rocks, nowhere on the paths, the crashed bottle swallowed by the tide. No one ever connected any foul play to anything happening on Aunty's grounds. They all believed Aunty's rendition of what went down, and how she damaged her face trying to save my mother. The fire inspector declared the cottage fire an unfortunate accident: woman fell asleep with cigarette in mouth, it dropped, she awoke aflame and ran to the sea. Disappeared.

But, yes, indeed, we should have questioned that ball-gowned woman's story and followed her. I should not have stopped Manny in running for her. And I know this for sure now, for as I watched my unblocked memory unfold like a movie in the bathroom mirror on the airplane home from Milan a week ago, I figured out the identity of the screaming woman on the rocks and what happened to her.

She was the bloated woman in Aunty's hospital bed in the barn.

Which meant Aunty lied about her coming *after* the fire.

And my doubts about the woman, my guilt for not believing my sixth sense, for not stopping her, they are true.

We are animals. Born of sticks and wind, mud and bone. We should never deny instinct, the wise mother of a mad daughter known as reason.

🐦

I see myself at Princeton over the last two years. I'd converse beyond quick passing hi's with only one professor, my Philosophy of Aesthetics professor, who invited me to solemn, contemplative dinners with his rather young wife off campus.

The professor set me up with a summer volunteer job, coaching reading to refugees of global sex trafficking, none of whom can afford to pay for toothpaste, much less the luxury of a reading guide. The professor said their individual and collective acts of survival and their processes of healing were aesthetic, but I'm sure he meant to deliver that last part, their processes of healing, as an analysis of me. Did any of their survival stories sink in? What had I heard, what had I learned in these two years? As I realized yesterday, right before running into the hole in the ground to hide, one of those refugees' stories taught me something rather valuable, and quite practical for survival in a certain specific situation of confinement.

Two years I spent with the professor, his wife, my reading students, and in this way, I stayed constantly busy and did not return home to Rye much at all. For me, the symbiosis of me working with the refugees and them helping me stay protected in a consumption of study, that was the true aesthetic value of all those volunteer summers. A beautiful consumption keeping me in a tranquil haze, a gorgeous fog.

Otherwise on campus, I sat on benches and stared at birds. I took long walks around Princeton's brick buildings and towering, flowering trees, alone. I practiced my faith by swimming laps, one hour, every morning, in Princeton's student pool. I ate cupcakes and drank coffee in village cafés, reading books, writing term papers, at a corner table for one. I'd find myself in random places outside, transported, it seemed, from my bed. Always alone, but I didn't realize I was alone for two years, until I blinked in the mirror of the airplane bathroom on the way home from Milan and recognized the woman in the barn as the same ball-gowned woman from the night of the fire. I realized one week ago in a sharp awareness that I'd been going through motions, devoting myself to one thing: a monk's life of study. I didn't realize anyone was knocking on my door. Much less Manny, of all people. Much, much less important memories full of evidence.

When Manny made me realize in my active mind that the woman in the ball gown on the rocks and the woman in the barn were the same, which realization meant my doubts and guilt were true—the ability to accept my mother's death did not cement further in my grips. No, any such ability flew far away, further than it had been over the last two years. I had come to Aunty's to emerge in full, to swallow acceptance, but that plan cracked when I found the woman in her barn, it cracked again when I saw Aunty boarding the attic door, and it shattered on the runway once we landed, home from Milan. And still, these weren't the biggest shocks. I didn't realize there were larger cracks and shatters to come.

I returned to Manny on the plane. I said nothing. He held my hand while I closed my eyes and steeled my mind to relive that night again and again. I gripped Manny's hand back, seeking to soak in from him strength to add to the strength I was building in myself, determined to stay straight and not block events anymore. I saw in my mind's eye the ball-gowned woman's bloated face in Aunty's barn. I saw red rage in my eyes, a rage I didn't know where to direct. To Aunty for clearly lying? To the ball-gowned woman, who seemed guilty on the rocks two years ago? To whom? Myself? I decided to say nothing to Manny about the woman in the barn and the connection he'd made in my mind.

And I wondered what else I forgot or missed. I wondered who else, beyond Manny, might have called to me in my abyss. My father? What had he said that I had not heard? Aunt Sister Mary, what about her? Who else? What else? Perhaps my mother clicked her coded flashlight messages, pressing the flashlight button like a nail gun with a soft *chih-chah*, only I wasn't looking. I wasn't seeing. I wasn't listening for the *chih-chah*.

Chih-chah, chih-chah, chih-chah is bleeding into my brain right now.

It's two weeks after arriving at Aunty's, and although I just blacked out in thoughts of my reunion with Manny, Milan, and my last two years at Princeton, I find I'm not dead. I feel a coming to, for, unless it's the storm or my delusions getting the better of me, I'm sure I do hear a distinct *chih-chah* piercing the air. I open my eyes. I'm still outside, on the ground, in the storm, above the burned basement hole. My companion still passed out on my legs. Maybe I slipped only seconds into memories.

I don't have my glasses. No contacts. Impaired vision paired with a blinding storm—no wonder the angel of death appears a shadow wrapped in black gauze. But it is actually more distinct, more solid. Focus. Squint.

The black shadow stands behind the woman with the hatchet. The shadow is holding a nail gun to the sky like a cranked-out gangster with an automatic weapon. The shadow is pulling the trigger, nails flying high, arcing like cherub spit in a fountain and plummeting down all around, raining with the real rain. The shadow yells at the back of the woman with the hatchet to stop or she'll shoot.

She'll shoot. She'll. She. The angel of death is a woman.

The black shadow is not the angel of death. The black shadow is a woman with a nail gun. Aunty's nail gun. But she's not Aunty.

I close my eyes. The vision of the woman who is not Aunty, but who holds Aunty's nail gun, is too much. I question this microcosm I'm in, how all this came together, me here, her here, my companion, the hatchet woman, a raging storm, what a medley of disconnected strands of life sewn together for an unbelievable moment. Is it philosophy to say everything is connected, or is it physics? Was this unbelievable moment predictable by some tangible calculation? Either way, everything is connected or impacts everything else, whether by philosophy or physics, doesn't matter. There's my reading-student refugee's story of survival, the one I found yesterday did impact me in a tangible way, and I didn't realize I remembered it until yesterday. And, I wonder now, the thing that happened to the senator who visited Boston with her daughters two years ago and wound up at Saint Jerome's, even that is connected. If the senator's awful event hadn't happened on the same night as the fire, I'm near certain I wouldn't be here above this hole in a hurricane.

CHAPTER ELEVEN

AUNTY

Two years ago

I'm on my way to Saint Jerome's for my night shift. After my all-night session guarding Johanna in the cottage—after I found my barn's floorboard disturbed and my stash of pentobarbital gone—and after I stole away and drove to fucking Cate and Kent Dranal's house at five a.m. to leave my taunting mistress note for Cate Dranal—I warned Johanna to keep clear of my house, to go back to Rye. I didn't feel my house was safe. And now I'm on my way to work the night shift. *Keep telling yourself you are working your night shift. Get even.*

I hope Johanna listens and stays put in Rye. I wouldn't leave my house for work until I saw her pull away, toot-tooting me a cheery goodbye and blowing me a big air kiss from her top-down, baby-blue convertible. After my long night of no sleep and a one-hour nap once Johanna awoke and showered, I worked my nerve to tell her everything. She listened like I knew she would, holding her purr beast Popover in her lap. Popover glared at me, loyal to Johanna. We resolved to talk on the phone tonight. She better stay in Rye. I know she'll want to meddle and check in on me, since she now knows *everything*. I know she'll want to sneak back to the house and wait for me.

Right after I clock in at Saint Jerome's, I'm going to call her and keep calling to make sure she stays away from my house. She agreed we can't go to the cops right yet, given all the background on the pentobarbital. And although she won't admit it outright, she thinks I'm imagining what really happened at Proserpina's.

"Honey cakes, do you think it might be like—I'm sorry, after Daddy, um, died, I'm sorry. But you know, and you are very stressed?" Johanna said, being the most delicate she could be in bringing up our father's murder, which was my fault, and my nervous breakdown because of it.

She didn't bring up the miscarriages, especially given what I told her this morning. I was surprised she even brought up our father's death. I'll never forget—although I've tried so hard to forget—the one morning a week after the estate manager did what he did to me when I was fourteen, when the house-call child psychotherapist couldn't get me to sleep or stop shaking, and I couldn't stop myself. Our mother whispered to Johanna outside my then Rye bedroom door, "Princess, we must never discuss how Liv is handling this, or what happened to Liv in the coach house. I've taken care of things with the cops. They'll keep the estate manager in jail on other charges, so that we can keep this our family secret. We don't need the press circling like sharks, like they do the Kennedys all the time. So Princess, it's your job, baby, to keep things light for Liv. You're so good at being our funny girl, baby, my special princess. Okay?"

"Yes, Mama. I love Livvy so much, I'll do anything for her. I won't mention a thing," Johanna, Mother's special funny princess girl, had said in return. And, true to her word, and Mother's directives, we didn't discuss what the estate manager did to me and how he caused our father's death, ever.

This very morning, when Johanna lightly touched on the subject of our father's death and my reaction to it, and she suggested I might be imagining what happened to Vicky at Proserpina's yesterday, I smiled at Johanna. I'd been cured of the issue with Daddy and my reaction. I had setbacks with each of the miscarriages, it's true. Upon the second loss, I kicked my longtime boyfriend David out of my life upon a near-murderous fit. Throwing literal vases and candlesticks at him, screaming how his sperm was toxic, that he was just a sperm donor to me, there was no way to repair the damage my words and actions ripped in the relationship. And I didn't want repair, anyway. In comparison to Kent, I still consider David no more than a failure of a sperm donor.

There was another setback when I heard why Johanna's sister-in-law, Sister Mary, really left the church—how unfair to me what that woman gets, and for no purpose. When Johanna told me, I left her standing in the cottage I built her, and in an eyes-flickering rage, I went to my own gardens and murdered my ring of sunflowers and several hydrangea bushes with the stabbing force of my sharp hoe. I thrust so hard I decapitated the metal head from the wood stick, which I cracked in half on my bent knee. At some point, Johanna sedated me. Days, maybe a few weeks, of mindless depression during these *outbursts* or *setbacks*, sleeping in a black room. But I'm a nurse. I'm practically a psychotherapist myself. I am good at being clinical. I can cure myself. So no, no, I did not imagine Proserpina's and Vicky's peanut poisoning. I've never imagined anything—gone catatonic a few times in my life, is all.

"Jo-Jo, no, honey. It happened, okay. I'm scared," I said, pleading to her with my eyes.

Johanna shook her head with a concerned brow but did not protest. She's too unwilling to agree evil exists. Nevertheless, as she pointed out, and she's right, the media would pounce on this story, given our well-known name and the fact we were born filthy stinking rich. There are the Kennedys of Cape Cod. And there are the Vandonbeers and Pentecosts of North Shore. We are pretty much the three most illustrious family dynasties in all of New England—except the Vandonbeers and Pentecosts never *outwardly* went the road of politics: *power* is an ugly word in my family. We're still paying penance for playing a disgusting role in the Salem witch trials—which was a politically motivated mass murder, if you didn't know, all about power and greed. And yet unwitting tourists flock to Salem to further monetize this mass murder, but I digress. It's gross. Instead, the Vandonbeers and Pentecosts stick with private dinner parties and charitable balls and private land and business deals and *hidden political maneuvers.* Johanna and I are the only remaining purebred Vandonbeers, not counting irrelevant second aunts and distant cousins, who, if we were royal, would be plotting to poison us for the throne.

So although I'm innocent—*am I innocent?*—the tabloids would judge this rat's nest salacious; even the high-and-mighty *Boston Globe* wouldn't resist. This is something the rich learn early, good or bad or honest or obnoxious as it may be. As our mother often said and Johanna repeated today, "It's best we handle things on our own, Sugar Cheeks." Johanna said "Sugar Cheeks" as if we're iced tea–swilling plantation owners, which we most definitely are not. We're 100 percent Yankee, blue blood, old money. There's a secret Underground Railroad chamber under the coach house at our Rye estate about which we remain quiet and proud. Never know when we'll need it again. I sure needed it when I was fourteen and Daddy was murdered, because of me.

The first thing I'm going to do when I get to Saint Jerome's is hunt down Kent and tell him his wife killed Vicky and stole my pentobarbital. *This is insane.* Of course I had no way to call him this morning, and he didn't call me. If I had tried to call him, I feared Cate would answer. He told me never to call his cell for this reason. He says she checks his phone records and audits him.

I'm an idiot. He's screwing other women. That's it, that must be why he told me not to call. He knows I don't text, I'm not on social media, I don't email, so I was just an easy target he could fuck without a trace. *Without a trace, what a riot. How ironic. No trace? Well, there's a trace all right. He's screwing someone—everyone—else. Did he leave traces with them too?* This is what I ask myself, because I need to hate Kent in order to extricate him from my life and my mind. His wife being a murderess is enough ammunition, but I'm piling on. I am deep in over my heart with Kent.

One week ago, we stood in the bathroom of the Kisstop. He held me from behind while we both faced the mirror. Swaying together to no music, he settled his head on my right shoulder, his hands on my naked belly, full of his child, the one I've ached for my whole life. *There's a trace of our love, all right.*

And this baby seems to want to stay. Not like my first two pregnancies, which I lost, both at twelve weeks. I'm at fourteen weeks now. "Heartbeat's strong," the doctor says.

Oh God, here we go. I'm crying again. I wipe away tears at a red light, so taken to think of holding our child.

I'm beyond the age recommended to carry, and there are risks, of course, with this. But in my gut, this child of love, is perfect and fine. A week ago, Kent and I swayed and swayed, staring at each other in the mirror, him holding my belly, our baby, and him saying strings of possible baby names as we swayed and stared. We traded whispered *I love you*s and didn't blink, didn't blink. His shirtless chest, his unbuttoned pants—I didn't apologize for stalling his dress. His thumbs looped the hip arches of my gold lace thong, which matched my gold lace bra. I wore nothing else. We swayed some more and because we were still staring in awe, we both started crying. Like I'm crying right now. Both of us struck by the dumb luck of falling in love. Which is a joke, of course: love is a curse.

How could he have faked his sobbing for me, for our child, crying into my hair and turning me to kiss me so deep my knees sank? I don't believe he faked those tears. I believe he was sincere, and we are in love, and although it's awful that he's married, for him, and this sounds cruel, but it's true, his marriage has become a terrible technicality. People might hate the cheaters in this, Kent and me, but I know the truth. And he was meant to tell her the truth yesterday. *Did he?*

I'm all over the place on Kent. I hate him. Then I'm defending him. I'm justifying our love as true and a higher power. I need to get a grip. Johanna said to get a grip. I'm getting a grip. I'm gripping the steering wheel so hard my fingers are white.

Last week when we cried at the Kisstop, he said he'd leave his wife for good this time. We've been at this affair six months. Not one email, not one phone call, no electronic trail between us. The Kisstop room he expenses to the hospital, some deal he made when he signed on as chief surgeon. It's a private hospital, so they can cut whatever deal they want, and they wanted Kent's name and patient list, so they agreed to comp him a comfy bed so he could avoid a "grueling" forty-minute commute on nights he pulled double shifts.

Why didn't Saint Jerome's pay for a car service? Kent set up a fuck nest is what he did. I beat the steering wheel after slamming to a stop at another red light on Route 1. *How many women has he trolled through those Kisstop sheets?* "No, no, no, no," I mouth aloud to the horn, talking to myself. *Kent only takes me there. He loves me, he does.* And around and around I go with myself.

His wife has killed. She broke into my barn. She stole drugs. It absolutely had to be her. Nobody else knew of the vials. She knew Kent had some pentobarbital vials when she found them in his Jeep. So I'm theorizing—and I have to be right, it's the only logical conclusion—that Kent did tell her about us last night and then she figured out it was me he got the pentobarbital vials from. She must have pulled his connection to me and found I had more vials when she came snooping and spying in my barn. He must have told her we're in love and he's leaving her and we're opening up a private clinic on my property and raising this baby together. And then, and I'm guessing, but this must be the case, she came to my barn to ruin our clinic, but found the vials. How else? Who else? This has to be the case. She is not dumb. She is a calculating witch. She put it all together. That is the only logical answer as to why my barn was disturbed and the vials missing. This is dangerous.

Get a grip. Get a fucking grip. I press clenched fists into my sitting lap so hard, I hope to bruise my thighs.

I park underground where I always park and immediately know something is wrong. Kent's gray Jeep is not in his usual spot. He's not here. There's no way I can face an evening shift with all this on my mind and him not here.

I race inside to beg off work, but there is chaos. I'm in ER this month, and son of a bitch, some asshole shot up a Catholic church by Government Center, and half those bodies came here. *Shit.* TV crews, reporters swarming outside. Mother of all fucks! Passing colleagues pepper me with drive-by updates, pulling me through drawn curtains, dragging me between clogged hallways, shepherding me to scoot through screaming families to join the fray of patching victims. This is how it is when I nurse. I lose time. I get immersed. I work. *This is why I need to nurse, to deviate from my dark obsessions, to stay focused, to be productive in a positive consumption.* Normally when I work, I think of nothing else, and so now, tonight, my obsession in getting to Kent has subsided to faded blinking in the back of my mind, but it's there, like low-grade nausea. I don't know how long I've been working.

Seems some fascist ass bag neo-Nazi shot the church up, nailing in his volley of bullets that senator the news has been squawking about—the one visiting Boston with her two daughters, both of whom she "dresses like royalty." The senator's spleen is in my right hand. She won't make it. Her daughters are hostages of the shooter on the run. There's a manhunt. I'm hip-checking an overaggressive detective this very second, pushing him out of the way, while I reset the senator's spleen for the surgeon.

What the ever-living fuck! FUCK!

"*Who let the fucking detective in? Get out! This needs to be sterile!*" I shout. They can't do anything to me; no law enforcement can touch me. Not while I'm fixing humans. And really, not ever. I'm a Vandonbeer. *I should remember this. This fear over the vials. Of being arrested. This fear is unnecessary. You need to accept your power, once and for all. Use your connections. Your secrets.*

No. Stop. Work. Just work.

I'm grabbed to enter an emergency surgery to extricate a bullet from the back of a schoolteacher, who, by the only saving grace, visited the church on a whim and didn't bring any summer students with her. I'd give away all my love for Kent and all my money if it meant these senseless mass shootings would stop.

As I shuttle in on the schoolteacher's surgery and command answers on blood type and complications, I slip a question to the attending physician on where the hell is Kent Dranal.

"Not here," she says.

We work two hours on the schoolteacher, with me being pulled to other fabric-walled ER stalls to mine other bullet holes, stitch other sutures, insert other drug lines, deliver other blood. Nowhere in any of this does Kent appear, even though protocol says in such an emergency code green, he's to be beeped to come in off the street or wherever the hell he is. Plus, he's supposed to be on shift anyway.

Manny is always there whenever Mop snaps her fingers, and vice versa. Same for Johanna and Philipp. There's no jamming things to be right, no doubts for them. With Kent it's all imperfect. But we have this baby, and the baby is perfect. The baby is perfect. Everyone else has everything perfect. Show up, Kent! Make this perfect!

But he doesn't show, and now it's eight p.m. There's a short lull as they cart the schoolteacher to one of the upper floors—ICU, to be exact. A tense static overtakes the air, like we all might fry as we await the prognosis on the senator. Guards and detectives and the feds clog up any free space. But there is, yes, this short lull when no one talks, and only static holds the world together. As the silence wanes away, I overhear two other nurses at the station where I've come to sit for a quick sip of water. They're whispering.

"I can't believe our chief surgeon missed this mess," Karen with the ponytail says.

"I know. Cate Dranal called, after we beeped for him, said Kent's got the flu," Betty, the nosy bitch of the ward, says, air-quoting "the flu" and rolling her eyes.

My heart beats in my throat.

Kent has never in his life called in sick, and he'd never allow Cate to call for him. Last year he worked for a week with painful laryngitis, never straining a complaint about his inflammation.

I race to the break room, intending to call Johanna in private. But when I get to the key card–locked door and I reach for my ID with the security strip to swipe and enter, I fumble at my breast pocket where it usually hangs and find nothing. I hadn't noticed earlier, because I've been stuck in emergency mode for hours.

Where is my ID?

I know it was on this shirt all night.

I think on all the places I've been since last night.

Where is my ID? Oh shit. Oh shit. Not there. No. Please.

I check with the lost items captain. "Hey, LIC, you got my ID?"

"Nope," she says. I check all the ER stalls I worked in, all the halls. Nothing. The hospital enforces strict rules on sterilization, so the crew in charge of picking up and mopping and wiping down everything would have found and turned it in. Nope, none of the cleanup crew has seen my ID.

I'm running to my car, frantic to search, hoping to hell the ID fell off my shirt and is in my car. *When the hell did it go missing? No, not then, please, no, not then.*

My Audi is almost alone in this part of the underground lot. The lights are dim by the two corner stairwells and bright like a spotlight over a Range Rover four spots down from mine. The Range Rover's black-tinted windows could hide anything, anyone. There are no other cars.

Shoes clicking on the underground floor above clatter around, like I'm a fish in a fishbowl and some child is tapping the glass with his nails. I'm seeing flashes of gray, mixed with blue-and-red taillights. I need to focus, calm. Breathe. I run to my car door, fumbling with the key fob to unlock it, and, because I'm a wreck, of course drop my fucking fob. It rolls under a back tire of the Range Rover.

On hands and knees, I'm blinded now, by tears, by panic, by my nurse shirt rising over my face. I grab the fob and freeze. Footsteps behind me. I stand, turn, and watch a woman descend from the upper floor through my floor. She's a blob of movement to me; I can't make out any features, so I stall like a lizard trying to camouflage. I don't think she notices me, and she moves on down the stairs. I trip-run to my car, electronically click it unlocked, scrabble inside, and see no ID.

Nothing in the driver's seat. No ID on or under any floor mats. Nothing under the two seats. Nothing in the creases of the leather cushions. Nothing. No ID. Absolutely nothing.

I played with the ID all night, and I know it stayed clipped. Shit. Shit. Shit. Did it unclasp when I leaned into Cate's awful minivan, when I got stuck in the seat belt? My God, what have I done? But what does it matter? If Cate already knew about you and was indeed the one who broke in and took the pentobarbital last night, before you left the mistress note, what does it matter?

I tell myself to shut up. It matters. *Because I incited her more. I escalated this. Play is in her court now. And if she didn't take the vials, she knows about you now.*

I am literally fighting with my own self.

I scrape into my pocket to find my flip phone and call Johanna. She doesn't answer her cell.

I try the Rye estate. Ring, ring, ring. I picture the rings echoing down the long, empty wings of that giant mansion. I think Johanna said Philipp is working late. Mop's not there, she's finishing up an extended seminar on ancient religions. She's not home for the summer until next week. So that leaves . . .

"Pentecost estate," a stiff, formal female voice greets me.

Johanna's sister-in-law, the ex-nun, answers on the eighth ring. I grit my teeth to hear her unworthy sanctimony. While the main house has an answering machine, the coach house doesn't, because the current estate manager, who lives next door, thinks it's too modern and not befitting of the grandeur of an old Vandonbeer estate to have more than one answering machine. The estate manager is a grade-A asshole with a fake Chilean accent. He's the third estate manager since the one who held me down and shoved his special metal shirt pin in my mouth when I was fourteen.

Three of the four Rye estate wings are filled with museum antiques from around the world. Johanna hates them, but Philipp Pentecost respects our Vandonbeer family pedigree and inheritances, and also his Pentecost inheritances, which he's added to the mix. And since Johanna loves Philipp, she's repainted how she sees her life as living in the movie *Night at the Museum*, one of her favorites, because she's got a "free-pass" star crush on Owen Wilson. Besides, Johanna and Philipp, and Mop when she's there, live mostly in the fourth wing, which Johanna has "Johannified" in pinks and ribbons and fabrics and upholstery, a blended shabby chic and beach elegant, just the way she likes.

Sister Mary Patience lives in the brick coach house, *the* coach house, the one I won't look at, much less step foot in. The one with the secret Underground Railroad chamber in the basement—where I hid in a catatonic state after fleeing the scene, naked but for a torn shirt, failing to help my father off the floor when he collapsed from the effort of fighting off my rapist. Daddy's heart couldn't stand the shock or effort.

The brick coach house happens to still have one of the estate's old rotary phones, same rotary I didn't use to call 911. Me, useless, like a dumb doll. The doctors said Daddy would have lived if I had fucking called.

The ex-nun Sister Mary Patience Pentecost has answered that same rotary phone now, squawking, "Hello . . . hello," in my ear.

"Oh, hello, Sister Mary, is Johanna there? It's Liv."

"Johanna left an hour ago, Lynette. Said she was going to your place." Before I can respond, she rushes in, "What's going on? What's the matter? Philipp just got home from his office. He's out at the pool, should I go get him? Lynette, is Johanna okay? Your voice is wrong." The woman is as astute as an AI robot from the year 4050, Planet Vulcan. And she refuses to call me Liv, like everyone else does. It's odd, her refusal, since I'm at the Rye estate, my own damn old home, almost as much as Johanna's at my home. There are almost no boundaries—our living arrangements are fluid. Well, they were much more fluid before Kent, but then I started staying home more, to feel twenty minutes closer to him. *I'm pathetic.*

As for Sister Mary Patience Pentecost and me, you'd think two grown women who share a niece, both of whom remain unmarried in their forties, would be closer. But there's a tension between us, a chance she stole from me that the universe should have given to me. She thinks I don't know why she left the church. Well, I know why. And she didn't leave anything—the hypocrite was kicked out, defrocked. She doesn't deserve Johanna's time away from me. Doesn't deserve Mop's time ever. Doesn't deserve . . . She's still squawking, "Lynette, Lynette, Lynette," like the incivility of an island bird squawking you awake at dawn despite your island hangover.

Perhaps she knows I judge her. She must assume Johanna told me the truth as to why she's retired—euphemism—from the church. Truth is, I think Mop's got some things in common with Ms. Mary Patience Pentecost, more than the two will admit to each other or themselves. But it's not my place to spread the gossip, and I do not accept any role in forging a bond between them. *You are a terrible person, Lynette Viola Vandonbeer. Get a fucking grip. No, I am not terrible. Yes, you are. Just listen to Mary Pentecost on this call—she's talking, you're spiraling. Find Johanna, focus only on that.*

"Lynette, Lynette, are you there? Is everything okay?" Sister Mary squawks hard at me again. She has almost no soft edges when she speaks. She's tall and skinny like a boobless scarecrow, so your skin itches just to see her.

"No, nothing's the matter. I'm at the hospital, and I thought Johanna was staying in Rye. There's no problem, Sister Mary. None at all. Whoops, got to go, they're calling me."

She tsks, I know it, as I hang up, which is fine—means she bought it, I think. Thank God for the drama I maintain in the community theater.

I'm shaking in my car, seeing shadows move in this underground parking lot, worrying about where my key card is, obsessing on where Johanna might be in relation to Cate Dranal. I call up to the nurses' desk, get Betty the nosy bitch, say I got sick and am going home. I know Cate Dranal's lurking around my house. She found my note and also my key card, and now she's waiting for me. *Is this delusional paranoia? No, this is real.*

Who knows what Cate Dranal did to Kent Dranal, but I suspect she did something. *Where is he?*

Johanna's ignoring my calls as I drive. I know her. Her playlist of Paul Simon and Ray LaMontagne and the incongruous intermixing of rap by Missy Elliott is blared high; she's singing along, the top is down, and her damn bedazzled phone is lighting up and being ignored in the back seat, next to Popover, who's yawning, immune to Johanna's constant solo concerts. One other thing she's doing, she's twirling a tape measure on one finger, planning out how she'll ask her Zimman's designer to decorate the new baby's suite in my home. This is how she'll surprise me; this is what she's thinking on. She's not taking my fears about Kent's murderous wife seriously. She thinks I'm imaging things. I'm not.

She answers my ten thousandth call.

"What's that, Sisterloo?" She answers in song, the words a trill and a lilting C.

"Do not go to my house," I say, short and in no melody.

"You're imagining things, Liv. Please, honey, I'm worried."

"Please, Johanna. Go. Home."

"Okay, you know what. How's about this. I drove to Gloucester actually, to eat dinner at the new hotel, the Bennington. It's *faaaaaaaaabuulous*, by the way. They let me bring Popover in and everything, gave him tuna in a crystal bowl! I was about to leave and pop over to your place, because I don't listen to no big sister when she's all crazy and I know we got more talk to do. How about you drive right here to the Bennington when you're done at the hospital? I'll get us a room and we'll sleep here tonight. And we'll go to Zimman's in the morning. Babycakes, you're upon your second trimester—we have to get a move on."

Johanna never listens to the news, so she has no clue there's been a mass shooting in Boston, involving a senator and the kidnapping of her two daughters. Johanna, the special funny girl family princess, is blissfully clueless. I wish I could be. And now she wants me to sleep in a new hotel, ten minutes from my house. Whatever. Whatever will keep her away and safe.

"Good. Good. Yes, Johanna. Yes. Stay there. I'll go to the Bennington once I'm done with work."

I don't tell Johanna I'm in my car and off my shift. With her safe, I'm going to make a stop on the way. I'm going straight to Danvers, to check directly on Kent and get my damn vials back. Screw this anxiety and worry. I'm facing things, bringing it all out in the open, exposing Cate for what she did to Vicky. She'll threaten to turn me in for possessing the vials. But damn whatever happens in the press—I can control this. I don't know why I tried to deny my power before. The Vandonbeer name can also be used as a shield, I can't forget that. We have connections. We have money. We hold extortion-level secrets on strategic powerful people, people who made their posts in large part on our decades of donations, some under the table, exported and laundered, not reported. We learned centuries ago to always lie low, set the traps, and be ready. Power is an ugly word in our family, yes, but the truth is, we can be ugly. I can shut this shit down any number of ways. In many, many ways, I am above the law. I am ugly. I have power. I can't be afraid to use my weapons of connections, extortion, secrets, and shame. I don't fear the weak, the sheep, the low-down, the press, or the law. I own it all. I'm a Vandonbeer. I am a damn Vandonbeer. I can be an ugly, powerful bitch, all right. People think we abolished royalty long ago. We didn't abolish royalty. Royalty went underground; we rule through puppets, charities, corporations, private equities, and empty vessels they call politicians. *Citizens United*, please. It is exactly what you think it is: ugly power.

I've tried all my life to pretend like I'm normal, like I'm not ugly and powerful. But I am a fucking Vandonbeer, so I'm done playing games.

I punch my thighs so hard as I drive, I know I leave bruises.

Am I really that powerful? Can I do this? Am I deluding myself? *Drive. You must do this.*

CHAPTER TWELVE

MOP

Present time

There is a woman in black with a nail gun, firing into the sky and screaming at the woman with the hatchet. My companion awakes and vomits on my legs. I can't take this. I can't take this. *I can't take this.* I try to stand, and all my remaining blood rushes down, throbbing at the part where I tied the cloth tourniquet. This time I crash back down to the ground for what feels like the last time and for good. I slam my head against the soft rock. Feels like with the force, the rock reveals it is not a pillow, but rather a throwing star that slices through my cranium and lodges in my brain.

One week ago, Manny and I landed back in Boston after being in Milan for a week. After I connected who Manny and I saw on the rocks the night of my mother's disappearance to the woman in Aunty's barn, I kept my silence, didn't say a word to Manny. I said I was feeling overcome by the recollection of the woman screaming on the rocks and that I needed to fetch my journal, which I left at Aunty's the week before. I told Manny I'd meet him back at his home in half an hour and we'd go to Rye to speak to my father about a wedding.

I also called the mechanic who'd towed my red Volvo the week before, and the mechanic said it'd be about another week until I could get my car back. I was going to have to rely on Manny for the driving for another week. So be it. Not having my own car was the least of my worries.

I fixed my intentions on the woman in Aunty's barn. And I really did leave my journal in the gray-and-green guest room. I didn't call ahead to Aunty to tell her I was back from Milan and heading over. I had planned on getting the journal and investigating the woman in the barn.

It was high tide when I set off from Manny's house a week ago, so I skipped plunking into the middle beach and stayed within the higher trails through mounds of bayberry, blackberry, blueberry, and then on into the catbrier and brambles and arthritic trees. When I came to the secret trail that meets upon Aunty's ring of willows and maples and perennial beds, I stalled to watch her leaving and locking her barn again—I suppose she was attending to her rounds as house nurse for her "friend." But, I thought, *why does she lock her in?*

Why the lock on the outside?

I should have screamed this question and forced her into reality. But she again wore no eye patch and she smiled wide to a bird in a tree with her broken teeth. Her wispy gray hair flew about like she was the maddest, oldest witch in the coven, the one the other witches stay away from.

So I waited until she returned to her pink house and her bright kitchen, which glowed yellow and sunny against the flawless blue sky. From the backyard through one of the kitchen's two bay windows, I could see her wall of now sparse collection of antique yellowware bowls and platters, the few pieces scattered in no pattern on an open antique wormwood shelving unit, which anchored to the wall perpendicular to the one with her black gas stove. Aunty stood with her back to the bay window, selecting a yellowware bowl. I couldn't get over how little of her collection remained. About eight pieces out of the original, I don't know, dozens and dozens. She prided her yellowware collection. *Colonial Living* magazine once featured it in a four-page spread.

What happened to her yellowware?

I slipped around to the front door, entered, yelled "hi" to her and "back from Milan," but ran through the Mermaid Library before engaging her, and into the green-and-gray guest bedroom. Beside the twin bed was a long dresser with four rows of drawers. I expected to snag my journal from atop the dresser. But there was no journal. I raced to the guest bathroom, ransacked the cabinet, and found no journal, for *why would there be a journal in a bathroom cabinet?* I looked under the twin bed, the gray braided rug, the green comforter and gray sheets, and still no journal. I hadn't used the dresser, but nevertheless, I set to yank all the drawers. I forgot about the woman in the barn, frantic that if I didn't get the journal, I couldn't return to Manny in time. It made no sense, but the grief fog and fury had returned. Any little pebble, like not finding my journal, threw me off. I didn't even allow myself to think on the boarded attic and bedroom doors upstairs.

My skin itched, I wanted my journal and out of Aunty's house so bad.

Where's my journal? Where's my journal? Where's my journal? Whatever she's doing upstairs and in the barn, her problems. Not my problems. I need out. I don't want to be dragged down. I want to move on. In my life. With Manny. No one else. I want my journal. I just want love back. It was wrong to come back here.

Inconceivable irrationalities entered my mind: *if I don't find my journal, I won't be able to leave with Manny, and he'll leave me. I'll lose him forever.*

Where is my journal? What's going on in the barn? No, find the journal. Get out of here. What about upstairs with the boarded doors? The metal scraping in the attic? Get the journal. Get the journal. Get the journal. Get out.

The top drawer held nothing but pillowcases. Slam.

The second drawer held nothing but bundled Christmas cards from well-wishers over the years. Slam.

The third drawer held one thing, a piece of paper. I skipped it. Slight push and turn of my head in a wince. *Did it really say that on that piece of paper?*

The fourth drawer held a spare bath mat, the pink robe I wore last week, and, thank God, my journal. Grabbed journal. Slam.

What was that piece of paper in the third drawer? Did it say "I know what you did to Vicky" on it?

I returned to the third drawer. I ignored, although why I don't know, footsteps behind me in the Mermaid Library.

The paper was a note that indeed said on the outside fold, *I know what you did to Vicky*.

The inside held the handwritten words of a mistress taunting a wife. This note holds the truth to why we are in this hurricane right now, me bleeding out life, my companion too.

But was being a mistress the ultimate cause to our present horror, or was it a symptom, or the final cause? Weren't there a number of causes leading up to our horror in this hole in a hurricane? Suppressing grief, denying mental illness might be other causes.

One week ago when I found the mistress note, Aunty entered the guest room as I shoved the note in the pocket of my black pants.

"I'm leaving now," I said. "I'm going to Rye with Manny."

"So you're going to keep the note then, Mop?" Aunty said.

"You wanted me to find it, didn't you, Aunty? That's why you hid my journal. I know you want to be free of whatever you've got going on. But I'm not ready to hear it yet. I don't know if I ever will be. This is your problem, and I think you know you need help. But I'll tell you one thing. If that woman in the barn is connected to what happened to my mother, I will find out, and I will get justice against whoever hurt her. Whoever."

I stared her down with a vengeance, pupils raised high in low-cast lids, chin down, sending my message, strong in my outward voice, but weak in my core, for as I said the words, I wanted to jump out of the window, slide down the basement bulkhead, and run. I scratched my arms and shivered on the spot, so desperate to be free of her naked, broken face and her, blocking me in the doorway.

Aunty stared at me with one sad eye, like a helpless cow rehearing the eternal cries of her calf being slaughtered. Withdrawn, defeated, depressed, and lost in a lonely field.

Maybe I shouldn't have left just then. Maybe I should never have come. Maybe I wasn't strong enough. Maybe I was the strongest I've ever been.

I pushed past her in the doorway, and when I did, her body felt as light as an empty piñata. She stumbled aside, one arm crossed across her ribs, holding her other straight arm, wincing as if I threatened to hit her. I headed back to Manny's through the bramble trails, the mistress note in my back pocket. The journal in my hands.

About halfway, my cell rang. I paused on the layered rocks along the shoreline, standing in the same spot where Manny and I had seen the woman screaming two years ago—the woman in the barn two years later. Sea wind brushed my cheeks, tousled my hair.

"Mop?" Aunty said on the phone.

I inhaled as my answer, catching a mouthful of salty air.

"Mop, I'm heading to Rye too. Going to change and then I'm leaving, like ten minutes. I'll meet you there. I want to discuss all of this with your father and with you. I'll meet you there. Please, I'm ready for help. Please," Aunty said.

This.

This call.

What would have changed had I not answered this call? Would I have continued on to Manny's? Would I have left for Rye with the intention of remaining voluntarily numb to Aunty, shutting her and her crimes out? Would I have listened to whatever she wished to reveal to me and my father, not knowing what I was about to uncover in going back to her house?

As I hung up, I ticked my head to the side in a click of my neck, as if this click was the press of a "Start" button on once again, to resume the intent to investigate the woman in the barn. A wave of high tide slammed me awake to the day and to a renewed mission. I had a sudden urge to visit with the barn patient on my own, without Aunty's meddling and incongruous explanations hovering over. I had no clue what Aunty intended to tell me and my father in Rye, but I sure wasn't going to listen to any of it without my own insights into the matter. So I stalled on the rocks with the phone dead in my hand, and I plotted my next steps.

I didn't look over to Manny's lawn beyond the middle beach. Didn't consider how he might be watching me. Instead I focused on the flight of a seagull, swooping through the bluest blue over a fisherman's green boat, apparently trying to steal his catch. I was ready. I was intent. I was present. I smelled the salt in the air. *I'm here.*

I looked to the rocks and the tide pool beneath my feet, and I waited a beat or two in meditating upon the microscopic fury of a tiny crab, cementing my intention in the stone of me. I turned back toward the bayberry mounds, the bramble and catbrier hedges, and headed into the thicket of trees around Aunty's. I passed by the cottage remains of my mother's demise, and I paused at the path head behind the haughty, spiral sunflower congress. There, I waited, watching her enter her Audi, back up, and drive off. As the only black item on her property, when her car disappeared, a heavy shadow lifted and thus her departure lit the world aflame in a wavy rainbow. Like I'd died and gone to a distorted heaven.

Still, I waited, to be sure, and once the coast cleared, set off for the back of the barn, so as to enter like I had the first day I arrived back at Aunty's.

As I brushed through the rosemary and basil garden, kicking up whiffs of herbs, which made me hungry, and was about parallel with the boarded window of the side room on the barn, where the woman lay, a finger tapped my shoulder from behind. How I didn't hear the approach, I don't know. Maybe I wasn't present after all.

I screeched and hauled around, shrinking and preparing my hands in self-defense. But upon seeing his face, I clenched up and melted in a fast breath relief. Relief I wasn't to be harmed, but still heart-pounding fear he'd find the secret in the barn.

"What are you doing?" Manny asked, fixing me with a somewhat frightened, somewhat clinical look.

I knew I had to act my way out of this. I wasn't prepared yet to let Manny in on the true insanity. And there was only one way to get him to step back and not venture beyond to investigate where I was headed.

"Oh, huh, you scared me," I said, jumping a second time. "I thought I'd go grab one of the props from our summer stage, from when we were kids. I was thinking it would be cool to do a little playacting for my dad to tell him about the wedding. He's going to freak, Manny. He'll be so excited to focus on something good for a change."

Manny smiled, and whenever he does this, two lines appear on his cheeks connecting his eyes with his chiseled chin. The appearance of these lines works a chemistry in me, so I smiled back and bit my bottom lip, crackling light taking the place of my heavy heart. For this response, Manny grabbed my hips, and so I had the opportunity to sell this whole charade and solidify my lie about getting props from the barn, but in a true way, for I just about die every time Manny pulls on my hips—closer, closer, closer to his hips.

"Aunty's not here," I said, suggesting he could pull harder, and thus allow me to sell this story for a song, seal the deal with the solidifying agent of sex. I sucked his neck.

I do love Manny. I did plan on telling him everything. I did. I just wasn't ready yet, because I wanted to give him all the facts. I hope he can forgive me. I hope he's still alive.

I unbuttoned his jeans, he unzipped my pants, we kicked our clothes into the rosemary and basil. He pinned my body against the side of the barn, the boarded window to my right. He pushed up inside me while I stood, my right leg raised and bent, so he could enter at the right angle and thrust. Our sexual geometry, just right. We pulsed against the barn's side room in a rabid passion, my back banging against the peeling paint. He felt like the greatest scratching sandpaper to an unquenchable urge, and I reciprocated by soothing his heat in an agreeable wet. God, he moaned like a pleased beast, banging, banging, banging me against the wall of the barn's side room. I didn't care that the mechanic rabbit who guarded the sunflower congress had hopped and frozen on a stone to watch. For a displaced moment, I was free of everything and only with Manny in some heaven dimension on earth.

And then he dropped his head on my shoulder, exhaled as if he'd finished a grueling sprint, and pulled away one inch, which felt like ten miles to me.

"Holy shit, Mop. That was amazing," he said.

"It was," I said, because it was. It was fast and furious and heated and crazy and raw and outside, but it was amazing. Despite the miles on my tortured mind, I must remember, we are young.

I looked to our scattered pants in the herbs and settled again on my intention.

"Babe," I said, catching his jeans with my foot and kicking the pair to my hands to hand to him. I did the same with my own pants, the underwear still inside. My cell and the mistress note were safe in a back pocket, but my journal had tumbled out. I headed to bend to the journal, which had rolled to the stone the rabbit stood on. "Head back to your house. I want to get another surprise for you. I'll be right behind. I'll be there superfast. Go, go, go," I said.

I knew if I smiled and demanded, he'd agree to go upon a twinkle in my eye and the promise of a surprise. I had no real surprise to give him, but I figured I'd figure on something.

The vertical smile lines on his face returned, and while I did consider a quick round two, he mercifully turned to return back down our secret path to his house and car to wait for me. I watched him snake away through those bramble trails.

Alone once more, I headed to the back of the barn. I found it barred from the outside once again, so I once again removed the board and entered.

Why is Aunty locking all entrances from the outside?

Inside, the inside was the same as always. The center with the four converted horse stalls: Aunty's tool stall, my mother's beach-glass stall, the gardening stall, and the painting stall. I paused by the corner with all my and Manny's former summer stage stuff, the stage made of shipping crates with the curtains of sailing sails and the box of props. I figured after investigating the woman in the side room, I'd find some kind of object to announce our engagement and some kind of surprise for Manny in the prop box.

I walked on to the side room.

And there she remained, sleeping away in a hospital bed. The same woman we saw two years prior, screaming in a blue-on-blue ball gown on the rocks by the water.

Her monitors hummed. Her liquid bag on a hook with line to vein dripped. I assumed saline. Maybe drugs, though. Aunty said she was in a coma.

I bent to open the side cabinet, which held gauze and linens. I did not know what to look for, but I looked for anything, so I had intended to ransack everything in the room. I suppose I wanted the woman's name, the ball gown she wore on the rocks—so I could confirm for sure what I already knew, or any identification card, anything. Maybe, I thought, Aunty kept nursing notes on her. Something. Anything. And what about the note I found in the third drawer of the dresser in Aunty's guest room? The one written by a mistress to a wife. Were there more? Perhaps one in response? Basically, I grasped for any clues to anything.

Who was the mistress? Who wrote the note? Sure looked like Aunty's handwriting.

As I tweezered my fingers in my back pocket to pull the note out, that's when she spoke.

"I heard you fucking outside my room," the woman said.

I rocketed up.

She rattled a metal chain connecting her leg to the bed, the chain obscured by a white blanket. I hadn't appreciated the chain the first time I saw her. I also didn't appreciate the orange beach-glass necklace around her neck: my mother's beach-glass necklace.

Chained up, locked in. Wearing my mother's orange beach glass.

CHAPTER THIRTEEN
AUNTY

Two years ago

Here I am, a block from Kent's. My Audi is three blocks away. Walking in the dark on his sidewalks could feel like coming home. It is not. Johanna's safe and waiting for me at the Bennington in Gloucester. It's go time, here we go. *Go, get out of the car and get this over with.*

Kent's Jeep is gone. *Where is Kent?* Cate's nasty minivan is gone, as expected: she has her triple at Mass General today, or, as I fear, she's stalking my property. The lights are black in their huge Victorian. The house looks dead. *Kent must have gone somewhere. Where?*

I look around the neighborhood. I suppose the white Cape with the drawn drapes, but the lights blazing and ten cars in the driveway, is murdered Vicky's house. These are her mourners' cars. A black wreath hangs from her boring black door, and on her front porch are a half dozen bunches of flowers and two trays of food from well-wishing neighbors, I'm guessing. A child's tricycle is flopped to its side, discarded in her front lawn; a sad spinning back wheel creaks around as wind plucks its spokes. Despair. The vision of her house and this lawn and the flipped bike, rank despair.

And Kent's looming Victorian of hideous hunter green and mauve, catty-corner across the street, is dark and black and dead.

If I can get inside, I'll find the vials Cate stole and regain the upper hand. Kent leaves keys under a brick by the back door. He used them once, one day when we made love in this house.

I know where their bedroom is.

I slid in her sheets, naked, him above me. I folded my neck to see between the V of our bodies, to watch where in our conjoining he came in, came out. It thrilled me to watch our entwined movement. And when I moaned aloud in this house, the walls absorbed my voice, like walls absorb the odor of smoke.

I am smoke in this house.

I am creation, creator, power in this house. Our child was conceived in the king bed upstairs. Looking up, I stare at the front master bedroom from a shadow by a bush on the sidewalk.

I know this house. I've lived in its plaster and beams a thousand million minutes in memory.

I own the darkness, all the shadows, the steam in the shower, the heat in the oven, the flames in the woodstove, the soot in the chimney, all mine. All his fantasies, of fucking me against their washing machine, on the counters she cuts vegetables on, those fantasies are constant fragments of me in this house. I can blend in, creep in the corners, find what I need before they return. I live as a phantom mist in this house, and thus my presence is merely that, nothing new.

I need to get the vials back.

I slither and feel like a slithering snake indeed, up his driveway, beyond the reach of candy-cane gas lamps; their glow is limp, futile to me, the aggressor. Why does it rile me so to see his driveway recently blacktopped, the pristine layer of tar a uniform black and perfect, no holes, no decay? Why would he invest in such maintenance when he should be working toward the dissolution of living here? I wish to jackhammer this tar. I wish to blow it up.

At the back door, I bend and kick the brick on the side of the stoop. I grab the keys and, with no shaking, turn the key and enter. Patches of black move along the walls inside, but as I adjust my vision, the world solidifies in shapes of gray.

I stall by the coats on the hooks in the mudroom. I finger the sleeve of his navy running jacket, the one he wore once at the Kisstop and from which he kept pulling mini Three Musketeers from the pocket— the trick-or-treat size. I wish, I want, no, I *need* to hold this jacket between my breasts and feel what he's worn, smell his smell. But I can't. Can't be caught. I let go the sleeve in reluctance; it falls fast and swings to hit the wall in a silent thud.

Hearing nothing, no sound, no snore, no breath in this house, I step farther in, scraping my spine along the hall, peeking into their pass-through, rectangular kitchen, and see nothing. No one. The breakfast bar with brown marble on the far end divides her predictable, out-of-the-box, no-originality kitchen from the grays of the living room. Of course that psycho picked brown marble—it's safe and boring and shows no individuality. I hate her. *I hate her. I fear her. I hate her.*

Still no sounds. No one is here. There are so many places to search for my stolen vials, but I will start with their bedroom. Kent showed me her safe in their closet once. And separately, on another day, he let slip when we were laughing in a druglike after-haze of sex how Cate was growing so forgetful in her age, creeping up as she was on menopause, she set all her pass codes to 3333. "She must have everything in threes," he'd said, laughing, but drained his statement along the way to a serious darkness. "Threes," he repeated with downcast eyes and nervous fumbling fingers. "I don't know what to do with her anymore, Liv. She has lost something, lost grip. I fear her," he'd said, staring into my eyes for help. This was before the first time she stole my vials and thus justified Kent in fearing her—me too.

And still, he said he'd been hinting at leaving her ever since, and she kept seizing this weakness in his possession of the vials to force him to stay. Time passed, and Kent and I learned of my pregnancy, and it was yesterday, only yesterday, when he was supposed to finally tell her he was leaving her for good. But he didn't, and she killed Vicky. We'd agreed enough was enough and we'd take the risk. And our baby, we agreed to raise our child together. Did he tell her last night, after Vicky? Did he tell her we were going to run a private clinic? Is that how she put it all together, came to my place, and found my vials last night? Did he tell her? *If so, where the hell is he? Why hasn't he called if the secret's out? Where the hell is Kent?*

Threes, he said, her code on everything. And she insisted he fold her underwear in threes. "She is obsessed with threes, and unnaturally so. She scares me," Kent said on more than one occasion. So as I tiptoe up the staircase with a red runner to the second floor of their renovated Victorian, I'm confident I can crack her safe and check for my vials by pressing four threes on the lock pad.

At the top of the stairs, I am met with exceptional familiarity. I've roamed this hall in my mind a million times. But I also suffer a slash of fear. I don't hear a soul, no human movement, no scream at my intrusion. It's a different sound, a different sense, and a different sight slashing my mind with fear. Like I was fine, but then someone came and snapped my neck to the side. A right angle bending a straight line.

Although from outside the house appeared black and dead, an interior bathroom, whose door is mostly shut, is lit. A sliver of light ekes out to form a white slash on the floor, and thus my slash of fear. I pause, wait, but nothing stirs within. Another item lending to my fear is a sound from the interior bathroom, a slow drip of liquid hitting liquid. The sound is as if the sink had only just been shut off. But by my vantage at the landing on the second floor, I can see into their bedroom to my immediate left, and their king bed is made, the room gray and empty. No one has broken the seal on their top cover tonight. Therefore, this slash of fear is not out of concern that someone is home and turned a sink off ten feet from me. The fear is something else. My instincts are screaming about something else; my neck is so tight I might merge vertebrae.

Upon closer inspection of the hall floor slashed crosswise in a line of white light, a slick of cleansing wet or polish marks a path from the interior bathroom, along one side of the continued red runner, and then, as I look back down, one side of the stair treads. Like a mop had been dragged to clean after something that had been dragged out of the bathroom and down the stairs. The slick of wet shine stands out; all else in the hall is layered in a film of dust. Cate is a barbarian—she doesn't clean.

For me, in looking at the wet wash along one side of the hall and down the stairs, taking in that vision and what it could mean, the slash of white light from the interior bathroom becomes alive and rises, forming curling vines around my legs. A stem of the light vine turns gray and pokes into my mouth, crawls down my throat, and coils to choke my heart. I inhale in quickened breaths, dragging the ominous air into my collapsing lungs; I begin to hyperventilate in this gray place, choking in gray vines. The oxygen is like moldy cotton. The drip, drip of liquid on liquid will not relent in calling me to inspect. There is more—my senses know there is more, there is worse for me to find behind the bathroom door.

I step closer, the air heavy against my shins, like I'm walking against the tide.

I pause. Still no breathing. No movement. No other humans.

I press open the bathroom door. The slash of light widens fast, alighting the hall in which I stand like the sun suddenly risen over a mountain, shining on the top of a lake to change from a muted dawn to blinding ice. I close my eyes from the stabbing glare and the truth behind.

I know the scent of blood. Smell is the sense blaring alarms in my brain.

I know the stench of it, from wounds, from bedpans, from puddles under beds, from surgeries, from birthing mothers, from holes in heads. I know blood as well as a bloodhound. I've worked with blood every day of my working life; the viscous odor never leaves my active memory. I keep my eyes closed in sensing its thick presence; I do not need sight to expose the truth in this room.

But visual confirmation is necessary for my mind and so, knowing full well what I'll find, I open my eyes. I grip a silver towel rack, bolted through the subway tiles of the bathroom wall. In an instant, I am displaced, set on a glacier and alone. The coldest chill I have ever known crackles in my core, as though I am an unsettled ice lake, splitting apart. On this lonely, arctic glacier, my sight is fogged, and I see nothing but gray blotches of cold air, cold clouds dislodged from the sky.

I rake the gray clouds with my hands to see through.

And there in Kent's white bathtub is a substantial layer of blood, pinking and rising with every plop of the water. But no body.

I am a nurse. I make quick conclusions.

A body was drained in the tub.

A body died in this house.

No detective is necessary to link the mop swipes on the floor, a cleansing trail to cover the trail left by the dragging of the emptied body out of the tub, down the hall, down the stairs, and to where?

I vomit in the toilet.

You are in a house of blood and death. You have ruined everything for everyone.

CHAPTER FOURTEEN
MOP

Present time

I don't know where or in what dimension of reality I am, and I fear that I don't really care. I think I'm wet or something, and all I see is black. I'm tired, tired, tired. *I'm tired.* I'm staying asleep. Someone is screaming outside my body, and I'm sure I hear *chih-chah* rioting over and over. Some metal sound. Wind. I don't know. It's too hard to open my eyes.

It's easier to live in the past, no matter how horrifying it is.

A week ago, after Manny and I got back from Milan and we made love against the side of the barn, I found that woman awake and chained at the leg, wearing my mother's orange beach-glass necklace. The moment she revealed herself as not in a coma is the starting moment to this last week's never-ending slide into insanity's greedy well.

What is this duplicity people are able to live in? I can only speak for myself. I know, for one, I do not want to live in duplicity. I want to live in pure truth. I want to live in harmony with my thoughts, my fears, my desires, and my actions. But I find this impossible, and it is also true, despite the wish to live in pure truth, that the impossibility to do so seems, oddly, natural. As if living in pure truth is unnatural.

Usually, a person's duplicity has to do with a war between heart and reason, whom to love and when and how. My duplicity a week ago centered not around whom to love, but what to trust of my love, what to believe, what to tell, and when. What if the double truth, the secret, were trotted out and tested? What if I did tell Manny about the woman in the barn a week ago? Would all this tragedy have been avoided?

Manny, are you okay? Where are you? Manny!

I stared at the chained-up woman in the barn and a quick philosophical question raced across my mind. I considered my aesthetics professor and recalled a question he asked me and his young wife at dinner one night.

"What is more beautiful, pure truth or balancing duplicity so well the actor acquires self-harmony?" In other words, his question was really, is false truth, or rather, a manufactured truth, the same in terms of beauty to the beholder, the actor who creates truth? Is truth really what we convince ourselves, and is that, what we tell ourselves, the beauty? Simplifying further, at its core, his question was really: *Is truth personal, subjective only?*

So what had Aunty told herself about this woman, chained in her barn, to believe she was living a truth? And what would I tell myself, but not Manny or anyone else, in order to accept this woman and cope? Could I find harmony, a beauty, in any of this?

And such impossible, impractical philosophical questions in a time of shock left me stone-cold, gape-mouthed frozen in the chained woman's captive glare. I think too much. And minoring in philosophy during years of grief only made this mental chasm in me deepen and fester. Without my mother to throw glitter and bright lights in the black well of me, I became the black chasm, questioning all, doubting all, and this woman chained in the barn, telling me she'd heard me fucking outside, was the bottom of the well. The sight of my mother's orange beach-glass necklace around her neck became a boulder on my shoulders, pinning me to the grime-slime of the well's bottom.

The woman growled. I backed up, pressing my butt cheeks so far on the edge of the linen cabinet I half sat, my hands as braces. She growled, she really growled.

"Fucking whore, just like your aunt," she said. "Fucking outside for the world to see. Do you know who I am?"

The vision of this woman, for me, tripled in some mad hallucination for a second, until I shook my head and blinked three times, swallowing reality. I couldn't think of anything to say in response, except one thing.

"Where's your ball gown?"

She squished her face to show complete confusion, turned her head slow to the boarded window, and then back. Sort of like a possessed doll in a horror film. No, not sort of, exactly like that.

"My what?" she said, keeping her hands limp on her sheets, which is something I began to focus on, for her lack of body movement became a blazing truth. Her arms didn't twitch; they hung dead to her sides. Only her head pivoted and her eyes bugged.

"You wore a navy-and-blue ball gown out on the rocks, two years ago. Where is it?" I suppose this crazy question was my attempt to jump the need to scour the joint for hard evidence, so as to obtain a direct confession that this woman was indeed the woman on the rocks in a ball gown.

She laughed. A throaty, scratched-record laugh, as if a sputtering engine coming to life.

I stared at her, didn't blink. I wanted an answer. That's all I could do, mentally and physically, for I couldn't move my own limbs. Her real paralysis became mine.

"A dress? Blue dress? Oh yeah, I suppose blue, right, blue," she said in a dead monotone, apathetic and weighted.

Although I could have regarded this answer with suspicion, as if I had given her some *Talented Mr. Ripley* clues for her to seize and falsely claim, I took it as a direct confession: she was indeed the woman on the rocks, in a ball gown, two years ago, the night my mother launched herself into the ocean. I wanted to jump to another confession. Forcing myself out of shock and fear, I leaned over her and into her dry, bloated face. I grabbed my mother's orange beach-glass necklace in a death grip and pulled, yanking it off her thickened neck.

"Did you start the fire? Did you kill my mother? How did you get her necklace?"

She laughed again, but stalled in her physical limpness, low-lidding me in a glare. The veins in her neck swelled with an effort to move her own arms, which twitched only as if in a slight seizure. She couldn't move, which I could tell angered her, or so it seemed. Her growling remained, as if she were a bloodthirsty puma in a jungle tree, waiting for her prey to step on the right spot.

"Your mother's necklace? Oh, right. You're the bitch's niece. Right. So your mother must be Johanna Vandonbeer. You are just another fucking Vandonbeer." She pivoted her eyes to look at the boarded window again; this action told me she had two positions: staring out the boarded window and staring at me, opposite the window. But was this truth or duplicity? Tricking me about her physical abilities? Perhaps wanting me to think her weak so I would let my guard down?

Her neck veins deflated and swelled to ropes, deflated and swelled to ropes in an apparent effort to work her own muscles. I wondered how long she'd been at these attempts. I wondered what was true. *I still wonder what is true.*

"Did you kill my mother!" I screamed in her face. Spit fled my furious mouth and landed in her dry-brush hair. I could have lit her on fire with the tiniest spark, if I wanted. And I wanted. I scanned the room for matches. Found none.

With the apparent effort of a Mack truck shifting to some nonexistent eighth gear to drive vertically up a building, she ratcheted her horror-doll head two notches to meet my face again. A zigzag stitch line marked her forehead, something I hadn't focused on before, given the shock of finding her. No other sounds in the world existed except her wheezy breathing and the undercurrent of her constant personal physical therapy. Even the lights in the side room, which might have hummed, even the monitors, which might have offered the white noise of beeping, even the drip of some liquid into her veins, ceased. We were well encased in a bubble of near soundless insanity, as if her mind and my mind had unfolded, turned inside out, and lay open to the physical realm of the room.

The question on the table, in the air, fighting against her play of paralysis, beating me to face and grab hold of emergence, to try to climb out of the well once again, was whether this woman killed my mother. She glared at me, and her nose gnarled.

"Did you kill my mother? My aunt says you are her friend. She says you had an affair with a married man, and the wife put you in a coma."

She *pffted* out a displeasure and rolled her buggy eyes, which had they not been bugged and unblinking, would have been swallowed into the bloating of her unnatural face.

"Your aunt has no friends. You know that. Please. Yeah, I heard what your aunt told you. She's a fucking liar. I'm not an idiot. I hide from her, you know. She has no idea I'm awake now. She'd put me under again if she did. You are basically my only fucking shot to get out of here. You're going to help me. But I know you won't unlock this chain without proof. Why don't you go and look in your aunt's wine cellar, behind her fake bookcase, to see what kind of woman she is."

I backed away, stumbled into the cabinet once again, shaking it with my force and causing a metal scraping to reverberate around the room. The sounds of the monitor and the drip, so too, the humming of the lights, returned.

How does she know about the fake bookcase?

I didn't wait for her to say more. Still clutching my mother's orange beach-glass necklace, I ran out of the barn and headed to Aunty's house, pregnant with unanswered questions: *What's in the attic? What's in the basement?*

I still had the front door key from the week before, so I entered Aunty's house. I suppose I could have retrieved all the house keys, for all the inner doors, from the birdhouse out back. But I wasn't ready for everything yet.

Off the marble foyer is a door to wooden stairs, which lead to a limestone-and-granite basement. I followed the way of natural substances, the marble to wood to limestone to granite, touching the sides of stone for pure truth, for what is truer than solid sand? As I reached Aunty's fake basement bookcase, I ignored the rumble of tires in the driveway.

I pushed the right way on the hidden swivel lock, like I did to play hide-and-seek with Aunty a hundred dozen times. It spun. And as it spun, I fell within the well of me, the cold slime of insanity's rocks scratching my shoulders in the descent. A scent of chalky dust and musty rocks pinched my inner nose. I fell to my knees on the real limestone, finding a new depth within which to fall. Out before me lay white bones in a fraying wool suit. A male skeleton.

I looked up to the room's concrete ceiling, as if a higher sight might answer me, tell me what I saw, whom these bones belonged to, and why I was here at all. My mouth hinged open; my eyes squinted in the darkness. On a nail on the inside of the doorjamb, above my head, midway up the wall, hung a clipboard with a pen tied in twine to a hole in the top. A metal clamp trapped about an inch of papers, like a patient's records.

Footsteps scattered the pebbles and seashells of Aunty's pebble-and-seashell driveway, and as I rose and backstepped out of the secret wine room to look down the basement hall and see out a basement window, I noted a black shadow had returned: Aunty's Audi. I had no time to hide, no time to think, no time for shock. I ripped the front page from the clipboard, shut the bookcase, ran up the basement stairs, and skidded as fast as possible into the Mermaid Library, so as to greet Aunty from the library and appear as though that's where I came from. As I slid, the door creaked open. I held my breath a couple of beats, hoping I'd hear no gasp from her, hoping to catch her off guard, coming in falseness from her library.

Where's my mother's necklace? Shit, I dropped my mother's necklace down there! She'll know. Aunty will figure it out. Relax. Breathe. For now, get out of the house. And dammit! My journal. Dammit. I left that on the cabinet in the side room with that woman! I'm toast. Aunty will know now where I've been.

Standing still in the library, I heard no gasp, nor did I hear her take any footsteps in the marble foyer, and I didn't hear her jangle her keys, like she normally would. I swallowed a great bucket of air and wiped my brow while contemplating those strings of cobweb tears, crying from the metal eyes of mermaid bookends.

I stepped into the foyer, holding a book, pretending to be absorbed.

"Ah!" I yelled, when I ran into her in the foyer. "Oh! You scared me. I came to grab a book I noticed last week."

She gasped back. "How did you get in here?" she yelled, revealing a real anger, a disgust. She scanned her one eye up the front stairs.

I didn't take the bait and follow her one-eyed gaze. I couldn't let on to my suspicions about the raccoon I was sure she lied about in the attic nor my knowledge of her skeleton in the basement.

I laughed, caving in my chest in a wince of apology. "Oh, I'm so sorry," I said, pretending I had no clue what angered her. I'd always been in and out of her house before, had my own keys before. "I took one of the door keys from under a mermaid last week." I handed the key back to her, to get her to drop her scowl.

When I did, she snatched it fast, another slap. Before, she would have laughed, accusing me of being off my rocker and to keep the damn thing, for I lived here too.

How did I not shake in Aunty's presence when I met her in the foyer? How did I not cry or reveal my fright? How I stayed calm and emotionless, acting out the instant part I decided to play in her horror house, I don't know. Perhaps duplicity was multiple folded by then: mine to Manny, hers to me, hers to the world, mine to her, mine to myself, hers to herself. Duplicity had multiplied, folded, expanded, and grown into its own beauty, a rose-garden universe of deceit, falseness itself, a pure truth.

"I forgot my purse," she said in the coldest tone, jumping back as she snagged her black Valentino from a mirrored shelf in the foyer. I thought of the foyer mirror as reflecting the wicked witch who speaks a spell about Snow White. Aunty set a shaky hand on the newel post of the stairwell banister, as if blocking me from going up. Appraising her, I noted she'd changed into the crisp green sundress she'd always worn before. And her hair, still grayed, was now combed and clipped in a twist. She wore her eye patch. Perhaps this vision of a mostly old version of Aunty helped me to play out my beautiful duplicity and suppress before her the knowledge of her secret in the barn and her skeleton in the basement.

"Yeah, I really wanted to get this book from the library," I said, thumbing backward to indicate the library. "Hope you don't mind."

"Oh, Mop. I love when you take my books," she said in a phony happiness, as if the statement erased her crazy yelling about me taking her house key. And when she said this and smiled like the joy of her statement would make her cry, she was 100 percent the new Aunty acting out the part of the old Aunty. I could feel it, I could, a cavernous wish for love again, to forget everything I learned and remembered. But I stayed like stone, holding the book so tight, I imagined the words squeezing out to fall and crack apart as letters on the marble floor.

"Well, since you're here, drive with me to Rye?" Aunty said as a statement question.

"No," I said, edging around her for the second time in under an hour, before she could pin me trapped in the library. I stood at the front door, one hand on the knob, the other holding the book. "Manny's waiting for me. We'll meet you there," I said, not turning to tell her to her face.

Racing toward Manny's, I chucked the book to a clearing in the brambles, intending to collect it later. Then I checked to confirm I still held the mistress note in my one back pocket, and in the other, the quick-folded "patient" record I'd ripped from the hanging clipboard, over the dead white bones of the secret in the basement. My journal. Well, dammit, my journal lay on the cabinet in the side room of the barn. My mother's orange necklace with the bones in the basement. I was cooked, the worst spy in the universe.

But I was out. On my way to Manny's. And whatever Aunty intended to reveal at our house in Rye, well, I braced for that.

On the one page of patient record I swiped from the basement, daily entries filled one line each, one for each day, all the same: *Still dead.*

CHAPTER FIFTEEN
MOP

One week ago
The Rye estate

Aunty is keeping a skeleton in her basement. A bloodless, fleshless corpse. She keeps a woman chained in her barn. And here we are on the Rye estate's rooftop, eating brick-oven pizzas from the domed oven installed up here, as if tonight's just another surreal summer night for people in mansions. This was what I thought a week ago.

Someone from the kitchen staff poured me a deep goblet of bordeaux.

"A *margherita* with spinach, please," I whispered to the chef, who molded pizza dough at the mouth of the fire-breathing hearth. The ocean tumbled below, in control of the white noise of our Rye home. The sunset blazed orange and purple over the navy Atlantic. No clouds cluttered the still-bright summer dusk. My bordeaux cooled my tongue, a smooth wash, like slow love, pressed against a building, an unhurried kiss of ownership, in a mist after a rain.

Aunty sat across from me at our rooftop tavern table, fidgeting with her linen napkin. She hadn't touched a drop of the perfect vintage, so I knew she fretted on how to broach her most unimaginable topic with me and my father, when and where. Amber candles suggested a coming calm of evening, but summer light shined on, despite the bruise-blaze sunset.

Aunt Sister Mary Patience sat beside me, my father at the end of the table, Manny to the right of him. The men were discussing a variety of typical matters: golf scores; hotel development; offshore accounts; the tragedy that no one paid attention to, a book titled *The Panama Papers*; charitable boards; the Nasdaq; whether tennis is better than racquetball; how to rid the Rye pool of a pesky resident bullfrog while giving said bullfrog a proper habitat elsewhere; and the awful presidential election cycle and the falseness of the binary, media-created political system in America. Typical. Average. Regular old dinner topics in Rye.

I tuned all of this out and watched Aunty Liv fidgeting with her napkin and not engaging in any of the various topics. I also watched Aunt Sister Mary Patience watching, like she was logging Aunty's every micromovement, and also logging my watching of Aunty Liv.

"Oh, hey, I found this cleaning out the coach house's furnace. I'm having it replaced—the furnace," Aunt Sister Mary said, digging in her housecoat pocket, fisting something, and reaching across the table to plunk the item in Aunty Liv's palm. A round metal shirt pin. "Not sure how the pin got into the old-old furnace. Looks old. Was among some other odds and ends, a hair clip, pennies, a couple of marbles. Guys think it's stuff that fell through the floor vent on the first floor and then they never removed the old-old furnace when they put in the old furnace—well, anyway. We're redoing everything now, so, found things rattling around down in the basement."

Aunty Liv's one eye turned steel; she stopped fidgeting. Manny and my father noticed nothing, for their conversation had moved along with them. They left the table and walked, shoulder to shoulder, to the roof's edge to point out possible locations to build the pool bullfrog a man-made pond.

"You think you're so superior, don't you? Testing me like this? You think you can shake me with this pin and judge how I react," Aunty

Liv snarled at Aunt Sister Mary while squeezing the pin in her palm so tight, her fingers turned white. The sudden shift from Aunty Liv's nervousness to viciousness upon the simple plunk of a metal pin in her hand was like walking down the street and being shot by a drive-by shooter. No warning. No reason. Just instant violence.

"No, Lynette. No. I'm sorry. What? I just wanted to show you, ask you. I thought maybe, maybe you and Johanna might remember it from playing, when you were girls. That's all. It's so distinctive, the green and the blue and the outline of California."

"Oh, sure," Aunty said, her voice low, her lip curling on one end.

The kitchen girl with the bordeaux flirted with the chef at the stove, not caring about our conversation. Manny and my father chuckled about the shape of a potted boxwood on the roof, which the gardener had sheared into the shape of an eyeball. Such dichotomy between their worlds and ours, like three wholly separate dimensions on one roof. Three truths.

I felt dizzy. Didn't know where to look. What to listen to. A fog formed, but I fought. I fought through.

"You want me to believe you never heard about what happened to me in that damn brick coach house you live in now. How dare you! As if Johanna never said anything to you and how I mentioned this pin to the police. How he shoved it in my mouth and told me to bite it in my front teeth, tight, or else I'd choke on it. He wanted that little metal to keep me quiet, while he violated me. And here you so casually and caustically plunk it in my hand for a reaction. You. Are. Wicked."

I'd never seen Aunty Liv react so uncontrolled before. Nor had anyone ever mentioned to me what really happened to Aunty Liv in that coach house when she was young. She seemed willing to now air this impolitic, personal topic in a seething hatred, open and free, as if she'd been waiting for any alternative topic, even one of violent assault, more palatable than the one she came to Rye to confess. Obviously regretting the decision to come to Rye, she seized the opportunity to avoid talking about why she came in the first place in a rapid madness, funneling all her unhinged furor on Aunt Sister Mary, who'd walked into a trap she didn't know had been set.

"No. No. Lynette. I don't know what you're talking about. I knew you had some trouble. Johanna said the estate manager caused your father's heart attack, and you were the only one home with him." Aunt Sister Mary shook her head. "She never. Oh, dear . . ."

This version of a terribly struck Aunt Sister Mary, nervous and fumbling and regretful and embarrassed, certainly wasn't the Aunt Sister Mary that Aunty Liv had referred to over the years in buried comments as "judgmental" and "hypocritical" and "sanctimonious." Had I allowed such a harsh judgment of Sister Mary's identity based on Aunty's carefully placed words?

Aunty Liv cut her off, her working eye as bugged as the patch on her dead one, her face sideways. "And what about you, *Sister Mary*? Huh?" She said "Sister Mary" in a taunting sarcasm. "What about what you hide? Did you think I wasn't here the week before they kicked you out of the church? Did you think I didn't know you were hiding out in the coach house? And guess what . . ."

I had never heard any of this.

"Aunty," I said, trying to stop her. I had an immediate urge to protect Aunt Sister Mary, an urge I had never in all my life felt before. I could tell by Sister Mary's nervous fingers under the table beside me, she hadn't intended to shock or judge or taunt Aunty Liv. She'd just wanted to give her an old pin, maybe she'd even wanted to bridge some connection with her. But Aunty Liv took her handing her the pin as an intentional aggression, or, at least, this was how she *acted* about it.

"Guess what," Aunty Liv said, ignoring my interruption, still staring at Aunt Sister Mary. "I saw the man enter the brick house, yeah, sure did, a week before you—what are we calling it, huh—*left* the rectory? And I heard your screams . . . and . . ." Aunty Liv stopped talking when my father turned toward the table. We all held our breaths. My father's stature is imposing. At six foot five, with still-black hair and ice-blue eyes on ghost-white skin, when he lifts one eye at you and doesn't speak nor smile, it seems he's shriveling your soul by gaze alone. Like a modern vampire. But he smiled at something above our heads and turned away, saying to Manny it was true how the sunset matched the Knicks' team colors. He'd only been confirming which NBA team sponsored the sunset.

Safe again, but apparently willing to stop spilling Aunt Mary's secret, Aunty said in leaning back, "Fuck off, Mary. Okay. Fuck you for throwing my past in my face." She didn't wipe away the spit that flew from her broken teeth upon both utterances of *fuck*. And on the second utterance, she threw the pin in Aunt Sister Mary's face.

Aunty Liv told my ex-nun aunt to fuck off and threw a metal pin of California in her face, one week ago, while our house chef pulled a bubbling pizza out of a rooftop oven in Rye.

I didn't know how to process any of this drama, the crimes, the secrets, the total freakish oddness. My grief for my mother, it grew again. *Mom, what would you do? You'd know what to do. I need you, Mom. I miss you so much.* All I could think to do was escape and drive to my Rye fort, sit in the false necropolis, and call the sea to bring me my mother. But I didn't. No. A tingle of fight came into me. I wish it had been a wash, a full swell of strength to fight off the fog. But it was something, a tingling of a coming to life. I fought off the wish to sit in my dark necropolis.

I stared at Manny's back as a way to hook onto something. He still roamed the roof's edge, skirting around the potted cypress and box-woods, surveying the Rye lawns on where to put a bullfrog pond, and discussing some other inaudible topic with my father. Perhaps he felt my visual pleas on his back, for he turned around with the biggest smile.

"Mop, how about this? Your father and I were thinking that maybe we go to the Grand Chesterton this week, relax before grad school starts, and maybe, how about, we start planning the wedding to take place there?"

The Grand Chesterton is one of Manny's family resorts in Cape Cod. He looked so excited in that moment on the roof. He had no clue the amount of horror at the table between my aunts and me. And as if I were the type of girl whose thoughts could course-correct at the offer of a trip to a grand resort, I projected the most duplicitous agreement.

"Sounds great," I called back. When he turned again in a glass-clinking cheer with my likewise thrilled father (how sweet, in retrospect), I turned evil eyes on Aunty Liv. A definite betrayal of Aunty, in favor of Aunt Sister Mary, an act I never before considered.

"You're being rude, Aunty," I say in a wicked, low-hiss warning. "When I get back from the Cape, perhaps we'll discuss other secrets. Hmm?" Popover would have been so proud at my delicious, disdainful purr.

Aunty Liv pulled back, arms crossed. I leaned forward over the table. Aunt Sister Mary, beside me, clasped her wineglass to her chest.

"Oh, ha," I mocked in a cheerful lightness while leaning back. "Let's just enjoy the night. No reason to get upset over misunderstandings over old blood," I said, looking at Aunt Sister Mary in lightness. And in darkness, I turned to Aunty to add, "It's not like we have literal skeletons in our closets! Right, Aunty?" I winked at her and smiled. I did not blink, letting her know I meant every single word.

Aunty ground her teeth and smiled without breaking her lips.

Something about old blood and skeletons—they never really go away.

CHAPTER SIXTEEN
AUNTY

One week ago

I'm driving home from that disaster of a dinner in Rye. The pizza—I didn't eat more than three bites of one slice. I didn't say any of the things I'd driven all the way over there to say. I couldn't. I wish I'd never gone. But Mop knows everything anyway. She made that abundantly clear. And I already knew she knew. Before leaving my house, I found her damn journal in the barn with *her*, and I found Johanna's orange necklace in the basement by the bones. I put the necklace back on the bitch in the barn, as a reminder to be kind and not kill her.

Oh, Mop knows, all right. But does she know everything? No. If she did, she wouldn't be eating pizza in Rye, pitching me shit. No doubt, though, for sure, my jig is up. And Sister Mary with the fucking pin. *The* fucking pin. How dare she.

I didn't work this hard for thirty years to forget that night. Consume myself in other mental consumptions. No.

I didn't work this hard for two years to be thrown in jail. I won't rot in jail. I will retain control of my body and direct the thoughts in my mind, dead or alive.

I'm going to finish digging a two-person pit behind the barn. I'll take care of things.

Mop returns from the Cape in about a week.

I'm ready. I'm not going to jail.

CHAPTER SEVENTEEN
AUNTY

Two years ago

I just found Kent's bathtub filled with blood.

I just found Kent's bathtub filled with blood.

I vomited. I flushed.

I just found Kent's bathtub filled with blood.

Johanna won't pick up her phone.

Fucking Route 128 traffic and the fucking construction for the fucking new Whole Foods slows me the fuck, fuck, fuck down. I can't get to wherever the fuck Johanna is fast enough. Is she safe at the Bennington hotel in Gloucester? I can't get ahold of Johanna. I even try calling Kent's cell, first time ever. Nothing.

What a dumb ass. Of course I should call the Bennington.

Four-one-one patches me in.

"Hello, Johanna Vandonbeer's room, please?"

"Hold on."

Motherfucker! Hurry the fuck up!

"I'm sorry, ma'am, no one here named Vandonbeer."

I choke. My face boils. I hang up. I should ask this slack-jaw receptionist a million questions to test him to see if Johanna is there like she said, but my throat is stuffed with gray cotton. I can't speak.

Just like it felt, this feeling again, no! Just like when Daddy collapsed and I shivered alone, hiding in the basement chamber. No, stop, don't go catatonic. Drive. Focus on the road.

I should call 911. I should get help. But I need to get to Johanna. And I don't know what Cate did with my vials. *Will she frame me?*

Somewhere along this drive, I lost track of where I am. I'm confused. I don't know where I am. I don't know where I fucking am. *Where the fuck am I? I've never seen that tree before.*

There's Exit 14. You're closer now. Relax.

I'm a nurse. I'm a nurse. I'm a nurse. *Stop this panic. Breathe. Get to Johanna. And then call the cops.* I look at my phone and realize I failed to check a blinking fact: a voice mail. *How could you not check the voice mail? You idiot. Idiot!*

"Siri, play voice mail."

"Playing voice mail."

Play the fucking voice mail!

Siri says, "Message one from Jo-Jo, 8:49 p.m."

Then comes Johanna's high, happy voice. "Sugar Cheeks! No rooms at the Bennington! Can you believe it? Now just relax. It's all going to be fine. I'll meet you back at the house."

Eight forty-nine? Eight forty-nine? An hour and a half ago. Oh my God, I went catatonic at Kent's! No, no, no, no. Not again. I'm going to lose again because I'm so weak! How long was I out? Where? In the bathroom, transfixed on the bathtub of blood? In the hall when the light vines choked me? Oh no. No! DRIVE THE FUCKING CAR!

Whipping off the highway, around curves and turns, up hills, down hills, tight country roads, past Annisquam, the beaches on my left, I gain closer to my home at Haddock Point State Park.

Who leaves a bathtub full of blood and a drip from the faucet to ping it, making a circle of pink where water meets blood? Who does that? *Who does that? Who would be so skilled to drain a body the right way, from the right cuts, and not leave a whole house of blood?*

A nurse. Cate is a nurse. Cate drained a body of blood.

Oh God. Here comes the gray cotton in my mouth and eyes again, my heart out of my ribs again. Like when the estate manager burst into the coach house in Rye, like when he held me at knifepoint and ripped off my pants. Like when he pressed his little metal button in my mouth and told me to bite down with my teeth and hold it tight, or it would fall into my throat and I'd choke. The taste of that metal is what it was, but in memory, it tastes of gray cotton, like now, so I spit. Gray cotton in my mouth again. Like when Daddy burst in and whacked the estate manager with a metal statue, fought him off me. Like when Daddy dropped to the floor, clutching his chest. Like when Daddy lay dying on the floor, and I panicked and I couldn't breathe and I ran and hid in the chamber in the basement and I couldn't move and snot dripped into my mouth, tasting of more gray cotton, and I couldn't crawl out to lift the phone and call 911. Like when I caused my father's death. Like when my first baby died and they did the D&C to scrape away remains, and I panicked and couldn't breathe, thought my baby cried to me from a jar on the sink. And the second time, too, the second loss the same. And when I discovered Sister Mary had an easiness she didn't deserve, then, too, gray cotton too.

My lost babies cried to me for help, my father, my babies, and I panicked, my heart pumping like a speeding car, my breath as shallow as a fast wind, whipping across flat ice, unable to breach the barrier of cotton in my throat. Like whooshing and sweat and beating and no traction. I'm panicking. I lose control of the car.

I'm skidding, a foot from the guardrail. I jerk the wheel to straight, too far, I'm heading into the oncoming headlights of a pickup truck. I jerk back. There is no air in this car, only hot cement. I haven't breathed a full minute. My forehead is filled with hot lava and spinning, separate from the rest of my hot face.

I'm straight on the road, huffing, hugging, I'm so out of control, I pass my driveway. Slam on the brakes. U-turn in a burning skid. Speed up my driveway.

All the lights in my rose house are on. Every single light from finished attic to second floor to first floor to basement. All the lights in the cottage are on. All the lights in my barn are on. My property is ablaze in light. My blue front door is wide open. Johanna's convertible has the front spot in my driveway, closest the barn. Kent's gray Jeep is parked behind hers.

"Johanna!" I scream as I open my Audi door at the same time as jamming the gear to park.

I'm running for the front door, following a trail of lit tea lights, which start on my front stoop. *Who left a trail of tea lights?* Following through my foyer, the tea lights go up my front stairs to the second floor. I ignore what could be in the kitchen, or elsewhere. I follow the tea lights, the trail, leading me. I'm screaming for "Johanna!"

No one returns my calls.

At the top of the stairs, I'm in my second-floor hallway, and the tea lights go down my hall, past my bedroom, and around the corner to the foot of the L of these upper halls. I follow. I turn the corner. At the end of this hall is a doorway to the finished attic, and on the right, about midway, is the door to Mop's bedroom.

Oh God.

Where's Mop? She's at college. Not home until next week.

"Johanna!" I'm screaming. "Johanna!" Nothing.

Mop has always yelled to me from this room, "Aunty, Aunty," in her sweet voice. Used to be for hugs or cups of cold water or to read her another book when she was little and now, in recent years, it's "Aunty, Aunty, nighty night, love you," acting like a little girl as our comfort routine.

No "Aunty, Aunty" meets me back. No one returns my yelling. "Johanna!"

A quick flash of fur races past me, low to the floor. I paste myself to the hall wall, frightened. It's Popover, hurrying, now disappeared into Mop's room, following the same path of tea lights I'm following. Popover is escaping something. *What?*

I run down the second hall to Mop's room to the spot in front of her door where the tea lights end. I turn to face the same room Popover entered, Mop's closet, Mop's room. Popover's back is high arched; he's hissing at me from under Mop's desk.

And once again tonight, I'm suffering the disabling, distorting panic I've suffered at times in my life. I'm on an arctic glacier with gray cotton in my throat, in my lungs, and I'm sure this time, it will never clear. In skating on the glacier to the interior of the room; I breathe not. I see not. I am blinded by this vision.

I scrape the clouds away, the second time tonight. Clawing at the thick air before me as if rungs will appear.

In one blink, I take the vision in, before fainting to the floor and folding into gray clouds.

Kent is laid out on top of the covers as a corpse. His throat and wrists are cleanly sliced, and I presume these wounds are where Cate bled him. And now his lifeless body lies on Mop's bed. He's clothed in a herringbone wool suit, one perfect for a man at his own funeral. His arms are crossed at his waist. His legs are straight. He wears black shoes and black socks.

Cate must have worked hard to drain every drop into the tub and not spill elsewhere in their house, to be able to run only a mop in one straight line along the upper hall and down the stairs. Unless there was other cleaning I didn't see. Only a sick, twisted person would do such a thing. And I suspect with him here and the cleanliness of her crime, she aims to frame me. The tub of blood, a psychotic's tub I'm sure she plans to drain and bleach as soon as she's done with me.

What is she going to do to me?

What has she done to Johanna?

"Johanna," I croak out, as I come to in the moldy clouds on the floor of Mop's room, at the foot of her bed, where Kent lies dead. I have to fight this time. I can't grow silent and paralyzed again. *Save Johanna!* The only thing to ever keep me out of gray clouds is when I'm clinical, a nurse. I am a nurse. *I am a nurse.*

I hear singing in my kitchen.

I am a nurse. Go be a nurse.

CHAPTER EIGHTEEN
AUNTY

Two years ago

Some other part of me is driving my body, stumbling backward out of Mop's bedroom with Kent Dranal dead in her bed, drained of blood, his throat and wrists slit, lying there in the bright of the light of the room, at the end of a trail of tea lights, to make some psychotic point.

I can't breathe.

Whatwhatwhatwhatwhat, where is, where is, where is, where is Johanna? Oh my God, Oh my God. Go, run, run, run, run to the cottage, get Johanna. Who's singing in the kitchen?

My active thoughts and my physical condition are in a riotous turmoil. There's a dichotomy inside me: on the one side, my executive function is driving my actions and narrating to myself what's happening; the other side is pure panic. Perhaps this is the inner split of how those in shock operate, or a soldier in war is able to walk ten miles in desert sand with the head of a comrade in his hands, so as not to leave his brother behind. It's like I'm a computer with two hard drives, one malfunctioning, smoking out of the disc mouth, the other running rote C: commands for digitized navigation.

My mind is split; my brain is splitting. I grab my skull with two hands, squeeze in, try to stop the white-hot pulse.

Tripping. Feet tied together. I will fall now, untie my feet. The air is not air. Air cement. My neck is swallowing my face, push down, push neck down from face.

My legs are not tied, but I fall. I'm on the floor, my right leg bruised from hitting the bedpost. *Or is the bruise from when I punched myself while driving?* I reach for my neck; it is not swallowing my face. I am a nurse. I'm hyperventilating. I close my eyes, inhale through my nose. I am a nurse. I calm my rhythm with a count.

One, two, thr . . . *Johanna, Jo . . . Oh God. Noise in kitchen, bang. Johanna!*

The pain on my right thigh is a sharp eight on the pain scale, a cup-size welt swelling; the hematoma will be black and purple for a good two to three weeks. I am a nurse. I must pull myself to standing and inhale. Two simple steps: stand and inhale.

Johanna, Johanna . . . where are my feet? Look there, Popover cowers in the corner. Popover, Popover, go get Johanna.

"Johanna!" I'm screaming, I believe. *I am a nurse. Stand.* I stand. Kent Dranal is dead in Mop's bed. This is death. I am a nurse. The walls of the bedroom and the hall walls can serve as brace supports for my feet, which are weak and not working. I believe the eight-sharp hematoma on my right leg is not the cause. The cause is my brain malfunctioning in shock. I use the walls to guide me to the stairs and it is now, this moment, midway down the stairs, when I see a change in the foyer. The change leads through the main first-floor hall to the kitchen, where I heard a bang, above the continued singing. My legs are built of liquid muscles and rubber bands. I catch myself on every tread in my descent.

JohannaJohannaJohannaJohannaJohannaJohannaJohanna. My head, filled with bees, bees, the lights in the foyer, down the hall, to Johanna, Johanna, Johanna, Johanna.

I'm inhaling in quick breaths through my open mouth; my throat drawing sips of air, not allowing them to fall to my lungs or rise to my brain. I don't exhale. I'm a nurse; I must exhale. I must then inhale through my nostrils to feed oxygen to my brain. I pause to perform this biological need on the last tread. I take a second to appreciate the change in the foyer and hall.

Starting at the midpoint of the entrance marble is a line of tea lights, and next to each tea light is a vial of pentobarbital. *Are these my vials, stolen last night?*

I reach the foyer and look into the kitchen, only to see shadows moving beyond the doorway. The light is a moonglow amber, the effect I created by buying the right lightbulbs. I wanted my night kitchen alive against the darkness outside. It should *feel like* a gold glow, and the flowers beyond my kitchen window should be lit by the soft solars, so I can watch the swooping bats beyond the blue tangle of morning glories, which crawl beside the window boxes of hot-pink petunias. But it is no longer a gold glow; this now is a blinding surgical light with new meaning.

Johanna, Johanna, Johanna, Johanna, Johanna. Don't say her name, walk slow, then it won't be her at the end of the line of pento vials. Don'tsayhernameandwalkslow. My neck is choking me. Johanna!

Beyond where I can see, I believe from somewhere near my kitchen table, a woman's voice hums Simon & Garfunkel's "America": *mmm, mmm, mmm, mmm-hmm—mmm-mmm-mmm*. I know the lyrics like I know the range of dangerous blood pressure in correlation to ranges of body mass index. Johanna listens and hums this song constantly, like it's her breath. If you ever catch Johanna unaware, perhaps if you sneak up to spy on her working away at her fashion blog, or her arranging her sea glass into shapes, you can stand behind her a full ten minutes, watching her work away, and listen to her happy humming of the carousel rhythm of "America." And this is exactly what the woman's voice does now in my kitchen, but the voice is not Johanna's. Whoever this woman is, she's mocking Johanna. She must have been watching Johanna to know her song. I am a nurse. I make quick deductions. I am a nurse. I must step to the kitchen and confirm my theory.

Johanna, my love, Johanna. My eyes are blind. What is this light flickering in my eyes; what is this blood, this blood dripping down my thighs. She sings your song, Johanna. Did you teach her today? Is that what this is? Is she your friend and you taught her to sing your song? Johanna?

I'm crying, I cannot help it. I'm weeping to hear someone else pretend to be the voice of my beloved Johanna. My mental sides are mixing together, the hard drives of me, both malfunctioning. *No, no, no, think. Think.* I am a nurse. *You are a nurse.* Blood is not dripping down my legs. There is no liquid dripping down my legs. I refuse to believe there is blood on my legs.

My legs are liquid.

I pause. I inhale. I pause. I inhale. I am a nurse. My legs are not liquid. I inhale through my nose, which is clogged with emotion and phlegm, viscous is my interior and exterior. My feet are crumbling meat, my legs still rubber. The walls of the hall are a savior for me. I scratch at the wallpaper as if I can reach into the vines and the red and blue birds for traction and catch. My stomach and breasts are pressed flat against flat birds and vines, and I slide along my own hall, like a shadow creature, so as to avoid touching the toxic trail of vials and tea lights.

I reach the kitchen.

I'm standing in the entrance to my kitchen.

Where am I? How did I get here? Who is here? What am I seeing? I am blind in the light and the gray clouds.

I am not blind. I am a nurse. I am not blind, I'm just not believing. I am standing in the entrance to my kitchen. My yellow-lit kitchen. I am standing in the entrance to my kitchen. I am looking to my right at the humming Cate Dranal, who sits at my kitchen table. She is folding my underwear in three folds, picking each piece from my green laundry basket.

"Mmm, mmm, mmm . . ." Cate shouts at me as some grand greeting, wild-eyed with a savage smile. Her humming is a violent humming version of "America." She's sitting in my blue-painted chair. My chair. She's sitting at my table, in my chair, wearing a navy-and-light-blue ball gown. There are a few twigs in her hair, scratches on her melting pink-rouged cheeks, like she applied clown blush and then shoved her face in a bush, hard and fast, back and forth, raping twigs with her mouth and cheeks. Her ill-advised, CVS-brand black eyeliner, which she drew right inside the rim, like the deplorable she is, droops low into the dry, drooping bags under her bloodshot eyes. True-pink lipstick is not on her lips so much, but rather smeared around her mouth and staining her teeth.

Cate is singing Johanna's song. Johanna. Yellow light stings my eyes; the windows are swirling liquefied gray clouds. Johannawhereareyou? I can't look, no, I will not, no, no, Johanna, I will not look to the left of me. No. I know you are in here too. I don't want to see you. Johanna, stop moaning.

Dangling from Cate's finger, held aloft like ET pointing to home with his gold-lit finger, is my gold thong, a pair I wore for Kent Dranal on an occasion or two, or ten. One time, his teeth tore away at the lace hem around the leg holes. So anxious to arouse me, he tore the lace in two spots, leaving sagging loops away from the stitch line to the cotton and silk panel of my crotch. And yet, I kept them. I confess. Does Cate know her husband's teeth made the torn loops she slips her fingers through?

Don't look to the stove to the left; don't register the murmuring, murmuring, moaning. Don't look, don'tlook, don'tlook, don'tlook. Don't, no, I won't listen to the gagging, don'tlook. She's gagging. I'm gagging.

A trickle of blood teardrops down past my knee to my ankle.

That is not blood. That is only sweat. Don't look down. Don't look left.

I turn my head to the left, for vision of my black stove and to identify a voice from this direction. An undefined and muddled moan, obstructed by something, murmuring and possibly screaming. It is indeed Johanna, and she's in an impossible contraption. She is seated on top of my black gas stove, duct taped in place by at least an entire roll, her legs wound in silver adhesive, her hips, too, the tape anchored around the stove. *I'm a nurse.* Perhaps this took two rolls. *I'm a nurse.* She is sitting directly atop the right front round burner, her left hip spilling onto the middle griddle, where we make pancakes. Her arms are tied behind her back. Her mouth: duct-taped. She cries, she wails, the noises of a dying animal.

The stove is not on.

The stove is noton, noton. Oh, Johanna. Johanna. My, my, my Johanna. My Johanna. Here comes my neck swallowing my head.

I vomit.

My throat burns. Bile now on my feet, which . . .

My feet do not exist. I don't have feet. There's no need to look down at the vomit to see if it met my feet because I'm feetless. It's okay. Okayokayokay.

I cannot quit these tears. *I cannot clear these clouds.*

Can I speak to Cate who folds my underwear at the table? The woman who ignores my sickness on the floor, my sister on the stove, my cries, her cries? Might I speak reason to the woman who hums on, calm in singing more about "America" and folding my underwear in three? Can I beg Cate Dranal to help me and help my sister, even though she is an obvious psychopath, the very cause?

I stare up at Cate Dranal from my kitchen floor. I collapsed, given the absence of feeling in my feet, my hands barely missing the pile of my sickness. *My feet do not exist. Blood drips down my legs. No, my legs are blood. Only blood. I can't move. Johanna.*

Cate looks down upon me and hums.

Using my arms, which prickle, turning to liquid, too, I drag my torso sideways toward the stove. I'm like a limp animal, chewed free of a bear trap, legs mangled and useless.

Blood is draining from my femoral artery along the kitchen floor. Gettostove. FreeJohanna.

I am a nurse. Blood is not draining from my femoral artery. That's a mind's split fiction. I'm not cut. My legs are freezing cold to no feeling. I cannot move them. I reach Johanna's bound legs.

Cate Dranal launches herself from my kitchen table and barrels for me as I pick and pry away at duct tape in a panicked attempt to unwind Johanna. Cate's blue-on-blue gown is strapless, and I note the mottling of the skin on her arms, red blotches against the whitest of skin: she's either suffering poor circulation or unable to calibrate temperature. *I'm a nurse.* Or are those red blotches not red, but a rust red, like dried blood? Cate elbows my cranium, crashing me backward, landing me on my buttocks and into my open shelves, which host a collection of yellowware mixing bowls, platters, cups, figurines, tureens, gravy boats, and plates. I hit so hard, the antique shelving unit shakes and dozens of pieces fall and shatter to the floor, but in some miracle, miss my head. A shard slices my left hand at the fatty part between thumb and gun-barrel finger.

Johanna wails from her throat, her voice muffled under the tape.

Cate sets one hand on the burner dial under Johanna's legs, while holding a syringe, which I presume is filled with pento, to Johanna's jugular.

Johanna, my Johanna. Be quiet, love. Be quiet. Lookatmebeingquietforyou. I will sit silent and be quiet because quiet will make her stop and I am going to sit here on the floor with my blood legs and my bleeding hand and the bees in my brain and without my feet and I am going to make all of me and even my blood and even the bees be very, very quiet and we are going to be quiet and the woman is not going to hurt you, Johanna. Johanna, shh, shh. Johanna.

I am a nurse. My legs are not blood. My right thigh has a throbbing hematoma. My left hand is lacerated and requires ten sutures. My brain is not filled with bees; it is oxygen deprived because I am still only inhaling in bursts through my throat. I do not close my eyes to inhale through nostrils as I should. *You surely should. I surely should.* Cate keeps her hand on the burner dial and a needle to Johanna's neck.

Cate Dranal clears her throat, stops humming about "America." She looks at me with one eyelid dropping like she's having a stroke, but it's more that she's moving through a quick catatonic state. I should know. She's a reflection of me in this moment. Then she clears her throat again, and both eyes fly wide and she's staring at me on the floor, her syringe in one hand to Johanna's jugular, her other hand on the burner dial on which Johanna is trapped.

Cate speaks.

"Oh. My dear. Lynette Viola Vandonbeer. What a fucking lovely name. Rich bitch has everything she needs, but she wants a married man, so she takes him and fucks him. Kent told me everything."

Don't look at her. Look at Johanna. Tell her to be quiet. Be quiet with me, Johanna. Johanna. Don't look at my blood legs, sprawled here on the floor with the broken bowls. Nana's bowls are broken. I'msosorry. Don't look at my bloody hand or the bees buzzing around my head. Stop crying, darling. Look in my eyes and be quiet. Can you see my eyes? Are they too clouded? Okay, darling, I'll wipe them.

I wipe my crying eyes so Johanna can see me being quiet, which, medically speaking should not make physiological sense. But it is logical to me, so I wipe again. The blood from my left hand swipes across my face. I must look like a red raccoon.

"You look at me when I'm talking to you, bitch!" Cate Dranal shouts from her towering height, me crumpled on the floor by the shaken shelves, broken yellow pottery all around me. The heavy bottom of one of the big bowls we use to mix cakes, the one that is an inch thick, teeters by my hand, the edges around the bottom now jagged and sharp. The way Cate bends from her height to me and shouts is like she's an abusive mother with a wooden spoon at the stove top, shouting at a quivering child at her apron strings.

"You will sit there and listen to everything I'm going to say or I will turn on the burner and burn your sister alive, right here, on your stove. Or, who knows, I could also pump her with this pentobarbital, right into her neck, and I think this much quantity would kill her or coma her for fucking ever, and who knows, maybe you'll lose more tonight. I don't know what I'll do. But you will listen either way."

I will make you a nice cup of tea, Johanna. Tonight. Your favorite, my love. Yes, the caffeine-free rooibos chai, with milk and honey and two slices of cinnamon toast with no crust and buttered heavy. I'll give you the rest of the wine too. And we'll go away tomorrow. We'll get away, get away, getaway, way, way. And, and, and, maybe we'll go to, goto, goto, your favorite little villa in Positano and we'll sleep late, just like you like. I'll get you whatever you need. Please, please, be still, stop fidgeting. The needle cannot go into your neck. Please be quiet. I will be quiet. See. Please, Johanna.

I am not quiet. My mouth works against me.

"You fucking crazy bitch! I swear to God, if you hurt my sister, I will make your living life a fucking hell!" I'm seething, literal spit frothing out of my mouth. I don't know what I'm saying. I'm a nurse. I should talk reason into this situation, defuse the tension, like I'm trained.

Cate Dranal is laughing. A nasally laugh, clogged and halting, a car working to stop in the rain and the antilock wheels can't catch.

"Oh, really, please, *Lynette Viola Vandonbeer.*" She says my full name like a bully on the playground. "What a bitch's name. And your sister's name, please, *Johanna Vandonbeer Pentecost.* She's a cunt. You're a cunt. Fuck you."

Cate moves to crouch in front of me, blocking me from reaching Johanna at the stove. But at least her hand is off the burner dial and the vial away from Johanna's neck. She hikes up her gown to her knees, fisting the scratchy tulle lining, which is ripped in spots. She wears no lining, no underslip, no Spanx, because she's an animal. The stitching on this dress is uneven. It's homemade. It's awful. It's psychotic. She made this dress. *She made this dress.*

"Oh, do you like my dress, bitch?" She says in a taunt, pivoting her head with each word, side to side. "I made it. I thought maybe if you saw my beautiful gown, you'd invite me to your stupid charity ball this Friday. Right? Yeah, I read up on you. I made this dress all last night and today, in between dealing with Kent, of course." And she's doing her phlegmy, rattling, awful laugh again.

When she crouches, her hiked gown rides up her formless legs, and yet she keeps her indecent crouching pose, her knees hovering and splayed to each side, her pointed elbows jammed into the tops of her thighs—this position is much like a tracker in the woods, crouched to the ground, pontificating over evidence. I can see the crotch of her cotton underwear, a large earth-covering grandma pair. No wonder Kent preferred me and my Brazilian wax. I'm fixed on thoughts of Kent folding this exact pair of yellow underwear, which I presume came from a plastic package of three. This is not rational to concern myself with Cate Dranal's underwear. *I am a nurse. I am a fucking nurse.* Can I reason my way out of this? Is there a logical, or medical, solution?

Johanna, she's talking to me now! This is good, darling. Good. Good. Good. Be still, I will speak with her to free you.

"Get out of my house, you bitch!"

What am I saying? I'm losing this situation.

Johanna. Johanna. Johanna. Iamtalkingtoher, darling. We'll go away tomorrow, I promise.

Cate Dranal caws at me, like a crow with a dry throat. "You don't get it yet, do you? *Lynette Viola Vandonbeer.* You may be a nurse, but you're dumb. There's no way out of this. You don't get it, do you?"

Perhaps I do not get it. I look to her face, which leans in on me now. Her face is a full moon, but sagged and dry, showing her age. Her dragging, tactless eyeliner drags more. She doesn't care for herself, doesn't use toner or moisturizer. Doesn't give a shit about her appearance, not in a graceful-aging or benevolent-apathetic kind of way, rather in an aggressive, you-will-look-at-me-as-is entitled way. And based on the catch I hear in her throat, and the age weight she's showing in the middle and her hips, I bet she neglects a disorder of the thyroid. Likely hypo.

"Kent tried to help you before, with your stash of pento. I never knew where he got it, but I've figured it out now. When he told me last night that he was leaving me for you, that you're opening up a clinic here, and that you're pregnant, I figured it out." She looks at my liquid legs, raises an eyebrow. "*Were* pregnant," she adds on a chuckle and raises her never-plucked eyebrows at whatever she sees on my legs.

I won't look down. I won't acknowledge her last line, her correction to the past tense about my present pregnancy. I stare at her, breathing fast inhales through my nose. I see three of her face. She's still talking, three mouths talking, not entirely in sync, but saying the same words. Awful past-tense words.

"I'm not an idiot, *Lynette*."

Johanna. Just be quiet. Listen, darling. Let her talk.

Johanna is flagging. She's no longer screaming or thrashing about. Her eyelids are falling. She may be blacking out from shock. Will she remember tonight? I hope she doesn't remember tonight. I am a nurse. Traumatic experiences can cause a form of amnesia, selective, comprehensive, progressive, regressive—all kinds of amnesia.

"I never knew who exactly Kent was fucking, or actually, what I mean is, who *all* he was fucking. You're not his only whore, *Lynette*. Kent told me everything, then I came and ransacked your damn clinic, which is so fucking elitist and weird, and found your damn vials last night. He told me all about how you two were going to run a private clinic in your barn. He was very specific on how great your lives were going to be. So I didn't need your stupid fucking note and hospital ID this morning, but hoo . . ." She pauses to exclaim a loud relief sigh. "Sure was entertaining! And leaving your ID *in my house* like that, hmm. Hilarious! Oh, I got your ID from my car all right, put it right on in my house. Tsk, tsk, you stalker. Might explain the blood in the tub, yeah? You did it, Lynette. That's what the evidence says, at least."

She is framing me.

She's still talking. "And then what? While poor me worked all day, you dragged my husband's dead body to your crazy lair in his Jeep? And then you went to work, like nothing happened? Wow!"

She is framing me. *She is framing you.*

"I know what you're thinking. You have an alibi for this whole day—Johanna, your sister, right? Well, she won't be around much longer, no worries. What a waste. Kent didn't really love you. He loved what's under your skirt, and what's under your skirt is getting old."

No! He loved me. I loved him. But maybe you're right, Cate Dranal. I'm listening, because listening is the logical thing to do to save my sister. This is the procedure I am to follow. It is the medical rationality we need. I am a nurse, so I am listening.

Johanna, look, darling. Okay, don't look. You black it out. I'll take you away, love. My legs are bleeding, but it's okay. Do not worry, love. The bees are still there, yes, but do not worry, I'm making them spin clockwise now, so it's okay.

Again, I tell myself my legs are not bleeding, but I am not accepting this. I remind myself that the bees are really my brain vessels screaming for air, literally, the vessels are screaming at me to give them air or else they'll let the bees back in to fly daisy loops and with no organizing circular pattern. I stare at Cate Dranal. My eyelids are falling too. I force them open; I force a consciousness.

"Oh, *Lynette*! I could think of you and me as two women betrayed by the same man, right? I could consider him the common problem, not us! But nope, you're the problem. Whore. So here is what is going to happen. If anyone finds out about Kent and where his dead body is, the toxicity report will show pento, and homicide detectives would then see a very common pattern: jilted mistress, you killed him in my house, dragged him here, to your crazy lair. You're basically fucked. It's ironic, right? You kept your life so otherwise off-line—no electronic trail, nothing between you and Kent, which I know because I'm in all his accounts now. His password is so pathetic, it's your fucking dumb name—*LivViolaV33*."

She's still crouching when she scooches closer to me, so now her hips mirror mine and her dry face is in my face. Her feet must be stinging in restricted circulation below the knees. She continues. "Irony. Your electronic absence will make it easy for me to claim no connection or knowledge of you. I'll just act, golly gee, shocked." She snorts from her nose, and I notice she's never plucked the hairs of her nostrils. She sucks in her cheeks and makes a fish face, contemplating me watching her, and then she jerks to standing, looking in the corners of my ceiling. She indicates she's about to launch into a monologue—a villain, proud to unfurl her world-ending plot.

"No security cameras here," she announces loud, her flabby arms indicating the corners of the ceiling. The blue-on-blue top layer of her misshapen, homemade gown swishes against the torn tulle. She sets a dramatic finger to her chin to indicate she's analyzing out loud, her monologue to roll now. "Maybe a good detective working hard could put things together and link me. Maybe. But who cares? You might still scream and shout how I'm to blame, but I came here analog last night, found your damn vials, and have an airtight alibi today and tonight. I walked ten fucking miles to get here last night. No phone on me, no trace, no cell-tower pings. I know everything I've touched, and no evidence will stay. No fingerprints. Nothing. Kent's Jeep in your driveway, which I drove here tonight, him dead in the back seat, for right, yes, I did drive his body here, couldn't carry him ten miles. Whatever! Evidence of his car here, fits with my story. No one saw me driving or when. It's an old Jeep, no GPS tracker to time anything, no nothing. I made damn sure."

She smacks her lips and winks at me, as a pause and to accentuate her high opinion of herself—she's just so genius. "As for his blood in *my* house. I'm a nurse, too, *Lynette*. Not a drop of it escaped the tub. He went straight into airtight plastic once his body drained, and I dragged him *out the house*."

She says this last part, *out the house*, in a strange southern accent and twisted head, like she's talking to herself and this entire monologue of hers is a mottled stew of actors in a circle on a stage. "Fortunately, our garage is attached—" Still southern accent, but she switches back to her grating Boston accent with the next line. "Right! I insisted on an attached garage, *Lynette*, when we bought . . . our home." She pouts in a whiny voice upon saying *our home*. "You wanted to steal our home, Lynette. Well, fuck you. I bleached *my* bathroom floor after I removed Kent, you cunt. I'll drain the tub when I get home and marinate the porcelain in bleach a few days, if you play nice nice." She rolls her eyes to the ceiling, mocking herself for being sad in saying upon a forced laugh, "I wanted something of him in the house when I got home." She's making no sense. Her framing of me, her keeping the blood in the house, nonsensical. *Applying reason to lunacy is a futile insanity.* But she's twisted me up in this, and she could frame me long enough for me to lose everything. I'm a nurse, and the two stark facts I can't avoid, no matter what Cate Dranal drones on about are these: Kent is dead in Mop's room, and my sister is duct-taped on top of my gas stove.

Cate spits on her own laughter at her own psychosis and then, with shoulders sagging, weeps in ugly heaving, but not for long. She springs up straight and finishes in a breathless rant, "I sent a resignation email from him to the hospital. Kent's on a . . . vague and undefined . . . mission to help Syrian refugees in Greece." She swipes her lips to the side and air quotes the vagueness of "mission to help refugees" to once again accentuate the laughable genius of her own plan. "He's got no family, you know. No one will report him missing. Unless I choose to. I'm in control here. I don't have anyone either. Kent and I had only each other, for real, no one else. And you took the us of us away, Lynette, so you will pay."

She quick-crouches, sticking her yellow crotch direct in my line of sight once again. She's hissing, slow and in my face, "I am in control here, bitch. You're going to play along so I don't report Kent missing."

What is the woman with the syringe saying? Who is she? Are those words, or is she humming again? What is this wind that smells of cheese in my face? Breath? Johanna, Johanna, Johanna, darling, she's feeding me cheese, see, we're talking and eating cheese, so this is good. Please, this will be over soon. Be quiet. Hush.

Cate Dranal, yes, it's Cate Dranal. The proximity of her close face and cheese breath, these are smelling salts, jolting me to listen and burn her words to my brain.

"So as insurance for me and because I want you to suffer, you're going to drag Kent into your basement, behind your fake bookcase. I followed your dumb humming sister around tonight. She didn't hear me when she opened the bookcase to take out wine. Had her earphones on, singing Paul Simon." Cate's laughing again, her catching, awful, phlegmy cough-laugh, like an old, crazed lady. I think of *Flowers in the Attic*.

Johanna, it's just a story, darling. Like Flowers in the Attic. *We will be done with the story soon. I'll finish the book; you go to sleep. I'll sum it up for you tomorrow, like I always do, if you want. Shh. Shh. Sleep, love.*

"If you ever say anything about who killed Kent, or Vicky, my neighbor with her damn peanuts, remember, Lynette, I've got three things on you." She takes her free hand and pushes fingers to my nose to accompany her recitation of the three things she has on me. "One"—she presses my nose once—"Kent with pento in every fiber of his dead body. Two"—she pushes twice—"you were at Proserpina's. You can be blamed for lacing Vicky with peanuts. Yeah, you whispering in my ear, I figured that out, too, even before you left your stupid note. You have impulse-control problems, don't you, Lynette. Tsk, tsk. Anyway, I'll say I went to the bathroom and the police will assume you leaned over then. I mean, you were there! And Vicky was, in fact, sleeping with Kent!

Oh, hoo, Lynette, you're such a crazy bitch! Hoo, Lordy!" She pauses to collect her breath from a cackling in laughter through these words. "And three," she says, losing her demented smile and laughter, getting serious. She pushes three times, jamming into my nose like she's trying to push it to the back of my skull. "Drumroll, please . . . *mmm, hmm, mmm*," and she's off humming "America" once again.

Cate Dranal stands, walks backward toward Johanna, and continues talking, not humming. "You know where I caught your sister? She was smoking a cigarette on her bed out there." She pointed toward the guest cottage. "She'd just lit it, in fact. Left the cigarette teetering on the fold of the duvet. All it would take is the right gust of wind from the open window and . . ." Cate makes a whooshing noise and fans her hands in a dramatic display to charade "fire" as she mouths the word. She turns a circle like a contemplative professor. "So this gave me an idea. When you crawled your whore ass up the stairs just now and found Kent, and you were up there *forever*, geesh. Anyway, I ran out to that dumb cottage, lit another cigarette, and left it on the sheets. The one I lit sure teetered on the duvet. Whoopsy do!"

Cate laughs as she stares out the back bay window toward the cottage. She sniffs the air.

"Smell it, Lynette? Oh, and your sister is so dumb. She was reading some dumb-ass romance novel. Smut. Oh yeah, the title—" And here she does her awful laugh again, looking at my sister and lifting Johanna's dropped chin to look into her face. I spring on all fours. I'm a guard dog coming to life after eating a drugged steak. The thick, yellowware bowl bottom with jagged edges is under my right hand's grip.

"Yes, right, the book's title," Cate says into Johanna's face, "was *Dirty, Blond Cowboy*. You had no idea I stood at the foot of the bed until I kicked the baseboard. Must have been the spent bottle of wine. Anyhoo . . ." Cate turns to face me, but keeps her hand squeezing Johanna's chin so as to keep her head cocked upright. Something catches her eye outside, and she looks to the back kitchen window toward the guest cottage. I follow her eyes. At the level I am at, given how the window sashes low—the house being on higher level than the cottage—I see a brighter core within the lit cottage, a core of slow-growing orange. A fire on the bed.

"Oh, now, finally, here we are," Cate says, looking back at me, growing a large smile in a coming glee and perking up her posture. "I think this decides it, then. Poor Johanna, your sister, *mmm, mmm, mmm*—" She's humming again, transforming beautiful poetry into a theme song for a horror carnival.

"Yup. Here's what the papers will say about this twit Johanna: she fell asleep with the cigarette in her mouth, and it fell and burned the bed. When she woke up burning alive, she ran. Oh yes, that's it, Lynette, your sister, she ran to the cliff, flaming on fire, and she launched herself into the ocean. Remember these details, because all this shit here is what you'll say. The story you will tell. Or else you're going to jail for the rest of your worthless life. I'm going to pump her full of pento now, a dose enough to kill her. *Your pento.* You knew I'd have to kill her. It's all your fault. Can't have any other witnesses, other than you, whore, and you need to live, because you need to suffer. I'll be off now. You better get a move on and get to hiding these dead bodies, nurse. Fire trucks will probably come soon. Here's the third thing I have on you."

Cate Dranal sinks the pentobarbital—I think an entire vial's worth, but it's hard to tell—into Johanna's jugular, or close enough to it. *How old is this pento? Is it still as strong as when first bottled?*

I growl. I am not a nurse. I am an animal. On all fours, I gallop like a rabid lion and bulldoze into Cate Dranal, knock her on her *ass*, and beat a yellow bowl bottom into her *brains*. At some point in my beating, and I hadn't appreciated this before, she pulls from a side-sewn pocket on her gown a giant antique nail, one big enough to drive through beams. I have a pile of them in the barn, given how I insisted on using as much reclaimed materials as possible to build Johanna's cottage. Cate jams the point end of the nail into my right eyebrow and drags down, puncturing my eye and cutting my face; she then takes the large nail head and jabs hard in several thrusts on my mouth, breaking some of my teeth. But I keep bashing her head.

I am not a nurse. I am an animal. The throbbing pain beneath my action is distraction—keep bashing, keep beating her face.

Her eyes close. I believe she's dead.

I am not a nurse. No, I am a nurse. *You are not a nurse right now.*

I lift my body off hers, the child inside me gone. I miscarried, I realize, which I knew the second I felt liquid thighs. I look to the blood that has fled me, losing the life within, a child, my soul. I am a vacant animal now. A hollow hollow, a hole, a worthless vessel. Nothing. I must move the bodies before the fire trucks come.

I am a nurse.

CHAPTER NINETEEN

MOP

Over the last week
Cape Cod

This is the state I'm in, living in a falseness, an untruth. All I wanted to do this past week was tell Manny everything, so we could solve this mess or walk away from the past, together. But even when we were in Cape Cod with my father and Aunt Sister Mary, I said nothing. I played the part they wanted me to play, the bride planning her wedding, so we could all be happy again and so they would love me like before, unencumbered. I needed that. Needed the fog. And what to do with Aunty. Help her? Expose her? Was she guilty of actual murder, or what? There was indeed a literal skeleton in her basement. A woman in her barn. I took comfort in believing the skeleton wasn't my mother, for the patient record I'd ripped from the nail said, "Dranal, Kent; DOB 12/18/71." Plus, the skeleton wore a man's wool suit.

Cape Cod was a maddening deviation of me assuming the role of my mother, stepping into the suit of her identity and suppressing my fuller identity's other parts. I selected a date for my and Manny's future wedding, planning out where on the oceanfront Grand Chesterton lawn we'd marry and beginning the grueling talk of menu selections. The

GC, as the Grand Chesterton is known, is one of the finest five-star resorts in the world—and owned, of course, by Manny's family. No investors. No public offerings. No private equity firms or offshore shell companies, so the quality is not diluted for short-term gain and the books not cooked for Wall Street. Just owned by his family and true.

I had to be the bride. The willing, happy bride. But the dichotomy caused constant spikes of panic inside, made worse by the fact I had to act them away on the outside. As I smiled at the offer of garland roses for the bridal arch, did they hear my dark thoughts wondering if I was living, questioning whether what I saw was a mirage and I was chained in hell? Did the perky wedding coordinator with the datebook know her scribbled notes sent my mind to Kent Dranal's daily record confirming he's "still dead"? Did Aunt Sister Mary know how her face, swollen from too many glasses of wine in the sun, looked like the face of the woman in the barn? I took a lot of spa appointments, saying I needed the rest and relaxation, only to sweat and shake so much on the table, the masseuse would end the effort and I'd hide in the steam room, crying under a eucalyptus-drenched face towel. Manny went bodysurfing while I hid, and in between resort appointments with my father, we ate riotous expensive meals together, the four of us, and between those meals, Manny and I made aggressive love in our GC hotel room.

Aunt Sister Mary Patience watched every move I made, like a hawk-woman, beady green eyes and all. When I laughed, she squinted her beads, showing she questioned my authenticity and saw my duplicity. When I giggled over the GC caterer's suggestion that we serve bacon-wrapped scallops, as if we New Englanders would skip such an obvious, obligatory choice, Sister Mary raised her eyebrows in a silent judgment and said "hmm." Aunt Sister Mary glowering there, sitting on the fringe of our four-top table in the GC's swanky lounge-restaurant, glitzy gold accents around, as if Don Draper might roll in any minute and light a silver-capped cigarette on a lighter wedged in the breasts of a black-dressed waitress. No, none of this was me, and Sister Mary called me out with her squinted eyes. When one of the cleavage waitresses bent her boobs in my face, Sister Mary lifted her eyebrows, as if saying, *I sent this girl as a test, how will you react? This is not you, none of this is you, and you know it.* I suppose she expected me to cast dower eyes at the waitress for lowering her own standards, but once again, Sister Mary misjudged me: I don't judge women on the choices they make with their own free will. If the girl wants to wear a low-cut dress, I seriously could not care less. It's not my personal choice, but my personal choices do not dictate anyone else's: I'm barely firm in them myself. And yet, since Sister Mary challenged me, I complimented the waitress on her revealing dress, fake-giggled along with her, then winked at Sister Mary in touché. None of this was the real me. This part I played in duplicity, and the wiry coat of it, the rank stench of phony fumes, riled me at my own self.

Is Aunty Liv even aware of her own duplicity? Can she bring herself together? Can I? If she fails at duplicity, this dual, insincere existence, will I? She's always claimed me as so much like her. But how much of the total identity pie does she claim of me? How much will I allow, now, in my emergence?

Back at the GC's swanky lounge, my other aunt studied me in my mental struggle for full identity, full emergence. Aunt Sister Mary knew I'd never fake-giggle about catered items, about bacon, about scallops, about cleavage. She knew I'd never fake-giggle about anything, except perhaps the notion that there exist universal truths immune to philosophy's relentless doubt. She knew a glitzy gold lounge with half-clothed women is the opposite environment I'd prefer for my wedding. More appropriate would be a candlelit, underground, ancient library in Italy with a close female relative or female scholar as the officiant. Maybe three—four, tops—witnesses in attendance.

But these things we do in duplicity, denying authentic multiplicity, to feel love, even if false or hidden. To collect acceptance. To keep the peace by keeping things simple and binary. To avoid a sick reality. Chains of protection.

On the morning of the day we were to leave the GC, I woke early, passing through the lobby to get an early swim alone, in the adult pool. My father wanted to leave earlier than planned, so we'd be packing in our cars around noon, because Hurricane Angelo was to hit the entire coastline of Massachusetts. The Weather Channel expected Angelo's eye to hover over land the next day, but given the battering the Cape sometimes gets, and given the battering we expected in Rye, I had to agree, it was best we get back.

Yet given the hurry we'd be in after breakfast, I needed to squeeze in a swim, get back to my morning laps, for my own well-being. I'd been dangerously off them since arriving at Aunty's. Like most mornings, I was going to swim laps for an hour. I needed the sound of swishing water and popping underwater bubbles to soothe my brain. The safety of pressure on all sides, a pressure that buoys you, but that you can fight, reject. For my brain, swimming is a beautiful meditation and powerful level setting. Had I been at Aunty's, I would have donned my wet suit and swum my typical swim along the coastline and up to the Rockport point of Manny's property.

Guess who was waiting on the ground floor on an upholstered bench, opposite the mouth of the open elevators. A paneled wood wall with embedded Freemason's tiles of metalwork backdropped Aunt Sister Mary on the bench. She wore a shapeless dress with brandless black leather shoes, black shoelaces too. Her hair was in the tightest knot on the tip-top of her skull. I wondered if I pulled the pin if her brains would bubble out. No need for a facelift with such torque. Her eye sockets pulled to each side as if trying to see her own earlobes.

"Aha, Mary Olivia. I knew you'd be up early. I know you like your morning swims. Always training for your triathlons. Well, well, sit here," she said, patting the taut fabric of the GC's bench seat.

I sucked in my cheeks, drawing my inner mouth to my teeth. I flared my nostrils, as I scraped to the bench and sat where she pat. She always says this, how I'm "training for a triathlon," but doesn't she recognize I never do triathlons? I never train on the bike or run, the other key components of a triathlon. How can she not recognize that I just like to swim for hours? It is my calmness, the greatest of which comes when I am in the sea, doing laps, back and forth, whether in front of our estate in Rye, or along the rock line of Haddock Point State Park. It is the practice of my faith, if I were to believe in such things.

Once again, I did not correct her. I let her believe my swims are mere practicalities of sport. She, in her enduring Catholic insistence, would never be willing to accept my intangible confidence in nature. She'd never accept the exaltation I give in my mind to ancient humanist philosophers like Epicurus and Lucretius. Blasphemy, she'd think, I think. She's "so stiff," so "stalwart, impenetrable," Aunty Liv has bled into comments about her. *Is she so stalwart? She sure does act stalwart and impenetrable. What is truth? Am I permitting just a one-dimensional identity for her to allow for a simple definition, an easy way to reject her in whole? Maybe I need to try harder.* In some ways, I wish I had Aunt Sister Mary's fortitude, like a brick house. Like a granite church. So unlike my faith of water, which seeps through my hands if I try to cup it. I am a colander; she is a stone bowl.

"I know there's something going on between you and your aunt Lynette," she said.

Bam. A direct slap to my facade.

"Seriously. Can't you call her Liv like everyone else? You're so stuck-up," I said, like a brat, which I hated to do. But I had to deliver a caustic slap, I had to pretend to act my brittle age, because I needed Sister Mary off the scent. I had never before talked to her like this, never told her she was stuck-up, never called her out for calling Aunty Liv by her formal name. I frankly never before and really now don't question Sister Mary's formality, nor do I wish to debate her choice to be formal. If stiffness is so important to her, so be it. But I had to slap her with my words on the GC's bench. And, being so stung by my words and shocked at how I acted, she leaned back, drew in her never-glossed lips, and swallowed.

"Mary Olivia, what has come into you? What exactly is going on? I know you're hiding something."

My first caustic slap didn't work. And so she forced me to up the smug and, like a candidate for president, deflect from my own sins, to hers.

I hated to do it. But I had to. I couldn't allow or afford Aunt Sister Mary asking questions or snooping around.

"So Aunt . . . *Sister* . . . Mary," I said, stressing the word *Sister*, but spacing out my words in a calm delivery. "Tell me. If you're so interested in getting into secrets, what's this secret you hold, eh? Why, exactly, did you quit the church, anyway? What about how Aunty Liv mentioned a man coming to the Rye coach house in the night, and you screaming?"

Frankly, I didn't know if Aunt Sister Mary had a secret at all. My mother never, ever whispered to Aunty Liv in front of me; she never gossiped about *anything* in front of me. My mother always told me to never be cruel. "Gossip is for the addle-minded," she'd say, adding a smile in her whimsical, frilly way and scrunching her nose all cutelike. She said things like, "Babycakes, I don't care what grades you get. What I'm most proud of is your teacher adding a comment on how courteous you are to her, and to the other students, and how you never gossip."

And it's true, before duplicity and insanity and selective amnesia came into my life, before I lost my mother, I did want to be kind, because it was natural for me, easy. I had no energy to focus on other people's flaws, for I obsessed on my own, with my own to doubt. And then over the last two years, I was vacant, or apathetic, or blindly invested in study or tutoring refugees, but not drilling into their backgrounds, and so had no cause or energy to gossip or be cruel.

But on the GC's bench two days ago with Aunt Sister Mary Patience Pentecost, I threw my instincts for kindness, and my wish to not engage in debate with anyone, out the resort's stained-glass windows to the holy rolling sea.

"So what's this secret, Sister Mary?" I taunted, like a child.

"What did you say?" She coiled back.

"I asked what your secret is, why you left the church, or was it, really, yeah, you were kicked out?" *Deflect, deflect, deflect. Get her to not want to ask again about what's going on with Aunty Liv.*

"How dare you!" she said while standing and slapping my face, for real.

She slapped my face.

I deserved it.

Standing above me and folding her long, lean body at the waist, she seethed in my face, "You know nothing. A man. A man coming to the coach house. It's not what you think, not some dirty sex with a nun secret, Mary Olivia. Not even close. But my truth is none of your business." And then she stormed off, but turned about ten feet away to say, "How dare you," upon a snarl.

Aunt Sister Mary Patience Pentecost was so furious, she left before we were scheduled, took an Uber all the way from the Cape to Rye, and barricaded herself in the coach house—something I knew when she texted me and my father: I'm home at Rye, in my rooms, don't call or knock. Leave me be. I have all I need in here to survive the storm.

I, on the other hand, drove home as scheduled, about midday, with Manny, my father taking his own car. I didn't let on to them anything about why Aunt Sister Mary left early. Manny and I drove straight back to his house by Haddock Point, and I told him I was going to go on and visit with Aunty. I asked him to let me go alone so I could visit with her for a couple of hours before dinner.

I could delude myself into packing my wake-up into a single second, the one physical event of Aunt Sister Mary slapping my face with a definite thwack. But that's too dramatic, too literal, too neat and tied up in a bow, easy for Hollywood, necessary for a strict ninety-minute movie. Like a cliché lightbulb pinged over my head in a Road Runner cartoon. The reality is, I'd been scraping and crawling for the lip of insanity's well, clawing to really emerge, ever since I slipped back down after finding the woman in the barn, clawed up but slipped again when I figured her for the woman on the rocks two years ago, clawed up a few feet but slipped again when I found the wool-suited skeleton. Straining through acting, crying in steam rooms, hiding my thoughts, pushing my mind at the GC was all me clawing, clawing, clawing on the rocks of my well, straining to emerge. Sister Mary's slap was the rope that met my hands stretching from the depths, seeking any help to pull me out. She pulled me out.

I was ready.

That was yesterday. And I haven't returned to Manny's since. I didn't get a chance to tell him about all these secrets at Aunty's. Did he find out on his own? Is he alive?

Yesterday, upon returning from the GC, I cut through the secret bramble trail and hit upon the space of the boarded burned cottage hole. I followed along through the stone path toward Aunty's lawn, brushing up the scent of rosemary and basil from the herb garden by the side room on the barn, and then, to my right, the spiral sunflower congress. The flower heads bloomed, swaying in their height in the high winds. I heard Aunty humming and singing in the side room to her patient woman.

"I whistle in the thistle, and I stop at the rock." She sang these two lines over and over. I walked softer past the barn, tiptoeing down the path to her front door. Deviating from the path, I visited her favorite willow, sprang the bottom latch on that birdhouse she and I made long ago, and extracted the hidden set of *all* the house keys, which includes the front door and the key to Aunty's bedroom, which has access to the attic.

The hydrangeas and all the other flowers bloomed in the August sunshine, seemingly lifting their petals to touch my skin as I passed. Keys in hand, I headed toward Aunty's blue front door. Oh, to emerge, to awake from cloudy dreams to definition and enhancements. To have purpose and questions and to be seeking answers and resolutions, however horrific. To be alive, to know I'm real. To be empowered, having chosen to take the keys, which were always there, and unlock rooms in literal and figurative ways. To have power. I clenched my hands in fists to bottle the thrill of being in command of my own mind.

The hibiscus petals at the entrance flopped as I passed, the size of them outgrowing the support of flower veins. But the flower's flopping largeness didn't stall me—a flashing from the windows above stopped me. Something overhead in the daylight glared. Glared again. Glared again. Three flashes. *I love you* in flashlight talk.

No, I thought. *No way. I'm imagining flashes, because I want lighted messages so bad.*

I stepped backward off the granite front stoop, craned my head to the attic dormer, and for sure this time saw, clear as day, three flashes.

I love you. Like my mother used to flash me from her cabin to my upstairs room at Aunty's.

Three more flashes from an attic dormer.

I love you.

And then a series that didn't quit.

I love you. I love you. I love you. I love you. I love you. I love you. I love you. I love you . . .

Aunty's singing in the barn wafted to me, giving a sense of safety: *Aunty is occupied.* "I whistle in the thistle, and I stop at the rock," she sang from afar.

More flashes from above.

I love you. I love you. I love you. I love you.

Flashing lights of *I love you* became a siren call.

My heart ran ahead of me, it beat so fast. I slipped through the front door, up the stairs, down the hall, scraped to the right key for Aunty's bedroom door, busted through Aunty's bedroom, up through her stairwell, and burst into the finished attic.

I stalled on the carpet, looking at a woman in a rocker, propped sitting by a dormer with flashlight in hand. Popover on her lap, and a kerchief blinding her hair to the world. A chain wound around her ankle and attached at the other end to a bed leg. *The metal scraping I heard on the first night.*

My mouth dropped to the floor, as did my body when I lost control of my muscles.

CHAPTER TWENTY

AUNTY

Two years ago

I am an animal nurse.

I lost my baby. My third baby gone.

My love is dead upstairs in Mop's room. Murdered.

My sister—I'm holding her wrist—is close to death and duct-taped on the burners of my gas stove. But she's not dead yet.

Her murderer is possibly dead or dying on my kitchen floor—her head bashed in by the bottom of the yellow bowl. My face is cut, my eye punctured, my teeth smashed, my left hand cut and in need of sutures. Blood on my face.

I am an animal nurse. I must act. I must be clinical so the gray clouds won't come. This is my job. Only my job. I push every emotion I should have out, like I'm trained to do in catastrophic emergency situations. This is war, and I'm on the front line, in the most critical medical tent. Like victims of a mass shooting coming to my ER.

Triage.

There's several forms of triage. I currently find myself in the mass casualty, low-to-no-resources scenario, and thus must enact the most complex of triage: continuous integrated triage. If I were in the ER,

I'd label patients on their chances of survival and dole out the limited medical resources to those with the best chance of survival, leaving to the side the ones with obliterated brains or blown-open hearts, as they have the least chance of survival. I'm known at Saint Jerome's as the best nurse to build the strategy for and execute incredibly effective, quick, and practical continuous integrated triage. I never undertriage or overtriage.

Shock will help me block reality. Adrenaline will boost my advanced efficiency skills. Here we go. I must act fast before authorities come. Psychologically, I'll pay later for pushing everything to the back of my brain, for activating only my executive function and none of the emotion or short-term memory in my hippocampus. But I won't have a chance at any livable later if I don't do exactly that. So here I am, a robot.

In tonight's case, I have one medical resource, me, and four people to assess:

Kent Dranal

- Assessment: Dead.
- Value: Zero. Already dead, he serves humanity no longer. He is worthless. However, his corpse frames me in murder and is thus toxic. I must deal with it.

Cate Dranal

- Assessment: Might be dead, significant head injuries, external bleeding on skull and in hair, suspect intracranial bleeding as well; unconscious. Needs CAT and/or PET scans and emergency surgery to remove likely hematoma, blood clot, bleeding in brain. I don't have the equipment to do scans here and am not trained to perform brain surgery.

- Value: Less than zero. She's possibly dead, possibly seriously brain injured. If she survives, she will exist with diminished mental capacity after a long road of rehab. She will be a drain on medical resources. Also, she is incurably and violently insane and serves no useful value to society. Rather, she is harmful to society. Like Kent, her body frames me in crime and is thus toxic. I must deal with it.

Johanna

- Assessment: She might die, is unconscious from unconfirmed quantity and potency of undated pentobarbital vial straight into her neck, unsure if hit vein. I can do nothing medically except wait to see the effects. I am holding her wrist, assessing her pulse, which is weak and dangerously spaced, but it's there.
- Value: Infinite. Johanna has the most value of anyone on earth, and with care and attention, and aggressive medical rehab and maintenance, she could survive to her prior state. I must deal with her, treat her in secret, if she even survives the possibly fatal level of injection she just received. If anyone runs toxicology on her blood and finds the pentobarbital in her, they'll link it to me.

So what if they link the pentobarbital to me? Shut up. Shut up and work! The reason, Lynette, you fucking imbecile, is you have no idea what Cate Dranal wrote of in her computer, or planted in Kent's emails—she has his password. She might link pentobarbital to you, which would link to your sister, and then there would be questions about Kent, who will be reported missing, and so will go an investigation . . . think. Then there's the matter of dead Vicky. No, don't think, stop thinking. Work.

Me

- Assessment: I need to avoid jail, have a serious eye injury, smashed teeth, slashed hand, but these injuries are not life threatening. I am suffering a miscarriage. Blood on my legs.
- Value: Limited and specific. My eye throbs, I can't see out of it, blood muddies my sight, I need stitches on my face and on my hand. The blood seems to have stopped flowing between my legs, but I need to be sure it doesn't start up again—I can't be leaving a blood trail of myself around this house and outside and highlighting for black light all the places I'm about to go. I will treat myself first, so I can deal with all three bodies before authorities come, so I don't go to jail. My relative value to humanity? Well, having lost my third child, almost none. The only value I hold now is the immeasurable value of bringing Johanna, who holds the most value, back to a life worth living. And if I fix her, after that, I am of zero value and can be gone from this cruel life. I refuse to be captured and thrown in jail for even a second of breath on this earth.

In the ER, I would never include in my assessments the relative value of each human life in comparison to the next. So while I much prefer to save the life of a child, as opposed to some haggard drunk past his prime, if the child is brain-dead and the drunk has a bleeding cut I can stitch so he doesn't bleed out, and it's only me, and there are no other resources, I'd, in the normal course of business, devote my care to the drunk.

But here, I *am* assessing the value of each of these lives before me and including in my quick assessment myself.

As I cut a piece of duct tape from Johanna, I look out the bay window to the fire, bright now inside the cottage, but still contained on the bed. I estimate about a half hour before the world descends upon me.

Triage.

I'm the best at triage.

The best triage nurse. Terrific.

I grab an absorbent washcloth and a long section of duct tape off Johanna and, given how thick the gluey adhesive is on this brand of tape, duct-tape the washcloth through the thumb and forefinger of my cut left hand. Next, using a corner of a towel from the laundry basket, I dab away blood on my face and press hard to stem the flow for a good two minutes. I fold the open skin together and slam another section of duct tape I've cut from the slumping Johanna over my sliced eye. The pain is unlike any pain ever experienced, but since it is so excruciating, this is my new normal. I work. The tape should hold the fold of the cut and quell the blood while I work; it won't last long. I need to work fast. With the rest of the towel, I wipe my legs of the blood and all the spots on the floor where it dripped. I wipe up the vomit too. The heaviest of my blood and the vomit is now soaked up in the towel. I'll run a mop last, after scooping up all the broken pottery. First: heavy fluids and bodies cleanup. Next: sterilizing cleanup.

In case I start bleeding again, I grab a Kotex from the kitchen bathroom, stick it to a pair of fresh underwear, and pull them on. The bloody towel and old underwear I shove in the oven.

First, Kent.

In nurse training, they teach you how to leverage the full weight of a man, up to double your weight, over your back to drag him to wherever you need to treat him, or in my present case, stash his dead body. I run up to Mop's room with another section of duct tape. Before slinging the bloodless Kent over my back as trained, I slap the duct tape over the slice in his neck, because I can't bear to look at it, and I can't bear to consider his head flopping back and his neck slice ripping more. If his head detaches, I'll sink into the floorboards and dissolve. I won't be able to pick up his face and cradle it to my chest. Having slung him over my back, I drag him to the top of the stairs, lay him headfirst toward the top stair, his body long. I slink around him, descend three stairs, and pull at his shoulders. The wool of his suit jacket is scratchy and real and I feel a blip of grief. *No, stop. Stop. The wool is wool. Just wool.*

In a sliding thunk, sliding thunk, every time his feet hit another tread, we make our way to the first floor and reach the foyer. I drag him across the white marble to the basement door. I repeat the shoulder-drag-sliding-thunk down my basement stairs, then slide him along the limestone floor to my bookcase, the one that is really a door to a hidden wine room. I turn the secret dial lock, push the bookcase; it swivels; I drag Kent inside, exit the wine room, swivel and lock the bookcase in place.

This process, as I clock my stopwatch, takes a respectable seven minutes.

I return to the kitchen, being efficient by grabbing pentobarbital vials along the way in the hall that connects foyer to kitchen, and, being further efficient, blow out each tea light with each bend to each vial. I enter the kitchen and stuff two fistfuls of pentobarbital vials under a loaf of bread and a package of hamburger rolls in the tin bucket with the tin lid—all this by the stove where Johanna is taped in place. She's still slumped; Cate Dranal still unconscious on the floor with broken pottery everywhere.

I need to stop the blood flowing from Cate Dranal's head gash, so I yank open my "glory hole" kitchen drawer, which holds all my random shit: pens, lighters, matches, paper clips, tacks, scissors, tape, the top flap of a Girl Scout cookie box—Thin Mints—saved for no fucking reason, a bouncy ball from a gum-ball machine, and, of course, superglue.

I grab another full bath towel from the basket of my laundry Cate Dranal folded and, with one end, soak up the blood from her hairline. Before more can billow out, I empty the entire contents of superglue into her open wound. This will hold the blood in, with hope. While it dries, I cut more of the duct tape from Johanna.

Now I fold the bloodied end of Cate's head towel in on the non-bloody middle and wrap, wrap, wrap the towel around Cate's head, in case the superglue doesn't dam well enough. Then I duct-tape the wrapped towel around, around, in the middle of her face. I don't want to drag Cate Dranal's blood through the house. I move her contained head and shoulders to the side a half pivot, and with another towel, soak up the blood on the floor. Again, I'll do sterilization mopping last. I ball up the third towel and throw it into the oven.

I pull Cate by her nasty feet down the hall to the foyer. Along the way, her yellow butt is a push broom, collecting the spent tea lights; the tea lights jumble and bounce like lottery balls against her bottom, but then fall around her body to skid across my marble foyer and clatter into the foyer's baseboards. No bother, I'll collect those as I pace the foyer, waiting for the fire trucks to come. I position Cate Dranal's towel-taped head toward me at the top of the basement stairs and shoulder-drag-slide-thunk her down the stairs, like I did with Kent, her toweled head in my gut. Cate's head blood is starting to dot the towel from the inside, and soon it will soak through.

I bring Cate inside the secret wine room and slump her body next to Kent's dead one. Her crazy-stitched, blue-blue ball gown drapes over Kent's wool suit in slashing angles. I remove the towel from around her head, so as to fold it under where her blood is now dripping, because I'd rather funnel the drip-draining blood onto this one towel, as opposed to taking my chances of it soaking through in a diffused way through a wrapped towel and dripping within my wine room. Plus, to be honest, had I not removed the towel, she would have suffocated.

Maybe let her suffocate?

No! You're a nurse.

Get back to work!

I leave the wine room, swivel and lock the false bookcase door.

I check my stopwatch: collecting and stashing Cate Dranal took another eight minutes. I run up to my kitchen. I check the bay window as I turn my attention to Johanna on the stove. The fire is now licking the ceiling above the burning bed.

I cut Johanna free with my kitchen scissors and ball up the duct tape as I remove it, working as fast as if I had to extricate an entire three-piece tuxedo from a man in a drunk-driving accident. Which, indeed, I have had to do, sadly enough, four times in my life. I stuff the ball of tape in the oven with the bloody towels. What fire investigator is going to first check the oven in the nonburning house? What cottage fire investigator would even question the glue lines left by the duct tape on the stove in the nonburning house? I'll deal with the tape and towels later. Now, I build the distraction, misdirect investigators to *outside* this house. Is that what happened in the JonBenét Ramsey case? Didn't they spend the first critical hours outside the house?

Johanna's so much lighter than Kent and Cate. About half as light. I shimmy her up on my back, and in the movement, her Tory Burch flats fall to the kitchen tiles. No bother. I need them anyway. Good thing we have the same size feet. Good thing I know the tide schedule like I know the hours of my weekly hospital shifts.

I kick a few pieces of the broken yellowware as I cross-bear Johanna on my back toward the hall.

It's hard work walking up the front stairs with the dead weight of Johanna, but I'm sure adrenaline fuels me, and my core muscles are in shape from all the real triage work at the hospital, all my screwing of Kent at the Kisstop, him screwing me back, and all the gardening I do. All the endless hours I spend standing, painting the ocean from the ocean rocks, and doing calf raises as I do, so as to multitask: art with exercise. I eat my own grown food, buy organic meat. I can do this. I am strong.

I am a nurse.

I am an animal.

We pass an oval window in the stairwell, and the full moon shines on the top of my head and the top of Johanna's, which rests on my right shoulder. Her arms are draped in a circular *X* around my neck so I can hang on to her, me folded over, and stomp and strain up the stairs.

What must the moon think to see such a vision, captured in an oval frame? One sister draped over the back of the other, who trudges up the stairwell to cross the moon's path.

I am a nurse. I can't think of what the moon thinks of me.

Who cares what the moon thinks. Keep working. Focus.

My thighs burn, but I lift, I push.

We reach the second floor. The fastest way to get Johanna into the attic is halfway down this hall, through my bedroom, and up the stairwell in there. For a short relief, I set her on the floor and pull her with her head at my knees and sitting backward. Her body crumples the rug runner as I pull, so I'll pull it straight again after securing her upstairs.

We reach my unlit bedroom, my canopy bedposts jiggling as I pull past. I secure Johanna on my back again and strain our way up the stairwell into the attic. No time to place Johanna comfortably in the puffy bed, so I lay her gently on the plush beige carpet. I remove my nurse's uniform, my shoes, my socks, and then remove Johanna's dress and pull it on. I leave my shoes and socks in the attic but ball my own uniform under Johanna's dress, making myself look pregnant.

I am not pregnant.

I lost our baby, Kent. Love, I lost our baby.

Shut the fuck up. Concentrate. Be a nurse. Don't let the gray clouds come. You are only a nurse. This is your job.

I pause to whisper a quick apology to Johanna as I pull off her slip and use it as a glove so as to yank a handful of her hair from her skull.

I know forensics.

I know because whenever there is a criminal or crime victim in the ER, the detectives and cops swoop in on us, demanding we collect clothing and immediately seal it in airtight bags, that we scrape under fingers and swab every orifice for minuscule strains of evidence—skin cells, hair fibers, saliva.

I know if I tell investigators that Johanna ran screaming, on fire, and pulling on her own hair through the bramble paths, to launch her burning body into the ocean as the only possible relief, before I could stop her, me running behind, they'll look for microscopic scraps of evidence to prove my story, or disprove my story. Plus, this is time-consuming distraction work for them, *outside my house.*

After retrieving Johanna's Tory Burch flats from the kitchen floor, I fling out my front door, wearing Johanna's dress, my own nurse's uniform balled at the belly underneath. In one clenched fist, I hold a section of her ripped hair within a ball of her slip; in the other, I cradle her shoes. My bare feet make indents in the soft earth and then muddy footprints on the stone path to the burning cottage. These footprints of mine are okay. They'll match the story I tell.

The flames lick through the front door. I slip on Johanna's shoes and lift the hem of her dress to the fire and let it catch. Just enough, just a slow burn by my knees, and I run fast toward the ocean, leaving Johanna-size shoeprints in the bramble paths, scattering her pulled hair, here and there along the way, close so it catches in the vines stretching into the path, and where investigators can find it, where they'll be crouched to cast her footprints in plaster, my bare ones, too, which will come next. The burning dress singes vine leaves and bramble prickers as I pass, the fibers of the dress floating like fireflies and sticking within the tangles of vegetation.

As soon as I reach the granite rocks along the sea's edge, I drop the empty ball of her slip and remove Johanna's burning dress from my body with one arm, taking care to slide out and not burn my own skin. My other arm cradles my nurse uniform. I wear only a bra and underwear under the moon's watchful rays. *The moon is a brainless rock and is not watching you. Doesn't care about you. Nobody does. Focus.* I look around—no one here. I run to the top of the cliff in Johanna's shoes and launch her burning dress and slip to the high crashing waves, and then kick her shoes off my feet so they fling to the sea.

I check my stopwatch. Settling Johanna and running to the cliff top took an unimpressive ten minutes. It's been twenty-five minutes since

I noticed the burning bed. I look back toward my property and see the smoke rising beyond the high treetops of maples and oaks. People from surrounding properties may notice the smoke now, and on this sea wind, which will carry the scent of smoke and fire, they will detect *something amiss* to just smell the air.

Thankfully, the tide is rolling in and three-quarters to the high point, so it will be safe for me to scrape down the side of this cliff wall and run along the flat granite rocks along the sea, which will wash away my footprints. I pull my nursing uniform over my head as I run.

I plunk into the middle beach, covered in two feet of moving water, so I slosh through, holding my uniform high over my underwear. I am submerged to a half inch below my knees, so no cloth is wet. This is a relief. I wouldn't be able to explain that away. Or it would complicate my story. I tiptoe at the literal edge of Manny's grass lawn to the secret trail he and Mop cut long ago, and which no one uses, and stepping as light as possible, reach to behind Johanna's burning cottage. From the path's mouth, I jump to within an inch of the cottage's backside and run around the cottage. None of these footprints will matter. I'll say I did exactly this, trying to save my sister, not noting her lunging aflame from the front door until it was too late. Most of my footprints will be gone anyway, as soon as this fire sends flaming boards and siding and Sheetrock and other building materials to the ground. Running around the cottage is also necessary to prove the story I'll tell about how I punctured my eye and cut my face and hand. The fire has eaten through the plaster walls and is eating the frame. The exterior walls glow orange, and I note the darker circles of the large antique nails in the thicker support beams. These nails, these are part of the eye story, in a coming fiction and in a past reality.

I again reach the path I just ran down with Johanna's dress on fire, running this time in my bare feet, leaving my own trail behind Johanna's Tory Burch trail, returning to the sea. I again reach the cliff wall, jump up and down like I'm screaming for her to stop. Walk to the edge, lie flat, as if I'm searching or reaching for her fallen body.

I run back down the path to my house.

As soon as I reach the kitchen, I check to make sure my eye and hand are not bleeding through the cloth and tape. They aren't, I'm good. I ignore the throbbing pain. Next, I sweep the broken pottery to a corner and with no time to scoop up shards and pieces, slivers, and yellow dust, I take a twenty-gallon antique crock from the walk-in pantry, empty it of five umbrellas, tip it over, and cover the pottery pile in the corner. I place a potted plant on the crock's upturned bottom. They'll think this is some cozy decoration. I rearrange the surviving pottery on the shelving unit, sparse now. The released umbrellas are a colony of folded black bats, jostling among themselves, excited to be uncontained, but settling in a collective lean in a pantry corner.

I call 911 from the kitchen cordless, and because I don't know if a neighbor has called yet, and I don't know how long I have, I drop to my hands and knees, scurry like the demon-possessed to the cabinet below my sink, extract a bottle of bleach, and pour it on the floor. I scrub with a facecloth, the phone jammed in the crook of my neck, pulling off the greatest acting job I've ever done, cry-sobbing crazy to the 911 operator.

I scream about how I got home (I don't say anything specific about when I left work, leaving a timeline flexible to how I need to unfold facts) to find my sister's cottage ablaze, that I ran out there in my bare feet to try to save her, followed her burning to the ocean, watched her pulling out her own hair, and then failed to stop her from flinging her body over the cliff's edge.

"When I got to the cottage, I was so disoriented in running around, I didn't see a board with an old nail had separated from the house and I ran into it, and slid down, and I'm cut too. In falling, I snagged my hand on something sharp, and cut that too. My eye is punctured," I add, after two full minutes of straight rambling about my sister. The operator buys it. I pull the duct tape from my eye, throw it in the oven, along with the bleach cloth, and spritz odor neutralizer everywhere to get rid of the bleach smell.

I'll need to keep the firefighters and police out of the kitchen.

I crank open every panel on both bay windows. My yellow-and-green curtains don't flutter in the stagnant air; no ghost curtains billow to tickle me with humor. I am rejected by my own curtains, my own home. *What the fuck with this crazy bullshit? Curtains don't tickle, curtains don't care. Fucking focus.* The odor of sea salt and fire smoke reach my kitchen. This will help to neutralize odor in here as well.

"Okay, now, okay, calm down. I'm sending trucks. It will be okay. Please breathe," the operator says.

I hang up. I don't have time to calm down. There's a couple more things to handle before the fire trucks and cops arrive.

I turn on the sucking fan in the restaurant hood over the gas stove. Crank it high.

Next, I drive Kent's Jeep to the Wilson property. I've been picking up their mail for months while they're in Costa Rica. I unlock their barn (they gave me a key to keep an eye on), park inside. When investigators ask about neighboring eyewitnesses, I'll tell them how the Wilsons are in Costa Rica, and I'll give them their number, and they'll confirm. And no one is going to be searching here for Kent or his Jeep, anyway. There's no *known* connection of him to me, and there'd be no inquiry that he'd be involved in my sister falling asleep in a cottage with a lit cigarette in her mouth. If Cate Dranal told it right, Kent's not even missing—he's helping refugees in Greece. Nevertheless, I'll be sure no one starts looking for Kent, but that's cleanup phase II, something I'll handle in the coming days.

Now done with Kent's Jeep, and back from running through the line of forest and a couple of trails between our properties, I pace my marble foyer, waiting. I pick up the spent tea lights Cate's ass jostled and stick them in a drawer in a side table in the library. Metal mermaids are my only witnesses.

CHAPTER TWENTY-ONE
AUNTY

Two years ago

Here are the fools with their sirens and flashing lights. Woo, woo, woo, fuck all you. You'll get what I give you, here I come. I bolt like a sprung spring from my foyer, screaming. Before I bolted, I made sure to set the lock. As my front door slams shut behind me, my home is barred to anyone without a key. I have spare keys in a birdhouse Mop made me, long ago. I want to keep these fools outside as long as possible, so that any remaining cleansing fumes in the kitchen dissipate. And so I have time to sneak a call to my overpaid lawyer.

My face is bloodied, throbbing, the pain in my slashed eye unimaginable. My mouth of broken teeth so painful, I no longer feel pain. My entire head is a bursting blood blister.

"My sister! My sister, oh my God, a cliff and my sister with her shoes and burning." I'm in hysterics for them, pointing in the direction of the ocean. I need to make sure my words are not in perfect, grammatical English. Smoke and flames from the cottage reach high over the oaks and maples. I hope the firefighters dragging massive hoses through my perennial beds and lawns right now are able to save Big Boy and the swing on his big limb. *That bitch is ruining my lawns and might take my favorite tree and maybe killed my sister, killed my love. I will track her down in hell and haunt her life an eternity.*

"Ma'am, ma'am, calm down. Where is your sister?" a man's voice says.

"She's, oh my God, I tried to stop. I tried to stop her." While keeping one hand on my throbbing eye, with the other I grasp the body of the man voice, some guy of some authority—he's wearing some man jacket with labels and ranks and patches and whatever. "Please, over there, the ocean, find her. Maybe she's on the cliff wall and I can't see. Maybe she didn't drown. Help her!"

By giving these fools hope of saving a human woman, I know they'll go where I say. And they do. Upon Man Voice's command, uniformed people race toward the ocean.

"A woman. On the cliff. Go, go, go. And get the coast guard on this. Now! Go!" he says.

Man Voice turns to me. "Ma'am, your eye. We're going to need to patch you up. Over here, with the paramedics. The firefighters will get the fire under control. They're already on it. If your sister is alive, we will find her. I'll stick with you. Let's talk."

So.

We'll talk.

Me and Man Voice will talk.

We'll chat as I stave off excruciating pain and some paramedic works on my busted face. And I'll tell Man Voice some things, through hysterics and broken English. I'll tell him that in the course of seeing the fire from my kitchen, I panicked and miscarried. I won't mention the word *blood*, won't let the idea of such liquid swirl in the vernacular of his mind. But by mentioning a panicked miscarriage, I'll plant the seed if for some reason I missed a spot of blood in the kitchen and some fool, who inevitably insists on coming inside, sees. But I didn't miss any spots. I checked several times while waiting for these fools. I am an efficient and effective nurse. I don't leave blood behind.

Oh and also, in a subtle and weak woman way, I'll direct Man Voice to stage his teams in the barn, outside my house. Because surely they'll respect how traumatized I am and how intrusive such tragedy is. They'll want, yes, because they're good fools, right, to respect the sanctity of my home. Which is not a workplace for law enforcement, paramedics, and firefighters. It is not a police station or firehouse. It might be a hospital and a morgue, though, but these fools don't need to learn that.

They can drink their Dunkin' Donuts boxes of coffee in the barn, because I'm not some fucking host. And they can jibber-jabber all they want on their walkie-friggin'-talkies and cell phones in barn stalls. My side room of medical equipment, just stuff for home health care, a private business, you understand, don't you, Man Voice?

Just as long as I keep the lot of these fools outside my house long enough to get in touch with my flaming bitch of a lawyer, who will fix everything. She'll fix it, all right. I'm a Vandonbeer.

"Fuck all these fools."

—A line Aunty scrawls over and over in a notepad as she watches detectives in her yard from her kitchen's bay window

It is five days later now, and my walls of staying emotionless and fending off the coming insanity and PTSD from what I just did and went through are starting to crumble. I know I'm sliding, but I keep fighting and acting. I need to pull this off.

Obviously, I had to cancel the annual Mighty Mary Trust gala. This bitch ruined everything. So many patrons let down, but what can I do? *Stay on track. Survive. At all costs, no jail.*

I'm about to drive Kent's Jeep back to Kent's house.

Diversion—this is the lesson I chose to take from some of the theories reported about the infamous JonBenét Ramsey case. Keep them looking outside the house, act distraught, pull it off, long enough to hide the evidence *in the house*. Also, have and use your connections, your power. And this is exactly, *exactly* what I've been doing for five days. Now it's time to deal with Kent's Jeep, which I'll enter soon. Time to deal with his house too. I'm dressed head to toe in black, my hair wrapped tight in a black scarf, like the tightest of turbans, black sunglasses on—at night. Black gloves, no fingerprints.

The fire investigators and detectives confirmed the burn pattern matched my story of Johanna smoking in bed. They tweezer-bagged several of Johanna's dress fibers along the path, her hair, cast her footprints, and mine, just as I said shit went down. They interviewed family members and friends, hospital workers, charity people, and everyone told the constant story that Johanna and I are the closest sisters ever. My drama acting came in quite handy, to prove how distraught I was in losing my sister. Doctors treated me on-site. No surgery could save my eye. They gave me stitches and a patch, antibiotics, and pain meds.

I absolutely leveraged the fuck out of the Vandonbeers' ugly power. Whatever dark secrets we've held, some for more than a century, over powerful people in politics and law enforcement, well, I pulled on them through my most expensive, well-connected Stokes & Crane LLP lawyer to send the clear message that the investigation was to start and end on my story of what happened. Yes, indeed, that *is* how things work for those interweaved in the establishment, the 0.01 percent of the top 1 percent—a constant chess game that plays out over, in my case, a couple of centuries. Did Judge McAdams really want his medal-decorated great-great-great-grandfather's brass statue in a well-known Boston park dishonored with the documented proof (which the Vandonbeers hold in a safe in Rye) of him raping ten slave girls and impregnating eight (which DNA testing on the bloodline would prove) before moving north to fight the right side of the Civil War? Fuck him, fuck the judge.

Fuck everyone. Did Commissioner Ryan really want it leaked that he fixed a mob trial in the mob's favor, because Johnny Bighead, the consigliere of the Boston mob, held some illicit pictures of Ryan paying four different human-trafficking victims to dress as men, wear strap-on dildos, and gang fuck him in the ass at a Southie motel? Commissioner Ryan's detectives and police might be honest, sure, ignorant of the affairs of their commander, but they'd follow commands from the top.

Does it really matter how I made the soup? I made the fucking soup.

They never found Johanna's body, found only her burned dress and one of her shoes (the other one washed up later, and in a stroke of amazing luck, I found it after investigators left one evening; I plan to throw it in the dirty hole of her burned cottage, as an offering). They never recovered her slip, the one I used to rip her hair out of her head and scatter the strands; the slip likely got tangled somewhere on the seafloor, obscured in rocks and underwater seagrass, undetectable.

In a miracle in parts, and thanks to the high tide, no investigator discovered my path through the middle beach nor through Manny's lawn or in the secret trail. They never did look in my oven in the critical first hours, because again, why would they? So I had time to collect it all, throw the stash in the secret wine room, and cook a turkey to obscure any oven remnants. They never found my false bookcase, nor my wine room, and no family members who know of it—only Mop and Philipp—had cause to mention it. David, my old sperm-donor boyfriend, might have known about my wine room, but he surely said nothing, for he, as the state's attorney, was part of the web of connections doing my bidding, hidden among the layers of plausible deniability. Oh, no, he wouldn't say a word; he wouldn't get tangled in my mess, not with the announcement I know he has coming, the one where he confirms that, yes, he is running for president next term after all. Good for fucking you, David. Good for you, Commissioner Ryan. Judge, you too. Good for you. I got what I wanted. I got cover. I got dirt on all you motherfuckers, and when the time is right, when I'm cleared for good, Judge, your family statue is coming down for "repairs" that take a literal forever; and Ryan, you will "retire early to spend more time with family." Eventually, all your dirty truths will come out too. Bite me.

They never looked in my attic, either; I was soon cleared. I pulled off the greatest diversion ever. They never did search my home, top to bottom, like they did in the Ramsey case.

Probably the greatest stroke of luck or fluke, or whatever you want to call it, was that no hounds were brought in on the search. Perhaps a combination of a complete lack of available dogs and just plain incompetence and investigative apathy—the investigators concluded from pretty much hour one that Johanna did indeed launch herself into the ocean, given the not-so-subtle leaning of Commissioner Ryan, who'd been approached by my Stokes & Crane lawyer—but they did not bring in the dogs. And even without incompetence or apathy, bribery or extortion, they really couldn't use dogs, anyway. Every police hound in the tristate area was tracking that gunman of the church shooting in Boston and his two hostages, the eight- and ten-year-old daughters of a sitting senator, who died from several high-velocity bullets (three of which I'd held in my hand and plunked in an evidence bag myself). So that international-headline-grabbing active investigation, as horrible as it all is, saved me. Continues to save me. Those girls are still adrift with the gunman. But that's another story altogether.

About a day into the investigation, there was a three-hour stretch, after medics treated me and detectives questioned me for hours, in which, in the earliest of dawn, all these dipshits left me alone. Cops took a coffee break with the press, whom they quarantined to the Haddock Point parking lot.

That's when I pulled the bloody towels and balls of duct tape from the oven and shoved the evidence with Cate and Kent in the wine room. I then checked Cate's pulse to find it beating, but her still unconscious. I checked her vitals and upgraded her prognosis, which was concerning. So I duct-taped her mouth in case she awoke while I baked a turkey for the detectives. I also tied her arms and legs and locked her back in the wine room. I thanked myself for putting a swivel lock *outside* the bookcase.

Why did I do that in the first place?

Ah, I remember why. As part of my single-woman security system. I figured I could trap an intruder in here and hold him until the cops came. What a strange premonition. Perhaps delusion. Perhaps paranoia. I never got over my father's murder.

Also during this three-hour time period, I ascended to my lovely sister, who was still unconscious, her pulse and breath a little steadier, but still weak. I dressed her in a comfy pair of cotton pajamas and settled her into the attic bed with Frette linens. From my barn, I dragged in a feeding line and saline drip. I began my nursing care of my sister that day, treating her in coma.

And now, five days after the fire, I'm forced to attend to the now starving Cate Dranal, who just awoke. Just now.

Her eyes bleary, her trying to speak or scream under the duct tape in the basement, in my cold, limestone wine room.

I rip the tape from her mouth.

Her eyes sag in lethargy, but she's working that ugly mouth of hers.

"My house. They'll find you," she gurgles. I think that's what the bitch says.

I jam a half vial of pentobarbital in her neck, sending the bitch to death or coma—either will do at this point. And it's sweet justice, giving her what she gave to my precious Johanna.

It's midnight, no one is around, no more media awake, no cops, so I slink within my known shadows, all the dark spots I've cultivated over the years in my lawn, enter my barn, and drag another feeding line and saline drip into the wine room. This is the treatment she'll get, this swine. I don't change her into comfy cotton pajamas. Don't place her in a bed or settle a blanket atop her. Her blue-on-blue gown is disgusting and soiled, as are her awful yellow underwear. She stinks, she's swine. The superglue in her head wound is beginning to peel away from the grease layer formed on her skin. I stitch her face with fishing line and a sewing needle. She looks like a bloated zombie. Or a murder doll.

I don't care.

I am an animal. I am a nurse.

And I'm slipping. I feel it. But before I do, cleanup phase II: Kent's Jeep and house.

Maybe I'll move zombie doll to the barn once all the hubbub dies down. For now, she'll be treated in the basement, on the floor, slumped on the body of her dead husband, and without any covers. Fuck her. Fuck this bitch.

What day is it?

I need to check Johanna's vitals before I drive over to Kent's house and drain the tub.

Check Johanna's vitals. Rotate her in the bed so she doesn't get bedsores.

Oh, Johanna. We'll go away, away, way, way, when you wake, my love. And we'll drink tea, and I'll tell you what happens in books, in books, in the books I read. My lovely love, ly, love.

I've left Kent's Jeep in his garage. Drained and marinated his porcelain tub in bleach. Checked Cate's and Kent's email accounts, and indeed, Cate did email Saint Jerome's and Mass General that she and Kent took off to help refugees in Greece. I don't see any frantic emails from friends or family members looking for them, and I recall Kent saying they had none, anyway. The neighborhood, I sense, based on the front porch over there, is rallying around Vicky's tragic allergic death.

I stare out the window; time passes.

I return my gaze to the computer desk and note a list on a chirpy, pretitled THINGS TO DO notepad. Beside each handwritten item, Cate,

I presume, checkmarked each of her completed things to do and slashed it dead with a deep pencil cross off:

- ~~Auto–Bill Pay~~
- ~~Sell van, cash~~
- ~~Lawn guy, schedule~~
- ~~Stop mail/newspapers~~
- ~~Work emails/Greece~~
- ~~House timers lights/thermometer on Nest~~
- ~~Nest cameras~~
- ~~Greece ticket~~
- ~~Passport~~
- ~~Purse (V)~~
- L&K

This list is simple for me to decode. Cate, so insane but also still an insane professional, had to do an "escape to Greece and disappear" to-do list. A list of items that would button up her house and allow for minimal questions from anyone. A list that allowed her to come back if she felt the heat was off. A list that was so demented, the last two items literally spelled out her admitted crimes: "Purse (V)," of course, meant she had to burn or discard the purse with the peanuts that killed V, or Vicky. And "L&K," which she never got a chance to cross out, was of course, to deal with L (me, Liv) and K (Kent).

Beside the THINGS TO DO crazy-demented escape/murder/obstruct justice/cover up major crimes list is a computer printout of her ticket to Greece, my taunting mistress letter I left in her ugly minivan, and my hospital ID. I grab and pocket my mistress note and ID. I pocket also the Greece ticket, which I'll burn. Back on her computer, I find her bank account, which I will seed once funds are depleted for the auto–bill pay through a labyrinth of shell companies and a money-laundered name in Greece. Nobody will suspect anything at all because the mortgage will be paid and the utilities will be paid, and all the money-grubbers won't have cause to complain.

I find all the damn Nest cameras in the house, put them in a bag. I'll sledgehammer the cameras tomorrow and scatter the pieces in the ocean. I hack into her Nest account (using her pass code written and pinned on her bulletin board) and delete all the video of me on the property. I note the earliest date of the videos is today, so there's no video of her murdering Kent, which I would have, of course, saved. I'm done here.

Given all she has set up for this house to run on her preset commands and her notices to work, nobody should be looking for Cate or Kent. And there's no other trace to spark anyone to come crawling to me for answers. So if anyone does come around here looking for Cate, they'll conclude she disappeared, or tried to disappear. And big deal with that. I used gloves while in this house. I know forensics.

I'm a ghost.

I'm smoke.

I'm smog in this house.

Vapor.

Gone.

On my way out now, I stall in Kent and Cate's back mudroom. And here I'm fingering the sleeve of Kent's navy jogging jacket. I taste my tears before I know they're rolling. I reach into his pocket and extract the wrappers of and a few unopened mini Three Musketeers. I'll eat them in my long walk home on country roads and backstreets.

Here come the voices in my head again—they'll win this time. They'll talk to me the whole walk home.

Nobody loves you anymore. You are unloved and worthless. You don't even know your own name—that is how worthless you are.

What is my name? Where did I come from? How did I get here? Who am I?

CHAPTER TWENTY-TWO
MOP

Present time

My mother blinked when I first saw her in the rocker in Aunty's attic yesterday. After shaking my weak muscles back to life, I sat and stalled.

"Mwop," she slurred.

"Mama," I croaked, not believing. *I don't believe in such things,* I reminded myself.

"Here, to mwe," she said, lifting her arm slow.

When I didn't move, she braced her hands on the rocker's arms, pushing hard to lift herself. Popover slid to the floor.

I do not believe my mother is here. I do not believe my mother is alive. I must be delusional.

I scampered on my knees over to what I told myself was grief's illusion, couldn't possibly be my mother, and cowered next to her in the chair, telling myself she was mere vapor, a floater in my eye. But as my disbelieving vapor felt solid to touch, I next allowed only that whoever this solid vapor was, she was simply my companion, a *companion*. Acceptance and emergence, for me, has been like Chutes and Ladders, up, down, way up, way down. There's no magic lift to the top. And so my battle with sanity began once again, only this time it braided with a physical battle to the death.

My mother's eyes flew open wide, looking *behind* me.

I turned to see who had entered, buckling in fright.

My mother and I shivered together, me on the floor, her in the chair, shaking in the presence of the woman at the door with a bloody hatchet.

One day later, I'm still thinking of my mother as my companion as I shiver on the ground, watching a woman in all black point a nail gun at a woman with a hatchet. In a hurricane. Outside. At the burned-out basement cottage.

CHAPTER TWENTY-THREE
AUNTY

One year and some months ago, Christmas Eve . . .

I'm up, alarm clock, stop, I know. I slam your button, you shut up. Up up up I get, slip to my slippers, sip my bedside cup, and first, I must, because I must, I must, seriously I must, first I must check Johanna Banana, Johanna Love, on my rounds.

Her saline's fine, her food line good, empty her catheter; we rotate arms, legs, and knees. All the joints. Must move all the joints. Her cognitive prognosis is still critical, and I can't truly evaluate. She hasn't "emerged" since that night. That night forever ago, or last night, I don't know. She's still breathing on her own, thank God. Stealing a ventilation tube would be difficult, ordering one suspicious. Agh! I need coffee! Early-morning Johanna care, check!

Popover's automatic feeder worked again, check! I clean out his litter box, check!

He scowl-meows at me as I leave, him there curled on Johanna's feet.

"Screw you, too, Popover! Kiss, kiss!"

Now down, down, down to the kitchen, I get my coffee, eat a cinnamon muffin in peace.

Hello, there, morning sun! Nice yellow shine you leave on the December snow! It's a white Christmas. Woo!

Next on to the bitch, rounds continue, in the barn, in the barn, and nobody knows what's behind my locks.

I whistle in the thistle, and I stop at the rock. Oh wow! That rhymes. So funny. I whistle in the thistle, and I stop at the rock. Ba, da, da da da, dadada, I stop at the rock. It's a song! I whistle, wee-woo, in the thistle . . .

Oh, that's good. It's a song.

Cate's face is so super swelled in sickness. What's the medical term? Oh yeah, disgusting fuck face. And she's in a little coma, poor lassie. Poor lassie, what a word! But she's like Johanna Banana, so sad, boo, sad. I dump her crap diaper in the trash, shove nutrition shit in her feed tube.

Good thing, oh, good thing, you should thank me, you bitch, I was trained for so many years. I know how to synthetize the synthetic nutrition stew they pump into coma victims, except my cocktail is real. So fuck you, here's the liquid breakfast you don't deserve.

I move Cate, bitchity bitch bitch bitch, to her right side, prop her back with perfect pillows. Need to make sure she doesn't get bedsores and make me deal with an infection, like five months ago, when I dragged her from the basement floor and she was a hair away from gangrene and well within a serious and relentless skin fungus that took fucking months to clear. But she won't get the physical therapy on her joints, like my baby sister girl, my sweet Johanna.

I scowl at the necklace around her neck, but it stops me.

I must be good.

Johanna's orange beach-glass necklace. I had to take it from Jo-Jo and give it to the bitch so I wouldn't choke the bitch out, so I'm reminded to be good. I know Johanna would be disappointed in me if I murdered her. I must be a nurse. I must make Johanna proud of me.

Be good. Maybe then someday if I get this all right again, Mop can come back and love me.

Kent is "still dead," like you wrote on his chart yesterday morning. Go ahead, after treating this bitch, check again on today's rounds, and write it again. Write it every day, because that's his assessment, and his prognosis won't change.

Is he really dead?

Yes! Focus, idiot!

I know, I'll sing the disgusting fuck face my new song!

"I whistle in the thistle, and I stop at the rock." This is better, much better. I sing and it makes me not think. Okay. It. Is. Good. This is a *good* song.

"Da, da, da, dadadada." I'm good at mouth drums. "I whistle in the thistle, and I stop at the rock . . ."

I'm almost done with the morning's rounds! Whoopee! I'll save checking on Kent until this afternoon, when it's dark. Because it's Christmas tomorrow and I'm busy, busy! Time for me to wrap Johanna's presents! Whee!

I'm flying like a bird through my winter lawn, into the foyer, down my hall with the bird in vines wallpaper, to my kitchen, and ah, there's the presents I made for Johanna . . . a sea-glass necklace (I need to replace her beloved orange one), a painting of the sea, and a candle holder set made from our favorite bordeaux wine. Made in my barn, just for you, Johanna. Now I wrap! And more coffee. Yeah!

Oh shit. Shit, shit, shit. Christmas is tomorrow. Do they expect me in Rye? That letter from my lawyer telling them to stay away and leave me alone, will they listen? Obey? Oblige? But I think, yes, where is it? Fuck. Yup. My lawyer forwarded me a letter from Mop. Lawyer told them they can only send things to me through her.

"AнHH!" I'm screaming. Can the neighbors hear? Calm down, there are no neighbors around. Wilsons are still in Costa Rica; they're there another year at least. Their house on timers, and whatever. The closest other neighbors are so long off, through twisted trails. Relax.

On to Christmas presents!

Whee!

A little over one year ago—A rainy June day

Damn. It's raining today. This is a down day. No light. No shine.

But it's June! And if it was sunny, like yesterday, which was an up day, and I thought, oh, fuck, I thought I could make it last. If it was still sunny, I could sit again with my flowers, smell the air around them, lick the wind of its salt and sugar. And now today, the rain, the dark corner in my bedroom, I will sit there, shadows covering me, and it will be safe. Here I go. Rounds are done. Three hours until next rounds and physical therapy.

I sit in my corner. Dark around me. Huddle knees to breasts, and if I moan, my voice drowns out Kent screaming from the basement, calling for me.

He's not calling for you, he's dead.

"Mmm, mmm, mmm," I'm moaning, okay, so neither one of us can tell if he is calling out or not. Let's not fight today.

Neither one of us? I'm you, and you are me; we're not us, we're the same.

Okay. Stop. Sit in the dark and try to nap.

In my kitchen, didn't I leave a green vase of pink peonies? I did. Yes, yesterday. If I bring those to Johanna, maybe that will lighten my mood. Your mood. My mood.

I'm leaving this corner. Going for the vase in the kitchen.

Yeah! Here they are, on MY kitchen table—not yours, Cate Dranal, fuck you for sitting in here—and ah, these pink petals smell so sweet, I'm going to draw this heavenly sugar scent up into my brain.

Okay, flowers, come on now, Johanna needs to smell you.

She's still not talking to me, her eyes still closed, she's still sleeping. I keep the nutrition and her hydration always constant, always good. She won't groan in her sleep when we do our three hours of physical therapy today, because the flowers will make her happy. It's me moving her muscles for her, and it's work for me, yes, but also, even though she doesn't realize, work for her.

Here now in Johanna's attic, I watch her breathe the scent of the peonies. How long? Don't know. But a noise and a darkness below are calling to me. I can't ignore the noise any longer.

Okay, I'm sorry, but Johanna, I need to go. It's a down day, darling, and you know what, you enjoy the flowers, okay. I'm going back to the dark corner in my bedroom to hold my knees before he starts screaming again or my throat swallows my face. I'll use the hall stairs down, because I need to check something in Mop's room. There's a noise coming from there. Remember how Mop used to call out to me for water late at night, "Aunty, Aunty, Aunty"? I miss her sweet voice. I think she's in there calling for me, "Aunty, Aunty, Aunty." No, no, no! Johanna, NO! She can't come visit us. No! I don't think Mop's really in her bedroom, but I'll go check. Okay, love. Now rest. Enjoy the flowers.

What is this noise coming from Mop's bedroom? Scratchy, whiny. Stop!

I'm closer now, down the hall stairwell to the second floor, not the stairwell in my bedroom, where I wish I could descend, straight to my dark corner. But this noise. I heard something faint this morning during rounds, but thought it was wind through the eaves. Now it's louder. I really don't want to look in Mop's bedroom, the place where Cate laid out Kent, dead, on Mop's bed. No! If I walk really slow past the doorway, maybe the noise will stop and Kent's body won't be in there again, dead again. But I need this noise to stop!

I'll pause here, outside Mop's room, and look in.

There's Mop's bed. Covers made. Pillows fluffed. Dust covering the dresser and desk. No one inside. But now that morning noise that grew louder is heard in a crystal clarity, ringing, singing, each syllable enunciated as a slap or morphed and scratched. All while I stand here staring in, hearing all, but seeing nothing.

"Aun . . . ty, Aun . . . ty, Aun . . . ty . . ." over and over. It's like this morphed sound of Mop calling for me that drops into a modulated, demented voice and then a record scratch. Here it comes again, calling to me straight from her empty pillow. "Aun . . . ty, Aun . . . ty, Aun . . . ty . . ."

I don't see anything or anyone in there. Right? Okay, breathe in. No Kent in the bed. But that noise! That calling! Is that him?

Oh my God, please stop! Blink your eyes! See nothing!

I can't step into this bedroom again. No more blood down my legs. All that started in this godforsaken room. Maybe the calling for "Aun . . . ty" is from my dead child, screaming from the grave, which was no grave, was flushed down the toilet once the mass passed. Maybe that child is mocking my love for a child who is not mine, is my sister's child. That must be what it is. My child laments from the sewer, angry that I love another child, who lives.

"Aun . . . ty, Aun . . . ty, Aun . . . ty . . ." It calls so loud and scratchy, demented, raking through my clawing hands, which cover my ears. I'm down on my knees in auditory pain.

I have no right to love my sister's daughter like she's my child. I have no right to love anyone. Look what happens when I do.

"Aun . . . ty, Aun . . . ty, Aun . . . ty . . ." Sweet voice—to modulated demented—to record scratch.

STOP! I stand up and run.

I'm storming in the barn. Grabbing wood and a nail gun. I'll board that damn room up, and the noise will stop.

Okay, calm down, breathe. It's okay, okay. You are okay. You are cradling everything you need. Remember what you learned in medical training. Remember! If you're feeling out of control, take decisive action. You can do this. Calm the fuck down!

I storm back up my stairs. I balance the loaded nail gun on top of two armloads of wood.

"Aun . . . ty, Aun . . . ty, Aun . . . ty . . ."

Stop mocking me! Stop mocking me!

I'm sorry, baby! I am! I have to do this.

I'm turning the corner of the hall, see Mop's room on the side, lit by the dim outside. Rain pricks at her windows. I can do this. I have to do this. You can do this. Go.

Slam! Board one, crosswise over the doorframe.

Nail gun, loaded and charged.

With a metal pop, I sink the first nail.

"Aun . . ."

That's right. Already your voice is muffled. This was a good idea.

I can't wait to finish and return to my dark, down-day corner.

Johanna, from her deep sleep, begged for Mop today. I know. She did, right? I've been all day in my corner thinking on this and on the screeching I boarded to block from Mop's bedroom. I walk past Johanna in the attic. I walk past her turquoise chair in the corner of the Mermaid Library. I walk to her ruined cottage, standing in the pricker bushes, looking at a hole.

My God, I kept Johanna separate from Mop, but I didn't mean to. Did I mean to? I kept her in a corner when we read in the center. I kept her in a cottage when we slept in the house. I keep her in the attic while we live out here in the world. I keep her to myself and away from Mop, so I can keep their love separate for me, but pull when I need. I need help.

No, you must fix this on your own. Go back to your room, go back. A whistle of wind in the trees, is that Kent calling my name? Yes, it might be. Yes. No. He's dead. I'll go check.

Aun . . . ty, Aun . . . ty . . . no!

Not again!

Three months ago

The bitch in the barn with no muscles just woke up! Just now! This minute! She startled me as I moved to put new sheets in her cabinet. Wow! She's screaming at me, but she can't see anything. Her vision is blurred and her eyes mostly shut. She's trying to lift her head, but she can't. She has no muscles left.

Wow!

Doesn't this mean Johanna will wake up too?

Only one thing to do with the bitch.

I reach under her bed. Extract a vial of pentobarbital, jam a quarter round in her neck, and race up to see if my Johanna is emerging too. I hope this vial's potency hasn't degraded over time. I'll monitor.

Johanna is somewhat waking, too, I think. To be safe, I'll chain her leg to the bed so she doesn't stumble around and fall down the stairs when I'm not watching.

And still, that garbage human in the barn gets to wake up in a more definite way than my precious Johanna? No!

No song for the bitch today! I will not sing for the bitch today, or play my mouth drums. No! No, no, no. Not fair. I whistle in the thistle, nope. Not for her today. How many times has she heard that song, every day for close to two years? She loves the number three. Maybe I've sung my two-line with drums song for her three million times. And she's addicted to it, that's why she woke up, because she's dying to sing along. Well, no, no song for you today, bitch. Go back to sleep.

Does pentobarbital's effectiveness degrade over time?

Did it work?

I should know.

I was a nurse.

CHAPTER TWENTY-FOUR
AUNTY

Yesterday

"I whistle in the thistle, and I stop at the rock," I'm singing to *her*. Did she flinch at my voice? I sometimes suspect she's awake. Perhaps she fakes her condition? I wonder if I should jam another dose in her neck to be sure.

Checking her body under her white linens, which she doesn't deserve, I see only the typical twitches her body makes, driven by her central nervous system, but not by intentional command, I think. *You could be wrong. Telling yourself things you want to believe.* Stop. Hurricane Angelo is going to hit hard. I need to test the generator to ensure this side room retains energy.

There goes her fluttering hand, rippling her covers, like a flustered mouse trapped in a pocket. Her breathing rattles as normal, check. Her pupils jump beneath closed lids, check. Her blood pressure, stable. Her pulse, steady. Check, fucking check.

This room in my barn smells of sweat today—this is new.

Is she awake?

No movement. No, can't be. Maybe, yes.

That is sweat. Definitely a heavy wetness on the air, denser when I sniff her pits. Her hospital dressing gown is damp. Shit. Now I'll have to rotate and change her. Bitch.

This is the part I hate most about caring for this beast. I unchain her so I can move and roll her over, make sure she gets no bedsores, and prep to change her dressing gown, also deal with her catheter. This is a vulnerable time: she's unchained, but I'll work fast. It's absurd to think I'm vulnerable. She's in a drug coma. But is she?

Is she?

The light in here is natural day. I haven't flicked on the overhead, no need. I prefer the mellow amber, as God intended indoors and out. An even, sedate amber, yes, is nice, but it is ruined by the stench of her sweat. So now it feels like dead amber.

This psycho ruins everything.

Is there anything worse than having to change her vile catheter? Nothing. Why do I do this to myself? I should stop feeding her, put a pillow over her blob face, bury her behind the barn, as I planned, along with . . . Fuck this. I've been thinking about it for weeks now, months. Mop hasn't noticed the two-people grave I've been digging out behind the back of the barn, beyond the hedge of brambles. The bitch needs to go. But Mop has seen her. Mop will ask questions. Mop is a problem. When she's back from Cape Cod, I need to deal with her.

I guess I'm gone now. A different person. Lost to who I was. I'm a plotter, and for no reason.

No. Stop. Fight. You can be better again. Mop will help you.

Maybe Mop wants to turn me in. Does Mop want to turn me in?

If Mop turned you in, you'd get the help you need. This is no way to live.

I'm staring at the wall in the side room, the side with the boarded window. Dipshit bitch is still out cold, but I swear she flinches when I touch her. I'm almost sure she's faking. I need my instruments by the boarded window. I'll test a few things.

I move around the foot of her medical bed, stand before the boarded window.

What's that? Was that flashing outside? So clear, the flashes cut through a crack in the boards and through this sedated amber room. White on yellow.

I'm peering through cracks between boards. I can't see much at this angle and with such little space for viewing, but as I squint to perfect my limited vision, I'm sure. Yes, indeed, from high in my house, in the attic where Johanna sits in the rocker, yes, there come flashes of light.

Johanna is signaling her flashlight "I love yous"? To whom?

I look closer, squinting and squishing my face for vision of my front door through this crack.

Mop. My God. That's Mop, looking up at the attic from outside! She's back from the Cape early. Oh no. Oh no. Oh no. She'll find Johanna! She'll never understand. I need to get there, explain.

"Hey, bitch," comes *her* voice behind me.

She was awake. She is awake. Oh, shit, she's awake. She's still unchained.

"That's right, bitch. You heard me," she says to my back. I'm wedged between her on the bed and the window, which I face. She should be unconscious in the hospital bed. She's unchained. *Oh God, no, she's unchained.*

The sheets scratch the still air with her quick movement on the bed. The bed shakes, metal scratching the floor. Sounds like she's positioning and steadying herself on her knees.

"You fucking bitch. Yeah. You bet. I've been awake for months. Exercising my muscles when you're not here. Been waiting on a perfect time, when I'm unlocked too long and you're distracted, and here's my chance."

As I turn, she jumps from the bed and out of the room.

Gray clouds in my mouth. I can't breathe.

I round the end of the bed and realize I stalled too long in gray clouds. She's returned, and she's armed.

The hatchet swings, thwack, hits my skull.

I'm falling, hit the rails of the hospital bed along the way.

Unsure of my injury, I'm seeing only black and warping light.

What a merciful release, my insanity fades and sanity is attained in this white, white light. What drips from my brow, what liquid cascades down, I do not care.

CHAPTER TWENTY-FIVE

MOP

Present time

Everything fell apart fast after the woman in the barn entered the attic with Aunty's hatchet, bloodied. I don't know how she knew to find my companion and me here—perhaps she heard us. Maybe Aunty narrated to her as she attended her rounds, giving away her sister's condition in the attic. Aunty doesn't realize how she talks aloud, her inner thoughts.

I also didn't then know where Aunty was, or what this woman did to her with that bloody hatchet. The woman entered, blood splattered on her white-and-blue dressing gown, eyes wild and crazed, and demanded I unlock my mother's ankle from the bed. She held the hatchet over her head as her motivating force.

If I were to believe in such things, I might believe that the witchcraft that raised my mother's body from the sea came with consequences, such as attendant evil as embodied in this bloody, hatchet-wielding woman. Like in *Pet Sematary* when the dead child rises from the grave as a tricked blessing, for he's depraved and soulless and slices Achilles' heels, literally and figuratively. But I don't believe in such things. I don't accept, today, one day later, although she lies upon my legs passed out, the hurricane rioting above, that this companion of mine is my mother.

She is awakening, out here in the hurricane, a day after I found her. She arches her torso like she's posing cobra in yoga.

"Mop," she says without the slur she had when she first said my name in the attic.

Yesterday, the hatchet woman burst in on me finding my companion alive in the attic. Everything was quick, but then prolonged and bizarre after that. It feels like the last day has lasted ten years. What she put us through, the depravity, the insanity, what I've seen and heard in the last day—I will never be the same. I can either choose to remain at the bottom of my own inner well, lost, or I can grow strong and resolute. I have no other choices: such trauma means I'll be planted in one of those extremes. I fight for the latter. I fight for strength and conviction.

"Unchain her and walk to the barn!" Crazy Hatchet screamed at us in the attic. She hoisted the hatchet high above her head, ready to strike.

Thankfully the ring of house keys I snatched from the pink birdhouse had one for my companion's ankle chain lock.

I carry-walked her, slow and gentle down the stairs, while Crazy Hatchet followed on our heels, laughing every time we tripped.

"She can't walk well, and I'm the one who had no PT! Weak Vandonbeer, a mutt's mix of races, really. Mutts, all you fucking Vandonbeers."

I have no idea what she meant by any of this. I concentrated on getting my companion to the barn. I didn't ask where Aunty was. I didn't want to know. But Crazy Hatchet offered anyway.

After we reached the center of the barn, by way of the unchained front barn doors—for it appeared Crazy Hatchet disrupted Aunty midrounds—Crazy told me to sit my companion and myself on the floor of the barn in the center. Two stalls to our right, two to our left. Next she tied my arms behind my back with quarter-inch rope, then my companion's, then our legs. Next she duct-taped our mouths. I had to comply because she kept the hatchet out of my reach and stood between me and my companion, who was too weak to stand and run on her own. If I didn't comply with being tied, I wouldn't have been able to save my companion from a hatchet swing.

"Do you know where Lynette Viola Vandonbeer is?" Crazy Hatchet singsonged, standing and lording over us, while we sat on the concrete barn floor.

I shook my head in fast micromovements, as if shivering in a Sub-Zero freezer.

"Oh," she said, puffing out her chest and standing tall, as if my answer truly surprised her. "Okay," she said and turned and walked over to the shipping-crate stage in the corner, the one Manny and I used to use. As she wore a blue-and-white hospital gown, tied in the back, the fabric didn't cover her spine or naked ass crack. "Your aunt's dead, over there." She pointed with the hatchet, toward the side room, her back still to us, and nonchalant.

My companion gasped and gagged under her duct tape; I stared on. I didn't know what to believe. I wiggled my toes in my companion's ribs to tell her I was here with her and to be quiet. She seemed to get the message and swallowed her tears. The bond between mother and daughter has been proven to be interweaved at the literal cellular level. Pieces of my mother's biology are in me, and, true fact, pieces of my cells are in her brain, racing around in the neurons of her mind. Perhaps this is why I struggled at such a profound and disturbing level in trying to accept her death, for I knew in my body and soul and mind, cells and breath, it was not true.

Crazy Hatchet dragged the stage closer to us in center and as she did, the prop box atop shifted, and the sailing-sails curtains swayed.

"What's in this box? Hmm," she said, calm, disconnected to the fact that blood soiled her dressing gown. She fingered the hatchet by her side, rocked bare feet like a savage, and held two women in ropes and duct tape in the center of a barn. In flipping off the lid, she shook her head and *pff*ed, as if indicating what she saw was obvious. "My dress and underwear. Of course."

She held her find for us to see: that awful, hand-stitched, navy-blue-on-blue gown I saw her wear two years ago on the rocks. As she pulled it from the box, rust-red and brown bloodstains blotched both blues.

She extracted her dress and underwear from the prop box, lumping them on the floor of the stage, and then sent forth a horrifying laugh. How her shrieking laugh reverberates to me now, one day later, as I scrape my fingernails into the muddy dirt, outside the burned basement, trying to lift my body off the ground while a woman in black holds Crazy Hatchet in a standoff by aiming a nail gun at her face. That shriek, here by the hole, cuts through thunder, slices sideways rain, so shrill and insane.

And yesterday she sure did shriek in her laughter on that sailing sails–curtained stage. My and my companion's shoulders rose around our ears to muffle the painful screech. Nothing worked. Then she stopped. Yanked her bloody hospital gown off, pulled on the dried-blood, homemade gown, and hiked up her yellow underwear. After pacing the stage like an inpatient in a corner of an asylum's rec room and staring dumblike with dead eyes to a pigeon in the rafters, cooing at him in a lethargic bird language as he flew beam to beam, she plunked on her ass in a *pfft*, landing in a thud on the shipping-crate stage. Fist to chin and elbow to thigh, she sat staring at me and my companion, blinking every few seconds, for several endless hours. As in, the remainder of the day and into the night, she stared and stared and we could do nothing, say nothing.

Well, that's not entirely true. I was doing something. With my feet.

At some point around sevenish, I'm guessing, based on the lower lighting, my iPhone rang in my back pocket. All day it had been vibrating with text messages I knew had to be from Manny, wondering where I was, so I knew that sometime around dinner he'd call, concerned. And indeed, he did. Before Crazy Hatchet could explode, as her immediate red face and jerk of the head indicated she would, I shook my head in a way to tell her it was okay.

"Where's your phone!" she thundered. But like a dentist, she asked a question to a patient without the ability to answer back. Realizing this, she scooched her ass across the stage and stood. Her wacko dress scrunched up as she did, revealing her yellow underwear. She stomped over to me, pushed me face-first into the concrete, and since I couldn't brace my face and not wanting to break my nose, I turned my head, forcing my cheek to crack on the concrete. Fishing around in my ass, she found my phone. It rang and rang and rang.

"Says Manny. Who's that?" she yelled.

Still, I could not answer.

She ripped the duct tape from my mouth.

"Who is Manny! Will he be looking for you?"

"Yes! Yes! He will look for me if I don't answer!" I said, because I did not want Manny coming here, looking for me. I didn't want him hurt by this awful woman. I needed to get a message to him to not come, and bonus, if I could send a coded message, to call the cops.

"Ha! You think I'm an idiot. You're not going to answer or send him a message. How hilarious!" And that shriek again. Oh, how it cuts my soul in long strips to remember. So high, so evil and aching.

"He will start looking for me soon!" I pleaded.

"Whatever. I'm not dumb. All you young bitches think I don't know technology. I'll text him back for you. He's the one you were fucking against the side of the barn the other day. I get it."

Sitting next to me on the concrete, taunting me with the phone in her hands, she showed me every move she made on my phone, as if I were her best friend in the world, surfing the internet for hot guys together. She waited out the ringing, and presumably Manny left a message. Then she went to my text screen and easily found Manny's last message: Mop, aren't you coming back for dinner? Pick up. I'm starting to worry.

Then she wrote back as if she were me: Staying at my aunt's tonight. She's sad. I'll call in morning. Don't worry.

My only hope was that Manny would detect the problem with the text, the fact that "I" referred to Aunty as "my aunt," which I had never before done. He should have remembered that I always called her Aunty, like a proper name. But wasn't it delusional hope that he'd somehow jump to the unbelievable conclusion that I was being held by a madwoman with a hatchet in "my aunt's" barn? Indeed, delusional, strained, contrived. Telepathy offered better odds, and I can't perform telepathy. He'd never come to that conclusion about the text.

Crazy Hatchet replaced the duct tape and took my iPhone back to the stage and spent the whole night reading the internet, interjecting surprise, although subdued and apathetic, at stories she missed in her confinement in Aunty's barn. She'd *pfft* and say "of course" or "I knew it" to whatever news she read, revealing the high opinion she held of herself: she knew all and all possible outcomes. So superior of knowledge, an omniscient, doubt-free being in a bloody gown. She regaled us, too, with celebrity obituaries and ended each reading with a high, scratching, rattling laughter that shreds my soul to remember. At around, guessing here, maybe one in the morning, my companion passed out on my legs, which was a good thing, for her body covered my working feet.

CHAPTER TWENTY-SIX

MOP

Present time

This morning we awoke on the floor of the barn to the sounds of weak moaning from Aunty in the side room. I still didn't know her condition. I guessed it was bad, based on the blood on Crazy Hatchet's discarded hospital gown. I and my companion stirred on the floor. I hadn't realized I'd fallen asleep until screeching awoke me.

"You DIE!" Hatchet yelled from the stage, cranking her head toward the side room, through which we could not see, for the doorway was down the wall, away from us.

But Aunty's moaning continued. Crazy Hatchet again scooched off the stage, stomped into the side room, and what I heard next curdled my soul. My companion stiffened and shook on my legs.

A thwack, thwack, clatter and cling of metal beat down upon the moaning, a fleshy metal thwacking, until the moaning stopped. Next came an exaggerated throat clearing, deep inhale, and forceful spit.

"No more from you, whore!" Crazy Hatchet said in the side room. And when she reappeared before us, fresh blood splattered her blue-blue gown and sprinkled her face and hair. My companion sobbed under her duct tape, convulsing on my legs. I stared up at the woman who just beat my aunt to a very presumed death with the metal bedpan in her bloody hands.

She bounced her weapon in one palm, holding it with the other. Blood plunked down and splattered in front of me. The woman ignored my companion and addressed only me.

"I've been thinking all night," she said, grinding her teeth in a literal and loud way, like trying to scrape ink paper for a dentist fitting your mouth for implants.

"And I have to kill you both, you know that. I can't have any witnesses. And it's perfect, makes a perfect three: you, your mother, your aunt. One, two, three . . . one, two, three," she said in a trailing of thoughts she seemed to have with herself. She lowered her head to us on the floor. "But you deserve to know what happened that night, two years ago, and why I will shut you and your dumb mother up forever, because I can't be blamed, I can't be framed. That's what I've decided, and you need to know why. So we're going to have a play. Manny won't be coming to see, boo hoo. He tried to come here last night, but I stopped him. He's dead behind the barn now. Right there, right out back," she said, pointing with a lazy arm to behind the barn. "So you have no reason to live anymore, bitch, and you will watch my play and then die. Boo-fucking-hoo." She turned to her stage and readied items she'd set up, mumbling to herself a chant, "One, two, three . . . one, two, three . . . one, two, three . . ."

My mother used to offer cushioned warnings about how Aunty Liv would sometimes have "outbursts" or go catatonic and stare. She'd say this after catching me staring off into the middle distance, and when she did, she'd hug me and sit me down by pressing on both my arms. "Babycakes, you know your aunty Liv, she gets quiet, too, and stares like this. Doctors say she can get catatonic. This is why she's a nurse, darling. She says the control and concentration helps her to stay straight. But this scares me. Are you okay?"

"Mom," I'd say, "I'm just thinking on a question raised in my book. That's all. Trying to figure on the answer."

"My smarty girl, my thinky thinker," she'd say, and kiss my nose.

This morning, my companion mother couldn't sit me down and kiss my nose to break my catatonic state. I just stared, unable to begin the thought of Manny lifeless outside. An impossibility. Something I'd never agree to believe.

My mother shook her body against my legs to nudge me to blink. But there was no way I'd blink first, not before the bitch on the stage, who stared back. Who would be the victor in our now declared battle to the death? I told her with my eyes that I'd be the vicious victor. Whether out of defense or vengeance, I fixed upon destroying her. How dare she say such a thing about Manny. Manny could not die. He is eternal.

Crazy blinked. I stared on. I turned off my thoughts on Manny, on her claiming to murder him behind the barn. I watched her as she moved around her stage, preparing herself for her one-woman play.

No idea why she felt she had to show us what happened *that* night, the night of the fire. I only know that insanity creates fabrications of reason in each person's mind so inexplicable to the outside, there can be no way to diagram any sort of rationale. I steadied myself to watch, so she would focus only on me watching, and not on my feet. Calming my breathing and lowering my eyes, I gave the appearance of meditation so intense, Gandhi would be proud.

This was this morning, and already the hurricane had started. Wind picked up outside the barn, not in the riotous way it is right now, at night, at the height of the storm, but in a rising strength, enough to know that children would be at Ocean Lawn flying kites, high and higher.

Crazy Hatchet moved to the stage, still holding her hatchet, pointing the blade at me. A slap of wind shook the rafters. I continued my low-lid stare; she jabbed the air with the hatchet in my direction. My companion stiffened; this threat to her daughter stopped her crying. I could almost *feel* my companion embolden, as only a mother can. A mother in protection. And yet, in that moment, this morning, I could not bring myself to look at her with daughter eyes in pleading, as a child, begging for protection, for I could only accept her as a vessel of a human, no more than my companion.

Crazy Hatchet flung one side of the sailing curtain farther open to reveal she'd set some items up in the night. Atop a cardboard box, she'd duct-taped a broke-neck, balding doll in a sitting position. Manny and I used to employ this doll in our plays—LexiCat, we called her. A couple of the ubiquitous tissue rose petals from our rose-thief-fox play stuck in her hair. Crazy had obviously extracted LexiCat from the prop box. She moved around slump-shouldered and lethargic, as if this entire act, the self-imposed drudgery of her having to put on her show and her having to be in the barn with her hostages, bored her.

"That's your bitch mother, *Johanna Vandonbeer Pentecost*, right there on your aunt's stove. I duct-taped her on the burners. Remember, Johanna?" She addressed my companion this time, and *pfft*ed out her lazy nonchalance. Her chronic *pfft*ing was a nervous tic. She indicated that doll LexiCat, duct-taped to the cardboard box, was a rendition of my mother duct-taped on top of Aunty's black gas stove.

"Now I will play the role of me and your whore aunt slash sister," she said, nodding to me and then my mother. She blinked three times, slow, and seemed like she was grazing in a field. She swished the other sailing-sail curtain farther open to reveal another box and a chair behind it, so a table and a chair, and a basket of laundry on the box. She took three steps to the chair, sat, and started folding the laundry in the basket: underwear and towels. She hummed the mellow carnival tune of Paul Simon's "America," the cadence one for a night spin on a slow carousel.

"I was innocently folding the laundry in your aunt's kitchen, folding her underwear, well, in threes," she said, adding her awful laugh, as a distinct spike to the otherwise slow, bored monotone in which she spoke. I think my eardrums shriveled this time.

I didn't need to analyze the insanity. To fold another woman's underwear in her kitchen, after duct-taping her sister to the stove, this was something I held no doubts about.

"*Mmm, mmm, mmm, mmm, mmm, mmm, mmm, mmm, mmm,*" she hummed again, and now I don't think I can ever hear another Paul Simon song without thinking of a horror house of mirrors. It's too bad, for he's a true poet.

"Now," she said, standing. "Pretend I'm still sitting there, being good, folding her laundry." She towered above me from the stage, me still slumped, tied up, on the ground of the barn. "And well, there I was, folding underwear, minding my business and humming. Your mother, you, Johanna," she said, pointing the bloody hatchet at my companion, "were helping me concentrate by staying good and quiet and taped on the stove."

"Ayup," she said, swiveling around toward the laundry basket on the table and the phantom ghost of herself sitting there. Sashaying the blood-crusty skirt of her homemade dress, she continued, "So there I was." At the edge of the stage, she paused, and in a slow cautious bend, set her hatchet on the corner of the shipping-crates stage, wormed her hand, still cautious, behind the folds in the curtains, and pulled out one of Aunty Liv's yellowware bowls. She must have retrieved it from the house while I dozed off in the night. She bounced the bowl with one hand into the palm of her other, like she did the bedpan.

"But in came your whore aunt and ruined everything! She beat me with a bowl!"

Crazy Hatchet leaped toward the mock cardboard table so unexpected and fast, holding the bowl aloft in a gesture that she was about to beat her own shadow in the chair, that she miscalculated her steps, wedging her still bare feet in the slats of the shipping crate.

A hush overcame the barn. I moved my ankles and feet faster. Had I been freed in full of my ankle tie, I would have taken my chance and run then. It's a good thing I didn't, for a million psychics would fail to anticipate what was about to happen next.

A knocking at the barn's front door cut a quick hush in the barn. We must have missed it before, Hatchet's voice and her shrill having masked it and also masked the roll of the tires and quiet engine of the car in the driveway that preceded the knocking. We missed such noise given her consuming monologue and her spike of screeching laughter. And so, evil thwarted her own self.

The barn door creaked open, then flung wide, and the bright morning sun invaded and blinded the darkened barn interior. Wind bent the highest part of the trees outside and loosened yard objects, such as Aunty's various garden flags, flew about behind the man in a green coverall at the entrance. Also behind him, my red Volvo.

The mechanic had come to return my Volvo. He'd said in a message somewhere in the last week that he'd drop it off when it was ready, and he'd walk the three miles back to the garage, for he liked this stretch of road. Being in the haze I'd been in over the last week, I hadn't called him back to warn him about the chains at the end of Aunty's driveway, and in that moment, looking up at him from the floor of the barn, I realized she'd unchained them on the night we ate pizza in Rye. She must have left them unlocked when she returned. I don't know why. I can only speculate on her lessening defenses.

I assume he heard the commotion in the barn, knocked, heard more commotion, and opened the doors. Crazy Hatchet, about twenty feet from him, her leg wedged wrongwise in the shipping crate, didn't hesitate. So while he startled at the sight he stumbled upon, his mouth wide open to see a bloody woman in a bloody gown, leg stuck in a make-do stage and two women on the floor tied and duct-taped, she snatched her hatchet on the cardboard-box table and threw it like a master Indian hunter with such force and precise aim, it hit the mark on the center of his face and stayed.

Aunty in the side room awaited her chance too. At this very moment, she limp-crawled quick from her confinement and out, past the split mechanic and into the sun. From the crown of her dented head dripped blood, down onto her shoulders and torso, like a red candle, melted of the flame. Aunty didn't turn to look at me and my companion. Didn't look at the mechanic. She crawled like a bloody animal, hands and knees on the seashells and pebbles in her driveway, and disappeared in shades of sunlight that blinded our darkened pupils. Growing hurricane wind lifted her gray hair, blending her in the coming storm.

Crazy Hatchet went wild, screaming and screeching, "You bitch," as if her voice would slow Aunty's slothful, yet seemingly fruitful, escape. Hatchet worked her leg, trying to free herself, and this is when I didn't waste another minor second on watching the mechanic twitch or animal Aunty disappear into stormy sunlight. This was the best chance I'd get to haul out. I was not only desperate to free myself and my companion but also desperate to check on the wellness of Manny.

Now, tonight, in this hurricane, I bring myself to think of that moment, the seconds before standing, horror-struck I might find Manny, dead behind the barn. This something in thought so unbearable to me, as if I lost my own soul. My real soul, detached, dissolved, making me nothing but skin. This possible reality was so far beyond frightening, a fraction of acknowledging it diminished the horror of the scene in the barn and the tremendous risk I was about to take for me and my companion. But the time was prime, no better moment than when Crazy threw the hatchet at the mechanic and wailed and flailed about in a riotous furor over Aunty. I'd been waiting for something, didn't know what, but that had to be the moment, and so, I acted.

Turns out, there is something I did learn, an invaluable and, turns out, practical—not metaphysical or philosophical—lesson in tutoring those human-trafficking refugees. Seems I did get their backstories. I was listening, storing their stories to the backup hard drive of my mind. One story flitted to the active hard drive of my mind during the time I sat tied in the barn.

Pradina was one of the refugee sex-trafficking victims I tutored. I coached her through a reading of my tattered copy of *The Mummy Market*, which is criminally out of print, for it's a classic.

Pradina, a sixteen-year-old girl who dreamed of competitive swimming, was snagged from a corner in Honduras, about a two-hour walk from her two-hundred-square-foot shack in the mountains. She used to talk of a monkey who stole her breakfast banana and papaya bread every morning, so she walked hungry to the city factory in which she cleaned bathrooms. She did laugh about the monkey and her long mountain walk, so I assume part of her home life, she did indeed mourn. I connected with Pradina over her wish to swim. In retrospect, the perspective she gave me was a thousand-volt lesson on privilege, how I shouldn't waste it and how I should spread my born-into gifts: Pradina had thousands of roadblocks and hurdles just to be able to find a muddy pond in which to swim one lap, whereas, if I wanted to swim competitively, I need only train off the coast of two estates, in one of two Rye pools, Princeton's pool, and register in any race among thousands of options.

Pradina had been tied behind her back and at the ankles once, after being held for three months in a literal pit and raped every day by a man named Stink. Stink was known as the "prep cook," charged with preparing victims for a trafficking ring's trade. On the day the ring was set to transfer Pradina to another pit, Stink tied her up, like an animal about to be thrust in a pile for a barbecue. Pradina said people tied as such waste their energy on the hands, trying to deknot with fingers. But, to Pradina's teachings, your legs are "powerful trunks of muscles," and if you're tied at the ankles, like she was, like I was, best to keep flaring the heels out and out. This option is usually undetectable and will loosen the rope fibers while also working up lubricating sweat. In her case, her legs were lazily tied together, as were mine, one rope around both ankles, not crossed in the middle. This parallel between Pradina's and my ankle tying gave me confidence to focus on my ankles and nothing else.

"Do not focus on the horror of what happened or the fear of what is to come. Focus only on the best activity with the best potential to escape; this will give you your greatest asset, a sense of control, and thus the greatest chance to win," Pradina had said. "Focus and stay on course with that one activity. Truly, it is mind over matter." Her words echoed to me in the barn like ancient verse, prophetic advice, divine direction. There are no words more pure than Pradina's. In this, I do believe.

In Pradina's story, about an hour or two into her truck ride from one pit to another, her right heel wormed out. With her legs free, she scooted to the end of the open bed of the moving truck and, when slow enough, jumped, rolled down an embankment, and ran with her hands tied for four hours through jungle and farmland. The best part of Pradina's story was how she rested on a rock on the edge of jungle and open field. Dozing for a second, she was awakened by the sound of scraping down the tree behind her. A monkey with nimble fingers worked the loosening of the rope on her wrists and took her rope, scurrying back up the tree, freeing Pradina's hands. When she thought the hero or thief, whatever he was, was long gone, a banana dropped from the canopy above, where his monkey face appeared through the thickness of leaves, and his monkey hands poked out to dangle his stolen rope. He either paid Pradina for the rope with a banana or mocked her. She ate the banana, thinking of her monkey in the mountains and how this hero-thief brother monkey might be part of the monkey network, and this was the network's way of saying thanks for all those stolen breakfasts back home. Thereafter, Pradina somehow found a missionary who connected her with the UN. I'm not sure of the legalities—they aren't the point. As for Pradina's belief in a network of brother monkeys and nature's connection to all, I did fall into her belief when she told the story, but then I pushed it away as fantasy. But today, I see Pradina's wisdom, and I agree with her fantastical belief. Nature saved Pradina. And nature would save me. I believed. *I believe.*

This morning, I finished working my ankles while I wished for a nimble-fingered brother monkey to untie my wrists. Pradina's story lent me the forethought to forgo my hands and focus all my energy on my feet. She gave me hope. She gave me focus.

I did what Pradina did. But I had it better than her: I had my mother's beach-glass stall right behind me.

My mother had done the same as me, for when I nudged her a couple of times as a way to say, *do what I'm doing*, she listened to the message of a daughter's touch. The second Crazy Hatchet loosened herself from the stage, limp-springing (I think she broke an ankle) toward the open barn doors toward the mechanic or Aunty, I'm not sure, I sprang and ran to the beach-glass stall, and my companion did too. *My companion, my mother, my love.*

With my hands still tied in back, I grabbed my mother's wire cutters, fished the point end into my back pocket, and, nodding my duct-taped mouth to my companion, indicated we needed to run for the back barn door, which was closer to us than to Crazy Hatchet.

We made no mistakes of hesitations and ran for the back door. Aunty had failed to re-bar the back or Crazy Hatchet had unbarred it or Manny had, and if the last were true, that lent to Crazy's story that he was dead. I shook to push the back exit and find it unbarred.

My body did not hesitate to escape, but my mind held back, afraid to find Manny lifeless.

Something bit me in the calf on the way out. It was not until we were in the sunlight that I realized she'd flung her hatchet clear across the barn at me, having retrieved it from the mechanic. The only fortunate part of the blow was that the distance thrown diminished the force. Had she been closer, my leg would have been severed.

I scoured behind the barn for Manny, ignoring the searing pain in my leg. The competing needs to escape and find Manny distracted me from collecting the hatchet in the doorway.

My frantic search was fast and thorough, for my companion and I had no time to lose. There was no disturbance behind the barn. No body, no footprints, no broken plants, no moved bricks, nothing. So Hatchet either lied or Manny lay elsewhere.

From within the barn, I heard a scowling howl. "Let me go!" Hatchet screamed. Then a thud, which I presume was her falling. Perhaps the mechanic grabbed her ankle in his last dying act. Maybe Aunty returned. Maybe one was our hero. I don't know, but whatever happened within the barn, the thudding, the scraping, yelling I heard, allowed enough time to lapse for me and my companion to make it to the burned-out basement hole, jump into the false door, nearly breaking our legs in the fall, for we couldn't use our tied hands to climb down. Underground and hidden, I wormed the wire cutters from my back pocket, turned my companion around by directing her with head nods, turned my back to her back, and clipped with care at her wrist ties. Once free, she removed the duct tape from our mouths and cut me free. Then we worked to tie a tourniquet around the bleeding hatchet wound on my calf—using the kerchief holding her hair back—and shivered together, in disbelief, grief, mournful reunion, blood loss, muscle fatigue, hunger, thirst, and fear.

All day went by. We did not speak. She was weak, and we didn't want our voices to carry on the wind. And besides, about ten minutes in, about when I thought we could test our luck, haul out, and escape to Manny's, my companion passed out. I couldn't carry her out. We were stuck. And having been separated from her for what felt like an eternity over two years, there was not a chance I would test the waters on my own without her. The wind whipped up as the day bore on, and the witch woman yelled along with the wind in search of us. If you didn't know there was a hidden hatch door, you wouldn't know we could get underground, so I believe she passed by our spot, which is hidden by vegetation, several times.

I believe she scoured Aunty's house ten, twenty times.

Now, I wait in an impossible hope for Aunty to somehow save us in her death state. All day in the hole, every single damn time my companion awoke and I thought I could convince her to use all her strength and follow me out, Crazy Hatchet's voice would near and kill the plan. And ten minutes later, my companion would again pass out. All day, cycles like this. The sounds of Hatchet bleeding to us underground, above the increasing winds. By some miracle, the blood from my wound had collected in my scrunchy sock and my sneaker until I was in the hole, at which point it flowed all around until tourniqueted. So no blood trail betrayed our whereabouts.

Scraping, cycling, fitful winds sang songs of rising laments, all day and into the night. I begged the Ocean Goddess to save us. My companion dozed in and out of consciousness, her head in my lap.

CHAPTER TWENTY-SEVEN
AUNTY

Earlier today

I'm lying on the floor of my barn's side room. *You're lying on the floor of your barn's side room.* She's hatcheted my skull; she's beaten me with a bedpan. I've entered my death process. I'm dying. *You're dying.* I won't, I can't, I won't, *you can't,* let Mop and Johanna die. I won't, *you won't,* give in to this lovely darkness. I won't fail, *you won't fail,* I can't fail, *you can't fail,* to make the call this time. It won't be like with Daddy. No gray clouds of moldy cotton. Only darkness awaits me after I finish this one last, necessary task, that is all. I just need to crawl into the light, now flooding, a man standing in the mouth of light. He's in green—perhaps he's the gravedigger. He's opened a door for me to crawl out and find a phone. And then, then darkness may shroud me.

Go! Now! Crawl out now! I need to go, now, and crawl out, now.

With the aches of a thousand flus and every virus I've ever had, my muscles tight and resisting, inflamed they feel, under my fire skin, I press up to palms and knees and push. I'm an animal, all right, dying and draining, muscles failed and failing, forward pressing, repeat. A rising fire in my throat foretells of retching.

I pass the gravedigger in his green suit. He's on the floor now. I keep going. Pulsing virus balls ache within my body. Blood flows anew from the gash in my skull and covers my dead eye socket in a liquid mesh.

Get in the house. The cordless in the library. And then you'll be best positioned, in there, to spring your premade grave.

Save them. Spring the grave. In a limited range of movements. In one confined room. Triage. Efficiency. I'm a nurse. *You're a nurse.*

I press on through my foyer. I believe screaming or wind or both is behind me. Blood drops from my face to my white marble foyer.

The library. Turn right. I turn right and enter the library.

The cordless under my Roosevelt gun. Perfect. *The cordless under your Roosevelt gun, perfect.*

I can't let Mop and Johanna die. I won't let that happen. With my literal last breath, I must make the call. I will not fail this time. Not like with Daddy. *You cannot fail this time. Not like with Daddy.* No gray clouds, no loss of consciousness. Fight. *Fight.* I press. *Keep pressing.* My muscles pulse up on my inner skin, breaking through fat and cartilage.

I nudge the table with the cordless with my bloodied head. Next I ram harder, using every ounce of strength remaining. The cordless drops to the floor, beside my right hand.

Thank goodness the batteries didn't pop out.

And now, with that motion, the remote to the CD player falls too. Blood from my skull drips on the phone and CD player remote.

With the last ounce—as in, it hurts so much to do this, requiring so much effort, I gag, cough, and choke to near final death—I press one button on speed dial. My hand then falls of its own will upon the remote, and "Die Rose," always primed to play, blares from the speakers at full volume.

As I listen to the forever ringing of my placed speed-dial call, "Die Rose" plays on in instruments and foreign operatic words, and I recite the poem lyrics in English in my head. My eyes droop, my shoulders droop, my body is falling toward the floor. Oh, "Die Rose," you accompany this never-ending fall, fall, falling to the floor and the never-ending ring, ring, ringing of the phone. Your lyrics about a regretful rose about to die.

The answering machine at Rye picks up after nine million rings in eternity. But I am in free fall to the floor, and "Die Rose" is weaving knots of foreboding in my mind. I can't speak now, can't say a word to the woman who I know will listen to this recording first. She is far away from me now, three galaxies of telescoping darkness, maybe, and I am listening to the ting-ting of piano keys and opera poetry in some unknowable space while I continue falling through my own floor, through the basement, the earth, and out beyond. But I know her. I know her secret. I know she's proud for what she did, despite being kicked out of the church for it. And I don't blame her. I'm proud for her too. She's a relentless, tireless, constantly suspicious, headstrong woman. If anyone is going to figure out why I say no words, for I can't, it's her. I'll pass the baton to Aunt Sister Mary to save our shared niece, our girl, and save our Johanna. I wish I could scream, wish I could say the word *help*, but I can't. I couldn't dial more than one programmed button. If I could, I would have dialed 911. With my final breaths, which are shallow and nasal only, I send a wordless SOS to the only one who will agonize and overthink on the words unsaid.

Leaving the phone line open, I try, although I know I'll fail, to crawl up the wall, which holds my glass-cased Roosevelt gun. If only I could crank down on the glass box and open my grave. Crawl out there and die in my intended death well. Above me would be my spiral of sunflowers, which I would command. And I would at once strip this ugliness and be pure power, beautiful power.

"Die Rose" has begun to play again. I think I must have set it to replay, or perhaps it is the only song I will ever hear now, in my eternity.

CHAPTER TWENTY-EIGHT
MOP

Present time

The woman in black pointing the automatic nail gun at the chest of Crazy Hatchet yells down to us through the pounding rain. "Do not move, you two! I'm going to shoot her now! Don't move! Stay low!"

This is a moment of awe for me, not because I waffle smack-dab in the gray zone between conscious and unconscious, but because this is a literal physical show of an existential crisis. Never have I seen one unfold—all before were theoretical hypotheticals, suggestions of wars over personal morals, questions presented by philosophers and professors. But before me now, an ex-nun in black garb holds a nail gun at the chest of the woman with a hatchet in a hurricane. The pause it took for Aunt Sister Mary to speak her warnings to us to lie still on the ground was a pause during which Crazy Hatchet lowered her hatchet. And while she raised that hatchet high again when Aunt Sister Mary squinted in the rain to aim her firing, things didn't *need* to go down as they are going to go down. I think, although perhaps I'm delusional, but I'm sure the standoff could have ended in our favor without further bloodshed, had Aunt Sister Mary kept the pause and her gun lowered.

But done with her warnings to us on the ground, her green eyes full of fire now, like the glow of flames mirrored in a Christmas ball, alive, glazed, possessive, possessed.

Aunt Sister Mary Patience Pentecost shoots Crazy Hatchet with a spray of pressurized nails. *Chih-chah-duusch, chih-chah-duusch, duusch,* is the sound of nails sinking into the woman's chest, I think. I think they sink into her chest. *Did they hit their mark?*

I can't believe she actually shot her. *Aunt Sister Mary, of all people, is capable of violence? Capable of physical defense and protection? Revenge? Vengeful justice? She must really love us, for real, regardless of how this must weigh on her. She's a zealot.*

Aunt Sister Mary's eyes are wild and wide, but determined and relentless, and she does not doubt her action. *She does not doubt what she's doing. She has unadulterated faith and conviction in protecting me and my companion, my mother.*

Aunt Sister Mary Patience Pentecost is trying to save me and my mother. My mother. My mother is alive. I believe this. For it is true.

How did she know to come here? When I last saw her yesterday in Cape Cod, she stormed off, mad at me, and drove home early. I really hurt her, tweaking her for her secret on why she left the church. How did she know to come here?

The rain is still a billion drills, and I suppose I shouldn't feel like it's been raining twenty hours, it's just that time is stretching too long and warped for me. I think, although it's so hard to say, it's only been a couple of minutes since my mother and I emerged from the burned-out basement hole. Maybe hours. Time seems irrelevant, such a pedestrian theory, in this otherworldly dimension where the embodiments of religion and nature join forces and fight for us.

Although I thought all was well and that Aunt Sister Mary Patience Pentecost shot her full of nails, something is wrong. Crazy Hatchet drops her hatchet and charges Sister Mary. Sister Mary, startled by the rabid animal's fast approach, twists, drops—by accident—the nail gun, and races away, toward the high ocean. I believe she's doing this to pull Crazy Hatchet away from us and only to her. Aunty Sister Mary pulls her black housecoat above her knees for freer legs, and I wonder what was that whipping gauze I saw around her before. Shadow? Aura? Delusion? My fractured sight without glasses?

CHAPTER TWENTY-NINE
MOP

Present time

The highest crashing waves, the riptides, the coiling, recoiling Atlantic—no one is meant to survive the ocean in storm. Not many are meant to survive the Atlantic's arctic chill when she's calm, let alone now, at night, when she coils like a demon. But she is no demon. She is a goddess, full of anger.

It takes a boat of adrenaline. Perhaps all the fate and faith whipped up in the lightning strikes me, for I bolt after Aunty Sister Mary and Crazy Hatchet, winding my way through the storm-ravaged bramble paths. Perhaps I limp, the cloth tied on my calf still tight to stem the flow of blood. No limp will slow me. No wind will rock me. I will not allow any more losses in my life tonight. Perhaps the ocean is, yes, she is a literal goddess. The air she commands as her army whips on the forceful winds into my lungs, making me a relentless soldier. Perhaps I do believe such things. Perhaps my god is this nature in a frenzy around me, and Aunt Sister Mary is the church in which I embody my religion, the granite church I must save.

I come upon the sea's edge, the great slabs of rock as big as rooftops, nearly all the slabs covered by beating waves. The women struggle before me, Aunt Sister Mary barely able to fend off Crazy, who, lost of her hatchet, wrestles and strikes au naturel. And she is winning, pinning Sister Mary to the stones and under the frothy water of the ocean's scraping edge.

I charge, taking no seconds to stall, like I stalled too long in fear two years ago at this exact spot in the bushes bordering the granite slabs. I bulldoze Crazy Hatchet on the rocks, like in retrospect and with twenty-twenty hindsight I wish I had two years ago, for this is indeed the exact spot at which I first saw her. She falls back, missing the greedy Atlantic, my leader, the goddess, my high command, by an inch. She pops up, charges me, flings me closer to the water and away from the safety of bayberry and catbrier up higher on the slope of the land, where Sister Mary is collecting herself, seemingly planning to join the fray once she can stable her stance.

Hatchet doesn't know I am a faithful servant of the goddess behind her. She doesn't know I am safe here in the storm. Hatchet is the enemy of me, and thus the enemy of my goddess, who will protect me.

And I am the one who has trained like a mermaid.

I am the one who overcame the surface of our last ditch, here soiled, ready for the Sink to wash me clean.

I let Hatchet fling me closer to my higher power. Aunty Sister Mary screams cautions over the wind. I wish I could console her with my mind, for I am unafraid. Hatchet charges once more, falling for my trap. It is dark now, no lightning ripping the sky, and the storm has calmed some, only releasing hard, straight rain, not sideways trains of liquid spears, no whipping wind, just straight, hard rain. This is the moment to reveal my ultimate superpower.

I've swum this exact stretch thousands of hours. Oh yes, I have been in the Sink, the cycle down, down around . . . rocks and seaweed. In fact, I've entered the sea from this same spot—albeit under much calmer conditions and when at low tide—so I know I need only tread a certain way, for a certain time, dip deeper, timing swells, as if a fish, circle minor maelstroms, where they always swirl, and catch the current at the right spot, by the nose rock, to skirt the jut that marks the boundary of Manny's land. I can swim and tread and back float three hours without pause if nature requires me so.

My heart is strong. My mind is mended. My will divine. The sea my goddess. The weakness of my muscles and the gash in my leg are irrelevant in this spring of cauterizing cold and antiseptic salt—this water that buoys and heals me. Perhaps teams of mermaids are my teams of angels, guiding me along the right rip current and tide.

We fall together, this murderess who stole my mother, hacked my aunty, split the mechanic, possibly took my love, threatened my church, tested my sanity. The churning sea will swallow her in a second, while she, the sea, will be my salvation, for I've prayed at her altar all this time, and I do believe.

CHAPTER THIRTY

MOP

Several months later . . .
Italy

Detective Popover—that's what I call Mom's faithful cat now. It was Popover who led me to the sunflower congress and Aunty's secret grave. They told me how they found Aunty, half sprawled up her own wall, slumped in the curve of floor and wall, as if reaching for the glass case holding her Roosevelt gun. But detectives said the gun had no firing trigger, called it a "rotted shell of a showpiece."

Once released from the hospital, I stood before that gun, staring, considering, wondering why on earth she would seemingly reach for it as her last act in life when there would be no way to use it as a gun with no firing trigger. Why, then, why reach for it?

I looked out the window to find Popover in Aunty's grass, watching me. When my eyes met his, he turned, pointed his tail, and walked into the sunflower congress. I followed, for I believe in such things, wholly now. I hold no doubts in nature.

Of course Aunty built herself a hidden grave. I'm a fool for not solving her Roosevelt gun puzzle before. By Aunty's standards, an obvious ruse. Pull down on the case, as if the whole thing were a lever, and bam, in the middle of the sunflower spiral, there opened a circular metal cover, itself obscured by turf. How real detectives didn't find this, I do not know.

They did find an ominous two-person-deep pit out behind a bramble line, behind the barn. Detectives surmised that was a grave, and freshly dug too. They speculated that Aunty had intended to dump bodies there. But whose?

I focused on the turf circle within the sunflowers and found only one conclusion: Aunty had another secret hiding place. I looked around within the spiral, and when I faced the house, the barrel of the Roosevelt gun, right there in the Mermaid Library, winked at me.

I twisted the glass case down like a big rectangular knob, ran back out, and the green turf was gone; only the open well remained. Aunty's aboveground planting beds covered the underground metal levers that connected with the gun case's levers, that ran within Aunty's walls, behind her library shelves and books.

When I figured out the contraption she built herself, and remembered how long that gun had been hanging in the case, I convinced my parents to burn Aunty's body and return her ashes to the well, as she intended. So that's where she is now, ruling the lawn with her sunflowers, which I'll plant every summer in a spiral, for I've inherited the rose house.

Where did I find myself? Where did I surface? At Manny's far-end beachhead, where—and how bizarre from Manny's point of view, I can't imagine—Manny was watching with his father from a high cliff. They both wore headlamps to cut through the storm, watching the coast guard working to save a sinking lobster boat offshore. Manny had called in the distress, seeing the poor lobsterman signaling for help, which Manny saw from the top of his property's lighthouse. Manny thought I was simply riding out the storm at Aunty's and needed family time, for that's what "my" texts through the night and day had said to him.

"But I was about to go over there, Mop. Those texts were so unlike you," he said. "It was the lobster-boat thing that stalled me."

Turns out, Crazy Hatchet had lied about killing Manny. Big surprise.

So I crawled out of the sea, ending my mermaid's escape, loose legged and stumbling, like a mermaid stripped of her fins, and Manny caught vision of me in the path of his headlamp. Divine providence, divine coincidence, a gift from the goddess—I believe it all. For had he not seen me, the currents would have claimed me, filled my lungs for good, made me a water being. As it was, all my strength drained in the second Manny's light feathered my drenched scalp. He ran and caught me, and 911 stole me away to treat my hypothermia and hatchet wound. Multiple bags of donor blood filled me back up, and after they jammed paddles on my chest to stem the cardiac arrest, I stabilized.

Now it is my wedding day, several months later. And we are in an underground library outside Florence, in the Chianti region.

My beautiful mother is fussing like a humming bumblebee around me, pinning wildflowers here and there in my hair, even though it's just us, just me, her, Manny, my father, Aunt Sister Mary, Manny's father, and his father's third wife. Manny's brothers and their spouses and children wouldn't fit in this cool cobblestone space, and the ceremony is going to be short, so they all wait for us in the cypress courtyard of another of the Acista Italian boutique hotels. The reception was designed by my mother, in chirpy concert and over lots of cocktail luncheons with Mrs. Acista Number Three. I'm pretty sure Mom didn't actually *need* to fly to Florence three times with her planning cohort for "site visits" and to "make sure everything is perfect," but I would never call her out on it. I'm glad Mom has a new friend.

Candle wax drips down squat candles and onto the stone floor. The spaces are filled with the colors of the rose thief: giant bunches of red roses, yellow roses, pink roses too. Everywhere. Candles and flowers and old books and stone, underground, with my mother and Manny.

It is the most near-perfect wedding in my mind. We just need Aunty here, but since that's impossible, I conjure her presence by imagining her in a shadow.

My mother, my mom, the lovely Johanna, she was hospitalized for two weeks too. They put us in the same room at Saint Jerome's (we could get whatever we demanded, given the decades of donations). Thereafter, for several months, my mother pained her way through grueling daily physical therapy with a relentless drill sergeant of a therapist named Brandt Ritz. We called him Butter, because Ritz crackers are buttery. She also suffered speech and psychoanalytic therapies.

When we were released from the hospital, we donated $2 million to the mechanic's surviving family. For his fifteen-year-old son, we set up a bottomless trust fund. But none of that, not a cent, would ever heal the son's bleeding heart. And I will never live down the guilt, for it's my fault, my gamesmanship, my obsession with retrieving love, that led me to leave my broke-down Volvo with his father in the first place. For my penance, I dedicate my life to working for sex-trafficking victims, starting with the one who helped save me in a foreshadowing prophecy: Pradina. The Mighty Mary Trust is reopened, I'm the chairwoman of the board, and I rewrote the mission statement so as to focus on sex trafficking, while also devoting a side trust to Aunty's original intended purpose. This is a full-time job for me, and I suppose you could say I've stayed in the family business, using our name and money for good. As I should.

My father taught me, too, about all the secrets we hold on others, and *how* we gather more secrets for our war chest. Information is the greatest weapon of all, both sword and shield. I understand that the Pentecosts and Vandonbeers hold silent, scary power, and we must maintain such leverage for the greater good. I'm okay with this. I allow myself a profitable dark side, too, for I accept the pure truth that those who play on the good side must play dirtier than the bad side, if ever there is to be any chance for good to triumph. Such is nature's rule.

Nature does not play nice and polite, waiting for evildoers to grow a conscience. She throws fits, like hurricanes. Love, too, such is love's rule as well—the unintelligible logic of impartial love, unswayed by man's laws. Nature and love fight to the death, with dirty, clawing, scraping, drowning, selfish, loving hands. Why would anyone choose anything other than nature or love as religion? Everything else is man-made and weak by comparison.

I'm pretty sure Mom's back to her old self months after our horror night in the barn and hole. In setting the flowers in my hair just now, she whispered, "My Mop-Bop! So lovely we canceled the GC for this splendid underground library! Who doesn't love a wedding in Italy! Who!"

Candles add soft light to this stony, shadowed, literary space. I am in a knee-length white cocktail dress with pops of the rose thief's colors, red, yellow, and pink, in the flowers in my hair and my flower-patterned shoes and the rope of wildflowers around my wrist as a cuff. Mom's design. She adjusts my wrist cuff while pecking my cheek.

We're about to begin. I wait now for my father to walk over and escort me down a short aisle, just ten feet long. All in performance of our ceremony.

Manny is in a delicious tuxedo, for that's what he wanted, and he sure is sexy as an underground Bond. The reflection of a candle flame licks the freckle under his eye, an extension of my own fire tongue, claiming my property.

I bite my lip in thinking on our wedding night, to come in just three hours.

Aunt Sister Mary sits in a corner, reading through her notes one final time, and as the officiant, she may be more nervous than I. My father looks over her shoulder and whispers a question about the reading he'll do. They smile at each other, happy siblings at a happy event.

It's time now. My father walks to me, bending a little since the stone ceiling is so low. He's a tall, dark vampire. I think he could live underground here and fit in quite well. He reaches me and kisses the top of my head. "Love you, kiddo. Love you to bits and pieces," he says, tears in his giant, bright dad eyes. I shiver in happiness, reminding myself how lucky I am. I look forward to spending my career with my father. We plan to do some good.

Sister Mary remains my church, although she doesn't know that's how I think of her. And my respect is tenfold, ever since she visited me in the hospital two days after I pulled myself from the sea and the doctors cleared me of the worst part of hypothermia and heart attack, blood transfusion too.

Then, she told me her secret.

First she explained how she found us at Aunty's that night. Aunty had called and gotten the Rye answering machine. The machine recorded the number, so tracking was easy. Aunty had said nothing, but the message revealed ominous terror. Aunt Sister Mary described hearing slight, somewhat inaudible gasping, or a nasally breathing, hard to tell, over-ridden by the blaring of "Die Rose" on repeat. I considered the timing of this call—it had to have been soon after she crawled out of the barn into the stormy sunlight.

My father didn't hear the message, for as soon as he'd returned from our trip to the Cape, an emergency in Hartford, Connecticut, with one of his businesses summoned him to drive before the storm hit its height. Sister Mary didn't listen to the message until evening; she'd been reading in silence all day, nursing her anger at me, which she said was really anger at herself.

But when she heard the message, Aunt Sister Mary rewound the recording and replayed. She says her antennae were up on a high wire. It was in the spaces she timed between the low whistle of background breaths, how long those took, that roused her trigger-happy suspicions to fire on all cylinders. "I should have called the cops straight away. But how do you convince others of your instincts?"

She peeled out of the Rye driveway in my father's black Lamborghini, the one quarantined to his show garage, the one hosting low-profile tires. She says she drove "faster than Batman in his piddly little Batmobile." I giggled, an authentic giggle, when she dissed Batman. Imagine an ex-nun, dressed in a black housecoat, in her midforties, looking like Olive Oyl, racing along the seacoast in an ornamental Lamborghini, during a Northeast hurricane, thinking she's better than Batman.

When she got to Aunty's and saw the mechanic, the storm raging around her, her eyes caught sight of the loaded nail gun in Aunty's open-door foyer. And she heard a woman screaming "Bitch" in the brambles.

After apprising me of how she saved me, Aunt Sister Mary huffed, sent a quick stare at me in the hospital bed, and opened a palm-size box. I did not expect to see the plastic, shriveled bracelet within.

"You asked me in the Cape about my secret. Why I left the church. You were right, I was kicked out. But I'm guessing you don't know why."

She took a calm breath, saddened but secure in what she was about to say.

"I would have gotten away with it had the doctor not sent the test results on a day I wasn't in the rectory," she said.

Aunt Sister Mary Patience Pentecost's story goes like this: a single-woman parishioner used to come to her for advice and prayer; this woman desired a baby so bad, but her ovaries were defective, she could not carry a baby, and adoption was basically impossible in her case. Sister Mary knew her for years, and herself desiring the "sensation of the greatest gift of nature, the highest of commanders, the physical sensation of pregnancy," struck a deal. *She called nature the highest commander. And she wanted to feel the greatest gift of nature, in a literal, living, not celestial, sense.* I connected with her on several levels the second she uttered these words. She shattered several false boundaries between us. We were finally *talking* to each other in a pure truth. Not a facade we'd erected, or others erected about the definition of each other, no ancient dogmas, nothing. Just our own beliefs, our raw identities.

The deal was, she'd lease an ovary and her womb, fermented by borrowed, injectable sperm, and hide the pregnancy by taking a sabbatical. She'd then give the baby up in a private, and confidential, adoption.

All went to plan, Sister Mary Patience delivering in the Rye coach house, hence the screaming and the "man in a coat" who came running in one night, never to be seen again: a private, house-call doctor. I had missed the whole thing, for I'd been in high school, partaking in a semester abroad program in France. But Aunty Liv had been in Rye that night, so she had alluded to it, the screaming, the man, Sister Mary holed up in the brick house. These are the details Aunty spewed the night we ate pizza on the Rye roof.

Test results were sent to the rectory, the test results confirming the baby's DNA and lineage and blood type and other physical attributes and health.

"I had asked the doctor's office to call me with results. And I was sure I changed my mailing address to Rye, changed it pretty thoroughly, as I recall, from the rectory address. But with all the administrative nests between hospitals and doctors' offices, there was one database that didn't get the instruction or update, and thus, the results were mailed to the rectory. And since the office secretary opened everything that came in, that's what she did. She read the results, all right, tattle-told on me to Mother Superior, and before the end of the day, the entire story unraveled. At my hearing, I told the truth. They kicked me out."

She nodded to the open box in her hand. Inside was the newborn's plastic bracelet, the one they put on babies' ankles in the neonatal room.

"Her name's Mary Olivia. I asked that she be named after you," Sister Mary said, a happy tear rolling down her face.

My father and I have walked the ten feet down the aisle to Manny and Sister Mary. Manny grabs hold of my whole right arm. I grab hold of his whole left arm. We merge our sides, unwilling to let this just be a hand-holding.

My mother behind us blossoms out a happy sob. Oh, she's sobbing and tittering now. I hear her whisper, "Philipp, our baby. Oh, Philipp, our baby girl."

Mr. Acista whispers from his corner, "She is a beautiful bride. They are a perfect couple. We are so pleased."

"So pleased," says Mrs. Acista Number Three.

Aunt Sister Mary clears her throat to shh everyone and begin this ceremony. Manny and I wrote the sermon for her together, our customized sacrament.

"Once upon a time, the rose thief snuck into a colorful lawn. He might have flown there as a seagull, he might have hopped there as a rabbit, he might have slunk there as a crafty fox. He wanted rose petals is what, and he wanted them for love . . . ," Aunt Sister Mary begins.

I smile at my aunt.

ACKNOWLEDGMENTS

No way could I have finished this story without the undying support of my husband, Michael Kirk. I am lucky. Truly. Huge thanks to my son, Max, for his creative inspiration and odd-beautiful input.

My beta readers, mom (Kathy Capone), cousin (Beth Hoang), and sister-in-law (Kim Capone), once again did not leave me down in the well. Invaluable feedback and lifting support from them brought this book to light. Thanks to my dad (Richard Capone), who drew me a beautiful property and character map for this novel.

Forever gratitude to my agent, Kimberley Cameron, who is a tireless champion and guide. Cannot—like no way possible could I—navigate these waters without you. XOXO.

And to the Thomas & Mercer team. I am thrilled to be within this publishing group with the boutique, hands-on, top-notch care and attention. Every step of the way has been professional, educational, and supportive. My editor, Jessica Tribble, LOVE. Her edits: crazy perfect. My dev editor, Andrea Hurst, like my own personal professor. Their edits were challenging, and as such, exactly right. Both of you helped me see things I'd become totally blind to and in the process, gave me an education and brought Aunty Liv and Mop into their true, truest lights. Thank you. And to the copyeditor team, Sara Brady, Karen Brown, and Sarah Vostok, who caught things I can't even imagine having caught. And the cover designer, very big huge thanks.

ABOUT THE AUTHOR

Shannon Kirk is the award-winning author of *Method 15/33*, an international best-seller; and *The Extraordinary Journey of Vivienne Marshall*. Having grown up in New Hampshire, Shannon and her brothers were encouraged by their parents to pursue the arts, which instilled in Shannon a love for writing at a young age. A graduate of Suffolk Law School in Massachusetts, Shannon is a practicing litigation attorney and former adjunct law professor specializing in electronic-evidence law. When she isn't writing or practicing law, Shannon spends time with her husband, son, and two cats. To learn more about Shannon, visit www.shannonkirkbooks.com, or follow her on Twitter @ShannonCKirk.